The Dead Kid Detective Agency

Evan Munday

ECW

Published by ECW Press
2120 Queen Street East, Suite 200, Toronto, Ontario, Canada M4E 1E2
416-694-3348 / info@ecwpress.com

Library and Archives Canada Cataloguing in Publication

Munday, Evan
Dead Kid Detective Agency / Evan Munday.

ISBN: 978-1-55022-971-4
Also issued as:
978-1-77090-083-7 (PDF); 978-1-77090-082-0 (EPUB)

I. Title.

PS8626.U54D42 2011   jC813'.6   C2011-902864-6

Editors: Michael Holmes and Erin Creasey
Cover and Text Design: David Gee
Typesetting and Production: Rachel Ironstone
Printing: Webcom   5   4   3   2   1

This book was printed in July 2011, at Webcom in Toronto, ON, Canada.

The publication of *The Dead Kid Detective Agency* has been generously supported by
the Canada Council for the Arts, which last year invested $20.1 million in writing
and publishing throughout Canada, by the Ontario Arts Council, by the Government of Ontario through Ontario Book Publishing Tax Credit, by the OMDC Book
Fund, an initiative of the Ontario Media Development Corporation, and by the
Government of Canada through the Canada Book Fund.

Printed and bound in Canada

Only The Good Die Young

– Billy Joel

October Schwartz is not dead.

Now, there are plenty of dead folks in this book (you read the title before starting the book, right?), it's just that October Schwartz does not happen to be one of them. That said, it was her first day at Sticksville Central High School, and she sort of wished she were dead.

October had moved to Sticksville only a month earlier, and she didn't know anyone yet, unless you counted her dad and maybe the Korean lady who sold her gum at the convenience store. She'd spent the month of August reading in the cemetery behind their house and working on writing her own book. So her first day of high school was even more nerve-wracking than it was for most of the students at Sticksville Central. The way she figured it, everybody was going to hate her. They certainly had in her old town. Why should this one be any different?

There were plenty of reasons for the average high school student to hate her: she wasn't chubby, but she wasn't not chubby, which, to those naturally inclined to be unpleasant people, meant she was fat. Also, she wore more black eyeliner than most — barring only silent film actresses, really. Add to that the natural black hair she'd inherited from her mom and her affinity for black clothing, and she was like a walking teen vampire joke waiting to happen.

Plus, she was a little kid. Due to the advanced state of middle school in her former town, a futuristic utopia of almost 40,000 citizens — most of them employed by the town's snowmobile factory — she'd been allowed to skip grade eight altogether in Sticksville (only three hours away geographically), straight into the teenage Thunderdome of high school before she even reached her teens. She was twelve and headed into grade nine, where most of her classmates were well on their way to fourteen if they weren't there already. This part was to remain a secret from everyone, if she had her way. But even if her classmates didn't know, October was sure they could smell the tween on her — the stench of Sour Keys and Saturday morning cartoons.

As October pulled on a black T-shirt, she began to imagine burgeoning extracurricular clubs founded on the members' communal hatred of October Schwartz, its members wearing T-shirts emblazoned with hilarious anti-October slogans.

October's dad — Mr. Schwartz to you — taught grade eleven and grade twelve biology, as well as auto repair at Sticksville Central, so it was sort of his first day, too. But somehow, October doubted her dad was anxious about what people would think of his clothes and hair.

She left for school early that morning, because she was cautious about that sort of thing. About other sorts of things, she wasn't very cautious at all, as you'll see. She shouted goodbye to her dad, who was still busy shaving in the washroom. He didn't respond, but he was kind of concentrating, blaring music by Fleetwood Mac or some other band from the 1970s.

She walked into the backyard and out to Riverside Drive using the cemetery that bordered their backyard as a shortcut. Mr. Schwartz had been uncertain at first about purchasing a house so close to the town's lowly cemetery. Not that he believed in ghosts, but there was something unseemly about it to him. However, the price was good and he wanted to find a home before the school year started, so he dismissed his uncertainties. October liked it. She smiled crookedly as she passed through the wide expanse of decaying stone and forgotten names on her way to the first day of the rest of her life.

The air was crisp and a bit cold for early September, like a Granny Smith apple left in the freezer by accident. October lived only about twenty minutes from Sticksville Central, so it wasn't long before she pushed her way through the double doors of the school's entrance. She opened her bag and unfolded her schedule.

Evidently, October wasn't the only student concerned with arriving early. A veritable gaggle of other kids could already be seen congregating, conversing, and giggling inside the main corridor of the school.

One of these students — a tall one with auburn hair and a belt the width of a small diving board, who was standing with some friends beside the vending machines outside the cafeteria (spoiler alert: she's a witch) — caught sight of October Schwartz and pursued her like a fashionable, but very silent homing missile. October, who was attempting to avoid contact with anyone and everyone, hurried past her. But she wasn't quick enough to avoid the belt enthusiast's loud slur:

"Zombie Tramp!"

Mortified, October made a sensible, strategic retreat to the girls' washroom, which was thankfully empty. She gripped a porcelain sink and stared dolefully at herself in the mirror. Two minutes into high school and things were off to a horrible start. But, above all else, October was determined not to cry at high school. Ever. She was still twelve, but she wasn't a baby.

She tried to fill her mind with thoughts different from her new "Zombie Tramp" status: her birthday, her dad, and her new classes. What did Zombie Tramp even mean? Why Tramp? Why not Zombie Floozy? Yet, because she was staring into a mirror, her mind kept drifting back to her big, stupid face.

Her dad often told her she was "darn cute," because he was related to her, but October never believed him. Her dad was no prize himself; how would he know what cute was? October did a quick self-analysis in the mirror. She might have overdone it with the eyeliner today, and maybe she should have taken more effort with her hair. Around her neck, she wore a gift left behind by her mom, a silver ankh necklace. It was probably the eyeliner and all the black that was encouraging the Zombie Tramp comparison.

A short girl with a ponytail entered the washroom and October turned on the taps, pretending she was washing her hands, then hastily exited, wiping her hands on her black jeans. French class would start soon, and October wasn't sure where her classroom was yet. Or her locker.

When October found her locker, at the top of the arts corridor, she also found another bit of unpleasantness. That very same tall, trendily dressed girl, the one who played so fast and loose with the term Zombie Tramp, was standing right beside her locker. The girl faced the other direction, chatting with a group of similarly attired compatriots who had formed a semicircle that blocked most of the hallway.

"Did you see what she was wearing?" the pointy-faced ringleader asked. Rhetorically, it would appear. "Uh, *hello*, Janet. Last year called. They want their boots back."

"And their hair! *Haw!*" added a little wisp of a girl with a very large laugh. Other girls chimed in; a girl with a goose neck and blonde hair, and a shorter girl with a shirt that read, "So many boys, so little time!"

As the symposium continued, October quietly opened her locker, slid her knapsack inside, and extracted her binder and pencil case, hoping none of the girls would notice her. She felt a little like she was playing Operation, trying to remove the patient's bread basket without touching the metal edges. Tragically, she was never any good at that game.

"Hey! Zombie Tramp is back!"

Oh, piss right off, October thought.

"You're new in town, right?" her tormentor with the prodigious belt asked, whipping around to face her. October stood, silent as a tomb — well, not some of the tombs encountered later in this book, but as silent as tombs usually are.

"Well, you can go back to wherever you came from. We've already got a couple of goth skeezebags here. Don't require any more . . . 'specially not the extra-large variety."

Her minions stared at October, waiting for her to spontaneously combust from the insult.

"That means you're fat," whispered the girl who apparently fretted about the ratio of time to boys.

"Ashlie Salmons," said an authoritative voice behind October. "Don't you have some class to be at?"

When October turned to identify the speaker, she saw an older man with glasses and thinning white hair standing in the hallway.

8

His arms were folded across his pudgy torso, strangulating his tie. October guessed he was a teacher at the school; otherwise, he was, like, the worst student ever. He frowned at Ashlie Salmons (who, dear readers, is that auburn-haired super-creep we all hate now). The older man arched a bushy, white eyebrow.

"Ms. Salmons, class is about to start. Wouldn't it be great to begin the school year by arriving on time?" A smirk split the older man's face.

Ashlie and her friends scattered like cockroaches in a lit room. Well, perhaps not that quickly. They scattered like cockroaches with some sense of decorum.

"Thank you . . . uh, sir," October stammered.

The older man's smirk made a subtle transition into a smile. "Not a problem, young lady," he said. "You look new. Ashlie Salmons began attending Sticksville Central last year, and certainly made an impression on her classmates. But I've figured out how she operates. She can smell fear." He chuckled a bit as he sniffed the air like a dog, then turned on this heel. He continued to speak to October as he walked away. "Don't worry too much. Their bark is worse than their bite . . . Actually, I think their bark *is* their bite. Either way, have a good first day."

He left October stunned outside her open locker. It certainly didn't seem like a teacher should talk that way about other students. But maybe she was naive about what high school teachers were like. She had French class in two minutes, so she'd soon find out.

☠

The remainder of October's morning wasn't nearly as eventful as her pre-class locker encounter. French class wasn't particularly scary or dread-inducing. It was, to the contrary, October's best subject. She was, how you say, *un connoisseur de la français*.

I said it was *her* best subject, not mine.

She was surprised to see the same older man who saved her from certain doom at the hands of Ashlie Salmons sitting at the front of the class. He was her French teacher, and his name was Mr. O'Shea. He seemed pretty nice, not at all the sort of person who would make students scatter in the hallway. But maybe all teachers had that effect. At the end of class, Mr. O'Shea assigned them a paragraph to write about themselves (*en français, naturellement*), due Thursday.

Second period math with Mr. Santuzzi, however, wasn't nearly as pleasant. Santuzzi was a tall, muscular man who wore a tight powder-blue suit and had a dark, handlebar moustache. He explained his lessons like he was barking orders to a deaf battalion of army recruits.

"A lot of you wonder why you have to learn math," Mr. Santuzzi boomed. "You say, *I know how to add, subtract, multiply, divide. I've got a calculator. That's all I need to get by. Why do I need to learn about quadratic equations and conical sections?* Put your hand down, I'm not taking questions! There's a very simple answer to that stupid question: You need to study math because I will *fail* you if you don't."

Then Santuzzi launched straight into his first lesson, reviewing order of operations. OOPS, for all you math fanatics. October (and the rest of the class) were assigned one hundred exercises for homework on the very first day. What is with that? October could read the other students' minds through watching their eyes; they were already inventing a stockpile of horrible nicknames for Santuzzi.

Mr. Santuzzi's class was followed by a multigrade assembly for all the Sticksville Central students, held in the gymnasium. The principal, Mr. Hamilton, walked up to the solitary microphone in the centre of the basketball court and welcomed the ninth graders, then welcomed back the returning students. He was new to Sticksville Central High School himself, having recently relocated from a high school in Toronto, where he was vice-principal. In his speech, Mr. Hamilton made it clear he was incredibly proud to be principal at one of the best schools in southern Ontario. Given her experiences so far, October figured his old school must have been a juvenile detention centre if he thought Sticksville was so swift.

High school, he told the assembled masses, sets the tone for the rest of your lives. What sort of people would they grow up to be? Gesticulating wildly, he encouraged students to get involved in school, sign up for extracurricular activities, and meet new people. October took it under advisement, but her mind wandered from the principal's first day oration. In just a few days, it would be her birthday, and her dad was legally obligated to treat her like gold. Gold that required cake and presents.

She wondered how his first day of school was progressing. Had he been harassed by any mean, trendy girls?

☠

Picking a lunch table in a high school cafeteria is a lot like diving into a cage of bloodthirsty ocelots while smeared in bacon grease. It's terrifying, there's a fifty-fifty chance that you'll die, and no matter the outcome, you're getting bacon grease on you. This is particularly true when you're the new student at a high school. Doesn't help if you're at least a year younger than everyone, too.

October slunk into the school's cafeteria, brown lunch bag in hand, and surveyed the two long rows of folding tables. She tried to imagine where it might be safe to sit. She spotted Ashlie Salmons, sitting with her squad of super vixens: Big-Laugh-Little-Girl, Goose Neck, Novelty T-shirt. Ashlie glanced at October but said nothing. Maybe she feared there were teachers lurking in the lunchroom. Everyone seemed to already have friends and mealtime companions, and October hadn't spoken to anyone but Mr. O'Shea all day. She cautiously selected the empty end of the table closest to her right, seemingly occupied exclusively by fat kids, Dungeon-Masters-in-training, and asthmatics, and opened her lunch bag.

"Zombie Tramp!"

October's eyes widened in fear. The voice wasn't Ashlie Salmons's. It was a boy's voice. The deadly nickname was spreading around the school faster than mono. Grade nine was going to be misery from day one.

She swung around to see who had called her that vile (but by now, quite familiar) name, fully expecting to receive a piping hot hash brown to the face. She was surprised to see a gawky, tall boy wearing a bowling shirt and pinstriped pants, entering the cafeteria. He said it again, and October realized he wasn't talking to her, but to a short Asian girl dressed all in black, standing between the two aisles of lunch tables — and she was smiling! The two of them had a good laugh about how trampy a zombie the girl was.

Before long, the two realized a chubby goth girl (October) was staring at them. They moseyed right over to her, plunked down on the lunch bench across from her and, seemingly, began training for the World Championship Belt for Poor Posture.

"Is there a problem?" the other Zombie Tramp asked. She suddenly seemed a lot more threatening than the boy.

"Um, I don't think so?" October guessed, trying to seem breezy.

"Then why were you staring at us?"

"It's — well, just — it's a funny story, sort of . . ." October said. Very breezy. "A girl called me Zombie Tramp this morning. I, uh, thought you were making fun of me."

"Yeah?" the tall boy said. "Was it that girl over there?"

"Ashlie Salmons, yeah."

"Yeah, my cousin says she's a nightmare," said the Asian girl. "Her mom is like the Crown attorney or high judge of Sticksville or something. But Ashlie got left back . . . she's doing a victory lap for grade nine, which is totally sad. I got the Zombie Tramp treatment this morning, too. Well, I'd rather be a Zombie Tramp than a RICH, SNOTTY, HIPSTER Tramp!"

Ashlie Salmons glowered from several tables up.

"So, I guess we should be friends now," the girl said. "You know, out of our mutual hatred. My name's Yumi Takeshi. This is Stacey Mac-somebody."

"Uh," the tall boy corrected.

"He's got a girl's name. I think his parents hate him," Yumi said.

So the two Zombie Tramps and the boy with a girl's name sat and ate lunch together.

✠

The afternoon started with music class with Mrs. Tischmann. October played trombone relatively well. She had initially chosen the instrument in grade seven because it was so very loud, and she stuck with it. Since it was the first day, Mrs. Tischmann eased them into class, asking them how music made them feel, emotionally speaking. Mrs. Tischmann was a wide-eyed woman in a sweater that had double-crossed the wrong bedazzler. Her curly blonde hair was beginning to turn grey and she wielded her conductor's baton like a natural extension of her body. October thought she was kind of loopy, but a lot nicer than Mr. Santuzzi.

The Stacey kid was in her music class. He played percussion. Or, at least, hit things with sticks fairly rhythmically. Ashlie Salmons was in Mrs. Tischmann's music class as well, but she played clarinet and sat in the front row, so October barely even had to see her face.

Mr. Page taught Canadian History, which promised to be a more exciting class than the words "Canadian" and "History" might indicate. Mr. Page was kind of funny, in the way that one's dad is funny (which is to say, not very). During the first class, he told several inexcusable jokes, but was so enthusiastic about them they were almost amusing. Almost.

The things Mr. Page spoke about that October actually heard sounded pretty interesting — Plains of Abraham, Louis Riel, Canadian railway system — but the end of the school day was fast approaching, and with it her attention span was rapidly diminishing. She planned to spend most of the afternoon and evening working on the fabulous horror novel she'd been writing in her spare time over the summer. Hopefully, Mr. Page wouldn't add any homework to what Mr. Santuzzi and O'Shea had already assigned.

The horror novel was a new obsession. Since moving to Sticksville in August, October had been bored out of her skull. Mr. Schwartz suggested she go outside and find some neighbourhood kids, but there was no way October was doing something like that. Who did her dad think she was, one of the Little Rascals?

"At least go outside, pumpkin. It's a beautiful day." Mr. Schwartz said frequently throughout August.

Eventually, October went outside and into the Sticksville Cemetery. She liked walking around the grounds and reading the inscriptions on the headstones. Some of the people had been buried over a century ago. She could barely decipher some of the letters cut into the stone. During one of her cemetery sojourns, October was inspired, surrounded by so many skeletons under the ground, to write a book. A scary book. Writing a book would certainly stave off boredom, she thought.

How wrong she was. Reading a book might stave off boredom, but writing one, as October discovered, is the very definition of

boredom. In a little under a month, October had only written three pages, yet had procrastinated countless times through a series of increasingly creative methods.

She had a title, *Two Knives, One Thousand Demons*, and a general concept: something about a really cool chick defending a small town from hell's hordes of demon soldiers with only two knives. And there would be at least eleven decapitations. And no romantic subplot. But other than that, she hadn't progressed very far.

Nevertheless, now that the school year had started, October

was looking forward to working on the book again. Perhaps she needed the added pressure and constant stimulus of school work to get her imagination flowing. Despite how difficult and boring she found the writing, she never failed to attempt working on it daily. For all the good it did.

☠

Once home, October ran to her room to retrieve a couple Stephen King novels (a continual source of inspiration), then back down the stairs she rumbled. As she slid open the glass door to the backyard, her dad walked in the front door.

"Hi, Dad," October said. "How was school?"

"Hello, October." Mr. Schwartz looked bedraggled. "I didn't hear you leave this morning. Busy day, busy day. Good kids, though. How about you? Meet any friends?"

"It's possible," said October cryptically.

Mr. Schwartz took off his shoes and jacket. "October, I don't feel up to making dinner tonight. How would you feel if I ordered some Chinese?"

"Sounds great, Dad. I'm going to go outside and write, okay?"

"Okay, pumpkin. Just be ready for dinner at 6:30," said Mr. Schwartz, and he lay himself down on the living room couch.

October passed through the backyard into Sticksville Cemetery. She sat down, propped her back against a crumbling old tombstone, and tried — really tried — to write. As valiant as her efforts were, she couldn't help thinking about other things. October blamed her upcoming birthday for her writer's block.

In just eleven days, October would turn thirteen. Not only was that date her thirteenth anniversary of life on earth — which is totally important, if you think about bat mitzvahs and that kind of thing — it would also mark ten years to the day when October's mom split, leaving little more behind than the silver necklace October wore.

October was just three years old when her mom ran out, and her dad would never discuss what happened. It made him incredibly sad. And Mr. Schwartz's sad could be pretty sad.

There was still one photo of Mrs. Schwartz in the house, on the nightstand in her dad's bedroom. October thought he must have destroyed all of the others. She wasn't sure why he kept that one in particular, but more importantly, she didn't really understand why her mom left in the first place.

She never knew her mom; she couldn't begin to imagine what she was thinking, what her motives were. Her dad rebuffed October's inquisitions every year on her birthday: *Why did Mom leave? Where did she go?* Maybe he'd finally think she was old enough to know the whole story on her thirteenth birthday. She'd be a teenager, after all. In the Jewish tradition, she'd be a full-blown woman.

That date was only a few sleeps away, so you can imagine it would be difficult for October to concentrate on writing. All kinds of troubling thoughts were spinning through her head.

So instead of writing, she leafed through the current Stephen King novel she was reading. October had read them all by this point in her life, and was now revisiting some of her old favourites. *Pet Sematary* had long been a treasured possession, with its terrifying cat illustration on the worn paperback cover. And she couldn't pass up the opportunity to read *Pet Sematary* in an actual sematary . . . or cemetery. (For the same reason, I only read *The Lion, the Witch and the Wardrobe* while locked in a dresser. True story.) And allegedly, the book was so horrifying that Mr. Stephen King himself was unwilling to finish writing it for years. If that's not a scary book, I'm not sure what is.

A minute later, inspired by Mr. King's words, October's pen started spilling words on the page like it was leaking — and they were good sentences, too. One important plot point from this flood of words was how the demon hordes actually wound up on earth. October ripped off a bit from *Pet Sematary* and had a heartbroken father attempt to raise his child from the dead in an extremely misguided instance of fatherly love.

The ritual October had written made her especially proud. After finishing it, she read the words aloud, just because they were so killer.

"Billy's father climbed to the top of the hill, gazing down

on the lonely graveyard below. Blood seeped from the self-inflicted wounds in his palms onto the dry grass and he spoke the forbidden words:

> 𝕬𝖘 𝕹𝖆𝖙𝖚𝖗𝖊 𝖙𝖚𝖗𝖓𝖘 𝖙𝖜𝖎𝖘𝖙𝖊𝖉 𝖆𝖓𝖉 𝖉𝖆𝖗𝖐,
> 𝕿𝖔 𝖙𝖍𝖎𝖘 𝖉𝖗𝖊𝖆𝖉 𝖌𝖗𝖆𝖛𝖊𝖞𝖆𝖗𝖉 𝕴 𝖉𝖔𝖓𝖆𝖙𝖊 𝖒𝖞 𝖘𝖕𝖆𝖗𝖐.
> 𝕬𝖘 𝖙𝖍𝖊 𝖙𝖊𝖆𝖗𝖘 𝖇𝖊𝖌𝖎𝖓 𝖙𝖔 𝖇𝖑𝖎𝖓𝖉 𝖒𝖎𝖓𝖊 𝖊𝖞𝖊𝖘,
> 𝕿𝖍𝖊 𝖎𝖓𝖓𝖔𝖈𝖊𝖓𝖙 𝖞𝖔𝖚𝖓𝖌 𝖆𝖓𝖉 𝖙𝖍𝖊 𝖉𝖊𝖆𝖉 𝖘𝖍𝖆𝖑𝖑 𝖗𝖎𝖘𝖊."

Many pages later, the sky started to get dark, and October realized her dad would be expecting her home for Chinese takeout shortly. She stood up and examined the tombstone she rested her back against. Vegetation and moss had eaten their way through crevices in the marker. The stone was so old and weathered it was hard to read anything on its surface. "Cyril Cooper" was buried below, according to the headstone. October had to stare at the numbers for half a minute before the dates, 1766 – 1779, became apparent. Cyril Cooper had lived well over two centuries ago. And died at age thirteen.

☠

FROM THE DIARY OF HENRI LAFLEUR - DEFENSE D'ENTRER!

November 14, 1968

(The following diary entry has been translated from the French, for your reading enjoyment.)

Dear Diary,

Hallo, it is me, Henri. I suppose you already know this.

A thousand apologies; I have not written in so long. Ever since I left for school, I have found it very difficult to keep a record of my days. But much has happened since I came to Montreal.

The big city of Montreal is much different from my little town of Baton Nuit. Mother and Father warned me things would be much different in the city. They said it would be difficult to adjust. The English influence is widespread here. Almost as many people speak it as French. And even the French spoken here is hard to understand. It's an unusual stew of both English and

French. Nothing like how people speak in Baton Nuit. I feared at first I must have appeared like a country bumpkin here, but I wanted to study literature and the University of Quebec at Montreal is the place to do it.

I moved into the first bachelor's apartment I could afford. I didn't know what the neighbourhoods were like in Montreal. How was I to know how English Westmount was? And wealthy? My apartment certainly doesn't look like any mansion.

My landlady upstairs comes to my door to pester me daily about rent, even days after I've written her a cheque. Nice cars, cars I could never afford — Bentleys and Jaguars — prowl through the streets. I see them on my way to wash dishes.

Yes, I have a job. I wash dishes at a restaurant owned by a troll named Bernard. He possesses no good qualities that I can observe. His nails are always clean, perhaps. But he did introduce me to The Figaro, a wonderful movie theatre at Mount Royal and Papineau that shows all the new American films with French subtitles.

My first month here, I drifted through the old city like a shabbily dressed ghost. I coasted from home to class, from class to work, from work to home. I would sit in my depressing little apartment like a shadow in a darkened room. No one wants to be friends with the backwoods hick. So the movies became my only friend.

As you know, I don't like many English things except the movies. All my favourite movies have been in English. Mother and Father used to drive us a half hour into town so we could sit in that small theatre for the most recent Hollywood pictures. Now, I could go to the movies every night, if I wished. The Figaro is just a few blocks away. Bullitt, Charly, The Odd Couple, Ice Station Zebra, Barbarella . . . Even better are the horror movies — Rosemary's Baby, Night of the Living Dead. I have seen the latter one at least four times.

For the first month or so, the movies were my only happy moments. But that sad and lonely business all changed when I had a chance meeting with Jean-Paul.

Jean-Paul is everything I am not, but everything I try to be:

charming, good-looking, popular with the girls. He is already losing his hair, but still he is attractive with women. His smile, or his unkempt hair — something about him is like catnip to them. He changes girlfriends more often than I change pants.

I helped him out with an essay in our French Romantic Literature class — real easy stuff. I was worried he'd take advantage of me and my offer, but ever since that essay, Jean-Paul has me attached to his hip. I've been to five parties with Jean-Paul acting as my guide. It's like I'm living the life of a rock 'n' roll musician, in some way. I finally feel at home with Montreal.

Some of Jean-Paul's friends are on the odd side. They've been swept up in some of the more radical student movements. A few are pretty dedicated to Quebec separating from the rest of Canada. Just the other day, a bomb went off at the chamber of commerce, and that separatist FLQ group was claiming responsibility. Jean-Paul and his other friends were discussing the news at a St. Laurent bar, grinning like cats that had eaten English canaries. It made me uneasy.

There was a girl at the last party Jean-Paul took me to: Celeste Boulanger. She was a giantess, and a gorgeous one at that. Six feet tall, with dark brown hair to her shoulders, and tortoiseshell glasses. I have decided I will ask Jean-Paul about her next time I see him. See if she's single, if she likes country bumpkins. I may be falling in love.

My birthday didn't start out
well. Like an hour after I
woke up on Monday morn-
ing, Dad still hadn't got out
of bed, and I had to spend ten minutes coaxing him out of the
room so he'd get to work on time. Every once in a while, Dad
has a lot of trouble pulling himself from bed. When that happens, I have to beg him, bargain with him — *I'll mow the lawn
this weekend if you get out of bed in the next two minutes*, that kind
of thing — and generally do whatever I can to get him to work
on time. Once, I had to dump some ice-cold water on the back
of his head, but I did that only once. Lesson learned.

I just didn't want Dad to lose his job here. How would it
look if he took a bunch of sick days his first month on the job?
It had been a problem at his old school.

We'd moved to Sticksville from our old town because my
dad had a nervous breakdown at school. I liked where we lived,
but there was no way Dad could teach there after he flipped
out in chemistry class and smashed a whole bunch of beakers
and test tubes and stuff in full view of the class. Nobody got
hurt — my dad couldn't hurt anyone — but he got fired. I've
been told teacher's unions are strong and stuff, but it seems like
even they can't help you out if thirty sets of parents are scared
for their children.

Once Dad found another school willing to take a chance
on him, we were on the road to Sticksville at the end of July,
all our belongings in the back of a U-Haul. So now I'm in this
town in the middle of nowhere, unless you consider a half hour

from the American border somewhere. At least in my former town there was the chance I could go to Toronto on weekends once I was in high school. The closest city to Sticksville is Detroit, about an hour away, and Dad says I can't go to Detroit on my own until he's dead.

Yes, my dad is clinically depressed. And it's okay. At first I was weirded out, but now I'm used to the frequent bed battles. I'm getting comfortable with it, but I'm not totally there yet. I can't imagine telling some teacher or Yumi and Stacey that I was late for school because I had to pull my father into the bathroom and barricade the door until he started his shower. Especially only days after starting at this school.

Dad finally spoke. "When I woke up, I had forgotten what day it was . . . Then I remembered," he mumbled through his pillow. "Has it really been ten years?"

I nodded and tugged on Dad's left arm, limper than a jump rope. "So you say. I don't remember anything before I was seven."

Dad buried his face deeper into the pillow. "Happy birthday."

Once I'd forced Dad into the bathroom, things improved. Within fifteen minutes, he was struggling with his necktie at the kitchen counter.

"October," Dad called. "Lasagna for dinner tonight?"

"That would be great, Dad. Thanks."

"You sure you don't want a ride?" he asked. "You might be late . . . we're a little behind schedule."

"It's okay, Dad. I will be fleet of foot."

"Okay. Have a good birthday, October."

I shut the door and fleet-footed it over to Sticksville Central.

☠

Bad news: Mr. Santuzzi was on the warpath.

He was teaching us algebraic factoring or something and

halfway through class he had some kind of brainstorm. He figured the best way to teach class was with a stupid pop quiz. I was complaining about it to Yumi and Stacey Someone-or-other at lunch. The nice thing is that since the first day, we'd been sitting together at lunch. School was a bit easier knowing I had a couple friends.

"Santuzzi's a hardcase. My cousin says he wears a toupée," said Yumi.

"I can kind of see that."

"She says he used to be in the military, too."

"Yeah," I sighed. "He told us on the second day that he was an ex-soldier."

Stacey, meanwhile, was singing along to his Walkman through a mouthful of curly fries. Though his attention seemed divided between these two activities, butchering some song and eating, he was still attempting to follow our Santuzzi-centric conversation. His eyes strayed back and forth like he was watching a ping-pong match in slow motion, which is something I imagined he would conceivably do.

"Why do you have a Walkman, Stacey?" Yumi asked. "Where do you even get one of those? Are you a time traveller?"

"No," he said flatly, shoving his hands in his pockets. "Just poor."

Yumi, momentarily distracted by Stacey's vintage musical device, turned back to me. "We got something for you," she told me.

"What? Why?"

"Well, isn't it your birthday today?" Yumi said.

I must have turned the colour of the ketchup on Stacey's fries. I hadn't told anyone. How had Yumi discovered it was my birthday?

"Your dad let it slip," Stacey said, as if reading my mind. He slipped off his earphones. "We ran into him outside the auto shop. We were kind of talking about you at the time and he introduced himself."

I began to feel my lunch reverse back up my throat, and I buried my face in my hands. Now my only friends, sort of, knew my dad was a teacher here. And things had been going so well.

Yumi rummaged around in her black bag, decorated in this sweet skull and crossbones, for the "something" they had for me — a Nice Knowing You card, perhaps? Eventually, Yumi pulled out a hard, flat, squarish object wrapped in the obituary section of the local newspaper, the *Sticksville Loon*. Like that wasn't worrying.

"You guys didn't have to get me anything . . . you barely know me. We just met days ago," I protested.

"I anticipate great things," Yumi declared. "Plus, I have an ulterior motive."

So I tore open the gift, which was pretty obviously a CD. I guess Stacey didn't pick it out. Would have been a cassette. And I had no idea what this CD was. I mean, I'm no music expert, but I can separate my Taylor Swifts from my My Chemical Romances. I listened to the radio and checked out bands online. But I'd never heard of The Plotzdam Conference.

"Thanks?" I said.

"Do you like it? Do you know The Plotzdam Conference?" Yumi gushed.

"No. I don't think so."

"They're local — from Sticksville. They're an Orthodox Jewish klezmer punk band."

Well, that explained the album's title: *Oy Revolt!*

"You'll love it," Yumi declared with certainty. "They're so cool. They're punk, but they've got, like, a clarinet player and an accordion. And they all wear yarmulkes! My cousin met the bassist once and said he was super-nice."

Don't get me wrong, I was totally flattered that these friends I barely knew gave me a birthday present, but I was also confused by something Yumi'd said earlier. "So, the ulterior motive . . . You guys want me to convert to Judaism?"

Yumi and Stacey exploded into laughter. People at the other end of the table stared at us as if we were all on fire. It's pretty much an unspoken rule of the cafeteria that kids like us should barely be seen, and definitely not heard. So we were drawing some unwelcome attention.

"No," Yumi gasped, regaining her composure. "We want you to come to their concert with us — if you like them, of course."

"Concert? . . . Oh, I don't know —" I stammered.

"It's just at the Sticksville Y. They have bands there once a month. It's really fun."

"I don't know. I'm not sure my dad will go for it. I've never been to a concert by myself before."

I'd been to concerts before. Or *a* concert. I once went with Dad to see Bruce Springsteen and the E Street Band, the highlight of which was when this fridge-like man in a clearly ironic "Born to Run" tank top puked all over us before the first encore.

It was so nice that Yumi and Stacey liked me enough to take me to a concert, but Dad would not be okay with his just thirteen-year-old daughter delving into the seedy world of rock music on her own. His vision of rock concerts (aside from those featuring Bruce Springsteen) probably involved biker gangs and street drugs being as readily available as concert T-shirts at the merch table.

But now I really wanted to go. Even if this band was the worst collection of pimply boys to ever drag their knuckles across guitar strings, I wanted to go. My new friends had asked me to join them for a concert at the Sticksville YMCA. The band was not important.

"I'll ask my dad about it," I said.

"There's no alcohol. Stacey's dad is driving us. Your dad can call him if he's worried." Yumi began writing Stacey's dad's number on a napkin.

"When is it?" I asked.

"Not this coming Friday, but the next," Yumi said.

"I thought they were Orthodox Jews," I said. "And they're playing a show on the Sabbath?"

"Okay, they're Orthodox Jews. But they're not super-religious."

After school, my goal was to work hard. I'd brought *Two Knives, One Thousand Demons* with me to the cemetery. To be honest, I'd hit a bit of a wall in the writing and the last few days I'd spent my writing time making suitable names for the demons – Annihila, Count Gangrenous, Typhio – which, if you think about it, probably isn't the best use of my time. I mean, there are a thousand demons to name, and most of them are likely to end up getting killed by one of the two knives in the title before they have the chance to introduce themselves. I wasn't getting much done.

Also, I probably sabotaged myself a bit. I'd borrowed Dad's old Discman so I could listen to my birthday CD. The music reminded me of the polka band that played at my grandma's eightieth birthday, but, like, fast-forwarded. The prospect of seeing these polka-rockers live started to feel somewhere close to thrilling. Nevertheless, I figured I'd hold off asking Dad for permission to go to the show until a little later. I was already planning to ask him for something much more important today.

Dinner time arrived, and it was a way more formal occasion than usual. It was, after all, my birthday. As always, Dad's

lasagna was fantastic, and he appeared in a way better mood than he had this morning. When we were both nearly finished our second helpings, Dad produced a gift wrapped in red paper from beneath the table like a magician.

"Thanks, Dad," I smiled.

I tore off the red wrap and to my surprise, uncovered a book by Stephen King that I'd never even heard of, which was a serious feat. I'm not some fair-weather King fan. I'd even read *Duma Key*. This book was called *On Writing*. As terrifying titles went, it was just above *Hearts in Atlantis*.

"I know how much you like Stephen King," Dad said. "And this book is his thoughts about his writing process. I thought it might be inspirational. You know, for your own literary master-work."

"Wow. This is so great," I said, flipping through the pages. It was, actually, a pretty thoughtful gift.

"Well, it's conditional. It's yours only if I get to read the first draft of *Twenty-nine Thousand Demons*."

"It's *Two Knives, One Thousand Demons*," I corrected, then walked over to the other side of the table to give my old dad a hug.

I sat back down, picking at the remaining noodles on my plate, my big question on my mind. I had been thinking of how to ask about Mom for days. When the best time would be, and when Dad would be most amenable to spilling his guts. Seemed like it was now or never.

Deep breath, and, "Dad. Can I ask you about Mom?"

"I knew it!" blurted Dad, furrowing his brow. "I knew it. Every birthday, more questions about your mom. Can we not—"

"Please, Dad. You never tell me anything. I'm thirteen now."

"Fine, fine," Dad said, though he didn't look fine at all. He looked like someone had sprinkled broken glass inside his slippers. I'd never seen him so uncomfortable.

Then total silence. We both sat there, looking at the salt and pepper shakers like they'd somehow provide an easy way into this conversation. I realized that was probably not going to happen. So, out of fairness to my dear, distressed dad, I thought I'd open with a joke. Set everything at ease.

"How did a square like you hook a looker like Mom?" I asked, trying to make clear I was joking. "I've seen the picture."

"Ahem. Very funny," Dad was grateful. "Your mom and I met at a school — the school I used to teach at. She worked in special education and I was teaching biology and chemistry. We met in the teachers' lounge, actually. . . ."

"Teachers' lounge?" Colour me horrified. All I could pic-ture was my dad as a teachers' lounge pick-up artist, wide-collar shirt unbuttoned to his navel, and a gold necklace with an apple or "A+" on it. Nightmares for the rest of my life. "Could you at least make something up that sounds romantic?"

"Hey, you wanted the true story. I don't know what she saw in me, to answer your question. Maybe I was funny or nice to talk to. I don't know. But I was smitten. She was amazing." Dad turned to look out the window at the charcoal black night sky, almost on the verge of tears. This was going to be impossible.

"And when did you have me?" I asked.

"I guess nine months after that."

"*Dad!*"

"Okay, I'm just kidding. That was about a year and a bit after we got married. Your mom thought you were the most beautiful thing she'd ever seen — I'm not making that up."

"Okay, Dad." I was disgusted. "No need to get mushy."

"It's true."

"Then why'd she leave?" I muttered under my breath. I guess Dad heard my not-so-secret question.

"I don't know," he confessed and folded his arms over the back of his head.

"Well, what happened, Dad?" I whined. Could whining work in my favour here? It was ridiculous to say Mom loved me but then vanished without so much as an explanation. Do you do that to people you love? To the most beautiful thing you've ever seen?

"You don't need to know. Come on, let's get you some birthday cake."

"Dad!"

"I don't know what happened, pumpkin."

Faced with my expression, which I was trying hard to make into the perfect combination of hurt and skepticism, he'd be forced to continue. I was basically a highly-skilled police interrogator.

"Back when we lived outside Toronto, your mom and I went to the movies and left you with a babysitter. We went to see *The Rocky Horror Picture Show*, in fact. Peggy was taking care of you. Do you remember your babysitter, Peggy? Anyway, your mom was dressed as Columbia and I was Eddie," Dad began.

"Weird," I whispered. As much as I wanted to hear about what happened to Mom, I didn't want to have to picture her and my dad out on some kinky, costume-themed date.

"When we went into the city, your mom ran into some guy she knew at the movie — I never caught his name, but he was dressed as Brad from the movie, just in his underwear. I guess he was an old friend from school or something. Imagine running into an old friend and he's in his Jockeys. Anyway, we went out for coffee with Brad afterward — we probably looked pretty ridiculous in our outfits — and they talked for an hour.

"At home, I pressed your mom to find out who her friend was, but she wouldn't tell me anything. I may have started an argument about it, I'll admit. We fought all night, and in the morning, she was gone. Half her clothing had vanished, her suitcases were missing."

"She didn't even say anything?" I was confused. How could Mom leave without even saying goodbye or good riddance? And on her daughter's birthday? My birthday!

"Not even a note. Your birthday party was a bit, um, solemn that year. . . . I thought she'd be back in a few days."

"And did you ever find out who that mysterioso guy was, Dad?"

He shrugged. "After a couple of weeks, I realized she wouldn't be back. I gave the silver necklace she left behind to you that Christmas, and took the rest of her clothes to the Sally Ann."

I nearly started to cry, because I knew that the Salvation Army thing was a total lie. I found the other half of Mom's clothes and things when we moved in to this house. They're all in a couple Rubbermaid containers at the bottom of his bedroom closet. I almost stopped asking questions, knowing how this must make Dad feel, but I was desperate to know why Mom left: why her friend was super-secret, and why she'd never even tried to call.

"What about Mom's family? Do they know where she went? Do they know who Brad is?"

"She has a brother in Montreal," Dad said. "We used to keep in touch to find out if either of us had heard from her. I haven't talked to him in a couple years."

Dad stopped talking; his eyes were all moist. He rubbed his face with both hands and exhaled deeply.

"Now this is a fun birthday, isn't it?" he dryly commented.

The kitchen chair scraped across the super-tacky linoleum floor we have in the kitchen when Dad rose from the table. "October, I'm sorry, but this has been difficult for me. I'm going to go to my room to rest. Happy birthday. I'm very proud of you, October. You've become a beautiful, smart, and very brave girl." Dad rumpled my hair like I'd just turned six, not thirteen, before departing for his bedroom.

As for me, I had lots to think about. Just sat there at that kitchen table, leftover tomato sauce hardening on the plate in front of me. It seemed like Dad had spilled his guts, but it only brought up more questions. How could Mom leave without any explanation? Even to her own brother? To me, her daughter? Who does that? No one, right?

So maybe Mom didn't just run out on us. Maybe she was kidnapped by an unhinged sociopath dressed like an old friend in his underwear. That could happen, right? Who would ever know? But then, I guess abductors rarely take two weeks worth of their clothing and luggage when doing their thing, so that was probably unlikely. Still, there was something way mysterious about Mom's departure. Mysterious and unsettling.

Whenever I needed a good place to think, I went somewhere also mysterious and unsettling; the cemetery just behind the house. The only problem with that was how late it was. As a result, the cemetery was mega-dark and equally spooky, and Dad was pretty adamant about not letting me visit the cemetery during the night. But today was a special day — my birthday — and Dad had just finished telling me how proud he was of how brave I am. What's braver than walking around a creepy cemetery at night?

So, quick as a bunny, I hosed down those lasagna-caked dishes and shoved them into the drying rack. I suspected Dad was asleep by this point, so I made sure to be extra quiet when I slid open the glass door to the backyard. The thing about the night version of the cemetery (and my backyard) was this: it was way more terrifying than I expected. Blotches of shadows crisscrossed tree trunks like heat rashes. Everywhere I walked, it was like these alien insect sounds were following me, and even though the moon was like the size of a satellite dish in the sky, it didn't provide much in the way of illumination.

Once I got deep into the cemetery, I found the gravesite I sat beside earlier, Cyril Cooper's. It was as good a sitting place as any, and given how dark it was, I was in no mood to go on some great sitting-place hunt.

My mom's story was really bothering me. Before, I had always imagined that Mom left a note for me that Dad kept secret, that she'd been sending letters or birthday cards with no return addresses for years. Y'know, like some kind of tragic TV movie. All would be revealed on my thirteenth birthday, ten years after the fact. The anniversary was like some kind of mythic event; it would mark a new era of understanding. Mom would have this ultra-compelling reason for ditching us, it would be obvious.

None of that stuff happened. No secret letters, no big revelation. Mom didn't even care enough to say goodbye. I'm not proud to admit it, but I started crying. I couldn't help it. The more I thought about Mom leaving, the more it happened. But I wasn't in school, so I figured this little cry didn't count.

Then something strange happened.

Okay, so I wasn't totally certain, because my eyes were somewhat blinded by tears (again, not my fault), but I thought I saw a young girl running through the patch of trees in the distance. The girl didn't quite look like a girl, more like the afterimage of a girl; I could almost see through her body. At least, that's what I thought I saw. Regardless, I frantically wiped the tears from eyes and called out. I wasn't going to let anyone see me in this unfortunate state. "Who's there?"

I swivelled around, my eyes much clearer now. The cemetery certainly looked empty: just the grave of Cyril Cooper, the other motionless graves and tombs, and me, all standing around like jerks. I cautiously stepped toward the more wooded area where I swore I had seen the girl, and called out again, probably more calmly this time, "Hello?"

Still, nobody answered. But as I got closer to the trees, I could hear a faint squeaking, like someone was pushing around a shopping cart with a busted wheel. Trudging (probably stupidly) deeper into the darkness, I couldn't find anything. Maybe I had imagined the girl. The squeaking, however, became quicker and louder the closer I got to a large willow tree at the edge of the cemetery's miniature forest.

I looked up into the tree, which in retrospect was a very bad idea, because the next thing I did was scream. This awful brown bat, fur hanging off it like a diseased rat, dangling on a tree branch like a rotten fruit, dive-bombed me and its gag-inducing wings brushed across my face. I sprinted out of that graveyard full tilt, waving my hands around in front of my face. It felt like it had dug into my hair and was flying around, but that probably didn't happen. All I knew is that by the time I reached home, I was out of breath and my hair was bat-free.

That was enough excitement for one birthday. I hopped into bed and resolved that if I were going to visit the cemetery at night in the future, I was going to steer clear of that willow tree — or at least come prepared for bat attacks. Some sort of motorcycle helmet or goalie mask would be key.

But I couldn't swear off the cemetery altogether, even if it had been infested with bats (as seemed the case). I know I was all emotional and stuff, but I was positive I'd seen a girl about my age running — almost playing — in that cemetery. Though maybe it would be better to leave well enough alone, or however the saying goes. But it's like with my mom running away, my curiosity gets the best of me, just like the unfortunate dead cats in that other saying.

☠

Following a good deal of convincing and cajoling, October's dad eventually did let her attend The Plotzdam Conference's most triumphant concert at the YMCA. Mr. Schwartz spoke to Mr. Whatshisname (Stacey's dad) beforehand, and demanded that October be home before midnight. October was so thrilled about the concert she nearly forgot about her terrifying bat-and-possible-ghost encounter in the cemetery. Most of her evenings since had been spent with her headphones in her bedroom, listening to *Oy Revolt!* Not since Neil Diamond have a bunch of Jews rocked so hard. October kept the repeat button on her dad's Discman locked, playing the CD over and over again. Rabbinical students probably didn't study the Torah this much.

The concert itself, when the big night arrived, astounded October. The bands set up their amps and other equipment in one of the small YMCA gyms. The blue mats for gymnastics or Greco-Roman wrestling or whatever they were for were piled neatly in the back corner. The rest of the gym quickly filled with Sticksville kids, talking and laughing. October had never seen anything like it. Yumi and Stacey attempted to point out other kids they almost knew in the audience. They almost knew a lot of people.

Before The Plotzdam Conference took the stage, October and her friends were subjected to Phantom Moustache, comprised of three skinny dudes that October recognized from the halls of her high school. Their strategy was to compensate in volume for what they lacked in musical knowledge. Phantom Moustache were remarkably loud and screamy and not very musical at all, but the other kids seemed to love it. People danced and pogoed up and down. A few attempted to lift a scrawny friend into the air, but the gathering in the gym wasn't large enough to support crowd surfing, so the group just shuffled around the floor with the friend held aloft, as if the captain of the world's saddest football team had just scored the winning touchdown.

October, however, was not nearly as impressed by Phantom Moustache. She scrunched up her nose and whispered to Yumi, "These guys kind of suck."

"Ha!" Yumi guffawed, delighted. "This is so exciting! You're becoming a music snob!"

"Why is everyone so crazy about them?" October asked.

"Because they're from Sticksville Central," Stacey, who tended to eavesdrop, said. "It's like our high school's official band."

Yumi nodded her head, either in agreement or in time to the music. Keeping a steady rhythm was not the drummer's specialty.

Phantom Moustache ended their final song and on the other side of the gym, past all the sweat-stained and dishevelled high school students in uneven haircuts and leather jackets, was a person October recognized from the hallways of Sticksville Central. She gulped in not-inconsiderable horror when she realized this was no fellow math student or band kid, but her advance-aged French teacher, Mr. O'Shea.

Despite having a good several decades on the majority of the crowd, October's teacher was not dissuaded from bobbing his head like a deranged rooster, his wispy white hair flopping back and forth. Yet as soon as October spotted him, he returned the favour, noticing her at the back of the room. And then it was too late. As if gasoline had been spread across the gym floor and Mr. O'Shea were an open flame, there was no escaping his inevitable arrival.

"Ms. Schwartz," he said. "How pleasant to see you here. The kids had a little circle pit going there for a while. . . . What are you all doing back here?"

October and her two friends were positioned at the very back of the gym, lined up shoulder to shoulder, as if awaiting execution.

"Uh, saving our energy for The Plotzdam Conference," said Yumi.

"Yeah," October agreed. "And, no offense, Mr. O'Shea, but shouldn't we be asking you what you're doing here at all? Do you like this music?" The very idea somehow made The Plotzdam Conference several degrees less cool.

"I suppose this band is all right. It's an interesting sound," he mused. "To be honest, I'm just here to drive the boys and their equipment home."

"You're a roadie for The Plotzdam Conference?" Yumi said, both bewildered and impressed.

"The clarinet player is Mrs. Tischmann's son, so I sometimes give him and a couple of the other boys a ride. My hatchback can fit much more sound tech than you'd think."

October didn't know what to say after that. Mr. O'Shea's whole presence in the YMCA gym on a Friday night was just wrong. Like Clark Kent and Superman standing in the same room. Something was off.

"Come on," her French teacher insisted, corralling the three closer to the band. "I've saved a good spot near the front."

October thought she maybe didn't want to stand so close to the front, but she also feared that disagreeing with Mr. O'Shea — the band's roadie — was like disagreeing with the law of gravity.

You could disagree with it all you wanted, doesn't mean you won't fall and break your legs when you jump off the roof of your house.

In reality, standing closer to the band was not quite as dangerous as jumping from the roof of a house. To the contrary, October had a great deal of fun. Clarinets and accordions were wielded like double-necked guitars (which, in full disclosure, were also wielded). The concert ended with a rave-up version of their minor hit "Keepin' Kosher," moments before Stacey's dad arrived in his beige Pontiac Sunfire. At just ten minutes before midnight, the Sunfire rolled into October's driveway and deposited her on the front step where her worried dad waited impatiently.

In spite of the possible presence of Mr. O'Shea at any concert, October decided she was definitely going to have to do that again. Little translucent girls running through cemeteries were, frankly, the last thing on her mind.

☠

October Schwartz was no slouch when it came to school work. She studied, did her homework assiduously, and, in due time, became bored in some of her classes. Music remained interesting, as they usually played songs during class. Even though the trombone parts in high school music classes are not among the most complex of musical compositions, performing kept her mind busy. And math class was never dull, as Mr. Santuzzi vigilantly scanned his classroom for any signs of students goofing off. Consequences for doing so were often dire and creative. The legends of his military service seemed more and more valid as he began threatening students with push-ups and saying things like, "If this were the Armed Forces, Mr. Rooney, I'd have put you in the hole by now!" October didn't know what "the hole" was and had no intention of finding out. So in math class, October's eyes were pinned to the blackboard. She feared the potential consequences of daydreaming.

It was, however, surprisingly easily to think about other things during both French and history. After about a week, October began bringing her writing notebook to class, so she could surreptitiously write notes, ideas, and lines of dialogue for her book — "I'm here to study demonology; this is the dissection lab!" She had already daydreamed a couple of great scenes, and hadn't committed them to paper so she'd completely forgotten what they were about by the time she arrived home. She wasn't about to let that happen again.

October sat toward the rear of Mr. O'Shea's French class. This Monday morning, Mr. O'Shea was reviewing conjugation for the modal verbs, but October had already reviewed them a few times at home. She quietly opened the notebook with "Two Knives, One Thousand Demons" stencilled on the front and started writing about how her heroine (she had recently been christened Olivia de Kellerman) encountered a quartet of demons in an abandoned Italian restaurant's kitchen while the rest of her class reviewed how to say "may not have visited" *en français*.

Olivia de Kellerman was just stabbing one of the demons (Margaret Thatcher III) in the throat with a lemon zester when, as if from a faraway tunnel, October heard Mr. O'Shea calling on her.

"Ms. Schwartz?"

October raised her head (which, to the rest of the class, had been nothing more than a mound of shiny black hair for the past ten minutes) and saw Mr. O'Shea staring back at her.

"Ms. Schwartz," he smiled, though not unkindly. "If I didn't know better, I would imagine that you're not paying attention in my class. But then I would have to have a rather wild imagination, wouldn't I?" His eyes goggled behind his thick glasses. The class began to descend into hushed comments. Big Laugh lived up to her nickname as she belted out a few at October's embarrassment.

"*Attention, étudiants!*" interjected Mr. O'Shea, quieting the room. "Ms. Schwartz, see me at the end of class, *s'il vous plaît.*"

For the remainder of class, October, ashamed and visibly reddened, faithfully conjugated French verbs and thought no more of demon-slaying. She had always thought Mr. O'Shea was a relatively nice teacher, but she dreaded what sort of punishment he might dole out in their after-class meeting. After all, Ashlie Salmons and her crew feared him. And he was tight with a rock band.

The bell rang and the other *étudiants* picked up their books and filed out the door. October, in no rush to learn her cruel fate, slowly gathered her belongings and dragged her heels while approaching Mr. O'Shea's desk. He just grinned and adjusted his spectacles. He had a young man's face, though October guessed he must have qualified for senior citizen's discounts at buffets throughout Sticksville. Maybe the band kept him young. His hair was a very bright snow white and there was not much remaining to judge the colour by.

He eased himself onto the front corner of his desk.

"I'm sorry to have embarrassed you in front of your peers, but I would appreciate you paying attention to my lessons, no matter how excellent your French may be."

"It's okay," October said, not looking directly at him. "I should have been paying attention in class."

"What was it that you were so tirelessly toiling upon?" Mr. O'Shea inquired. "At first, I just assumed you were working on French, but you were writing too much . . . and having too much fun." He laughed a little at the thought of his class possibly inducing fun. "Were you working on other homework?"

"No!" October almost shouted. His insinuation she was goofing off by doing other schoolwork offended her deeply.

"Well, would you care to educate me?"

October didn't see why she had to tell Mr. O'Shea anything, but then she considered that she might avoid punishment by telling him the truth — writing a book is a pretty harmless activity, after all.

"It's nothing. I was working on my book," October said, then hastily looked out the window, her feet nervously tapping on the floor.

"A book?" Mr. O'Shea seemed surprised. "Really? Could I . . . may I see?"

October slid the notebook from the top of her little pile and handed it to her French teacher.

"*Two Knives, One Thousand Demons*?" he read. "Intriguing title. . . ."

"It's a horror story," October explained, as though Mr. O'Shea was going to mistake it for a self-help book.

O'Shea flipped slowly through the pages, trying to decipher October's chicken-scratch handwriting (officially worse than a medical doctor's) for words he recognized. "I like a good horror story," he said.

Mr. O'Shea didn't seem like the kind of guy who enjoyed a good horror story to October. He seemed like the kind of guy who enjoyed a good story about incredible cats.

"So what happens in it?" Mr. O'Shea asked. "It is Lovecraftian?"

"Lovecraft . . ." October repeated, puzzled. "No, sir. There's no romance at all. Straight horror and action."

"No," he chuckled. "I was referring to H.P. Lovecraft. He wrote a number of classic horror stories. Before your time. Actually, before my time!"

While October almost cracked a smile, Mr. O'Shea rifled through the bookcase behind his desk. From the top shelf, he produced a yellowed paperback, its tattered cover featured a strange illustration of a giant octopus-type thing.

"*The Outsider and Others* by Howard Phillips Lovecraft," he announced. "Here, you should borrow it. Let me know if you like it."

"Yeah? What is it about?"

"Well, it's a collection of horror stories," he explained. "The title story is about a lonely man who lives in an ancient castle and who hasn't seen another human being in years. Eventually, he leaves his castle and goes wandering the countryside. Soon, he finds a new castle, and there's a party going on inside. He barges in on the party, but all the guests run away in horror. When he turns down the next hallway, he realizes what they were running from —

Mr. H.P. Lovecraft

there's a horrible, rotting ghoul, with chunks of its skin falling off, roaming through the castle . . . but then he notices it's not a hallway at all — it's a mirror!"

"Gross! That's *so* awesome!"

"Sorry," Mr. O'Shea said. "I guess I gave away the ending, but there are plenty other stories in the book. They're all pretty good."

October took the ancient book and piled it on top of her binder, textbook, notebook, and pencil case.

"Thanks, Mr. O'Shea," October said, slowly understanding that she had, in all likelihood, avoided any and all punishment. "And I'm sorry about today in class."

"Tell you what," Mr. O'Shea said as he took back October's notebook. "You let me take this down to the staff photocopier so I can take your book home for a quick read-through, and I'll pretend your indiscretion in today's class never happened. You and I both know you're ahead of the rest of the class, so I don't expect you to pay attention all the time. Your French is actually quite impressive given you've skipped a grade. But let's try to keep the authorship to a minimum during class, okay?"

October nodded.

"Alright then. You're free to go, Ms. Schwartz. I have to go check on my car. Confidentially, I think I might need to have my head examined. I had a brake problem, so I brought it to the school auto shop. That may have been a mistake," said Mr. O'Shea.

"My dad teaches auto shop."

"Well, let's hope he's better than the last instructor. I'll see you in class tomorrow."

"Thank you, Mr. O'Shea," said October.

"*En français*," he scolded.

"*Merci.*"

October left O'Shea's class feeling very satisfied with herself, and a little eager to read this Lovecraft book she now had in her possession. That satisfaction rapidly fizzled when she realized their little chat had made her late for Santuzzi's math class.

☠

"He told you what?!" Yumi shouted in disbelief.

"Um . . . he said that the class was a unit . . . and that I was letting down the unit," October recalled. "Then he said that if we were in a wartime situation, I would be the first to get *fragged*."

October sat at her usual cafeteria table, recounting the grim scene that had unfolded when she arrived almost fifteen minutes late to Mr. Santuzzi's class. In addition to the military-themed lecture, she was also to endure an after-school detention.

"*Fragged*? That's hilarious!" Yumi doubled over in laughter. "What does that even mean?"

"It's when soldiers shoot their commanding officer in the back," said Stacey. "Happened a lot in Vietnam."

Yumi exploded into another bout of laughter, and nobody could be sure if she was laughing because Santuzzi had said it, or because Stacey No-last-name, secretly a Vietnam vet, knew what it meant.

"So, I'm at school until, like, five today because of the detention," lamented October, and she dropped her face into her hands.

"What? Oh no!" Yumi said. "But I was going to ask you to join the curling team with me! Sign-up and the first practice both happen today after school."

"Curling?" Stacey asked, thoroughly amused.

"Yeah, so?" deflected Yumi. Then she hurled her pitch to October. "It's really fun. Trust me, Schwartz. All the girls worth talking to go out for the curling team. Please join with me, please, *please*!"

Yumi Takeshi, while not as intimidating a lecturer as Mr. Santuzzi, was nearly as persuasive. She compensated for her lack of menace with persistence and annoyance.

"I don't know," October said. "This sounds like it might be a lot of work . . . and exercise."

"It's only two practices a week. Plus one game a week, once the season starts."

"That sounds like a lot of time I could spend — oh, sleeping, watching TV, reorganizing the canned vegetables in the kitchen cupboard."

"You'll meet new people! You get a broom! Mr. O'Shea is the coach!" Yumi was throwing out anything that could possibly be viewed as a bonus to curling. A broom? Plus, Mr. O'Shea was coaching? Was that guy everywhere?

"Okay," October relented. "I can't go today because of

detention, but you can sign me up!"

"Yes!" exclaimed Yumi, pumping her fists in victory. "This is going to be so wicked. Curling is the best sport ever!"

For the uninitiated, curling is a winter sport played on an ice surface that combines the fast-paced action of shuffleboard with the innate thrill of cleaning your house. That said, curling can occasionally be a very exciting and competitive game to *play*, but spectators of curling should keep in mind that the appearance of the Zamboni machine should be regarded as the absolute height of excitement in any game.

Ashlie Salmons and her roving pack of fashionable she-wolves happened to pass by during all this curling banter, and leapt on it like a predator on an immobile gemsbok.

"Playing with brooms, girls?" Ashlie said. "Training for future careers in the custodial arts?"

"At least they *have* future careers!" said Stacey, which wasn't nearly as clever a comeback as it seemed to him at the time.

"The curling team's just perfect for Zombie Tramps like you," Ashlie continued. "It's where all the degenerate wastes of skin pass the time. Have fun."

With a flick of her perfectly brushed hair, she and her goon squad exited the cafeteria, giggling as they went.

"I can never come up with a decent comeback!" Yumi said.

"Want me to mess her up?" asked Stacey, but everyone knew (himself included) that he was only joking. Ashlie Salmons could merely stun October and Yumi into silence; for a male social outcast like Stacey (who already had a stupid name), it might involve his total social banishment for the rest of high school.

"She's on the volleyball team," said Yumi. "Like that's any less moronic."

"Oh, barf," said October.

"What?"

"My dad's coaching volleyball."

☠

Detention with Santuzzi was not quite as bad as October had

anticipated. He had her write a five-page essay on how math class is not unlike a military squadron. Though how he expected her to know what a military squadron was like was beyond her. October could only assume extra credit would be awarded for references to exit wounds, napalm, and/or Charlie Foxtrots.

While October tried to develop a military metaphor for pop quizzes — an ambush? Too obvious — she considered Mr. Santuzzi, seated behind his desk in his tight grey vest and pants. His clothing always appeared two sizes too small for a man his build, and ever since Yumi had mentioned a hairpiece, his hair looked more and more like a muskrat that some mischievous sorcerer had enchanted to lie still on his scalp. Santuzzi was concentrating on his desk, aligning all the papers, books, and writing utensils to perfect 90-degree angles with the desk edges.

October wondered what could have driven this former serviceman into teaching. He certainly didn't seem to like teenagers. In fact, he seemed to despise them, a blight upon his otherwise satisfactory days. From what little her dad had told her about Mr. Santuzzi, he wasn't too fond of his fellow teachers, either. If she were to believe Yumi and Stacey's rumours, Santuzzi had been forced out of the Canadian military because he was "too thorough in his methodology." Yumi claimed her cousin hacked into the Canadian military's soldier database, where she read that cryptic dismissal statement. The information seemed suspect to October; was there even such a thing as a soldier database?

Yumi also imparted to October a long-standing school rumour that Santuzzi had once been kidnapped by three senior students who disagreed with his grading system. They caught him off guard, bound him with rope to his wheelie-chair and rolled him across town to one of the boys' garages. They demanded he change their marks or they would never set him free. While they were busy threatening him, Santuzzi had secretly freed himself from the ropes using a broken glass shard from his wristwatch. He then handily subdued the student kidnappers, beating one within an inch — no, a centimetre — of his life with a metre stick. Because he was a victim of abduction, Yumi sagely reasoned, he was never charged with aggravated assault — it was self-defence. He still used that metre stick to this very day, student blood dried into its fibres; or so the rumour went.

"Yeah. That sounds entirely probable," Stacey scoffed.

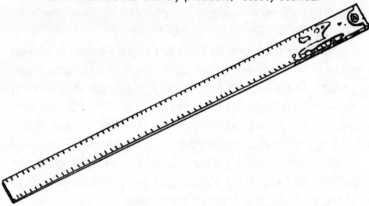

"That's probably the phoniest story I've ever heard in my life," October said. "Why would they let him teach after that?"

"I dunno," Yumi had said. "Teachers' unions are pretty strong. Or maybe," she raised her hand, as if painting a picture with her open palm, "all that happened in some other town, and he changed his identity to start a new life in Sticksville."

"What are you looking at?" Mr. Santuzzi barked, aware that October had been studying him and his possibly checkered past. "Eyes down. You have five pages to write before five, remember? Five by five. Unless you want another assignment: *How is October Schwartz like a failing student?*"

After that, October powered through the essay. The Santuzzi story still sounded like a hoax, but she was reluctant to discard any rumours she heard about her math teacher. He was certainly bad news; the only question was *how* bad.

☠

Through the orange, black, and brown shadows of her backyard, October crept to the cemetery. She held a silver flashlight in one hand to illuminate her path. In the other hand, she had a copy of Lovecraft's *The Outsider and Others* that Mr. O'Shea had lent her. As a horror book, she figured it was probably best read in the dark.

44

Yes, she'd recently had a rough experience in the cemetery, but that wasn't about to stand in the way of an unbeatable reading experience. And yes, her dad wasn't keen on her sneaking into the cemetery at night, but he'd retired to his room about an hour ago, which was pretty well an open invitation for October to sneak out.

Pushing past the gate that separated her yard from the Sticksville Cemetery, October guided her flashlight beam back and forth, looking for a comfortable spot to sit. She captured a large tree stump in the disc of light and established her makeshift seat. Her back turned to Cyril Cooper's headstone, she propped open the paperback and held the flashlight above the pages. Her dad had warned her against reading by flashlight; it would make her eyes bleed or shrivel up or something. But sometimes, just sometimes, you've got to risk blindness to read a scary book in the pitch-black night.

Sixteen pages into the book, October couldn't really see what the fuss was about. The first story featured a lot of cargo ships and decaying fish (which was gross) and despair, but not much that could be labelled "scary." There may have been a sea monster involved, but it was so vague, she couldn't even tell. As October became frustrated, reading and re-reading the same sentences by accident, she began to hear distant whispers.

Immediately, October was reminded of the half-invisible girl she'd seen on her birthday — right before that bat got up close and personal with her face. What a mistake it was, heading back into the cemetery in the middle of the night when there were weird girls running around and summoning bats! What if the whispering voice was that girl's? Why would a girl be skulking around the cemetery at night? A girl besides October, that is; her presence there was completely normal. There was no way that girl was a ghost, was there? Because that would just be stupid.

October didn't know how she felt about ghosts, but it was too late, she had already made the logical leap that turned this vision of a girl into a possible phantom. She didn't totally believe in ghosts, but she had read too many horror stories to be certain they *didn't* exist. This paradox was exactly why October was so frightened; even more so when she heard other whispers. While she couldn't hear what was being said, she was nearly positive they were not just voices in her head.

She dropped the book into the cold grass and waved her flashlight around maniacally, trying to determine who was whispering, and where. She searched the area closest to her backyard, the row of aboveground tombs, the grove of trees — and then she saw her.

A girl about twelve with a constellation of freckles and her blondish hair in a bun peeked out from behind a large willow. Her skin was whitish blue and paper-thin. October could nearly see through her. The flashlight panned down to the section of the girl's tattered skirt that was unhidden by the massive tree. The young girl must have noticed the movement of light, because her eyes widened, her mouth opened in a silent gasp, and in an instant she disappeared completely. Winked out of existence.

October froze in place on the tree stump. Not physically, mind you. Though the evening was slightly chilly, it wasn't nearly cold enough for that. October was instead frozen by the enormity of what she believed she had just seen. Forget belief; she was sure she had seen something. A spectre of a girl, spying on her from behind a tree. A girl who magically disappeared.

The cemetery behind October Schwartz's house was home to a ghost. Suddenly, it didn't seem like such a fantastic place to read anymore.

☠

After a couple of weeks, the thrill ride that is curling kind of lost its magic for me. Though I'd have been happy to get back to afternoons of watching television and reading in the graveyard, Yumi was still really into it, and I wanted to be a good friend, so I stayed on the team. She had jumped to the head of the class, or the team — whatevs — to become skip of the junior girls, which is like the captain in curling. She was like Mr. . . . uh, Coach . . . O'Shea's brain in action on the ice. Mr. O'Shea was one of the genuinely cool teachers in school, so that was a bonus. My participation on the team also meant I got an easy ride in French class (not that I needed it).

Mr. O'Shea gave me my first-ever critical analysis or review on my book at a Thursday night practice, but that didn't happen until we ran through about a half-million drills. We had to set up guard stones, practice takeouts, and make sure all the opposing stones were *hogged*. At that point, I could barely get the stone into the house — usually it either rocketed all the way down the ice, crashing into the boards at the other end, or stalled halfway there, like my dad's compact car on any hill steeper than a 15-degree angle.

The worst thing about curling — and it's hard to pick just one thing — is that we had to drive to practice halfway across town to this arena called the Temple of Ice, because apparently you can't just dump buckets of water onto the gym floor and crank down the thermostat. Ice sports had to happen at the Temple of Ice, which was completely heinous because hockey

The Peanut Butter Solution

teams practised there, too, so the arena was always crawling with these pimply hockey guys. They laughed when we busted out our brooms and slipper shoes.

Okay, so I'm getting a little ahead of myself. If you're anywhere near a normal person, you probably haven't the slightest idea what a *stone* or *button* or *takeout* is, and *hogging* probably sounds like something filthy. I'm not going to turn this into a curling instruction manual or anything, but I should explain a couple things:

There are, like, these ice lanes. You take a stone, which is a big . . . well, stone . . . with a handle on it, and you glide it down the ice, trying to get it close to or inside the house. If you were on the roof of the arena, the house would look like a big bull's eye. So you glide your stone as close as you can, and two teammates take brooms and sweep like crazy in front of the stone's path if they want to speed the stone up or change its direction or what have you. Crazy, right?

So you go on like this, taking turns, and the other team can knock your stones out of the house, kind of like bocce ball or croquet. Again, two games you've probably never played if you're under a hundred.

Thing is, I was horrible at it. I couldn't throw the stone very well, I could barely keep from falling over in the stupid slipper shoe, and despite what Ashlie Salmons might believe about my future career as a street sweeper, I was no good with the broom, either. My arms just wouldn't move quickly enough, so Yumi, the skip, was always screaming — "Hurry! Hurry hard!" — then laughing like a hyena as soon as the play was over. It was so not funny. And she's like a curling prodigy or something, which is relentlessly annoying. I had to redo my turn several times because I burned the stone, which meant I touched it with my broom. You try to keep control of that broom!

I was up, stone in hand, and instead of gliding the stone magnificently like a boat off to sea, I *might* have accidentally tossed it into the air, and it *might* have come crashing down, nearly cutting off Yumi's foot and cracking the ice. Mr. O'Shea figured we should leave, just in case the hockey players had heard what we'd done. Yumi and the other two curling juniors — Tricia MacKenzie and Lena Aldroty — went to the girls' locker room to change. And yes, we only had four players. No alternates or understudies or whatever you call them in sports. Benchwarmers, I guess. If anyone gets sick, we're totally disqualified.

Mr. O'Shea kept me back because he wanted to talk about my book. Awesome, no? Well, maybe not. Even though I thought my story concept was total genius, I worried what someone like Mr. O'Shea thought about it. He was used to reading Lovecraft — which ended up being very good; not super-scary, but really creepy and atmospheric — and things with more literary merit. No one was choking demons to death with a bathtub chain on his reading list, I bet.

It took a while to hear what he thought because he couldn't even find the photocopies and notes he'd made without his glasses. His blue duffel bag was laid out across the bench, spread open like a dissected frog, and changes of clothes and books were scattered all over the floor.

"You okay, Mr. O'Shea?" I asked.

"Yes, yes. Sorry, Ms. Schwartz," he rubbed at his temples. "I can't seem to establish where I last put my glasses. I've been so distracted lately."

I wasn't sure how I could help, but I felt embarrassed for the guy. I didn't want him making a scene in front of the hockey players.

"Uh, where did you last see them?"

"I had placed them in the bag, along with a snack and my notes and these books . . . Ack, I don't think I even brought the right books. I had meant to pack *At the Mountains of Madness* for you to borrow. Oh dear, I really am a mess . . . and, well, here's the glasses case, but no glasses."

Mr. O'Shea then popped his case open and closed like he was operating a puppet. All he needed was to throw his voice and he could have been a stand-up comedian; except he'd need better personal hygiene if he were going to be on a stage. His fingers had peanut butter all over them. It seemed really strange, because if I was going to rank the personal grooming habits of the teachers at Sticksville Central (the thought had crossed my mind) he'd be close to the top of the list, right up there with the moustache-manicuring Mr. Santuzzi and light-years ahead of most of the computer science teachers who — and this is not a generalization — all seemed to have permanent sweat stains around their mega-wrinkled short-sleeve dress shirts. Which was kind of how I figured the mystery out.

"Mr. O'Shea, what's on your face?"

"My face?" He looked horrified. "I don't know. There's something on my face?" He pressed his fingers gingerly against the various regions of his skull. "Well, now there's peanut butter all over it, thank you very much."

"Yes, but before, there was dried peanut butter on your temples," I tried to explain.

"I see."

"What sort of snack did you bring to practice, Mr. O'Shea? A peanut butter sandwich?"

"Yes, but . . ." Instantly, Mr. O'Shea ran to the garbage can just inside the arena's entrance. Soon he was pawing through trash like a starving sewer rat. "Nice work," he said once he'd returned with his glasses in a little zip-lock bag. I guess he was impressed or probably more just relieved to have his glasses back. "How did you figure it out?"

"Usually, you don't have dried food on your temples," I explained. "And when you opened up your glasses case, it reminded me of my old retainer, and how I'd always stuff it in a napkin or something at restaurants, and my dad would always have to spend an hour rooting through the garbage."

"You're a regular Sherlock Holmes. Good thing you're smarter than your curling coach," he said. "Otherwise I'd never have been able to read you the comments I made on *Night of the Thousand Demons*."

"It's *Two Knives, One Thousand Demons*."

"Really?"

"I'm pretty sure."

"Maybe you want to consider changing it?"

Listen, old man, you're nice and all, but are you insane? The title's the single best thing about the book so far.

"I've made a lot of notes, but I should preface everything by saying I very much enjoyed the book. You need to work on a few things, but overall, this novel is shaping up to be an impressive piece of horror literature! Even more impressive when you consider you're only thirt—"

"Shhhh!" I hissed. "The other girls will hear. I'm kind of trying to keep that a secret."

"Oh, they're all in the locker room. Besides, they won't care that you're a year younger than them. It would explain why you're not at their level in curling."

Mr. O'Shea was just hilarious. Comedy gold spilled from his lips. He might have been a lot of things: French teacher, curling pro, Plotzdam Conference roadie, horror fan, but one thing he was certainly not was a thirteen-year-old girl. And this thirteen-year-old girl thought it'd be a pretty solid idea to keep her age a secret for now. Still, it was nice that he'd liked the book so far.

"So you liked it? Really? What did you like best?"

What Mr. O'Shea liked best, apparently, was that the story jumped right into the action. Boom! He had some Latin name for it — *in medias res* — but I'm not even sure if I'm remembering it correctly. He towelled off his face and told me all about it.

"Too many books of the supernatural try to explain themselves. They'll spend pages and pages describing the science of the zombies or the monsters, and I always find it inane. Zombies aren't real, we all know that, but we're reading to be entertained, to disbelieve for a while. You jump right into things: *There are demons. Deal with it.* It's great!"

He went on about a bunch of other things — he liked that I'd limited Olivia's weapons to two knives (and the occasional bathtub chain) — but I'll spare you the boring details. Don't get me wrong. I loved hearing all about it, but it's kind of personal. The only thing he really felt needed work was Olivia, my main character. Said she needed more depth, that she was only one-dimensional.

"Olivia is a compelling heroine, but we don't know anything about her. She kills demons, she's good at it, yes, but what else?"

"I don't know," I stammered. "Does there have to be an else?"

"I want the else. Give Olivia some layers — why is she doing this? What else could she be doing? Maybe give her a bit of mystery."

By that point, Yumi had arrived from the locker room, and when she gave me the nod, I realized I had to go. We both thanked Mr. O'Shea and he began repacking his duffel bag. I didn't even have the chance to change clothes, so I smelled like curling practice all the way home.

Something about Mr. O'Shea's comments bugged me. I can take criticism, but more depth? Add a mystery? I'm writing a super-violent horror book here, with intense gore and adult situations. Who's reading for layered characters? Still, he'd read the book closely, and apparently had given it more thought than I had.

I think I'd like Mr. O'Shea more if he wasn't always right.

☠

Spontaneous combustion can really ruin your night.

Here's just one example (and I'm sure there are plenty others): I was walking home from curling practice; normally I'd just cut through the cemetery and go in the back way. But that night I reached Riverside Drive and started having second thoughts about taking the shortcut. I think it must have been because of the girl I saw the other night.

I was facing the front gates of the cemetery and it wasn't even super-late. Like, 7:40 or something, but it was starting to get dark. The last time I'd spent any time in the cemetery while it was dark, I may or may not have seen a ghost — even though Mr. O'Shea's all like "those aren't real" — and it creeped me out. I wasn't really overly jazzed to stroll through the gothic, old cemetery.

But whatever. Scared or not, I couldn't stop, like, living my life. I couldn't start acting like a baby now, afraid of the dark; I'd kept the secret so far. Besides, it shaved a full ten minutes off the trip home.

First, I felt sweat starting to soak through my shirt. Not totally unheard of — after all, there may have been a ghost lurking in the area, which made me tense. And member of the curling team or not, I maybe wasn't in the best shape. I've been known to sweat while climbing the stairs. Not a big deal.

But then, my back felt warm — unnaturally so. But it wasn't coming from my back; it was coming from inside my backpack. Just as I took it off to figure out what was so hot inside, my backpack totally *burst into flame!* So I threw it onto the grass, went into stop, drop, and roll mode, and ground my backpack into the dirt, which was somewhat tragic. I'd been doing a pretty good job of keeping it clean and, you know, *not on fire* until then. I sat there panting for a couple of minutes until I figured my bag was cool enough to touch. When I opened it to survey the damage, it was a bad scene.

The bag's outside didn't seem too bad — a bit extra-crispy, for sure, but the fire had come from inside. My math textbook was nothing but cinders (Santuzzi wouldn't be happy about that), my lunch container was melted and fused into a weird hourglass shape, and most unfortunate of all, *Pet Sematary*,

Stephen King's finest novel of 1984, was nothing more than a pile of well-written ash.

Really only one thing was undamaged: the composition book marked "Two Knives, One Thousand Demons."

☠

Until the middle of the month, October avoided the cemetery at night like Mr. Santuzzi avoided random acts of kindness. (To wit, the math teacher gave her a week of detention when she showed up to class with a crispy black wafer, asking for an exchange of textbook.) She continued to spend time in the cemetery during afternoons, when she could see everything in clear daylight, but was quick to hurry home at the first sign of dusk. The whole notion of ghosts haunting the graveyard just seconds from her home unnerved her, and she made a conscious effort to focus on the less supernatural matters in her life.

One of those less supernatural matters was curling, and even though she'd been just atrocious at the beginning, she had graduated to almost decent. Mr. O'Shea, at least, was fairly pleased with the strides the novice junior team had made.

"We have our first game coming up on October 14th," he reminded them. "And I think you're really going to knock some socks off."

Knock some socks off, October thought. *Who says that?*

October tried to find time to practice her trombone, too, but her dad often complained that it gave him a headache, and it was difficult to spare the hours with curling taking up so much of her free time. October was expertly keeping busy in a concerted effort to not think about ghosts in the cemetery — the cemetery that was a one-minute walk, or, say, spectral projection, from her bedroom — but no matter what she did, her mind always wound its way back to those spooky evenings. While coasting down the ice at practice, the phantom girl's face appeared in her head. When reading in the safety of her house, she imagined the pages were heating up, scalding her fingers. But when she put the book down, she felt it was no more than room temperature. Every day she heard ghostly whispers. Even the volume of her trombone couldn't drown them out.

☠

With October's — the month, not the girl — second week, so arrived the official start of curling season. October — the girl this time — was seated that Tuesday afternoon with both the junior and senior girls' curling teams in a short, cheddar yellow school bus driven by Mr. O'Shea. He was driving them to New Hammersmith, a neighbouring town, to play Robert Bishop High School in their first match of the year. "Driving" was probably an overstatement. Though Mr. O'Shea was seated behind a steering wheel and pressing an accelerator, October had been on faster tricycles.

October lowered the book she was reading and whispered to Yumi, seated beside her, "When does the game start? We'll never make it at this rate."

Yumi was putting on lipstick, which should give you a good indication of how fast the bus was travelling. "It's at 4:30, but New Hammersmith is just outside Sticksville. We'll be there in no time."

"I think we may actually be going backward," October said. "I'll probably finish my book by the time we get there." October had taken out another Lovecraft novel from the Sticksville Public Library. Yumi picked up the library loan.

"*The Dunwich Horror*," she said, evaluating it. "Disturbing cover. Is it scary?"

"Kind of," October decided. "It's really good, though. Mr. O'Shea got me into Lovecraft. He was supposed to lend me another one of this guy's books, but he keeps forgetting."

October looked to the front seat of the bus. It was hard to imagine the white-haired, balding man, going 30 kilometres an

hour in a 60 zone, could like anything close to cool, but she had to admit he was nearly there. Tricia MacKenzie, seated on the left side of the bus just behind Mr. O'Shea, was peeking her head up behind the seat. She was facing the rear of the bus, talking with one of the senior team girls. The way she stared out from behind the seat, combined with Tricia's freckled face, reminded October of the girl in the cemetery. A shiver ran down October's spine.

"What's up?" Yumi asked.

"Nothing. It's nothing," October said, but then continued, in a conspiratorial whisper, "Yumi . . . do you . . . do you believe in ghosts?"

"What, *ghosts*?" Yumi said, as if October had just asked her if it was ethically sound to eat babies.

Immediately, October felt stupid. She couldn't believe how stupid she was to ask that stupid question. Now her new best friend thought she was certifiably insane, ready to be hauled off by men in white overcoats.

"I don't know," Yumi said. "I never used to, but maybe three years ago my mom woke me up at night, saying she thought she'd seen a ghost down in our laundry room. Told me she thought it was the ghost of my brother."

"You don't have a brother," October interjected.

"I don't. Anymore." Yumi got quiet and stared at the seat cushion in front of her.

"Oh wow. I'm sorry," October said.

"It's okay. He was my older brother, Taro, and it happened,

like, six years ago now. Who knows what my mom saw. But I have a hard time just disregarding her."

October sat, thinking about ghosts and dead brothers and missing mothers, and wondering if she should tell Yumi what she had seen in the cemetery. Yumi had been conspicuously open-minded about the whole ghost subject, but October wasn't sure how far she should pursue the conversation.

"Why are you asking me about ghosts?" Yumi asked. "Is that what your book is about?"

"Sort of," October answered.

"Did you see a ghost?" Yumi asked.

"No," October said, and bit her lower lip.

"Did your mom or someone say they saw a ghost?"

"My mom left ten years ago," October answered, nervously playing with her ankh necklace. "We haven't really . . . talked."

"Oh," Yumi said, and her line of questioning ended.

October opened her book to where she'd left off. The bus was probably still hours from New Hammersmith.

☠

The Sticksville Central junior curling team soundly trounced their Robert Bishop opponents, six to four. October was elated. She and the other players excitedly discussed the details of the win during the lengthy bus ride back to school. It was now after eight, and Sticksville, outside the bus windows, was all inky black. Inside the bus, the girls laughed and cheered through a greyish haze. Mr. O'Shea smiled as he very gingerly banked the bus around the gentle bends of Riverside Drive.

Yumi and Lena congratulated October; they said her miraculous

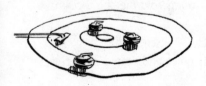 double takeout had won them the game. October didn't think so, and was a bit embarrassed because the double takeout was entirely accidental.

"Who cares?" countered Yumi, with logic that couldn't be argued with. "The invention of gunpowder? Also an accident.

We won!" The back of the bus erupted with a cheer of four teenage girls.

The short bus crept into the Sticksville Central parking lot around seven. Mr. O'Shea didn't even need to slow down for the speed bumps. The bus eased over them like a rolling tree sloth. October was amazed to see that a good number of cars remained in the darkened lot. Her dad had volleyball practice, she knew, but she guessed many other teachers must have other evening extracurricular activities she didn't know about. Or they had fallen asleep at their desks. Something like that. Mr. Hamilton, the principal, could be seen at one of the front windows, watching the small school bus return. A number of cars also idled by the front entrance of the school — dutiful parents waiting to retrieve their hard-working sons and daughters. Or possibly they were enterprising child-snatchers.

The school bus emptied and Mr. O'Shea tapped the horn as he waved out the door. "Good game, girls! I'll see you at practice!"

October said goodbye to Yumi, who leapt into her mom's minivan, and turned toward the school. October had to wait until volleyball practice was finished to get a ride from her dad. He'd kill her if she walked home alone this late, and, after the exploding backpack incident, she was not too keen to take a shortcut through the cemetery.

"Ms. Schwartz," Mr. O'Shea called out from the open door of the school bus. "Ms. Schwartz, do you know if your father will still be at school? I was hoping to finally pick up my car from the auto shop."

"Yeah," October yelled from across the front plaza outside the school. "He's coaching volleyball, but he should be done soon."

Mr. O'Shea heaved the door closed and methodically steered the bus into the parking lot, slow enough that October figured the stick shift must have been locked in neutral.

☠

October avoided the front door and circled around the school. The gym entrance was at the school's rear, which is where she planned to sit and read *The Dunwich Horror* until her dad was finished with volleyball practice. And if she could avoid running into her least favourite person and volleyballer Ashlie Salmons, that would be a miracle.

Miracles rarely happen here on planet earth, and so, as she rounded the corner and crossed under the outdoor basketball nets, October nearly put out her own eye walking into Ashlie Salmons's lit cigarette. Underneath the chain-link hoops, Ashlie and some guy — it looked like he could have been the guitarist in that Phantom Moustache band — were sharing a smoke and were drinking something out of a Gatorade bottle that was probably filled with something other than electrolytes.

"Whoa," shouted the guitarist, as October narrowly avoided colliding into him.

"Sorry," October spat.

But Ashlie, who looked quite alien in her shorts and T-shirt, had way more to say.

"Zombie Tramp! Can you leave me alone for one night?" Ashlie was visibly enraged. Her skin tone began to match the colour of her hair and she flipped her half-finished cigarette to the pavement, and stubbed it out with her ultra-white sneakers.

"Hey, I was still smoking that," the guitarist protested.

"Shut up, Devin. And you shut up, too," she whirled over to October like one sneaker was bolted to the blacktop. "I swear, you say you saw me out here tonight to anyone — to your dad — and I'll stab you in the neck. You'll be real happy, too, because you can be a zombie for real."

October instinctively reached for her throat. She couldn't seem to generate a single word.

"Cripes, Ashlie, calm down. What are you worried about? What's she going to tell her dad? We're just out here smoking and —"

"Shut up, Devin. Zombie Tramp's dad is my volleyball coach. And if you recollect, I'm supposed to be practising volleyball right now."

"So?"

"So I don't want any of this getting back to my mother," she loudly whispered.

"Ashlie, I —" October began.

Before October could get any further however, who should arrive on this evening basketball-court interlude but October's math teacher, Mr. Santuzzi. He emerged from the darkness in a lime green leisure suit, seemingly patrolling the back lot of the school. Perhaps his military muscle memory kept him patrolling the school's perimeter, as if keeping night watch.

"What's happening back here?" he barked. "What are you all doing here?"

"Uh." The guitarist's mouth froze, but his hands still had sense enough to jam the Gatorade bottle into his backpack.

"We were at volleyball practice," Ashlie said. "We just got . . . overheated. Mr. Schwartz sent us out here for some air."

Mr. Santuzzi's eagle-eyes surveyed the three and their motley attire.

"Is this true, Ms. Schwartz?" he demanded. "You're playing volleyball? You don't seem dressed for the sport."

"I hand out the orange slices."

This answer satisfied Santuzzi, who exited into the night as smoothly as he entered. Crisis averted. Or so October thought.

"You better not tell," Ashlie muttered as she yanked open the school's back entrance, and the guitarist made an awkward retreat. "Stabbed. In. The. Neck."

☠

The Dunwich Horror propped onto her knees, October sat in front of the row of bright red lockers that bordered the athletic corridor. The shrieks and yipes of bright white sneakers on waxed wooden floors could be heard from inside the gymnasium. October tried not to think about Ashlie and how she made her blood boil, and instead immersed herself in a world of deformed albino mothers, sorcerers, and books of the dead — no white sneakers or fashionable belts allowed.

"Sorry I'm late."

October looked up from her book to see a creature that looked like her dad, but he had a silver whistle around his neck and was wearing navy sweat shorts. How unfortunate.

"You're wearing shorts," said October, disappointed.

"I was coaching volleyball. What do you want?"

"Mr. O'Shea manages to coach while wearing pants like a normal adult."

"Mr. O'Shea coaches on the ice at a rink several blocks away," reasoned October's dad. "Once they keep that gym at a temperature below sub-Saharan, then I'll put on some pants. Deal?"

October's face belied that she felt that was no excuse.

"Like I said, I'm sorry I'm late. I had to have a private talk with one of the players. Do you have any classes with Ashlie Salmons?"

"Yeah. Why?"

"She ran out of practice. I couldn't find where she went. I hope she got home all right."

October didn't say anything in response. She couldn't really share her father's concern for Ashlie's welfare.

October hoisted herself up from the dusty floor and slid *The Dunwich Horror* into her bag.

"So did you win?" her dad asked.

"Yeah," October said. "We crushed them."

"Fantastic! Remind me to make a detour to the supermarket on the way home. I need to pick up some celebratory mint chocolate chip. You ready to go?" Mr. Schwartz lifted a duffel bag and briefcase from that same dusty athletic corridor floor.

"You're not going to drive me home in gym shorts," October answered.

"Sorry, lady."

Pushing open the grey blue double doors to the parking lot, October saw there were far fewer cars straggling behind. The short little school bus remained huddled in a corner of the lot.

"Oh, did Mr. O'Shea get a hold of you, Dad?"

Mr. Schwartz arched an eyebrow at his daughter. "What are you talking about?"

☠

Once home, October peered gloomily out the sliding glass door to the backyard. At another time, faced with the threat of a neck-stabbing (as exaggerated as it may have been), October would have sought refuge in the cemetery. But now some rotten, fun-hating girl ghost had taken up residence, started setting random things on fire, and basically ruined everything for her. Why was that girl haunting the cemetery? Could October have imagined it? She had to admit that imagining the same ghost twice seemed improbable.

☠

October arrived early to French class the next morning. She wanted to apologize to Mr. O'Shea that she and her dad had left practice before he'd had a chance to find them, and maybe get that copy of *At the Mountains of Madness* from him. However, Mr. O'Shea didn't arrive early like October, so she was kept waiting. The hands of the clock on the wall inched forward and fellow students continued to arrive, but Mr. O'Shea made no appearance.

Just two minutes prior to the bell, a short, thin, middle-aged blonde woman with thick-framed glasses entered and stood at the front of the class with a paper that seemed grafted to her left hand. October looked around to the other students to see if this woman's appearance made any sense to them. They looked similarly befuddled.

"*Bonjour*, everybody," the woman said. "This morning there will be a special assembly in the place of your usual French class.

Principal Hamilton should make an announcement over the P.A. system presently."

True enough, Mr. Hamilton's baritone voice soon entered their classroom from afar, asking all teachers to bring their classes to the gymnasium. The blonde woman led them down the monochromatic hallways. October wondered why Mr. O'Shea was absent, but didn't have much time to wonder since Ashlie Salmons, striding toward the gym with her drama class (drama queen), had quickly appeared beside her. Some student traffic jam closer to the gym entrance forced both October's French class and Ashlie's drama class to halt at the same exact point in the corridor. The pause gave October and Ashlie ample time to chat and share, something October had been thinking the two of them didn't do nearly enough.

"Hey, Zombie Tramp." Ashlie adjusted her belt and leggings as the crowd slowly lurched forward. "You have any idea what this assembly is about?"

October pretended not to hear her, which — helpful hint number forty-three — is a rather ineffective way of handling someone who is harassing you.

"I'll take a stab at it," Ashlie continued, unfazed by October's silent treatment, "I heard that Principal Hamilton is instituting an immediate ban on all Zombie Tramps. Something about impeding the spread of mono through the school. You and your other zombie friends are going to be first against the wall."

October simmered with anger and glared at Ashlie. She tried to will her eyes to shoot concentrated heat rays for the first time ever. It didn't work.

"It's hard to kill the undead," October replied through gritted teeth.

The logjam of students finally broke and both lines of students progressed toward the gym. Her dad was stony-faced as he tried to wrangle his grade eleven biology class. The entire school was seated on bleachers on one edge of the basketball court. October spied Yumi and Stacey several rows above, and climbed the bleachers to join them.

"Hey," said October.

"Hey," Yumi replied. "Who's the lady that brought your class in? I thought you had French with Mr. O'Shea in the morning."

"I do. I think he's absent. Maybe he got a cold from being out on the ice yesterday."

"Yeah," said Yumi. "Or maybe he's still driving here."

October and Yumi chuckled. Stacey had the look of puzzled indifference that teenage boys often wear.

Mr. Hamilton entered and walked over to the microphone that had been placed in the centre of the basketball court. The assembly looked hastily arranged, with a lonely mic stand propped in the middle of the gym floor, and two large speakers on either side. One of the tech boys was seated behind one speaker, pushing the glasses up the bridge of his nose, rebuttoning his Hawaiian shirt, and looking rather harried as he checked that the wires had been connected properly for the third time.

"Good morning," Principal Hamilton began, and the hum of dozens of conversations dimmed to complete silence. Principal Hamilton was a rather imposing man, over six feet tall, with a gleaming shaven head, and finely manicured moustache.

"I want to thank all of you students and teachers for joining me in the gymnasium on such short notice," Hamilton continued in his deep voice. "I'm afraid that the reason for this sudden assembly is a very sad circumstance, and rather than draw out the tragic, unfortunate news, I am simply going to describe to you what occurred last night.

"Late last night, there was a terrible accident in our school's automobile repair shop. One of our beloved teachers, Mr. Terry O'Shea, was crushed by a car that fell from the lift. . . ."

October gasped and unconsciously grasped at her necklace.

"Mr. O'Shea was rushed to the hospital when one of our custodians found him last evening," Principal Hamilton continued, "but the injuries he sustained were too severe. Terry O'Shea passed away at Sticksville Medical Centre early this morning."

☠

FROM THE DIARY OF HENRI LAFLEUR -
DEFENSE D'ENTRER!
February 12, 1969

(The following diary entry has been translated from the French, for your reading enjoyment.)

Hallo again. Henri here. You've probably forgotten all about me; it's been so long. But I have a good reason for not writing.

I am in love! Yes, in love! With that same astonishing giantess I was writing about earlier: Celeste Boulanger.

Much has happened over the past four months. Jean-Paul brought me to a few parties that Celeste also attended. At first, I was much too shy to talk to her, but things slowly progressed somehow, despite my inability to talk. By Christmas, we were making out on the tables of the University Student Life Centre and in the booths of some of the St. Laurent student bars. It was like the genie from the television show dropped into my life and made all my wishes come true.

My romantic life is quite excellent. I will not bore you with the details . . . I imagine it would be quite embarrassing to look back upon it years from now. Even what I've already written distresses me. Our three-month anniversary is coming up shortly. I am not sure if this is an occasion when you buy a gift. Is three months a milestone that couples celebrate?

To complicate matters, I already bought her a gift of sorts, though she's not aware of this yet. Celeste is studying fine arts at the University of Quebec. I can't pretend that I understand most of her work, as hard as I try. But to describe it: she makes sculptures out of various pieces of junk and garbage she finds. Bicycles with old television sets impaled on the seat, milk crates stuffed with discarded children's dolls, these sorts of things. She asked me to be on the lookout for an old clock for her new sculpture. But the clock had to work, and it needed a second hand. Finding trash in the city is not a problem, but finding trash that is functional (and meets specific requirements) is something entirely different.

As a result, I splurged and bought Celeste a new clock. I plan to surprise her with it this very evening. This morning, I walked into the storefront of the old watchmaker I have passed probably five dozen times on the way to wash dishes. The watchmaker was a short old man who spoke only English, which was frustrating, but he was able to butcher enough French for us to make our business transaction. I was able to purchase a pewter desk clock. I can't remember if Celeste was looking for a desk or wall clock, but I suppose either will do. It works and has a second hand. Everything else is just the gravy on the poutine, no?

But I write not to boast about my attractive girlfriend, as fun as that is. No, instead I write because I am concerned about my friend Jean-Paul and his group. This group now includes me among its number, I guess. We are growing more political, and I've gone along with them until now. You cannot mistake me for a friend or champion of the English — the English treat us Francophones like trash at the university, and not the way Celeste treats her trash — but sometimes my friends take their politics a bit too far.

Regularly, we read La Victoire, the FLQ newspaper, at Bernard's restaurant. They feel Bernard is a friend to the cause and that he won't report them for reading the paper. I imagine their feeling is correct, as we've had no trouble, or rather that Bernard is too busy eyeing the female patrons of his restaurant to care what anyone is reading.

We don't spend evenings out anymore. Instead, we spend time in Jean-Paul's apartment, which he shares with Claude. The apartment is the third floor of an old building. Jean-Paul's place is not much for decoration, marked more by the haze of cigarette smoke and with the sound of Jefferson Airplane songs distorted by Jean-Paul's speakers, than any wall hangings or furniture. We listen to music, talk about stories in La Victoire, discuss girls. Jean-Paul and the others always are ribbing me, suggesting I am more interested in girls and monster movies than I am in Quebec. They may be right, but I always insist I am committed to the cause, to the movement.

In January, an FLQ bomb went off near the home of the chief of police, and Jean-Paul, Claude, and Jean-Marc applauded when Celeste arrived to triumphantly throw the newspaper down on the apartment's kitchen table. But the police chief was a Francophone. What was the FLQ hoping to accomplish? I didn't understand. Jean-Paul said I was just a first-year student. I would understand when I was older. But what is to understand? I am no child.

At the very least, I am still certain that Jean-Paul is not a member of the FLQ himself. Only an avid enthusiast in their projects, I guess.

I couldn't believe it! Mr. O'Shea was dead. I felt like somebody had thrown one of those curling stones into my gut, and I know it wasn't just me. This ugly feeling took over the school and just, like, slept there for the rest of the day. Everybody shuffled around, barely talking to each another. It was like it was a snow day, but for some reason the school hasn't declared it a snow day. So everyone shows up to school on the for-some-reason-not-snow day, but nobody wants to be there, not the students or teachers, and the school's just oozing with gloom. It was like one of those days, but eighteen times worse.

I don't mean to compare Mr. O'Shea's dying to some bad weather. It was way worse. It was an avalanche of sadness, but I'm making myself puke and cry at the same time. Some of the other teachers at Sticksville were okay, but Mr. O'Shea was the only one I really liked, and the only one I felt understood me. At least, a little.

Every class that day was taken over by a silent sadness. Most of the teachers attempted to teach lessons, but it was nearly impossible. Class as usual was simply not happening in what used to be Mr. O'Shea's French class. After the assembly, our class had to return for a remaining half hour of French lessons. But the supply teacher knew about as much French as the average Siamese cat; she asked us to sit quietly at our desks and work on other schoolwork or read or do anything that didn't bother her, basically. I couldn't even begin to imagine how horrible auto shop classes would be. I really hoped they had cancelled them.

I didn't have any other work to do; I was all caught up in my classes, and the only reading materials I had with me were my Lovecraft books, which only reminded me of Mr. O'Shea. How was I not supposed to think about him? I sat at my desk, looking at the old library copy of *The Dunwich Horror* — almost looking through it. The cover started blurring into pixels or one of those Magic Eye pictures where you see the 3-D boat. I couldn't help but picture poor Mr. O'Shea in the hospital, surgeons trying to reset his broken, pretzel limbs. I started to feel sick to my stomach. I could feel tears climbing up my throat to my eyelids and forcing their way through, despite my promise. I wasn't going to cry at school. I really wasn't. But then I did. Me, the stupid baby, not ready for high school. I wiped the salty droplets away with the flat of my hand. By the end of the period, I'm sure my face was a mess, black eyeliner smeared in every direction across the top of my face, but I didn't care. Mr. O'Shea was dead. I didn't even want to go to the washroom to clean it off.

☠

For whatever ridiculous emotional or hormonal reason, I had imagined that after the assembly, Principal Hamilton would close the school for the day, or the teachers would spend their classes sharing memories of Mr. O'Shea, or some nice touchy-feely Hallmark junk like that. But the school day grinded on, and most teachers and students carried on with their routines, the only change being that everyone was now super-sensitive. Any sudden movement or irritation would remind people, "Oh yeah, Mr. O'Shea just died this morning after being crushed by a 2-ton vehicle. So maybe I don't really care what the value of x is if $y = x^2 + 4x + 1$."

Speaking of math, Mr. Santuzzi pressed through his math lessons like a true soldier. Maybe his shoulders slumped a slight bit in his tight pink shirt, and maybe he spoke more gently than I'd ever heard before, but those were the only visible indications that he was aware of his fellow teacher's recent death. But what do I know? Perhaps the mathematical findings of Blaise Pascal were a much more relevant and meaningful topic to our lives. Mr. Santuzzi only referred to Mr. O'Shea's death once, after noticing my face, which probably looked like I'd tried washing up with a spray paint can.

"Ms. Schwartz," Santuzzi said. "Why don't you go to the washroom and clean yourself up? We were all saddened by the death of Terry — Mr. O'Shea — but we should try to put on a brave face." *Saddened*, he said. *Were saddened* — past participle — as if our time for sadness were over, now a full hour later.

"This is my brave face," I answered.

"Yes," Santuzzi (apparently) agreed, probably because he was worried I was going to start crying again or throw myself out the window. "But you've got mascara or something all over. Maybe you can't see it, but you look awful."

"I know. It's my mourning mask," I finally spat.

☠

"I can't believe you said that," Yumi said, half laughing and half crying. I guess she was also a little overwhelmed by Mr. O'Shea's death. He was, after all, our curling coach.

"Neither can I," I said, my eyebrows together. "I'd never talk to Santuzzi like that normally. But I just don't care today. Everyone is sneaking around, pretending like Mr. O'Shea didn't die, and it's *really* bothering me."

Yumi slid down the cafeteria bench and patted my shoulder, like I'd just struck out at the World Series or something. I don't think she fully understood.

"I know what you mean, Schwartz. I liked him, too."

☠

Music class was a disaster. Mrs. Tischmann was determined to play some music, despite the general atmosphere of dread. But everything we played sounded like the soundtrack to a funeral. Stacey pounded the bass drum listlessly, like he was setting a beat to a public execution. The only good thing about music that day was that Ashlie Salmons had enough sense to be completely quiet and didn't say a word to me.

After a version of "Don't Stop Believin'" that sounded like we had all, long ago, stopped believin', Mrs. Tischmann ended class early in exasperation. I quickly packed my trombone into its case and returned it to the instrument storage room. Before walking out the door, I sidled up to Mrs. Tischmann, armed with a very important question: exactly when and where the funeral service for Mr. O'Shea might be held. I needed to know.

Mrs. Tischmann was a little dismayed. "Well, they haven't made any announcements about that yet, but I doubt they'll be informing students."

"But I'd like to go," I insisted.

"You shouldn't feel obligated," Mrs. Tischmann decided. "It won't be like what you imagine. I don't even know if I'll be going, October. We barely talked. I think it's best to remember Mr. O'Shea by the memories you have of him now."

"Okay. . . ." I said, attempting a different approach. I couldn't believe how cold this lady was. Mr. O'Shea just died; you don't have to pretend he's a stranger already. "I'd still like to honour him or something like that — pay my respects."

"Well, Mr. Alito is working on something for students to do right at this moment," Tischmann said. "He had his art class construct a giant card, which the whole school can sign tomorrow and leave their personal messages on. Someone will bring it to the funeral on the students' behalf."

A giant card? What kind of card do you give someone on the day of his funeral? And I kind of had a vendetta against those mass card signings from personal experience. When I broke my leg in grade five, the entire class signed a get well card for me, but the entire class despised me. Even Ellie Plexman, the girl who broke my leg in a particularly unorthodox game of Red Rover, signed the card.

"A card?"

"A card."

"So you're not going to let me know where the funeral service will be?"

"No."

"Fine," I grumbled as I walked away. Mrs. Tischmann was going to be no help at all. She didn't care. "I'll just ask my dad."

☠

Mr. Page had a very different idea of how to teach a class on the day of a death in the faculty. Since it was history class, he wanted all of us to remember Mr. O'Shea and to talk about how he contributed to the history of Sticksville Central and Sticksville in general. Mr. Page started telling all the anecdotes he knew about my curling coach and French teacher.

Mr. Page's class was a total release. A great weight lifted from my stomach like the roller coaster had finally eased into its final stop. I actually laughed. Mr. O'Shea — and I guess I should have figured this from the horror movies and the punk music — was a pretty crazy guy. And since he was so old, I guess he'd had time to accumulate a lot of funny stories. Mostly, I was surprised to learn Mr. O'Shea had taught at Sticksville Central for over thirty years, and even more surprised to find he was good friends with Mr. Santuzzi. That's like being friends with a land mine.

After Mr. Page finished entertaining our class with legendary tales of Mr. O'Shea's life, I could sense the relief washing through the room.

"As your homework tonight," Mr. Page announced, amid quiet boos, "I want you each to write a fitting obituary for Mr. O'Shea, based on the stories I've told you today." He ruffled his hand through his curly brown hair and wiped the condensation from his moustache. "It's a good way for us all to pay our last respects. A good obituary," he said, "can be just as meaningful as any eulogy."

And the school day ended as it began: with Mr. O'Shea dead.

☠

Dad arrived home late. I was writing at the kitchen table when he tossed his blue jacket on the counter and gave me a tight-lipped smile.

"What you working on?"

"History homework," I answered, lifting my head for a millisecond. That was when I guess Dad noticed the faded black smudges around my eyes and on my cheeks.

"I guess you're taking it pretty hard. He must have been a good teacher."

Yeah, Dad. He was one of the best. But I didn't say that. It would be weird. And maybe he'd get, like, professionally jealous. I looked down at my obituary in progress, which was going super-slow. The front doorbell rang.

"Uh, I'll be right back, pumpkin," Dad said.

Doodles of several of my one thousand demons were guarding the margin of my page. Even they made me feel sick; my book just reminded me of Mr. O'Shea. He was the only one besides me who'd read it. I needed to finish my obituary — I hadn't even started typing it up — but I was also, foolishly, considering how I could tie the history of curling in Canada into the essay. It was impossible. The history of curling in Canada was somehow even duller than the history of Canada in general. So I procrastinated. I procrastinated hard.

In the front hallway, Dad was still talking to people at the door, which was odd. Moving closer, I saw two policemen. One looked like an old-timey boxer — narrow, pointy face and a jet black handlebar moustache. The other was a young brown guy. He didn't look much older than some of the guys in school; his uniform looked like a Hallowe'en costume. Speaking of which (mental note) I needed to think of a costume idea. Hallowe'en was only weeks away. But I didn't feel much like dressing up.

Dad and the boxer were talking as the other policeman took down notes in a little black booklet. As I rounded the corner, the two cops turned toward me, their eyes darting back and forth at one another. The kid in the policeman costume scribbled some more notes, like I was evidence of something suspicious.

"Dad, what's going on?"

"October," Dad said. After he said my name, the one cop began writing again. "Can you just wait for me in the kitchen, please? I should only be a minute."

Three minutes later, my dad moseyed back into the kitchen, like he'd just been in the bathroom or something. I didn't even pretend I was working on the obituary assignment.

"What was that?"

Dad feigned confusion, as if police officers stopped by to chat every Wednesday night. "The police . . . the police had to ask me some questions. I am the auto shop teacher after all and Mr. O'Shea *did* die in the auto shop. They wanted to know some things about the lift, safety measures . . . things like that." He coughed. "In fact, I may have to speak to Crown Attorney Salmons in a few days."

"Ashlie's mom?" I said. Tragic.

"Did you have anything to eat yet? I know it's a bit late, but I can —"

"Can I go to the funeral?" I interrupted.

"What?"

"Mr. O'Shea's funeral," I said. "Can I go to it?"

Dad looked at me with some serious fatherly concern. "Now, pumpkin, why would you want to go to that?"

"I just want to go." I didn't think it required any further explanation.

"October," Dad sighed. "I don't know if you really want to go. A funeral . . ." he searched for words.

"Fine," I snapped, then exploded. It was like someone had set off firecrackers at the base of my neck. "I don't know what it is with you and the rest of the school, but apparently you think I can't handle death! You're answering questions from the police about the teacher who was *crushed* in your classroom,

but you don't want me to go to his funeral because — why? — because I'll realize he's *really* dead? I'm not a baby!" At this point, I started crying, which totally hurt my not-a-baby argument. Twice in one day!

"October," Dad pleaded. "I never meant —"

"I know you never meant to, Dad. You just haven't figured out that maybe I can handle the real world a *lot* better than you can," I shot back, sobbing some more, demonstrating how well I could handle the real world. "You can't even talk about Mom without falling apart! I can go to the funeral, Dad, and I'm pretty sure I'll be able to get out of bed the morning after!"

"October!" Dad shouted, but he said nothing afterward. He just watched as I clutched all my paper and pens together and stomped off, opening the sliding glass door and marching into the backyard.

Dad dashed to the open back door. I could hear him behind me and almost see him out the back of my head.

"October!" he called out into the darkness.

I let him wait a few moments, but I eventually replied. "Yeah, Dad."

"You'll come back, won't you?"

"Yeah. I will. I just need to go right now."

"Be careful," Dad said. "I love you." Then I heard the door slide back with a click, and I was alone in the dark.

☠

I wandered into the cemetery through the iron gate in the backyard. In the back of my mind, I remembered my close encounters with what I imagined had been a ghost. I remembered that I was terrified of this cemetery at night. But on a way more relevant level, I didn't care about ghosts, or kidnappers, or wild animals, or homicidal maniacs, or Satanic cults, or zombies, or any other things that might be in the cemetery. I didn't care that my dad was upset or that he hated me out here at night. I only cared that Mr. O'Shea was dead, and more than anything I wanted to be alone in the cemetery, dangers or no.

I was able to find the solitary grave of thirteen-year-old Cyril Cooper relatively easily, so I sat on the chilly earth on top of it, resting my back against the cold headstone. I could feel the engraving of his name against my spine. I tucked my legs in, knees under my chin, then wrapped my arms tight around my legs and started to cry. A hiccup opened in my chest and I began to bawl. For the third time. It must have been a world crying record, and it certainly wasn't my proudest day.

I felt truly awful; like the human version of stuff you'd scrape off your shoe. I'd just finished yelling at my dad and I really was not pleased with myself. I was terrible; I'd gone straight for his jugular, mocking his depression. I mean, I had criticized him for being afraid of death of all things! Who wasn't afraid of death? Might as well have torn into him for being a carbon-based life form while I was at it. One second, you're alive, talking with friends, and then you're not. Worm food. And if this graveyard was any evidence, no one seemed to care when you're gone. I mean, attendance at the Sticksville Cemetery was never ultra-impressive.

Everyone's reaction to Mr. O'Shea being extremely crushed by his own car was making me doubt my sanity. First, I was seeing ghosts and my books were lighting on fire, then I was breaking into tears at school. Not exactly astronaut material. Anyone who could have read my mind would surely have me locked up in a psychiatric ward. Maybe I really *was* my messed-up father's daughter after all. How else could I explain the little ghost girl I kept seeing in the cemetery? Or did I totally imagine my bookbag exploding? Either I was certifiably insane or I was cursed — I'd caused Mom to run away, Mr. O'Shea to die, and the dead to rise from their graves. I sighed heavily and tried to dry my cheeks with my palms, already wet with tears.

In retrospect, I wish I never had asked those questions, because — and I'm not sure how, exactly — they led to an answer. The answer came in a very unusual form moments later, as a pale, translucent girl stepped out from behind a nearby tomb and spoke to me. "Why're ye so sad?" she asked.

I shrank in fright. It was the girl I'd seen before — a small girl, a little younger than me, dressed in a high-collared shirt and kilt, like the daughter of a schoolmarm (whatever a marm is) in *Anne of Green Gables*. A flurry of freckles spotted the deep rings around her large, curious eyes, and her wispy hair was tied back in a bun. And — this was the most important part — I was certain that she was quite dead.

She didn't look much like I figured a ghost would. She looked a good deal more solid, though I could see through her to the tombs behind, and her whole body, clothes and all, was bluish white, as if she and her clothes had drowned together. I felt the sickness from earlier today return to my stomach. But

I had a plan: I pulled my legs tighter to my chest and shut my eyes, knowing the dead girl would disappear when I did, if only momentarily.

But I forgot to plug my ears.

"Did somebo'y hurt ye?" the dead girl, who inexplicably had a Scottish accent, asked. "Ye aren't usually crying when ye're here."

Though I was mad scared, I opened my eyes. The dead girl stared at me with wide eyes and folded her arms in front of her waist. She was patiently awaiting an answer. Oh, how I longed to explain that I was not being rude, I was simply unable to speak because the sight of a dead Scottish lass expressing concern for a sad goth girl in the middle of the night had totally paralyzed my vocal chords, not to mention every other part of my body.

"A'right," the little girl said, looking a bit disappointed. "Ye dinna have ta answer me. I was jes' trying t'be friendly."

The petite girl turned to leave, but stopped in her tracks at the sound of something bounding through the forest directly in front of her. With a crash in the bushes, another dead kid leapt from the woods and into the clearing. He was a fit young guy — well, as fit as sickly corpses can be, I guess — and dressed as a pirate. One of those noble pirates: the kind who wash their hair and don't get their hands or legs cut off. He wore a tricorn hat, tights (I think), and buckled shoes, but not an eye patch, hook, or scabbard in sight. At his side, however, he had a small drum attached to a belt that was slung over his see-through shoulder. A look of exasperation was plastered on his face.

"Morna," he said to the ghost girl. "You should not go so far, somebody might —" He stopped mid-sentence when saw me. Me, who was attempting to make myself as invisible as possible. This mostly involved me tucking myself into a ball of black hair and clothing, all while trying not to empty my bladder all over my nice black jeans. The boy looked like he'd been slapped across the face with a glove full of nickels.

"You!" he shouted. "You can't sit here! Get off my grave!"

It was then I understood that I was looking at (or rather, mostly through) Cyril Cooper (1766–1779). The guy from the tombstone. I screamed very loudly. And then the other dead kids came running.

☠

If you're just joining the story now, you've missed quite a bit of narrative, so you should know two important things before reading on:

1. Starting a book on the seventh chapter is highly unorthodox. Indeed, while often the real excitement doesn't begin until the seventh chapter (or perhaps later), you have missed the introduction and earlier, less supernatural adventures of the characters, and as a result certain events are bound to have less resonance for you . . . emotionally speaking. It's a pity, really. This sort of recap won't happen every few chapters.

2. October Schwartz, our plucky heroine, saddened by the death of her French teacher Mr. O'Shea, has just been approached in the Sticksville Cemetery by a group of dead kids — three male, two female. Actually, that part hadn't been mentioned yet, but it's accurate. And things are about to get weird.

☠

A scream escaped from October's mouth, but upon seeing that her scream only attracted more adolescent ghosts, October fell silent. She looked around in amazement as one of the dead kids began to speak.

"What's going on?" a heavy-set dead boy in high-waisted shorts and knee socks asked, gasping for breath. "I thought I heard

Morna scream so I came running." The dead boy bent over and rested his chubby hands on his knees.

"That wasn't Morna," the boy October had deduced was Cyril Cooper explained. "It was that girl, sitting on my grave." He pointed an accusatory finger at the terrified October Schwartz.

"Who's she supposed ta be?" asked a girl in braids and a tattered plaid dress.

"Is there a new dead girl?" asked a dead boy in baggy jeans and T-shirt, partially out of confusion and partially out of hope.

"Well, I haven't seen her in the cemetery before, Derek."

October peeked a bit from behind her knees, which weren't hiding her nearly as well as she had hoped. "I'm . . . not dead," she confessed to ghosts.

"What?!" gasped the dead kids in horror (and in unison, to boot).

"Ah, shoot," grumbled Cyril, and tossed his tricorn hat on the ground.

The girl who the other dead kids called Morna looked betrayed. "So . . . ye're not dead?"

"No," October repeated.

"Well, ye look dead. Tha' wasna fair," Morna said, anxiously twisting her hands. "I'm sorry, I shouldna said tha', but ye're so pale an' . . . I figured ye were dead."

"This is just great," Cyril shouted as he paced the soft ground like a caged ocelot. (Again with the ocelots.)

"But you," October began, in shock. "You're dead . . . you're . . . *ghosts*." October got to her feet and walked over to the tiny Scottish girl. She held out her hand and slowly advanced it toward the ghost girl's shoulder, waiting for it to pass through as if there was no shoulder there. She touched the Scottish girl's shoulder and screamed.

"Stop doing that!" commanded the roundish boy.

"What happened?! You're ghosts! Why didn't my hand go through?!" October shouted, seemingly more concerned that the ghosts weren't obeying generally accepted ghost rules than the reality that she was currently talking with five of them.

"Oh, we can control that," the girl said, then waved her

intangible arm through October's middle.

"Gah," coughed October.

"Okay, okay," said Cyril, who was moments away from a panic attack. "Everybody calm down. Calm down . . . Living Girl, could you give us a moment? Just stay right there — just — yes, not on top of my grave . . . while we, uh, converse."

Cyril, who appeared to be the unofficial leader of the ghosts, gathered the others and they huddled by a tomb made of aged marble. Occasionally, one of the kids would glance over at October, then duck his or her head back down.

October didn't know what to do. Her instincts told her to run home and hide in her bed and never return to the cemetery for the rest of her life. No more shortcuts to school. Ghosts might be entertaining to read about and write about, but in real life they are SCARY AS A TROPICAL ILLNESS and she just wanted to go home before they decided to turn her into a ghost, too. Could ghosts do that? It's an interesting question. Zombies could definitely turn people into zombies, but these kids didn't look like zombies. They weren't rotting in any way (though their clothes had seen better days and wide, dark circles ringed all their sunken eyes).

October desperately tried to remember what she knew about ghosts. At the same time (her mind was running a million miles a minute) she tried to determine if the fact that she now saw five ghosts instead of one and had pursued an extended conversation with them was a sign that she was *not* crazy, or that she was, in fact, even battier than previously assumed.

Despite the myriad logical and sensible and sane reasons October had to leave immediately, she also had a terrible curiosity to know if the kids really were ghosts. While she wavered — should she stay or should she go? — biting her lip and frantically tugging at her necklace, the dead kids interrupted.

"Living Girl," Cyril called. "Can we speak?"

"I have a name," October said.

"Apologies. What is it?"

"October."

"I didn't ask what month it was," Cyril said. "I wanted to know your name."

"October is my name," she explained, for the 37,518th time in her life.

"That's a ridiculous name," Cyril decided.

"Really?" October said. "Cyril? Morna? People who live in ludicrously named houses shouldn't throw stones."

"We don't live," the girl in braids deadpanned.

October then decided it might not be a good idea to mouth off to dead kids.

"October," Cyril said. "My name is Cyril Cooper."

"I know," she said. "I've been sitting on your grave for the past month."

He forced a polite smile and continued. "The girl who discovered you is Morna MacIsaac."

"I thought she was dead, I swear," she muttered.

"This is Tabetha Scott [he pointed to the girl in braids], Kirby LaFlamme [the larger boy in the tie and shorts], and Derek Running Water [as he introduced the boy in a modern-looking T-shirt and jeans]."

They all murmured hello. Derek Running Water waved in a wide arc and Cyril continued his introduction.

"As you've figured out by now," he said, "we are dead, and you are not. And that leaves us in a bit of a predicament. It was an honest mistake on Morna's part and there's nothing we can do about it now. We've seen you, and you've seen us."

"You should get more sun," Tabetha added, absent-mindedly twirling a braid. "Then maybe people wouldn't mistake you fer a ghost."

"What do you mean?" October asked. "How are you ghosts?"

"Well, we died, and then we woke up, just weeks ago, in this delightful cemetery as ghosts. It's not that complex," Kirby explained, as if he were explaining why one shouldn't douse one's face in an open flame. "But you shouldn't be able to see us."

"See," Cyril said, "most living folks can't see us. We're ghosts. We only come out at night. We are invisible and inaudible to most human eyes and ears, and we can become intangible whenever we want." He stopped to ram his head noiselessly through a tomb wall for a dramatic demonstration, just in case October didn't get the point already.

Cyril certainly did like to talk. He went on for ages about ghosts and ghost rules and ghost etiquette or something. When he was finally finished talking, October knew a whole lot more about ghosts. Later, when October was back in her bedroom, she would hurriedly write down whatever she could remember in one of the back pages in her *Two Knives, One Thousand Demons* notebook.

RULES FOR DEAD KIDS

1. Tangibility: Dead kids can become tangible/intangible at will. (So, they can pass through walls if they want to. Equally, they can knock over antique vases by accident if they are so inclined.)

2. Visibility: Dead kids are invisible to almost all living people, except those people who have had someone close die under sudden or mysterious circumstances.

3. Mortality: Since the dead kids are already dead, they can harm each other and themselves with no pain or lasting consequences. Like Tom and Jerry or Itchy and Scratchy.

4. Time: The dead kids' existence on earth only lasts a calendar

month after being raised. In this particular case, until October 31: Hallowe'en. After that evening, the ghosts disappear. They only appear in the evenings, as soon as it's dark.

5. Interaction with the living: They can touch living people — like, nudge them, shake their hands — but they cannot knowingly harm them. I guess like robots. (But robots programmed not to harm people. Not evil robots.)

6. Why they're dead kids: The dead kids will remain ghostly corpses until they somehow find justice for their horrible, horrible demises — something like that.

However, these rules only brought up questions for October. Especially rules number two and four. If ghosts were mostly invisible, why could October see them? And if, like Kirby had said, he'd been a ghost for just weeks, how could they know when their time was up?

"Have you ever lost anyone close to you?" asked Kirby. "Dad died and it was never explained? Sister murdered? Something of that nature?"

"No," October said. "My French teacher died last night . . . I liked him, but I don't think we were really close. And it was an accident."

"Maybe you were closer than ya' thought," Tabetha added.

"Okay," said October. "Maybe. But what's the deal with you only being around until Hallowe'en? How do you know that? Kirby said you all woke up here just a couple of weeks ago."

"Oh, we've been summoned before," Derek explained.

"Summoned?"

"Yes," Morna said. "Every ten years or so, someone comes inta th' graveyard, looking to raise th' dead fer some reason. We eventually figured out th' rules. I think th' last time was 2006."

"A group of Wiccan girls thought it would be fun to raise the dead on the first of October," Derek said. "But by midnight on the thirty-first, we were gone."

"Gone where?" October wondered.

"We don't know," said Kirby. "It all goes black. But usually, we're back in this cemetery in a few years. Judging by my estimates, it looks like we'll be out of here on Hallowe'en again. You don't need to concern yourself with that."

"Wait." October still couldn't believe she was having this conversation. "Someone raised you . . . from the . . . even more dead than this? Why would they do that? How would they do that?"

"Usually it's just someone playing the Dark Arts," Derek said. The Dark Arts sounded ominous, even if you were "playing" with them. "They say the wrong thing and raise us from the dead by accident. It can only happen during a full moon, but then, that's when most people like practising the Dark Arts."

"And the person who summons us can always see us," Cyril said. "Did you summon us, mayhaps? That could explain it."

"Didja say anything in the graveyard?" asked Tabetha. "Yer here all the time. Didja say some magic words? Maybe earlier in the month? Think, girl!"

"No," October protested. "What would I be saying? I'm always here alone!"

"She's always readin' by herself," Morna agreed.

A horrible realization came to young October — a realization that connected the ghosts, the burning backpack, all of it together.

"What if I had read a book out loud?" she asked. "Might that book remain in one piece if, say, my entire backpack burst into flame?"

"What book did you read aloud?" Kirby asked.

"Um . . . a book I wrote . . . about demons. And a passage about raising the dead."

"Wha' did ye say?" Morna asked.

"Oh, something about the innocent young and dead shall rise . . ."

"No!" Derek Running Water exclaimed. "You're like a witch! That's almost a word for word spell. It's all about raising things from the dead!"

"I didn't know! I was just reading what I'd written!"

"Well, that explains it."

The verdict was in. October Schwartz had raised the dead kids from some supernatural, black nothingness. And it appeared they'd be taking up residence in the cemetery behind her house until Hallowe'en. How terrifying was that? In truth, not so terrifying, once she asked them what they did with their time.

"We dead kids have it pretty good," explained Kirby, "We sleep for about sixteen hours a day, then run around in the cemetery at night, usually playing Truth or Dare, or sometimes, if we have time, staging elaborate musicals —"

"Musicals?" October said, though to be honest, she was more shocked by the Truth or Dare. She tried to imagine it:

"*Okay, truth!*"

"*Have you ever . . . kissed someone with wooden teeth?*"

"Yes, musicals," said Cyril. "This explanation is going to take a whole lot longer if you keep repeating everything I say. For the most part," he continued, "we do this sort of thing without incident. We usually congregate in the wooded area over there," he said, pointing to the place where October had first spotted Morna. "Who's going to venture into the dark woods within the already dark cemetery in the middle of the night, really?"

Yeah. I mean, really?

"Also, we are only around for a month at most," Cyril clarified. "Often we're raised some time in the fall, and our appearance scares off the person who's summoned us, so there's not too much to worry about. We like to keep the graveyard free of visitors. If anyone knew we were here, there would be parsons and newspaper men and professors of science crawling all over the Sticksville Cemetery."

"And how are you supposed to mount a decent production of *Phantom of the Opera* with all that going on?" Kirby shouted, clearly outraged.

October was dumbfounded.

"So what will you do now that I've seen you? I mean, I'm freaked out, but I can't just pretend this encounter didn't happen. And I live next door. I'm in this cemetery all the time."

"And ye've already seen me once," Morna said quietly, ashamed.

"Twice, actually," said October.

"Regardless," said Kirby, "of the exact number of sightings, it remains that you have seen us and, worse, talked with us . . . somewhat . . . mostly incoherent babble on your part . . . so that poses a conundrum."

"Uh," was the first response October thought of — incoherent babble? — but then she came up with, "It doesn't have to be a . . . um, conundrum."

"She's right, Cyril," said Tabetha. "We could jes' hide ourselves an' people'd think she was crazy. I mean, she already looks crazy." She whispered that last part, but October overheard and crossed her arms self-consciously.

"I guess you're right," Cyril said. "Okay, Living Girl. Thanks for raising us. It's been a gas."

"Wait! Where are you going? Are you leaving the cemetery?"

"No," Cyril said.

"Then where are you going?"

"Just over there. Away from you."

☠

"Wait!" October cried.

"What is it now?" complained the squattest dead kid, Kirby, as he swivelled around.

"How about," October suggested, "instead of you leaving and me, y'know, seeing a psychiatrist — how about we be friends?"

A beat skipped, then the dead kids roared with shrill, ghostly laughter. Man, did they ever laugh like a bunch of old ladies — even the boys. Speaking for the group, Kirby said, "Thanks, but no thanks."

"But, I won't tell anyone about you, I swear!" October pleaded. "You ghosts are a little scary, but also kind of cool. I'd like to talk more."

The dead kids seemed unimpressed.

"And I can help you fit into the world outside the cemetery," she continued. "I know you don't get out very often. All those years of darkness must have an effect. I can keep you updated about what's been going on in town, keep you up on technological advances, stuff like that."

"What's a technological advance?" Cyril asked.

"She means inventions," Morna whispered. "Remember the car?"

"Oh."

"I won't bother you," October said. "I promise. I'll only visit every now and then. I can raise you every full moon if you'd like! I live right next door so it's not strange for me to hang out in the cemetery at night."

Cyril silently consulted his dead friends with his eyes and a movement of his shoulders. Morna and Derek were slightly nodding their heads. Kirby and Tabetha looked cautious, but not entirely displeased.

"She could pick up musical scores for us," relented Kirby.

"Okay," Cyril said. "We can be friends."

"But that doesn't mean we'll give you a part in *Jesus Christ Superstar*," said Kirby.

"Yes!" October exclaimed, clapping her hands together. "So, want to play a game of Truth or Dare?"

As October had only recently discovered there were such things as ghosts and, additionally, that five of them were currently loitering in the cemetery behind her house, she had a ton of questions: Where were all the adult ghosts hiding? Who were the kids when they were alive, since it looked like they came from a cross-time Mickey Mouse Club? The dead kids proved as reluctant to give up information about themselves as they were to befriend living girls, so October figured a game of Truth or Dare would be a clever way to discover the answers she wanted.

A game of Truth or Dare with a bunch of adolescent ghosts was, in many ways, just as she imagined it would be.

"Truth," chose Cyril.

"Did ya' ever own any slaves?" Tabetha asked.

"You *always* ask this question!" Cyril protested, folding his arms.

"Well, it's an important question ta me," said Tabetha (who, it should be noted at this stage, was black).

"And I always give you the same answer: no."

"Well, maybe I think you're lyin', an' will slip up an' tell the real truth one day," said Tabetha, folding her arms across her chest.

"If you were clever," noted Kirby, "you'd ask a subtler question, like, 'What colour kerchief did your house slave wear?'"

"Shut up, Kirby," Tabetha said.

"Dare," answered Derek Running Water.

"Okay . . . go throw this rock through the window of that house over there," Kirby said with a laugh.

"Wait," October said. "That's my house, you jerk! Don't do it now. My dad will wake up and wonder where I am!"

October knew she was already pushing her luck. It was after one o'clock in the morning, and it was a school night. But her dad had probably already fallen asleep, and had probably done so feeling quite horrible after the argument he and October had. She reminded herself to apologize to him first thing in the morning.

Truth or Dare was a mixed bag. Some of the dead kids didn't seem to be having much fun, having exhausted all the possible inquiries a few summonings ago, but October learned a wealth of new information about them. All she had to reveal was what it was like to eat food and feel the warmth of a cat on her lap and boring things like that. Oh yeah, and Kirby wanted to know if she'd already started wearing a bra. Creep. The dead kids were all from Sticksville, though from different times, and they had all died suddenly and mysteriously. They were also all about October's age, but the main difference was they would stay that same age forever.

FIVE THINGS OCTOBER LEARNED ABOUT HISTORY
FROM PLAYING TRUTH OR DARE WITH DEAD KIDS

1. Some of the earliest Canadian settlers were British people chased out of America.

Cyril Cooper was a member of a Loyalist family who fled to Canada during the American Revolution. Loyalist as in loyal to the British Empire. God save the Queen (or in this case, the King) and the Union Jack and all that. Cyril was born in New York, but his dad's allegiance to the British Empire forced them to hightail it to Nova Scotia when Yankee revolutionaries started tarring and feathering people like his dad. They were kind of counter-revolutionary.

But Nova Scotia proved too cold and harsh, so they travelled westward to New France (that's what they called Quebec then), and then on to the area that would soon be named Ontario. His family became one of the honest-to-goodness earliest European families in the newly founded Sticksville. His dad was a shipbuilder and Cyril was learning to become one while he was still alive. Cyril also played drum for the local Lower Canada militia, hence the little drum. Cyril died one night after manoeuvres when he went down to the harbour across the lake from Detroit to help his dad on a clipper. He remembers nothing about how or why.

2. Ornithologists = Unsung heroes of the Underground Railroad.

Tabetha Scott was born in 1848, and with her father (her mom had died in childbirth), she came to Sticksville via the Underground Railroad. October had never heard about it, but Sticksville was, in fact, one of the northernmost stations of the Underground Railroad — a final destination for American slaves seeking freedom. Tabetha and her dad had been field slaves on a plantation outside Richmond, Virginia, but when she was ten, a man named Alexander Ross came to visit their master.

Ross said he wished to study rare birds that nested on the plantation, as he was an ornithologist, but he was also a station master for the Underground Railroad, and secretly plotted with Tabetha and her dad to find a way to sneak them into Canada and away from their life of slavery in the American South. Tabetha didn't bother to describe the journey, but we can all assume it was suitably harrowing. Sticksville had been home to Tabetha and her dad since slightly before the beginning of the American Civil War. Like Cyril, she had no idea of how she died — not even when and where it happened — but she suspected it had something to do with the white woman her dad had started talking to.

3. There's no such thing as "cheap" land.

The Scottish lass, Morna MacIsaac, had immigrated to Canada from Scotland in 1910. Her parents thought it would be a good move; Canada promised work and cheap land. After the journey, the MacIsaac family — Morna, her two sisters, her mom, and her dad — moved into a tiny one-room apartment in downtown Sticksville and struggled to pay the rent and keep themselves in clothes that weren't falling apart. They ran out of money well before they could attempt the trip out west, where the cheap land supposedly was.

Mr. MacIsaac worked in a local grain mill and the missus was a maid for the Coopers, who were wealthy townspeople and likely descendents of Cyril Cooper's family. Morna would often go to work with her mom at the Cooper's estate. She knew her body had been found frozen in a snowy alley behind The Bishop and Castle, the past and current local public house (pub, for us modern readers), but not much more than that. Gruesome.

4. Canada was home to *two* famous sets of quintuplets.

Kirby LaFlamme announced that he was one of the celebrated LaFlamme quintuplets. He wasn't surprised that October had never heard of them, because most people hadn't.

Kirby and his brothers — Kyle, Kurtwood, Keir, and Kip — had been born in late 1934, several months after the more famous Dionne quintuplets. The LaFlammes were the second quintuplets ever born on planet Earth (and also in Canada, coincidentally). As with their female counterparts, the Dionnes, Kirby and his family were adopted by the Ontario government who tried to make them something of a tourist attraction.

Unfortunately, not many people cared about the world's

second set of quintuplets, especially, Kirby said, since they were five not-so-cute boys. And, October thought, stuck-up jerks, if Kirby was any reflection of his clan.

The Ontario government never made much money off LaFlammetown, which they dubbed the tourist destination, but Kirby lived a rather luxurious lifestyle while other people weathered the Great Depression by scavenging for tin. He died mysteriously at age thirteen after he and his brothers made a CBC Radio appearance to promote LaFlammetown. He was the only dead kid who had been born in Sticksville.

5. Things in Oka are not okay.

Derek Running Water was the most recently deceased of the dead kids. He was one of the Mohawk Nation; his family lived on an Ontario reserve for decades, but when Derek turned eleven, his mother was hired for a hospital job in Sticksville. Derek and his mom left the reserve and they lived in Sticksville for a couple of years before Derek's mysterious death. In 1990, Derek became very upset about the Oka standoff. October had no idea what he was talking about ("I wasn't even born yet, man."), so Derek explained.

Land developers in Oka, Quebec, planned to put a golf course on sacred Mohawk land. A number of Mohawk Warriors barricaded the roads in Oka, and an armed standoff between the provincial police and the Mohawk Warriors ensued. A police officer was killed.

Derek argued with his mom. He wanted to go and be part of the protest, or even one of the sympathy protests that had sprung up nearby. His mom disapproved, especially since someone had been killed. She felt Derek should appreciate the life he had in Sticksville and not get involved with the Quebec Mohawk Warriors. She thought the matter was finished, but Derek snuck onto a Greyhound bus to Oka and joined the protestors. His mom had been right to worry. Shortly after reaching Oka, Derek Running Water died.

And so ended October's crash course in history: dead kid edition. You might want to mark this section with a dog ear to refer to it later, or cut the paragraphs out and glue them onto flash cards or something. Just in case.

"Okay, this one is for Cyril," she said.

"Truth."

"Where are all the dead adults?" October knew these kids must have become ghosts because of the mysterious circumstances of their deaths, their sudden and inexplicable ends. Surely there were adults with the same situation.

"Most of the adults know who killed them," Cyril said, "And if they do . . . when they're raised, that is . . . they usually go haunt that person. It's a revenge kind of thing. Ghosts find it difficult to live and let live . . . you understand."

"So adult ghosts leave the cemetery to haunt people?"

"Yeah, as soon as they're raised. And they usually don't return."

"And you don't ever leave?"

"Every once in a while, for fun," said Derek. "But we don't really know who to haunt. And we always make sure to come back here in time for the end of the month."

There should be a ghost handbook.

"I'll have to take you out somewhere fun before Hallowe'en comes," October said. "I should go now," she decided, when in fact she should have gone hours ago. It was three o'clock in the morning, for pity's sake. "It's late, and I'm going to be destroyed tomorrow. I'll talk with *most* of you later. Not Kirby, though. He's a creep." October quietly walked back to the gate that led to her backyard. If she were lucky, her dad had gone to sleep long ago.

Though she'd acted pretty calm and collected, October couldn't help but feel unsettled by the dead kids. It made her uneasy to know there was something beyond death, and that something was singing musical scales, minutes from her backyard. But after talking with the dead kids she realized they were like any other kids, just less tangible and with more interesting vocabularies. It comforted her to know that in some cases, you might be able to stay in touch with people you had lost. Well, through death, anyway. As far as October's missing mom was concerned, this news was no help at all.

If only October could talk to Mr. O'Shea and tell him how

much she appreciated the book he had lent her. She would have liked to just say goodbye, especially since it didn't look like she was going to be allowed at the funeral. Only one problem: Mr. O'Shea wasn't killed by a person or for any mysterious reason; he was killed by the shop's hydraulic lift. Unless you could haunt a piece of machinery throughout eternity, Mr. O'Shea's story was over. Case closed.

The next morning, I was so tired that I staggered through the school corridors like a prison guard with a sharpened toothbrush in my spine. My vision was a white blur, but as I got close to my locker, I could see Yumi Takeshi and Stacey Somebody standing there, waiting for me to arrive.

"You look terrible," Yumi exclaimed when she saw me stumbling my way down the hall. "Did you get any sleep at all?"

I chose to ignore that critical assessment of my appearance and began spinning my combination lock. "What brings you both to my neck of the woods?"

"You seemed really upset about Mr. O'Shea yesterday," Stacey said. "We just wanted to see if you were okay."

"Yeah," I said. "Yeah . . . I'm fine. I had something of a rough night last night," I admitted, trying to wave away their concerns with my hand, "but I'm fine now." I started to smile to make it more convincing, but the effort just made me sleepier.

Okay, so maybe I lied by leaving out the more important, more supernatural details of my evening. But what could I tell them? *Uh, I'm pretty tired because I was chillin' with a bunch of dead kids last night?* No way. And yes, I sometimes still say chillin'. It's still a thing.

"Well, I'm glad you're doing better," said Yumi, way too awake and energized at eight in the morning.

"Okay, gang," I said, rubbing my eyes, which felt like they were on fire. "It was very nice of you to visit me this morning,

97

but I want to leave the vicinity before Ashlie Salmons shows up. And I've got to get to Mr. O'Shea's class."

I shut my locker and realized what I'd said. From Stacey and Yumi's dumbstruck faces, I could tell they'd heard, as well.

"Yikes. . . . I meant *French* class."

☠

When I sat down in French class, that blonde woman who had been there the day before — the very harbinger of doom herself — was standing in front of the chalkboard again. Seemed like she would be teaching French for the remainder of the week, or at least until the school found a supply teacher who could actually speak French.

In the moments before class started, the supply teacher tried to engage the few students who had arrived early (including me) in a conversation.

"I know I don't speak any French," she smiled. "But there are several exercises and worksheets your teacher left. We'll be doing those today."

She opened a thick file folder and began sorting through the daunting stack of white paper. "I forgot my glasses," she said, almost to herself, like the smart one on *Scooby-Doo*. She spun around and looked directly at me. Meanwhile, I was busy trying to look anywhere but at her. "Dear, could you go down to the teachers' lounge and retrieve my glasses? I've left them in my coat pocket. My coat is a long brown one. There's a little plastic flower on the lapel."

"Uh," I said. "Are they going to let me in?"

"It's the teachers' lounge, not the Pentagon, dear. You'll be fine. Thanks."

The morning bell rang just as I approached the blue door puzzlingly labelled "Teacher's Lounge." Which teacher? Students scattered and within seconds, the halls were empty. I carefully opened the lounge door and called in, afraid of the repercussions of entering unannounced. "Hello. Anybody here?"

Nothing but silence answered, so I walked inside and headed straight for the coat closet. I didn't even bother to turn on the light; I figured I'd be all of thirty seconds inside.

I hadn't expected a Club Med within Sticksville Central, but I was shocked at how mundane and boring the teachers' lounge was. A fridge, sink, microwave, some cabinets, a few card tables with accompanying plastic chairs, and two couches that I swear I'd seen discarded at the side of the road. No television, no pool table, no massage tables, though there was a clock radio and coffee maker. So, theoretically, I guess my teachers could get hopped up on caffeine and start rocking to the CBC.

The closet held a number of long brown coats and I had to sort through them to find one with a plastic flower. I dug my hand into the supply teacher's coat pocket and out came a pair of horn-rimmed glasses. Just then, the lights fluttered on and the lounge door swung open. I immediately realized it would not look good if someone found me rifling through the supply teacher's stuff, so I hid. I hid because, apparently, I am the biggest loser ever. I realized this as I covered myself in teachers' coats and tried to control my breathing. I flattened myself against the closet wall and pulled several more coats in front of me. I'm pretty sure you could still see my Chuck Taylors beneath all the coats, so I hoped whoever had entered didn't have a coat to hang.

"What a morning."

The voice was unmistakable. It was Mr. Santuzzi, psycho math teacher extraordinaire. What constituted a bad morning for him? Did he run out of children's blood for his All-Bran? I really hoped he — of all the possible teachers who could have entered — didn't discover me hiding amongst the coats. He'd think it was a sneak attack and would retaliate in kind. I couldn't tell who he was talking to. Probably some teacher I've never talked to.

"I nearly ran Page over on my way to work," Santuzzi complained, though it sounded like Mr. Page would have more to complain about. Am I right? "Why does he insist on riding that ridiculous bicycle to work?"

The other teacher had no answer, I guess.

"It's like he's trying to make a point since he lost that position to the new guy, Schwartz."

I could hear them open the fridge.

"Are you going to O'Shea's service tomorrow?" asked the other teacher. So the funeral was *tomorrow*. Advantage: Schwartz.

"Of course," said Santuzzi. "I knew Terry for years. Apparently," his voice lowered, "according to Schwartz, the lift was completely functional. See, the lift has sensors . . . it won't normally lower onto a large object beneath it, unless you break it. But it looked like the switch had been kicked in. Terry must have tried to operate the thing, got frustrated, and dropped it on himself by accident."

"Grim," marvelled the other teacher. "It was kicked in? You don't think someone killed him?"

"What? No," Mr. Santuzzi was incensed by such a ludicrous claim. "O'Shea had a wrench in his hand. He bashed in the switch himself. And the auto shop is usually open, but Terry had locked himself in. It's possible it was . . . you know . . . self-inflicted."

"I can't imagine," said the other. "Was he depressed? You knew him."

"O'Shea?" sneered Santuzzi. "Why would a failure like him possibly be depressed?"

The two teachers extinguished the light and walked back out the door, leaving me all alone, smothered with coats and jackets. I don't know what Santuzzi meant by that last part, but Mr. O'Shea never seemed depressed to me. With Dad, I had a bit of experience in that field. And he wouldn't drop the hydraulic lift on himself, either by accident or on purpose. Who would do that? It sounded like such a terrible way to die.

I hurried to leave the lounge before any other teacher had

the chance to enter, running straight to French class, feeling ill with fury. Who was this Santuzzi clown, telling other teachers that Mr. O'Shea was some kind of sad-eyed, accident-prone walking disaster? When I got back to French class, already in progress, I handed the glasses to the supply teacher, who wondered aloud what on earth had taken me so long.

"I got caught up in some French research," I muttered.

☠

Mr. Santuzzi popped another surprise quiz on our math class, which is exactly the sort of thing that Santuzzi does. I was exhausted from the night before, so naturally, he *would* choose that day to hold a pop quiz. My hatred of him, if possible, was increasing and gaining strength exponentially.

Santuzzi handed out the quiz papers, walking up and down the aisles like a prison warden. He noticed the raccoon circles around my eyes and the expression on my face.

"Tired, Ms. Schwartz?" he asked.

"Me? Why would a failure like me possibly be tired?"

Zing, Mr. Santuzzi! Does that sting? In truth, I'm not entirely sure that was a snappy comeback, but in some way, I was getting back at him for those terrible rumours he was spreading about Mr. O'Shea. At the same time, I was calling myself a failure, so maybe it wasn't the sharpest insult. Mr. Santuzzi was also confused. He simply stroked his moustache and continued down the aisle.

I knew all the answers to the problems on the quiz, but I felt compelled to elaborate on the solutions, using answers such as "5x, *sleazebucket*" or "Q.E.D., *dirtbag*." And even though these were technically the correct answers, I guess I should have known better to not pepper personal insults throughout the test. Especially since the test required no words at all. But I was too angry with Santuzzi to care.

I told Yumi and Stacey about my test answers during lunch. Stacey laughed and slapped the wooden tabletop repeatedly.

"Santuzzi's going to flip his wig!"

"No, he won't," Yumi said. "It's sewn onto his scalp. My cousin told me. It'll never move."

I smiled a little and continued to eat the day's cafeteria selection, their rendition of beefaroni, I guess. Not a total winner.

"What did he say that made you so mad?" Yumi asked. "Apart from the usual."

I explained my adventure in the teachers' lounge and how I'd overheard Mr. Santuzzi spreading rumours about Mr. O'Shea.

"Wait, you were in the teachers' lounge?" asked Yumi. This was big news to her.

"Yeah."

"What's it like?"

"Pretty depressing, actually," I said. "Old furniture and old appliances. It looks like it hasn't changed since 1985."

"Is there, like, a wall of closed-circuit televisions," asked Stacey, "with cameras trained on different areas of the school?"

"They have a clock radio."

"But what did he say about Mr. O'Shea?" asked Yumi, getting back to the heart of the matter.

"He said the police had determined Mr. O'Shea lowered the hydraulic car lift on himself when he died in the auto shop, either by accident or on purpose! The room was locked, so he must have locked himself in there while my dad was teaching volleyball. And he took a wrench to the switch or something crazy like that. He said that Mr. O'Shea was dangerously depressed. Mr. Santuzzi said that; not the police. I don't think . . ."

"You think he was depressed?" said Stacey.

"Mr. O'Shea was, like, the only good teacher at this school, Stacey. And he coached curling, which is, like, illegal if you're clinically depressed. It's too risky," I said definitively. "He just wasn't."

"Maybe he had, like, a totally different identity outside of school: a clumsy, heartbroken failed saxophonist," theorized Stacey. "You never know."

"But he couldn't have dropped the lift on himself," Yumi interrupted. "He was Captain Cautious. He drove like a little old lady."

"I know!" I almost shouted, haphazardly flinging some of the beefaroni across the table. Other kids were beginning to notice our heated, death-centric debate, so I lowered my volume. "I know. And he left, like, over two weeks of French exercises. Prepared much? The guy was not sloppy. And who plays saxophone anymore, Stacey?"

"Weird," said Stacey, who was attempting to finish his science homework while still somewhat participating in the conversation. "But like you said, maybe he did it on purpose. He did leave weeks of lessons. He did lock himself in the shop."

"You don't know Mr. O'Shea," I said.

In a wise move for the safety of his face, Stacey stopped pushing the issue. I was certain that Mr. O'Shea simply didn't take his own life. All three of us sat quietly at our cafeteria table. Stacey continued determining the rotation rate of various planets, while other wheels turned in my head.

"He's probably right," Yumi said, referring to Stacey. "We don't really know much about Mr. O'Shea, outside of French class and curling. Speaking of which . . ." she added, "there won't be any more curling team this year."

"That's okay. I figured as much." While it was fun enough to sweep ice, I wouldn't exactly be losing sleep over a year without curling. "I still think there's something weird about that auto shop accident," I decided.

"Well, I'll get a team of detectives on it right away," chuckled Yumi.

If only that were possible. Although, upon further consideration . . . I did know five kids who couldn't be seen or heard and liked to sneak around at night. Yumi, I thought, you beautiful Asian Zombie Tramp! You don't know it, but you just invented the Dead Kid Detective Agency.

☠

After school, I sat at the kitchen table, working on some of the French exercises the supply teacher had assigned. My dad opened the door and took the seat beside me.

"How was school?" he asked, removing his blue jacket. He could never seem to avoid getting it covered with yellow chalk dust.

"Fine," I said. This was officially the only acceptable answer to "How was school?" Anything more, my dad didn't need to know. "I'm sorry again for getting mad at you last night . . . and I'm sorry for using your . . . illness . . . against you. Wasn't fair."

"It's okay," Dad said, and rumpled my already dishevelled hair. "I've been dealing with this for over ten years. I can handle a low blow here and there." He opened the refrigerator and pulled out some perogies for dinner. "And maybe I should have been more understanding when you said you wanted to go to Mr. O'Shea's funeral."

I nodded, and began working again on my French.

"Do you still want to go? It's tomorrow," Dad revealed.

"I know. But I don't think I want to go anymore."

Even though I really wanted to pay my respects to Mr. O'Shea, I was afraid I was beginning to look even weirder than usual to everyone else in school. In music class, I'd asked Mrs. Tischmann again where Mr. O'Shea's funeral was going to be. I knew the *when* — I'd figured out which closets to hide in — all I needed was the *where*. Mrs. Tischmann informed me she didn't think it was appropriate for students to attend Mr. O'Shea's funeral. I guess she thought she was doing me a favour and being all polite, but she chose to inform me of this belief at such a volume and with such harshness that the entire class heard. Everyone else looked up from their instruments like Mrs. Tischmann had just discovered a rotting groundhog inside her lectern. The woodwinds in the front row were particularly disgusted.

"Morbid much, Zombie Tramp?" said Ashlie Salmons.

It occurred to me in that moment that I might be earning something of a reputation, and not just with Ashlie. Secondly, I now knew Mr. "Rumour Mill" Santuzzi would be there, which would probably ruin the whole funeral experience for me – as much as a bad time like that can be ruined.

"You look tired," Dad said, snapping me out of all this self-reflection. "How late were you out last night?"

"Kind of late," I said, using the definition of "kind of" that was synonymous with "very."

"You know I don't like you in that graveyard late at night," my dad said as he placed a saucepan of salted water on a stove element. "It's not safe."

"It's right next door, Dad. You'd hear me if I screamed," I joked. But now that I thought about it, he hadn't woken up at all when I'd screamed several times last night. Way to go into a coma, Dad.

"I'm serious, October," he said, waving the wooden spoon in my direction. "In a dark cemetery, you could run into all sorts of sickos – kidnappers, murderers, budding terrorists . . ."

"United Empire Loyalists," I added.

"Unlikely . . . but always a concern, I guess," Dad said, very confused.

"I've never seen another person in that cemetery."

Dad frowned. The utter lack of people was apparently not very comforting, either.

"Okay," I said. "I'll try not to stay out in the cemetery too late," but as I spoke, my fingers were totally crossed under the table. Was he aware that there were dead kids back there? Dead kids that I needed to talk to tonight, and likely many nights afterward, if my plan worked out. It looked like I'd have to wait to sneak out until Dad got off this whole night-safety kick.

"Dad," I said, changing the subject very anxiously. "Was Mr. O'Shea depressed like you?"

"What?" Dad was too absorbed in watching the water in the pan boil to be shocked until a couple moments later. "No. What?! Why are you asking me this, pumpkin?"

"Mr. Santuzzi said Mr. O'Shea's accident in the auto shop wasn't really an accident. He might have dropped his car on himself purposely," I explained sheepishly.

"He shouldn't be saying that to his class."

"He didn't," I said. "I overheard him talking with another teacher about it."

Dad considered me very suspiciously, as if deciding whether I was really his daughter or a pod-person. Just as he probably knew "kind of" usually meant "very," I guess he also knew "overheard" was my euphemism for "eavesdropped." He emptied the bag of perogies into the boiling water.

"Well, I don't know where Mr. Santuzzi got that information from," Dad said. "The police haven't come to that conclusion. That's why they came to interview me about Terry."

My heart warmed to hear Dad refer to Santuzzi as "Mr. Santuzzi" and Mr. O'Shea as "Terry." Given these fond feelings, I saw if I could dig any deeper.

"Are you in trouble, Dad?"

"I don't know. I wasn't in that auto shop that night — I had locked it up — and it looks like an accident, but the police can't figure out how Mr. O'Shea broke in, or why he'd forced the pneumatic lift carrying his own car to drop down on him. Did Mr. Santuzzi say that Mr. O'Shea took his own life, pumpkin?"

"He was all like, 'Why would a failure like O'Shea want to drop a car on himself,'" I recounted, doing my best impersonation of Santuzzi. The key was to make it low and gravelly.

"October, he shouldn't be spreading rumours like that," Dad decided, but I knew there was an exception coming. "But I'm worried Mr. Santuzzi might be right."

Quelle shock! Mr. Santuzzi could be right!

☠

At eight o'clock that night, I turned the television on and cranked the volume up loud, even though I had absolutely no intention of watching it, or to spend any time in the living room at all. This was my thinking: if the television was on at a certain volume, Dad would get used to the noise and fall asleep, no matter how loud it was. And the mega-volume TV could muffle the sound of me escaping into the cemetery in the middle of the night. Sure enough, Dad shuffled off to his bedroom at ten thirty, never once commenting that I should turn down the volume.

By eleven, I figured it was safe to assume Dad was sound asleep. Old people go to bed so early. I went into the living room, opened the cabinet, and began emptying it of board games. I'd need some ammunition for my dead kid visit. They'd probably initially have reservations about my idea, so the more board games I could bribe them with, the better. The only game I left in the cabinet was Scrabble, my dad's favourite. He'd notice something was up if that went missing.

With a stack of board games — Hungry, Hungry Hippos; Jenga; Life; Monopoly — waiting on the kitchen table, I put on my shoes and black starter jacket, then slid the glass door open, pretty confident Dad wouldn't hear the little squeal of rubber on glass over the extra-loud edition of the eleven o'clock news. Once outside with the pile of games, I slid the door shut and slunk into the backyard.

The secrecy of the dark made me way more confident. I marched right through the back gate and deep into the cemetery. In no time, I found the headstone I was looking for. Among other unusual sights, the cemetery included an odd little grave with a bell over the tombstone. Placing the board game pile on the ground, I found a stick about the size of a shower rod and promptly began whaling on the bell.

"Who puts a bell on their tombstone?" I whispered to myself. From the woods, an answer came.

"There's a string that leads to the coffin. It's a safeguard, so if the person was accidentally buried alive they could alert someone."

My eyes scanned the bell and found a little string leading to a hole drilled into the dirt. How morbid is that? Planning for the chance that you're buried alive? When I looked up, all of the dead kids had already emerged from the forest.

"Sick," I said.

"Be quiet," spat Tabetha. "You wanna wake the whole dang neighbourhood up?"

"No," I said, standing astride the bell-marked grave with my summoning stick in hand. "Just you guys."

"What are all those?" Tabetha asked.

"Presents," I explained. "They're board games . . . for you. I figured you'd get bored in this cemetery."

The dead kids looked skeptical. Kirby stood with his hands in the belt loops of his silly little shorts.

"Nobody has ever brought us gifts before, Living Girl. What do you want from us?" he asked.

"Oh, I just had an idea," I said. I could feel their skepticism hit me in the face like an invisible force field. I took a deep breath and spoke: "How would you like to solve a mystery?"

☠

The five dead kids stared at October with their huge dark eyes. The weird girl from last night was already back, and this time, she had brought homework.

"Solve a mystery?" parroted Derek Running Water. "What are you talking about?"

October illustrated the situation, describing the death of her French teacher Mr. O'Shea. She, like everyone else, had believed his death to be the result of a blameless (though highly unusual) accident in the school's auto repair shop when he went to retrieve his Volkswagen Rabbit. However, she'd learned that such an accident was impossible without damaging the lift or breaking the switch beforehand. And given that her dad was being questioned and Mr. Santuzzi was claiming Mr. O'Shea clearly took his own life in a gruesomely creative way, October figured something was amiss. She had read enough horror novels to know a suspicious death when she saw one.

"So, tha's why ye were crying last night? Ye think yer French teacher was murdered?" Morna MacIsaac said. Her mouth hung open like an expectant mailbox.

"I don't know," said October, "but I know there's more to that accident than what everyone is saying. Either he did it on purpose, or someone was with him in that auto shop. Something weird happened, and I need to know what it was."

"Need is such an abused word," yawned Kirby LaFlamme, whose eyes rolled in his skull.

"Come on," October pleaded, stamping her foot in frustration.

"I know you can help me. You can walk through walls and stuff, and you're invisible to most people — and you can't really get hurt."

"Yes, and we're only around until Hallowe'en," reasoned Cyril Cooper, one of those dangerous Loyalists her father had warned her about. "And you want us to spend those days on this wild goose chase? You don't have much evidence to suggest this teacher was murdered. He was in an *auto* shop?" He chewed the words like taffy. "What was he doing there?"

"Getting his car fixed. His *automobile*," October said.

Cyril looked blankly for a moment, then smiled. "Oh, yes. Automobiles. The big things in which people move quickly about. Kirby and Derek showed me an automobile once. They go a great deal faster than a horse."

October shook her head in dismay. She started to think that it might actually be an extremely stupid idea to have a bunch of kids, most of whom died before the invention of the television, investigating a suspicious death on her behalf. Tabetha Scott, who had been silent about the mystery-solving proposal up to this point, suddenly walked directly through Cyril, positioning herself in front.

"Now, wait a minute," she insisted. "Before anyone starts talkin' 'bout horses an' automobiles, I've got a much more important question: What's in it fer us?"

The dead kids looked at one another.

"As much as I'm loath to agree with Tabby on anything, she has a point," Kirby said. "Why should *we* exert ourselves just so you can find out more about your corpse of a French teacher, hm?"

October didn't appreciate Kirby's tone, nor his colourful turn of phrase, "corpse of a French teacher," and furthermore, she had made a crucial oversight. She had been thinking of the dead kids as adults when they were adolescents like her. Sure, they were a lot older — Cyril must have been well over two hundred — but not much more mature. The search for truth and justice was not a convincing motive for them. They needed an added incentive.

"What if I promised to bring you back at the next full moon? It could only be a month away," she asked. "Apparently my words are pretty magical. I could read my novel out loud whenever I want and bring you kids back. You wouldn't have to wait ten years or whatever to come back to life. Or whatever this is."

She saw their eyes shining with promise in the darkness. It was hard for her to read a corpse's body language.

"Don't you want an adventure?" October asked, even though speaking to five dead bodies about adventure struck her as somewhat misguided. They'd probably had too much adventure in their lives already. "You spend most of your time here rotting in the graveyard working on your three-part harmonies. You could be helping people solve mysteries. You could be helping me!"

Was October beginning to convince them? Did they like the idea of returning to the cemetery? It was impossible for her to determine from their grey, impassive faces. Did Derek crack a smile?

"If we work together, we could be a really good team," she gushed. It was getting a bit embarrassing. "I'll ask the questions, and you can do all the cloak-and-dagger stuff, all the sneaking around. Plus, I brought you all these board games. You kind of owe me. What do you say?"

The dead kids didn't speak, but looked meaningfully at one another, just like soap opera actors who had momentarily forgotten their lines. Morna sat on a tombstone, kicking her legs, but she was deep in thought.

"I'm all for this," Kirby decided authoritatively. "We should be able to solve this mystery within a few days, then think of all the musical productions we can mount. A different show every season, if we're guaranteed to come back!"

"Oh, shut up," said Tabetha. "You don't speak for all of us! Maybe I'd rather not spend time with you dead bodies or sing songs for all eternity."

"Good! You don't have the voice for it!" Kirby barked back.

While Tabetha and Kirby bickered, the other three ghosts approached. A cold breeze snaked its way through the leafless trees.

"So, yer idea is that we help ye wi' yer French teacher, and ye'll bring us back t'life every full moon?" asked Morna shyly.

"Back to life?" questioned October.

"Back to living death," corrected Kirby. "That correct enough for you, Mistress Logic?"

"Then yes," October said. "That's what I'm suggesting."

Kirby and Tabetha stopped arguing and joined the other ghosts.

"Okay, Living Girl," said Cyril. "I think you have yourself a deal. We can start as soon as you're ready."

"But first," Derek insisted, "we've gotta play Hungry, Hungry Hippos."

☠

Maybe I was paranoid, but I wanted to wait until a few days after Mr. O'Shea's funeral before I sent the dead kids out to investigate. I thought it would look unseemly if I was jimmying open Mr. O'Shea's desk and his files were mysteriously vanishing from the front office while final arrangements were still being made.

I also needed some time to get used to hanging around with dead kids. With each meeting, I'd become progressively less scared, but let's be honest; these were dead kids I'd been meeting in a cemetery every night, and it was hard not to be jumpy around them. Every time I thought I was getting accustomed to them, I'd accidentally touch a clammy finger while playing Jenga, or I'd see a worm crawl through a rotting shirt, and I'd want to puke or poke my eyes out. It wasn't easy to instantly accept the living dead.

Somewhere around October 22nd, I felt I'd finally reached some place inside myself where I could be calm and collected around the five of them. I felt that we were officially a team — an unholy union of the dead and the living. That night, I arrived at the cemetery with actual investigative work for the kids to do. By that point, I'd already served three afternoons in detention with Mr. Santuzzi for my creative math answers — apparently he found my insults offensive, and not "edgy" or "in-your-face."

One thing I hadn't done was touch *Two Knives, One Thousand Demons*. I was afraid to work on it. I had read aloud from it and it raised the dead. Mr. O'Shea was the only person besides me who'd read it, and now he was dead. The book was cursed! My next paragraph could snuff out the sun for all I knew. It also felt wrong to work on a horror book Mr. O'Shea liked, given how horrific his own death was — even Olivia de Kellerman wouldn't have dreamed up a death like Mr. O'Shea's. Opening the pages of the *Two Knives, One Thousand Demons* notebook was like slowly pulling off a bandage, and I couldn't handle it.

I hadn't seen the dead kids in a couple days, and when I saw the five of them waiting by the clearing, they almost looked excited. Maybe this ridiculous plan would actually work. I had their first assignment ready — I'd even bought and prepared composition books for each of the kids to take notes. Cool, right?

"Evening, fleshbag," said Kirby, ever the charmer.

"Okay, whatever, Kirby," I said. I was so not in the mood for his weak insults. "It's mystery solving time. I've only got your help for about ten days, so we'd better get started. First thing I want you to do is go to the Sticksville police station and find the police report and the coroner's report for Mr. O'Shea. The police must have spotted something out of the ordinary — something we don't know about."

"A police station? With police?" said Morna.

"Yeah and there will probably be some cops at the station, even late at night, so you should be very careful when reading the reports. I've made these booklets . . ."

With a sudden epiphany (and not the good kind), I dropped my mass of black-and-white composition books on the ground and my head dropped like a sandbag attached to my neck. "Oh no. Can you read?" Stupid me. I had completely forgotten about the lack of literacy in earlier eras.

"Derek and Kirby can read," said Cyril. That explained why we were always playing Jenga and Hungry, Hungry Hippos, and never Trivial Pursuit.

"I can read both French *and* English," Kirby elaborated, quite impressed with himself.

"I'm a little concerned about breaking into a police station," said Derek. "I'm no big fan of police."

"An' there's no way of tellin' if one of the policemen might be able to see us," added Tabetha. "They're police. Good chance one of them lost someone violently or mysteriously, right?"

"Okay, I know it's dangerous," I said, "but to be perfectly honest, that's why I'm sending you – already dead – kids to the police station. They can't exactly throw you in jail."

The dead kids had a few more minor protests that I handily dismissed. If only our school had a debate team, I would definitely be the most valuable player in our motley crew of ragtag orators. Eventually, they agreed to go to the police station the following night.

Cyril looked down at my chest (but not in *that* way). "What's on your shirt?"

"It's a movie."

"What is?" Tabetha asked.

I forgot they couldn't read. "The shirt is for a movie called *Night of the Living Dead*. It's, like, this horror movie. Kind of a big deal."

"Oh," he said, clearly unsettled. "This dead stuff is kind of an ongoing interest, huh? Well, I'll see you soon. We should have some information for you. Or so I hope."

"Freakshow," Kirby whispered to me as he passed.

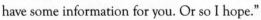

Gnawing through the eraser end of my pencil in math class, I could taste the ugly tang of the metal ring; a nervous habit of mine that I'm sure I'll get over. Could be worse. I could bite my nails, or smoke, like Ashlie Salmons (which I've totally never seen her do, by the way). After assigning the dead kids their first mission or quest or whatever, I had some serious trouble concentrating at school. I was mega-anxious about the dead kids' raid on the Sticksville police station, and just wanted to warp ahead to the next night so I could know what they'd uncovered. I wanted to be like Superman in the old movie and push the earth's rotation forward one day. This waiting was absolute torture, and it had only been a few hours.

Santuzzi's initial mild tolerance of my existence had completely worn off when I called him a dirtbag on that pop quiz, and our repeated detention sessions had not really forged any bond of friendship or mutual respect between the two of us, even though it did seem like he could read my mind. Whenever I started thinking about the dead kids, the mystery, or anything outside of algebra or geometry, he snapped at me like a Doberman at a child poking it in the eye. How could he know?

"Ms. Schwartz, I asked you a question. Exactly how many types of drugs did you take before class this morning?"

I was restless. It lasted through the day and after school. I had to force myself to work on *Two Knives, One Thousand Demons*, despite the potential risk to me and the world, and this time it wasn't the sadness about Mr. O'Shea or my fear of, like, ending human history that prevented me from accomplishing anything. I just couldn't find the inspiration. Maybe since befriending real ghosts, my geeky little stories of spirits and demons seemed totally lame. Whatever the reason, I couldn't think of anything but the dead kids' investigation. I really hoped no one at the precinct could see ghosts.

☠

When the clock struck midnight — the metaphoric clock that is; there was no public timepiece in the Sticksville Cemetery — the dead kids set out for the police station. Derek *supposedly* (my emphasis) knew where it was located, so he led the group. The crew of dead kids stuck to the side streets and ducked behind bushes or trees or mailboxes whenever they heard someone approaching.

They reached the police station an hour later. Geographically speaking, the station is not an hour's distance from the cemetery — more like fifteen minutes — but the dead kids took the back roads and Derek was no GPS system when it came to navigation. They got hopelessly lost twice on the journey. The parking lot of the station was deserted, but a few lights were still on inside the building.

Surrounding the building in a much smaller perimeter was a chain-link fence. Within that fence, tied to a post with a fairly liberal lead, prowled an unfriendly German shepherd.

"I'm pretty sure tha' dog can see us," said Morna. "Animals can always see us."

The shepherd began to snarl.

"Somebody better do something before the police hear it."

"I think Tabetha should do it," said Kirby.

"Me? Why me? Look at you. You've got the meatier arms, big boy. He'd love t'chew on you."

"I'll need both my hands to read through the police reports. Unless you can suddenly read."

"Who said we need to use yer arms?" said Tabetha. She lifted Kirby's worn dress shirt, dug her first deep into his fish white belly and broke off a rib.

"You're lucky I could find yer ribs in there," she said, then heaved it over the fence, into the open, salivating jaws of the attack dog.

"I can't believe you did that," Kirby choked.

The five dead kids walked through the front gate and passed the German shepherd, who observed them with detached interest as he contentedly gnawed on a section of Kirby's ribcage.

"I think there's a constable inside the front chamber," whispered Cyril. "He might be able to see us. Running Water and I will go in first, and we'll signal you if it is safe."

Morna, Kirby, and Tabetha nodded, and Derek and Cyril walked through the front door. The strange duo turned a corner and found themselves facing a large desk in the centre of a room. An officer sat at it, but thankfully had his back to the entrance. His attention was focused on a radio behind the desk; he seemed to be seeking out a particular station. Derek and Cyril madly scrambled onto the floor, crawled along, and pressed themselves against the front of the desk, sinking into it a little to be less conspicuous.

Their eyes bulged at each other in a manner that silently said "That was close!" and Cyril pretended to mop his brow, though it was physically impossible for there to be any sweat for him to wipe away, even if he'd run a marathon across the Sahara in a sweater-vest. Cyril pointed at his hand and then gestured upward, indicating that he was going to stick his hand up above the desk edge to see if the police officer could see it. Derek nodded and Cyril slowly raised his hand in the air.

"Cripes! What is that?" exclaimed the guard.

Cyril froze. Terror shot through his body and, looking at Derek, Cyril could see he felt the same way. The police officer had seen them. He could see ghosts. His partner was shot down in the line of duty, or his father was killed by muggers outside of a theatre. Something had happened and this man could see the dead. He had seen Cyril's spectral hand and now he knew there were ghosts in the room.

The officer stood up from his post, his face in a rictus of disbelief, and to their surprise, walked right past them, and stared at a spot on the floor. Atop that spot, a dog had recently left a steaming hot gift, fresh from its lower intestine. Well, let's hope it was a dog.

"I told that idiot McGarrison he shouldn't bring that mutt of his into the station," the officer said. "Now *I'm* the one who has to clean up his mess." He returned to his desk and began shoving things around, looking for an appropriate implement to clean up dog poop. Derek and Cyril breathed two large sighs of relief.

"He can't see us," Derek said, delighted he could now speak without fear. "That'll make things a whole lot easier."

"What about the other voices?" Cyril asked, still not entirely confident. "I hear others. Can't you?"

"That's a radio," Derek explained, realizing Cyril was concerned about the long-ago-recorded voice of rock 'n' roll legend Roy Orbison. "I've already told you about the invention of the radio several times. Do I have to again? The voices are coming from far away? Remember? The people they belong to aren't here in this building?"

"Oh, I remember," answered Cyril, trying to look like he had the faintest clue what Derek was talking about. "Let's retrieve the others."

Once inside, the first order of business for the dead kids was to determine where police records might be stored. They wandered through the halls as a unit, too worried about being this far from the cemetery to split up. Eventually, Kirby noticed a door with "Records Room" printed on the frosted-glass window.

"Wait," shouted Kirby to the others, who were continuing down the darkened hallway. "I think this is the place."

They walked right through the locked door and were suddenly surrounded by rows of bankers boxes piled in metallic bookcases. Only Derek and Kirby recognized that the boxes were alphabetically ordered by report category, then by the name of persons concerned.

The room was about the size of a basketball court, with several aisles of bookcases.

Kirby turned to Cyril. "We can find the things October needs in here," he said. "But it might take some time and we might make a lot of noise digging through these boxes. A distraction would be handy . . . so the guard doesn't come down this hallway."

Cyril smiled.

"Since only Derek and I can read these files, how about you, Morna, and Tabby play poltergeist?"

☠

The three illiterate, dead kids ran up and down the hallways on the east side of the police station, flicking and slamming light switches on and off as they went. The records room was on the west side of the building, so ideally, this inexplicable light activity would draw the guard away from the room's vicinity. Sure enough, the officer on duty came running down the hallway, heavy flashlight in hand.

"Who's there? Show yourself!" he bellowed.

Morna toyed with the light switch, causing the hallway to flutter between light and dark, as if it were lit by a strobe light. The ghosts watched the officer grind his molars and spin around wildly as he tried to identify who could be responsible for the light malfunction.

Leaving the officer suitably spooked, Tabetha led Morna and Cyril to another room on the east side of the station. The room contained seats, some recording equipment, and a large window into another room. The other room simply featured a desk with a lamp and two very practical chairs on either side.

"Look," Tabetha said, as she approached the large window. "On this side it's a window . . ." Then she moved her upper torso through that window. "An' on this side it's a mirror."

The others followed her as she coasted through the window, and though they couldn't see themselves in the mirror — ghosts don't cast reflections; wasn't that one of the rules? — they could see reflections of the table and two chairs. Tabetha walked over to the table and kicked the chairs away. She gripped one side of the table from underneath.

"Here. Give me a hand!"

Cyril and Morna grasped the other edges of the table and all three began to rock it back and forth, making an awful racket in the process.

"Louder!" Tabetha goaded, and they rocked the table even more. The guard burst into the room and saw the interrogation table moving of its own volition. The dead kids laughed at the panicked look on his face and continued to jostle the table.

"I've got to call someone," the officer said, taking one final look at the self-propelled table before madly scampering down the hallway.

"He's calling others," said Cyril, dropping his side of the table. "We've got to stop him!"

The three dead kids bounded down the corridor, hotly pursuing the confused officer. The man in uniform turned down a darkened hallway. Cyril followed, his little drum bouncing against his side. Morna and Tabetha found it difficult to keep up in their full-length skirts. The officer rounded a second corner and increased his speed. His destination: the front desk. He was quick, but the young Loyalist was quicker. Pumping his legs demonically, he passed through the guard's body and overtook him. Now that he was in the lead, Cyril suddenly realized he didn't know what to do.

Cyril jogged around the desk, whipping his head back and forth without any idea about how to stop the officer from alerting anyone. The officer, unencumbered by any doubts, dove behind the desk and reached for the office telephone.

Morna and Tabetha, following as fast as they could, entered the front lobby.

"The phone!" Morna screamed. "Get the phone!"

"The what?" said Cyril. He saw the officer on the ground grasping at a black object with buttons on it.

"The black thing he's got," explained Morna at the top of her lungs. "Pull it out o' tha wall!"

Cyril became tangible for a moment. He grabbed the black object and yanked it out of the wall, then quickly became intangible again. The officer backed away from the telephone suspiciously, then curled up into a protective ball.

Derek and Kirby appeared in the other hallway, Kirby carrying several sheaves of paper under his arm. "We've got it! Let's make haste," he suggested.

"Perfect timing," said Cyril, and he charged out the front door. Kirby carefully slid the papers under the front door, and retrieved them from the other side once he'd passed through.

"Are we getting my rib back or not?"

A few hundred yards from the station, the dead kids slowed to a normal walking speed.

"What is that?" Tabetha asked, pointing to the bright white papers Kirby carried.

"Photocopies, apparently," Kirby said. "Derek showed me how to make them. It's a bit like a lithograph."

This analogy didn't help Cyril, Tabetha, or Morna at all.

"These papers are identical to the papers in the reports," he tried to explain, using smaller words and simpler concepts, "but they are not them. They are imitations that a machine made."

It wasn't clear if Cyril understood, but he continued the conversation. "And what do the reports say?" he asked.

"I don't know," Kirby admitted, while scanning the copies with his eyes. "As soon as Derek and I found them, we made these copies and ran. We didn't have a chance to read them."

Kirby continued to skim through the papers, while the other dead kids stood impatiently beside him in the police station's parking lot. In the distance, all the lights of the station winked on in small waves. The lone officer inside must have decided a darkened police station was not ideal when tables were moving by themselves and telephones were pulling themselves out of the walls.

"Oh," Kirby sighed. "October's not going to like this." He looked up from the copies. "According to the police and the coroner, it was either a terrible accident or a self-inflicted death. Terry O'Shea's death was nobody's fault but his own."

☠

Today, I added to the list of growing indignities in my life the fact that my dad decided to pay me a visit at lunch. I was sitting with Yumi and Stacey at our usual table, which was — no surprise — available, and I was feeling incredibly ill, though if it was my worry about the dead kids' trip to the police station or the cafeteria's tater tots, I really couldn't say. Whatever the reason, the sickness in my stomach only got worse when my dad, in his suit of chalk, showed up at the cafeteria doors, searching wildly for something. It was probably too much to hope he was looking for a kitchen knife to help with a dissection.

"October!" he called out from across the cafeteria. I asked Stacey if he could shoot me, should he by chance have a handgun on his person. My high school social status, to this point on life support, was now officially dead. But being dead wouldn't be so bad. The dead kids seemed to have an okay time; they didn't have any embarrassing parents to worry about.

Dad power walked over to our table and flopped a hardcover book on the table.

"Hey, Mr. S.! Looking good!" Yumi was enjoying my mortification a little too much. I shot her a knifelike glance.

"Dad, don't you have class?"

"Yes, pumpkin," he twisted the knife. "But the students will be fine. I just stepped out for a second. I have volleyball practice tonight, and wanted to make sure you got this as soon as possible."

"Are you sure it couldn't wait?" I asked. "Did you have to visit me in the cafeteria?"

Dad wasn't an idiot. He realized what I was talking about. "Sorry to embarrass you in front of your friends," he said, scanning the empty cafeteria table with some skepticism. "But this book is from Mr. O'Shea. Figured you'd want to see it as soon as possible."

All was forgiven. A book from Mr. O'Shea?

"Yeah, apparently it was in his desk in the humanities office. There was an envelope that had your name on it. Did you know anything about it?"

I picked up the leather-bound book. It was a lot nicer than the paperbacks Mr. O'Shea had lent me in the past, but it was unmistakably another book by H.P. Lovecraft, an old edition of *At the Mountains of Madness*, the one he'd meant to give me for weeks before he died.

"Mr. O'Shea was going to lend it me, but he kept forgetting," I explained, attempting not to cry. I had already cried three times in the past week. I was already over my yearly quota if I was ever going to keep my thirteen-year-old secret a secret. No tears, I told myself.

My dad left, I guess trying to keep his impact on my social life to a minimum, and Yumi grabbed the book.

"Is this another one of those books he was always lending you?" she asked, flipping through the yellowed pages. The book must have been over thirty years old.

"Yeah . . . I guess it's mine now." As I spoke, a folded paper dropped out of the book and onto Yumi's cafeteria-grade meatloaf.

"You dropped something," noted the ever-observant Stacey, poking at the gravy-stained paper.

"Oh, gross. Not that I was planning to eat this meatloaf anyway."

I snatched the paper from Yumi's plate and unfolded it. The paper was a map of Sticksville. The west end of Sticksville specifically, almost at the American border. And in the middle of a blob of gravy an intersection had been circled in red, its address written at the top of the page.

"A map?" Yumi asked. "Of what?"

"I don't know . . . what's out in this neighbourhood?"

"The old movie theatre is out there," informed Stacey. "I used to have birthday parties there. But I don't think that's the address."

"What is this place?" I wondered aloud.

"Hey, genius," Yumi interrupted. "Ever hear of the internet?"

Disregarding Yumi's comment, I opened up *At the Mountains of Madness*. On the title page was an inscription, "To our Sherlock—," and at the bottom, "Best, Mr. O'Shea."

☠

After scribbling my name on the computer sign-up sheet, I sat down at one of the school library's six computer terminals and unfolded the map, gravy stains and all. In the google search line, I entered, 64 Walker's Line, Sticksville, Ontario, and hesitated before hitting enter.

At first glance, the book was just a nice memory of Mr. O'Shea handed to me on a plate (quite literally, Yumi's plate). That alone was nearly enough to make me cry. But given that the inscription suggested the present might be some kind of secret code, I could barely think straight. "To our Sherlock?" Clearly that was a reference to me finding his glasses at curling, right? Unless he had lent it to someone in the past named Sherlock. But who is named Sherlock? Isn't that like Madonna or Stalin? It's just a name parents avoid giving their kid.

But did this mean Mr. O'Shea was murdered? And if so, did he know it was going to happen? Why else would he have written this way cryptic note in his book, a book that might not have even made its way to me? That said, I felt it was clear the map was intended for me. If Mr. O'Shea had gone to the trouble to write a new inscription in the book, you think he'd notice he left an old map in there, right? The good news was, if this map was some kind of clue, I wouldn't have to spend every day twiddling my thumbs while the dead kids solved this mystery. I was now part of the action.

I initiated the search, and the first link was a commercial storage area: You-Store-It, at 64 Walker's Line. So either Mr. O'Shea had a storage unit there, or the owners of this storage place were somehow involved. I was going to have to check this storage area out, either by myself or with my handy, ghostly helpers.

☠

Dad had volleyball practice, so as soon as darkness fell outside my bedroom window, I ran into Sticksville Cemetery, eager to hear what the dead kids had learned at the police station. The anticipation was killing me, especially now that I had another . . . clue, I guess?

My eagerness gave way to disappointment as soon as I located the dead kids and learned the only new information was that: (a) Mr. O'Shea's death was officially ruled an accident, and (b) Kirby now knew what a photocopier did.

"There was nothing weird in any of the police reports?" I asked, not yet willing to believe the rulings of Sticksville's finest.

"Here are the copies," said Derek. "Check for yourself. They're pretty sure it was either an accident or that your French teacher did himself in by his own hand."

I hurried through the papers, flipping them like I was trying to animate the pages. I refused to believe there was nothing important buried in the report.

"What's this?" I asked, holding up one copy that was completely black.

"Oh," Kirby said, and focused his eyes on the ground. "I got excited when I learned what the machine did and tried to photocopy my face . . . I forgot that it wouldn't show up."

Shuffling the papers back into a neat pile, I felt my heart sink in my chest. The police reports showed no evidence of anything super-suspicious, and as bumbling and inept as I'm sure the Sticksville PD were, how could they have screwed something like this up? Nevertheless, I couldn't shake the feeling that Mr. O'Shea's death was something much more than a normal auto shop accident — as normal as those are, anyway.

"So, you up for another round a' Hungry, Hungry Hippos?" asked Tabetha.

Everything was ending so quickly. Even if the police didn't think anything strange had happened, I couldn't give up on Mr. O'Shea now. What did the police know about detective work, anyway? He had left me a clue, a map to a storage unit. This was no time to feed plastic hippos.

"We understand how you feel," Derek said. "But really, it was an accident. Don't worry . . . you'll get used to unsolved mysteries. We've all, kind of, made peace with our deaths, which will probably never be solved. Just give it time."

"No, it's not over. You've got to give me until Hallowe'en!"

"That's not —" started Tabetha, but Cyril interrupted.

"Okay. You've got until Hallowe'en."

"What're we supposed to do?" Tabetha asked, and the other kids nodded in agreement. "Sit on our hands? Ya' got no leads. Ya' want us to search every home in tha' town?"

"This should be a start," I said, and pulled out the map from Mr. O'Shea's book. "Your second mission."

☠

FROM THE DIARY OF HENRI LAFLEUR -
DEFENSE D'ENTRER!
February 14, 1969

(The following diary entry has been translated from the French, for your reading enjoyment.)

You are probably wondering why I'm writing again so soon. It has only been days, not months. Bad news, my friend. My heart is broken.

In two days, my world has turned upside-down. Yesterday morning, the northeast wall of the Montreal Stock Exchange exploded. Someone planted a bomb and twenty-seven people were seriously injured. Naturally, when I went over to Jean-Paul's that evening, I figured they'd be a little smug. Not happy or celebratory, perhaps, but whenever a bomb went off in Montreal, they seemed able to justify it. This bomb was clearly an FLQ project, one aimed at the city's financial centre, which is still largely controlled by English and foreign companies.

What I did not expect is that Jean-Paul was directly involved. As I walked into the apartment, Jean-Paul proudly told me he'd provided the explosives for the stock exchange bombing, and — even worse — I had helped! The clock I'd bought for Celeste's sculpture work was never used for artistic ends. It had served as the timer on the bomb Jean-Paul made for the FLQ. Jean-Paul had been an FLQ member for four months now. And, as I realized only at that very moment, so had I! This is what he'd meant by "the cause." Not just Quebec separation, as I'd thought, but bombs and robbery. Inadvertently, I had become a member of the FLQ. My present for Celeste was instrumental in the explosion.

I started feeling queasy at Jean-Paul's. Perhaps it was all the cigarette smoke — I could never get used to it — but more likely it was the enormity of what I'd done. I excused myself and went home early. Walking home to Westmount was a long trek, but I needed the time to think, and every passing pedestrian amplified my guilt.

Diary, I don't know what I should do. The police will find me out, I am almost sure of it. How many clocks are bought in Montreal on a given day? I can't imagine many. They will trace the bomb back to me and they will find Jean-Paul and Celeste, too. After the explosion, I found it impossible to think about Celeste. She has been asking about me, I know. She came into Bernard's restaurant looking for me. I'm sure Bernard liked that. Someone has been calling my apartment building's telephone all hours of the day and night. But I can't even imagine looking her in the face right now. She took my gift and turned it into an explosive device.

I can't see any other option than leaving Montreal. Maybe even Quebec. But where can I go? I know no English. Not enough to get by. And what will my parents say? They had been saving money for me to go to university for years, and now I've thrown it all away by buying bomb-clocks? I need to think of another plan.

My parents. Jean-Paul. Celeste. If I do what I am thinking of doing, I can never see them again. Some of the stock exchange victims are still in critical condition. Maybe I don't deserve to see these people again. Maybe Henri LaFleur deserves to die.

"What're we supposed ta do with tha'?" Morna asked.

Okay, so maybe my presentation of the map was a bit dramatic. After all, it's not like it was a pirate treasure map, written in blood on parchment and tied up into a scroll. It was a little photocopied letter-sized paper, speckled with dried meatloaf gravy.

"It's a map," I said. "To a storage area. I found it in a book of Mr. O'Shea's. I think he's trying to tell me something, like, from beyond the grave."

"Trying to tell you what, exactly?" Kirby quipped. "Where to find his old couch?"

"No," I shouted. Didn't the kids understand this wasn't the time to joke? I was trying to solve what I was certain was the murder of my teacher. "I think he has a storage unit there, or knows someone there. It must have something to do with his death. He wanted me to see it."

"You think he knew something about his own death before it happened?" Derek asked.

"Yes, maybe."

"And he left this information for you to find, rather than just give it to the police," Kirby said.

"Yes."

"An' why in tha name of John Brown would he do tha'?"

"Um, because . . . he thought I was a good detective," I said. Out loud, it didn't seem so obvious an answer. After all, Kirby had a point. The Sticksville police might not have been able to find a deal in a dollar store, but they were adults and solving mysteries was kind of their job. Surely they could make better use of this map if it had something to do with his death. Was I going crazy?

"We'll look at this tonight," Cyril declared, saving me from much more begging. "Thanks for bringing it. But remember, you only have us until Hallowe'en. After that, we can't really help you. The case could run cold in a month."

Cyril was right; I was on a deadline here. A literal one. If I didn't figure out what happened to Mr. O'Shea before Hallowe'en, I was on my own.

☠

It wasn't shaping up to be a banner week at school. A new French teacher, Madame Falcone, took over from the supply teacher and took charge of what used to be Mr. O'Shea's class, and I totally bombed one of Mr. Page's history tests (which, ironically, was about anarchist bombings during World War I). On top of all that disaster, I still had to finish my never-ending detentions with Mr. Santuzzi.

Every afternoon, Mr. Santuzzi and I sat alone together until 4:30. In the margins of my *Two Knives, One Thousand Demons* notebook, I had devised a hundred possible additional ways to prove Mr. O'Shea's death was no accident, just in case this storage area thing didn't pan out. But as I wrote, I also scratched out most of the ideas because they didn't make any sense or were just too impractical. Where was I supposed to get a metal detector, for instance?

The detentions were way depressing, and I resented spending Friday afternoon sitting in a classroom when what I really needed was more ideas and clues for the dead kids to investigate. If there was nothing of note in the storage area, I was doomed. By the calendar, I had only eight nights left of dead kid assistance, and I had no idea how I was supposed to find motives and evidence when trained police officers had failed at turning up anything.

Yumi Takeshi sat down across from me in the cafeteria that Friday. She was holding a newspaper in her hand, but I was brooding about the detentions and the go-nowhere investigation, staring dejectedly at the overcooked fries on my plate. I didn't see the paper until she poked at it with her black fingernail.

"Hey, check this," prodded Yumi. She opened the newspaper — if you can seriously call the *Sticksville Loon* a newspaper — to the real estate section. At first, I was a little more than confused; Yumi had never expressed any interest in buying a house, and I seriously doubted she had the purchasing power to do so, interested or not.

"What?" I asked. "What am I looking at?"

"Mr. O'Shea's house is for sale," she said. "My cousin pointed it out. It's this one. Just a couple blocks from my house." Yumi's finger landed on a square box with a little bungalow inside it. The photo had been taken at a bad time of day, and the colours were murky. I read the description below the photograph.

Beautiful bungalow. Well maintained.
Close to school, amenities. Perfect
first home for young couple. Avail.
immediately. 533 Arthur Lane. Call
Alyosha Diamandas: 905-555-2424.

"The body's barely cold and they're already selling off his house!" Yumi was outraged.

"What's going on?" asked Stacey as he sat down beside Yumi and fished his hand into his lunch bag.

"Mr. O'Shea's house is *for sale!*" Yumi yelled, hoping to inspire equivalent outrage in Stacey.

"How does your cousin know it's Mr. O'Shea's house?" I asked.

"She knows," Yumi said, as if that were an explanation in itself. "She knows lots of things."

Yumi rotated the paper around to an angle at which she could read it, and looked it over again. "I can't believe his kids would sell it so quickly," she muttered.

"Maybe he didn't have any kids," I said.

"True," Yumi said. "He did leave you a book. Seems like something you'd give to your kid."

"What about you, October," Stacey said, gesturing toward me (recklessly, I thought) with half a cupcake. Dessert for lunch again. "You still think there's something fishy about his death? Maybe it had something to do with the real estate market."

Even in the face of Stacey's outlandish, inane suggestion, I didn't say a word. The surrounding environment had completely vanished. It was like when it all goes white in *The Matrix*. Seeing Mr. O'Shea's home in a grainy real estate photograph changed everything. What if, instead of looking for evidence, I looked for a motive? Who would want to kill Mr. O'Shea and why? And what better way was there to learn about a guy, his life, his friends and enemies than by rummaging through all his crap? An idea hit me. In retrospect, it was not a particularly good idea, but it was an idea nonetheless.

Stacey was quietly polishing off his cupcake when I began asking him leading questions.

"Stacey, how tall are you?"

"I dunno. Five-eleven. Six feet, maybe? Something like that."

"So, you're tall for your age," I said with interest. I'm sure Stacey could see the crazy beginning to build in my face.

"That's what my dad says."

"How do you feel about wearing fake moustaches?" I asked, arching my eyebrow.

"What?" Stacey spurted. Clearly he was flustered, having lost control of this conversation.

"October," Yumi interrupted. "Have you been huffing glue? What are you talking about?"

"Stacey," I asked. "How would you like to help me set up a viewing of Mr. O'Shea's house? I think if I can take a look inside, I'll find some kind of clue. You know, about his death."

"This is ridiculous, October," Stacey said. "Who are you, goth Nancy Drew? Encyclopedia Brown? A *clue*?"

"No, listen. I'd do this myself, but I'm too young — I mean, we're the same age, but I look too young. No one will believe I'm old enough to afford a house. But with your height — if we disguise you — you can pretend to be my dad or something and we can both look around. . . ."

"That's messed up. I'm not pretending to be your dad," choked Stacey.

Yumi, whose smile widened as I outlined the scheme, said, "Oh, I'm not missing this! I'm coming along. I'll be your daughter, too."

"No! Nobody's being my daughter!"

"How good are you at lying, Stacey?" I raised my voice over his protests. "Because you'll need to be a good liar. Like, an expert in deception."

"I'm not doing this. A *clue*. Oh, maybe it was Professor Plum with the broomstick or whatever in the billiard room. This is insane," concluded Stacey, and he stood up from the table and stomped out of the cafeteria with a theatrical flourish.

"Don't worry," said Yumi. "He'll do it. He's a pushover."

☠

14

Later that Friday afternoon, after another Santuzzi detention, October, Yumi, and Stacey (who was, in fact, a *major* pushover) found themselves alone in the Takeshis' kitchen. Over the counter, they had spread open the real estate section of the *Sticksville Loon* to the listing for Mr. O'Shea's house. October lifted the kitchen telephone receiver and began dialling on Stacey's behalf.

"Wait," he said. "Nobody will believe that you're *both* my daughters."

"What's the problem?" said Yumi. "You and your wife adopted a little Japanese baby. Happens every day. Or maybe your soulmate is Asian and you two adopted a little white baby."

"And where is my wife? Shouldn't she be checking out this house with me?"

"Struck dead by lightning."

"Okay. Okay, fine," said Stacey. He wrestled the telephone from October's hand. "When do you want me to set up this viewing?"

"As soon as you can," chirped October. "Tomorrow morning."

"I can't do it tomorrow morning. Drum lessons."

"You take lessons to sound like that?" joked Yumi.

"Fine," said October. "Set it up for Saturday night. It'll make it look like you work weekends, *Dad*."

"Ha ha. You know, you girls certainly are having a lot of fun at the expense of someone who's going to wear a fake moustache for you. You'd just better hope this Alyosha guy is willing to show the place on a Saturday night."

What Stacey and, indeed, October and Yumi, did not know is that Alyosha Diamandas was perhaps the most feckless, avaricious real estate agent in Sticksville, if not the entire province. If Stacey had requested to see the house at two in the morning on Christmas Eve, he would show it. If Stacey had requested to see the house during Diamandas's own wedding, he would show it. Of course, such a scenario was unlikely, as Alyosha had a difficult time meeting women; he always seemed to be too busy showing houses to one person or another. In short, Alyosha would show a property at the drop of a hat — he didn't care about the who, the what, the where, the why, the how, or whose hat had been dropped. In fact, there was really no need for the elaborate ruse of Stacey wearing a moustache and pretending to be the girls' father. Three monkeys standing on each others' shoulders in a trench coat would have been granted a house viewing from Alyosha Diamandas.

Consequently, Stacey easily arranged a viewing for seven o'clock the following night. October and Yumi made plans to visit a party store the next morning to purchase some convincing facial hair for their male friend.

That night, before anyone purchased any moustaches of any variety, October checked in with the dead kids. She'd sent them on a mission across town the previous night, and knowing Derek Running Water's navigation skills, it was entirely possible they'd never made it to the storage unit at all. For this reason, among others, it was beneficial that October had a couple of mystery-solving irons in the fire. If the living dead crew had found nothing, there was always tomorrow night's real estate visit.

Luckily, the dead kids were able to accomplish their mission: they found the You-Store-It storage area using the map (and not using Derek as navigator).

"And?" October asked impatiently.

"And it looks like a grand place to store yer junk," Tabetha assessed.

"What Tabby is trying to say, in her overly folksy way," Kirby interjected, "is that it was impossible to find anything out of the ordinary."

"Ugh," October said.

"I'm truly sorry, October," Cyril said as he began to construct a Jenga tower on top of a low gravestone. "There must have been over three hundred storage units there, and we had no idea how to figure out if one of them belonged to your teacher."

"We searched a couple units, but didn't find his name or anything unusual," Derek added, proving the dead kids had done their duty. It wasn't as if they'd blown it off and played Twister all night in the cemetery. "We even checked the ledger or whatever at the front desk. No O'Shea listed at all."

October felt dejected, but wasn't sure what she expected the dead kids to find in the first place. A dartboard with Mr. O'Shea's face on it? A written confession posted on a storage unit? At the very least, she'd expected he had a storage unit there. Otherwise, it didn't make any sense for him to have left the map in the book.

"You don't happen to know the number of your teacher's storage unit?" Derek asked.

"No," October sighed.

"Then ya' won't mind if we play some Jenga?" Tabetha asked.

"No," October said. "But I can't join you. I've got a big day tomorrow, sorry."

Given the map hadn't done more than show her an ideal place to store her excess books, October was going to have to make the visit to Mr. O'Shea's house extra-special. She'd need to keep her eyes open, her wits about her, and be on the lookout (especially) for any paperwork about a storage unit.

"Big day?" Tabetha asked. "Doin' what?"

"Can you pick us up the score for *Cats*?" Kirby asked.

"No, I'm actually looking at —" October started, before being promptly interrupted by the cries of her dad, searching for his mysteriously absent daughter.

"October! October, where are you?"

"I have to go," October apologized. "Think any of you can lend me your invisibility while I try to sneak past my dad?"

☠

Later that very night, as October sat in bed trying to envision Stacey's face with a store-bought moustache, the dead kids of Sticksville Cemetery — following a few listless rounds of Jenga — had a very similar, not-so-bright idea. They, too, elected to snoop around Mr. O'Shea's old house to look for clues.

None of the dead kids subscribed to the *Sticksville Loon*, and if they had, they probably wouldn't have paid much attention to the real estate section. Instead, Derek Running Water thought about paying a visit to Mr. O'Shea's when he read the police report for a sixth time. Tabetha was chastising him for spending all his time looking over the photocopies of the report, suggesting October was crazier than a cat with two tails, and that the sooner she gave up on her quest to find something strange about her French teacher's death, the sooner life (or death) could get back to normal.

"C'mon an' play some Jenga," Tabetha insisted. "The girl's lookin' for things that aren't there."

"I appreciate her thoroughness," Derek said. He smiled at Tabetha and went back to the photocopies of the police reports.

He laid the individual sheaves of paper in the dark green grass and read by the dim moonlight. When the thought struck him, he immediately felt like an idiot.

"Kirby!" he shouted. "Look at this!" Derek ran over to Kirby, who was busily removing a centre Jenga piece near the bottom of the dilapidated tower. When Derek thrust the copied report in front of Kirby's face, the tower went spraying over the cemetery lawn. Kirby was not amused. Tabetha, who had just won, was much happier.

"Look. The French teacher's address," he said to the only other reader in the group. "We could find his house and rummage around. It would be totally empty. Maybe we could find some clues."

Usually reluctant to agree with anything he had not himself proposed, Kirby agreed that it was not too terrible an idea. The two brought the plan to the other dead kids, who all agreed they should sneak into the house the following night. Tabetha was wary at first, figuring it would be a complete waste of time, but was eventually won over. Still, in the part of her that was quiet (such a part existed), Tabetha doubted they'd find anything worth a lick in the old French teacher's house.

☠

Are you following this, kids?

Both October and her living friends, as well as the dead kids from the cemetery, have planned to search through Mr. O'Shea's house on the very same evening. October will be there, pretending to be poor Stacey's daughter, accompanied by an oblivious real estate agent. The dead kids will be there, walking through walls and doing all manner of ghostly things. Can you imagine the hilarious hijinks that might occur were the two groups to run into each other in the former Mr. O'Shea's empty abode? Luckily for you, you don't have to imagine it, because there's an entire section about it. It's not half-bad, either. But if you would rather simply *imagine* the encounter, go right ahead and skip to the next chapter. It's a free country.

141

☠

After October and Yumi had applied a fake light brown boxcar moustache to Stacey's upper lip with much more than the recommended quantity of spirit gum — they couldn't risk it falling off midway through the showing, now could they? — the faux family set out for Mr. O'Shea's bungalow. They had prepared at Yumi's house. To heighten the illusion of Stacey's parental status, Yumi gave him a suit and dress shoes that belonged to her dad. They didn't have far to walk, but Stacey still complained about his sore feet. They were two shoe sizes larger than Yumi's dad's.

A little walking and a litany of complaints later, the three arrived at 533 Arthur Lane. The house looked just as it had in the *Loon*'s grainy photo: a bungalow with brown shutters and a small attached garage — a garage that October realized must be empty. After Mr. O'Shea's vehicle crushed him, it must have been taken to a police impound lot somewhere. On the front lawn, a For Sale sign stood like a question mark. A glossy photograph of Alyosha Diamandas beamed at them from the sign's corner.

Cautiously, Stacey rang the doorbell. Within seconds, Alyosha Diamandas answered. He, too, looked remarkably like his photo. He was a short man, balding in the worst possible fashion, with a thin caterpillar of a moustache twitching above his nervous mouth. He looked up at the taller man who he imagined was supposed to be the two girls' father and welcomed him in.

"Come in, come in," he said. "Let me give you and your beautiful girls the tour. Then we can talk business." At that very moment, Alyosha shuddered like he'd experienced his own little earthquake. He disregarded the inexplicable chill as nothing and led October, Stacey, and Yumi into the living room.

At the very moment Alyosha shuddered — maybe you had already guessed — the dead kids of the Sticksville Cemetery had entered the former home of the former Mr. O'Shea, quite literally through the back door. They debated which room a French teacher might store information about his own death in, and agreed that an office or study would be a smashing start. That is, if there were an office or study. They immediately set out in search of one.

Back in the living room with the living people, Stacey tried very hard not to play with his false moustache. "Who was the previous owner?" asked Stacey, the dad.

"He was a teacher at the local high school," Alyosha Diamandas said as he paced the beige carpet of Mr. O'Shea's living room and fussed with what remained of his hair. "He lived here alone for several years. Decades, I think. Did you notice the wood panelling on the walls?" He gestured to the wood panels like a showroom model. "And a fireplace, too. It is not unlike living in a glamorous ski lodge, yes?"

"No wife or kids?" asked the Caucasian daughter (October). As close as she felt to Mr. O'Shea, she knew nothing about his personal life.

"He had none. He tragically passed away over a week ago," Alyosha said, then added, "Do not worry. He did not die here." Ghastly images sprang to mind of Alyosha Diamandas on his hands and knees, scrubbing away pesky bloodstains on the bedroom floor.

"No family members were bequeathed the home," Diamandas continued. "I have been employed by the school board. The money from the sale of this house is going to a scholarship at his high school."

October studied the framed photographs on the mantle of the fireplace. The frames featured pictures of Mr. O'Shea and other teachers — Mr. Santuzzi, Mr. Alito, the art teacher — as well as other people she didn't recognize, but none who could pass for a blood relative. Not even a mom or dad.

"Let's take a look at the kitchen, shall we?" said Stacey through his bushy moustache. He was trying to stay on topic so Alyosha didn't get too suspicious of their motives. The real estate agent glided through the long, narrow hallway and beckoned them to follow.

"Does the house have an office?" asked Yumi. "Someplace a teacher might have kept all his personal information?"

"Uh . . . yes," answered Alyosha. "Down the hallway."

"She's a computer geek," October quickly explained. "Needs somewhere to put her laptop."

"Ah," said Alyosha as he led the three into the kitchen. Stacey smiled back at October. *Nice save* was the telepathic message he tried to send.

The kitchen was shimmering white and country blue. Either Mr. O'Shea was one of the neatest bachelors in history, or the realtor had thoroughly tidied the house upon taking possession. The white of the kitchen gleamed with disinfectant; all utensils, and pots and pans, had been neatly stowed. Diamandas emphasized the large windows that overlooked the backyard (which was a featureless, black void at this time of night) and doorways that led to the bathroom and another hallway.

October knew she'd have to look in the office at some point, but she thought it better to wait until after the agent had shown them the room, so she could sneak a preview before returning for a closer search.

"Do you think the previous owner had any enemies?" asked Yumi. Stupid, stupid Yumi. October began to regret bringing her Asian sister along.

"Enemies?" the real estate agent grinned hesitantly and glanced over at the girl's father, as if for some confirmation that yes, this girl was indeed off her medication. The father simply fondled his moustache gingerly. "Your daughters are such inquisitive girls," said Alyosha, pausing in front of the hallway with his feet spread wide, "with such unusual questions."

Between Alyosha Diamandas's little legs, October suddenly saw five small ghostly figures appear at the end of the hallway. Her eyes widened in surprise, then horror, as she realized that Yumi, Stacey, and/or the real estate agent might soon see the dead kids as well. She could have a total disaster on her hands.

Alyosha spotted the shocked expression on the one daughter's face. "Something wrong?" he asked, peering closer at her ever-dilating pupils.

"Oh, snap!" shouted Derek Running Water as he glimpsed the tableaux in the kitchen ahead.

"Did someone hear something?" said Alyosha. As he turned to look behind him, October motioned wildly for the dead kids to hide, but they were way ahead of her. As soon as Alyosha had opened his mouth, the dead kids had leapt around the corner like field mice chased by a starving tomcat. (You thought I was going to mention ocelots again, didn't you?)

"I have to use the washroom," announced October, and she ran into the little white room adjacent to the kitchen and slammed the door shut.

"Okay," she could hear the muffled voice of the real estate agent outside the washroom door. "Just don't make too large a mess, yes? I still have to display the washroom for your father."

October crouched in a ball on top of the closed toilet lid. She didn't know what to do, now that the dead kids were in Mr. O'Shea's house with her. They must have had the same idea she had, and were searching the house for clues. She wondered if — hoped — they had maybe already left; she would have to cut their real estate adventure short if the dead kids were still lurking about. October peered into the mirror to see just how pale the shock of seeing her dead friends had made her. Her face was a whiter shade of pale than she'd thought, and more freckled. October reached out to test the temperature of her forehead when she realized that the face in the mirror was not her own, but the gaunt, Scottish face of Morna MacIsaac, who was in the midst of entering the bathroom through the mirror. Four dead kids followed her.

"What're ye doing here?" asked Morna.

"Shhhhh!" whispered October. "I think the real estate agent can hear you, and he's right outside in the kitchen!"

"If he can hear us, there's a good chance he can see us, too," Cyril whispered back.

"I can't believe you guys would just barge into the bathroom. What if I was, you know, doing stuff?" whispered October.

"*Please*. Like we want to see *that*," muttered Kirby.

"Okay, it's getting crowded in this bathroom," whispered October. "You have to go. Go, go. Like out of this house," she clarified.

"What?" said Tabetha. "We can do a much better job searching your teacher's house than you can!"

"This is our stock-in-trade," Cyril added. "We walk through walls, sneak into houses — it's our strong suit."

"That," Kirby whispered, "and scaring the life out of people. Scope this out." And with that, Kirby tore off his left arm, leaving a gory socket at the end of his shoulder. October let out a small scream. Kirby reattached his arm, Cyril hit him for being so pigheaded, and there was much subsequent shoving and jostling among dead kids in the clean, but small bathroom.

"Everything all right in there?" the real estate agent asked through the door, obviously concerned, or at the very least mystified, by the scream.

"Yeah . . ." said October. "I was just, uh, astonished by the beautiful handiwork on these faucets."

Alyosha must have found that a plausible explanation, because no other questions followed.

"We're going to the office," said Derek. "Keep him busy while we look through your teacher's junk."

"Fine. Good. Look for something about a storage unit," said October, while flushing the toilet for effect. "But be quick. I'll stall him, but I don't know how much more house there is to see."

October washed her hands in the sink, dried them on the blue hand towel, but still the dead kids remained, crammed in the bathroom with her.

"Well. What are you waiting for?" she asked.

"Do ye know where the office is?" Morna asked.

October rolled her eyes. "Down the hallway — near the front entrance. Now go!"

Outside the bathroom, Stacey and Alyosha were deep in conversation about the Sticksville housing market. What Stacey had to contribute to that conversation, we may never know. Yumi, bored to a near-comatose state, pounced on October the moment she exited the bathroom. Stacey joined them and left Alyosha to test the icemaker in the refrigerator by himself for a few seconds.

October quietly indicated to Yumi and Stacey that they should extend the tour as long as possible, and while they didn't know why they should do such a thing, or why October had spent nearly ten minutes in the bathroom whispering to herself, then screaming, Yumi and Stacey, being good friends, obliged.

They devised some questions for the realtor.

They asked Alyosha Diamandas questions about faucet fixtures, the benefits of city plumbing over septic tanks, feng shui in the bedroom, the architecture of the house, the rumours that London architect Nicholas Hawksmoor's work was influenced by the symbology of secret societies and the occult, ventilation in the summer, the ability or inability of squirrels to enter through the chimney, schools in the area, local politicians, the effect of the book *Peyton Place* on middle-class North American consciousness, rental agreements, and pretty much anything related or unrelated to the purchasing of a house that they could think of.

Eventually, Alyosha concluded he had answered enough of these potential clients' questions and insisted they view the office. Yumi agreed. Apparently, she was still in character as a computer whiz. October dashed in front of the rest of the group and ran to the office. Someone had to warn the dead kids of their impending arrival, and since no one else knew there were dead kids in the office, the task fell to her.

"Kids," sighed Stacey, with a conspiratorial shrug directed toward Mr. Diamandas.

October leapt into the office and saw the dead kids rummaging through boxes and cabinets and desk drawers. When October entered, they sort of froze in place. "Get out of here!" October shouted between her teeth. "They're coming! Go! Close everything and run!"

The dead kids moved quickly, but focused their energies on the running half of the instructions. Desk drawers were left wide open, files left vomiting out their sides, and boxes left scattered across the floor as the kids sprinted through the far wall. October yelped in frustration, sickened by the obvious signs of an old-fashioned ransacking that lay before her.

Alyosha Diamandas, Yumi, and Stacey entered the office two seconds later and looked around in bewilderment, or disgust, or something. Their eyes bulged, at the very least.

"What happened here?" Alyosha was stunned. "Little girl, you're not supposed to go through other people's things like this, yes?"

"Darling," said Stacey in a stern tone. "I thought I'd taught you to respect other people's things. I don't want to see you act like this ever again."

"Okay . . . Dad."

Stacey was going to be punished for this.

"I'll . . . I'll clean this mess later," said Alyosha, almost to himself. "Well, this is the office," he declared, sounding defeated. "I just have to show you the bedroom down the hallway, then we can talk things through in the living room, yes?"

"Sounds good to me, old boy," said Stacey, and he punched the real estate agent on the upper arm. He was laying it on, like, two layers too thick.

The party of four, whose unlikely relationship frayed with every second they spent together, departed the disaster area of the office and continued into the bedroom. Alyosha directed all eyes to the bed and pried the large white closet doors open with a flourish, waving his hand across the volume of space inside. "The mirrors make it look even larger. You could fit a canoe in there," he remarked, which October thought was an unusual illustration of the storage space.

However, October didn't, as instructed, marvel at the closet space. Something else entirely had caught her attention. On Mr. O'Shea's nightstand was a framed picture of a woman. The name "ZOE" was signed across its bottom, along with the numbers "36-21-33." The gears in October's head clattered. Not literally, you understand. She's not some kind of robot or something. That would be a weird plot twist at this point.

The framed photo struck her as odd; the real estate agent said Mr. O'Shea had no wife. If it was just a generic photo, part of the real estate agent's dressing, why the signed name and the, frankly, kind of gross and sexist listing of her measurements? And October was nearly certain she'd seen the woman in the photo before.

"Your daughter is not looking at the closet," Alyosha whispered. "I insist, it's a definite selling point."

"Oh, don't worry about her," Stacey said.

"Now, Mr. . . . I apologize, but I have forgotten your last name," said Alyosha, "but if you'd just join me in the living room again, we can talk business."

"I have to get something from the car!" October announced, and she ran out the front door.

"There's no car in the driveway," said Alyosha, peering out the window. Stacey took him by the shoulder and led him and his Asian daughter back to where their tour had begun.

Outside, October circled Mr. O'Shea's house until she found the dead kids hiding in the bushes of the backyard.

"Sorry," said Morna, who rose to her feet. "We're so sorry. We left tha' mess and — "

"Whatever," said October. "I don't care."

Morna was a little startled by her abruptness. Cyril picked up the conversation where she left off. "We didn't find anything. Kirby and Derek said it was all French examinations and things of that sort."

"Listen, just shut up for a second." And they obeyed. "You need to go to the bedroom, to Mr. O'Shea's nightstand — there's a photograph of a woman, okay? Cyril, you know what a photograph is? I need you steal it and bring it to the cemetery. Do it now. I'll keep everyone else occupied."

"October?" Yumi was outside and calling from around the house's corner. "Where did you go?"

"Run!" October whispered, and the five dead kids dove full-tilt into the back wall of Mr. O'Shea's house.

Yumi came jogging around the corner. "October, what are you doing out here? Were you talking to someone?"

"Just needed some fresh air," said October. Ladies and gentlemen, for your consideration: the worst explanation in human history.

"Well, come back inside," Yumi said. "We need to get Stacey out of there so we can go back home. We're not going to find any clues here if we haven't already."

"Not yet . . ." said October. "Let's give the living room another quick look while Stacey and the agent talk payment plans."

"You know this is killing him," Yumi had an overly sinister glow in her eyes. "I'm surprised he hasn't soiled his y-fronts already." She laughed, grabbed October's hand, and skittered back into the house.

Inside, just beside the large, canoe-accommodating closet, Derek, Tabetha, and Kirby approached the bedroom nightstand and lifted the framed photograph of Mr. O'Shea's mystery lover. At the doorway, Cyril and Morna stood watch, keeping an eye out for anyone approaching. The living visitors would have to pass the doorway on their way out, so their time was limited.

"Hello, Zoe," whistled Kirby. "October's French teacher was quite the ladies man. And signed with love, too."

"It's a love note?" asked Morna, stationed at the door.

"Be quiet," warned Tabetha. "They ain't love letters t'you, crazy Scotch girl."

"Measurements, too," Kirby noted.

"All right, pig," Tabetha shoved him and grabbed the frame. "We got the picture. Let's go."

"No," Kirby shoved back and wrestled the photo back from her. "It would be safest with me, don't you think?"

"Stop fighting," said Cyril. "Here comes our Living Girl once again."

Quickly, Kirby snatched the photo and ran it to the doorway to meet October.

"You have to leave now," October panted. She'd run ahead of the others, and with her announcement, the four other dead kids left through the bedroom wall. "They're leaving, and they're headed this way."

What October hadn't realized is that Yumi had followed a little closer than she'd thought. She was directly behind her. "October, who are you talking to?"

October spun around and sputtered like a dying car. There was nothing she could say. She could only hope Yumi couldn't see ghosts.

"What's that photograph . . . and that guy holding it?"

Yumi extended her hand and pointed at the framed photo, tight in the chubby little hand of the late, yet annoying, Kirby LaFlamme. Yumi, unsure if what she was seeing was a trick of light, reached out to touch him.

"Boo," he said.

Understandably, Yumi screamed. A lot.

And that's when Kirby ran for the front door, and October, who didn't know what to do, instinctively ran after him into the front entrance hallway. Alyosha Diamandas and Stacey dashed out to Yumi and frantically asked the shaken girl what had happened.

"I don't know! I don't know," she cried. "There was this light, it looked like a boy — I think it was a ghost!"

"Ghost?!" said Alyosha, in a manner you might expect a real estate agent to say "water damage?!" or "rat infestation?!" He tore off down the hallway while Stacey stayed behind with the thoroughly-spooked Yumi and attempted to make her feel better. It's hard to comfort someone when you're wearing a fake moustache. Maybe you'll learn this yourselves one day.

Some distance ahead of Mr. Diamandas, October and Kirby ran for their lives — their undead lives. Kirby fumbled with the photograph and shoved it into October's hands. "Take this!" he said. "I'm travelling light."

"Ghosts!" shouted the real estate agent from around the hall. He was gaining on them quickly.

"What?" said October. "Why are you —?" Then she slammed headfirst into the front door.

"Meet you at the cemetery!" shouted Kirby from the other side of the solid oak door.

October lay in a crumpled heap in the house's foyer. Her head rang and the room tilted and swerved in an alarming manner. Kirby must have just run through the closed door. How considerate of him. She heard the real estate agent approaching, so she took the photograph of Zoe and, with her remaining scraps of consciousness, stuffed it down the back of her pants.

Alyosha Diamandas lifted October off the floor and wiped the beads of sweat from his little moustache with his free hand. "Did you see the ghosts?" he asked. Not, *Are you all right?* or even, *What are you doing on the floor?*, which, October thought, would have been much more appropriate opening questions.

"What? Ghosts?" said October, playing dumb. She didn't really need to act; she felt a bit brain-damaged after being smacked in the face with a door.

Alyosha eyed her suspiciously as he adjusted his suit.

"No, I . . ." October scrambled. "I think I felt something rush past me, like — like a breeze. But I didn't see anything."

"A-ha!" Alyosha exclaimed, as if it proved something, or as if it were his favourite Norwegian band. (For fun, google "Take On Me.")

Stacey guided a shaky Yumi Takeshi into the foyer and grabbed her jacket to help her slip it on.

"Mr. Diamandas," he said in his most authoritative voice. "I'm afraid this house is a bit too exciting for my daughters and me. You'll understand if I'm no longer interested."

The real estate agent shuffled his little feet and ruffled his bit of hair. He understood.

On the walk back from Mr. O'Shea's house, the only sounds made were those of Stacey, again complaining about his shoes. October had a few things to complain about, too. Notably, the pain in her head and the uncomfortably square photo frame she was trying to conceal in her pants that was poking her in the rear. Finally, Yumi, still wide-eyed, leaned into October and whispered something in her ear. Though she faced October, her stare was focused far, far away.

"Remember when you asked if I believed in ghosts?" she asked, and didn't wait for an answer. "Well, I do now."

☠

It was much later that Saturday night when October entered the cemetery. She had experienced a far more thrilling evening than she was accustomed to. And to think, she'd originally considered going to bed early. Her dad went to bed almost directly after October returned from her "night watching movies with Yumi." But time was running out and she needed to bring the photograph to the dead kids as soon as possible.

October stepped deeper into the dark, carrying the photo in her bag. She hadn't looked at it much since she'd stuffed it into her pants while lying on Mr. O'Shea's foyer floor. She extracted the frame from her bag and studied the photo. She was unable to shake the feeling that this was, like the map, something Mr.

152

O'Shea had left for her. A clue for Sherlock. Then a ghostly head appeared over her shoulder, analyzing the photo alongside her.

"You scared me, Kirby," gasped October.

"That's what I do," he said, offering no apology. "I'm a ghost, remember?"

"What do you think about this?" she asked him.

"Your French teacher had taste," he offered; a creep on all occasions.

"But Mr. O'Shea wasn't married. And this girl looks about a third of his age."

"Ooh-la-la," whistled Derek, finding October and Kirby alone, huddled close together. "What have we here? A little dead-on-living action? Some trans-death romance?"

The other dead kids had arrived.

"Shame, shame," tsked Tabetha, lifting the hem of her dress coquettishly. The action didn't really suit her.

"Oh, please," said Kirby. "I'd rather kiss *you*, Tabby, and you know how I feel about that."

"Don't remind me," grumbled Tabetha. One had the feeling that if he had reminded her, he'd have received a kiss from her angrily clenched fist.

October knew this photo meant something. What kind of person puts his girlfriend's (or possibly secret granddaughter's) measurements on her photo? "Do you guys have any idea who Zoe is?"

"It's not Zoe," Derek Running Water said. "Whoever that is."

Kirby and October looked at the photo, then back at Derek. Clearly, the photograph thought the woman's name was Zoe.

"It's Phoebe Cates."

☠

Exactly. I was, like, who the heck is Phoebe Cates?

"Oh my God, I can't believe none of you know who Phoebe Cates is," Derek said, exasperated. "Don't you know, October? She's just the hottest actress ever!"

"Maybe she was more your time, Derek," I said. I confess, I'm not totally up on my hottest actresses. Not a going concern for me.

"*Fast Times at Ridgemont High, Gremlins, Gremlins 2, Drop Dead Fred?*" Derek counted the movies off on his fingers. "Do none of these films ring a bell?"

I had seen the *Gremlins* movies, but I couldn't tell you who any of the human actors were. Only the Gremlins themselves had made any real impression. I guess the same couldn't be said for Derek. "Anyways, that's a photo of Phoebe Cates, I'm sure of it. Break it open. I bet it's from a magazine."

Kirby smashed the glass on the side of a grave marker — a bit dramatic, I think — and pulled out the photo inside.

"He's right," Kirby said. "How many family photos do you have that feature reviews of motion pictures on the reverse?" He displayed a two-star review printed on the photograph's other side.

"Amazing," October said. "I was right. This is a clue, left by Mr. O'Shea. Wild."

So, it was a clue, but that didn't help. Why did Mr. O'Shea leave a photo of some actress, big in the 1980s, on his night-stand. Was she involved? Seemed unlikely.

"Speaking of which . . ." I changed the subject, "that was a pretty wild scene down there at the house. I guess the realtor could see dead people, huh? And didn't like them."

"Yeah, well, we didn't know you'd be there," said Derek.

"Or tha' short, horrible man," added Morna.

"Who? Alyosha Diamandas?"

"Yes," Cyril said. "We've met."

I thought of ways the dead kids and that unpleasant real estate agent could possibly be acquainted. Was the real estate agent dead? Despite Diamandas's unfortunate appearance, he looked alive. Maybe Alyosha Diamandas used to hang with the dead kids in Sticksville Cemetery before he grew up, when his interests turned from dead people to housing markets and stuff. Was I destined to become the next Alyosha Diamandas? Was that my cruel fate? All I had to look forward to was a life of late nights selling houses, of thinning hair, and creepy, oiled moustaches? The thought was too terrible to consider. Luckily, Tabetha set my mind at ease.

"Musical theatre and board games are recent hobbies," she explained. "We used ta break inta empty houses when people would raise us. Houses for sale, usually."

"But Alyosha Diamandas was waiting in most of them," remembered Cyril. "I think we became a real annoyance after the first few incidents. We haven't seen him for years."

The night's pandemonium made a bit more sense now.

"I prefer the musical theatre me'self," decided Morna.

That was one mystery solved, but still no progress on Phoebe Cates. Maybe the numbers meant something. Morna obviously had the same thought I did. "What do the numbers mean?"

"Those are her measurements," Kirby explained. "The first number is her — "

"She doesn't need to know that," I interrupted. If I could save Morna from Kirby's sure-to-be rancid explanation of the primitive practice of listing a girl's bust, waist, and hip size, I would. "Besides, it doesn't even make sense."

"Well, if ye can't make sense of it, maybe the numbers

mean something else?" Morna suggested.

"They could be the numbers of a combination lock!" Derek shouted. "They would totally work! Some of the storage units had combination locks on them."

"We could spend tonight checking them all," Cyril said.

"We don't need a combination lock, you dunce," Kirby reprimanded him. "We can just walk through the walls. What we need is the number of the unit."

"We don't have it," Cyril shouted back. "But if we try the locks, we might be able to find which one is his."

While Kirby and Cyril barked at each other (a nice change of pace from the usual Kirby–Tabetha antagonism) I remembered how the photograph was sitting on Mr. O'Shea's nightstand and realized I could save the dead kids some time. I dropped my bag onto the lawn and rummaged through it until I found my hand mirror.

"Give me that photo," I said. "See how 'ZOE' is in capital letters?"

They nodded their heads slowly, not yet understanding. In time, my good dead kids.

"The photograph was close to the mirrored closet in Mr. O'Shea's house," I said. "Watch."

With that, I held up my hand mirror to the side of the photograph of Phoebe Cates. ZOE became 305 in the mirror image.

"How would you kids like to go to the movies . . . the, uh, motion pictures . . . tomorrow night?" I asked. "You've done an excellent job tonight, despite everything."

"Don't we have a mystery to solve first?" Derek, nemesis of fun, asked.

I didn't have the heart to tell him I would be making him leave the movies early, or that I was only taking them because the old theatre happens to be right around the corner from the storage area. I wanted to be there as soon as they found out what was in Mr. O'Shea's storage unit.

"Meet me at the Sticksville Mews at eight o'clock tomorrow night. They're playing *Ghostbusters*."

"I dinna' like th' sound of tha'," Morna said.

"The theatre's just around the corner from You-Store-It," I said.

"I have a feeling," Kirby announced, "we're not going to see how that movie ends."

☠

Sunday morning, I called Yumi from my kitchen phone. Yumi's recent ghostly encounter had really disturbed her. I had completely forgotten about the spooky story about her brother and mom. Of course she could see ghosts! I called to see if we were still on for the special screening of *Ghostbusters* at the Sticksville Mews, as it was likely Yumi would not want to watch any movies featuring ghosts. Even if they were being busted.

In hindsight, it probably wasn't the most sensitive thing in the world to bring Yumi to the movies when I one hundred-percent knew there would be five ghosts in the audience, but I needed to get out to that remote Sticksville neighbourhood, and there was no way Dad was letting me go to the movies on my own on Sunday night. He was wigged out enough by my night cemetery residencies. Stacey was the only other option, and I wasn't about to ask him out to the movies. That would seem too much like a date, and while Stacey makes for a fine friend and fake dad, I couldn't even begin to fathom the two of us making out in the front row. Uh, no thanks. Yumi was going to be my movie date, by process of friend elimination.

"Hey, Zombie Tramp," I said.

"Um . . . hello? Who is this?"

Clearly, the voice at the other end of the line wasn't Yumi's. Whoops.

"Oh, uh, hi, Mr. Takeshi. Is Yumi home?"

Mr. Takeshi bellowed for Yumi at the other end, declaring that her questionable friend, me, wanted to speak with her.

"Hey, October." Yumi sounded like she was talking with a mouth full of water crackers.

"So, how are you doing? . . . With the ghosts . . . and stuff."

"Been better . . . didn't sleep much last night."

In the background, Yumi's dad yelled and swore and made sounds like he was rearranging boxes in a glass factory.

"What's happening over there?"

"Dad's looking for his shoes. We're supposed to go to church in a few minutes . . . I forgot and Stacey took them home."

"You gave Stacey your dad's only good pair of shoes?"

"It's okay. He'll wear his New Balance shoes and lose face for a week."

"So . . . did you still want to go to the movies later? We don't have to . . . we can just hang out."

"No, it's okay. Movie ghosts are still okay. I'll see you at your place at six."

Yumi hung up, the cacophony of her dad's mad search resounding through the phone cord. With a sudden click, I realized I had the whole afternoon to myself. I decided to meet up with an old friend: Olivia de Kellerman.

It had been weeks since I had written anything in the *Two Knives, One Thousand Demons* notebook that actually related to the story. I'd thought I'd given up for good, but I reconsidered and decided it was time to give novel writing another shot. We were making progress on the Mr. O'Shea mystery, and, really, he would have wanted me to keep working on the novel, if you thought about it that way. No one had died or risen from the grave for at least a week, so it seemed safe. I shoved the notebook, along with *On Writing*, a few pens, and a Kit Kat bar into my black book bag and set out for the cemetery.

A few hours later, a tiny pyramid of my crumpled pages rested in front of Cyril Cooper's tombstone. I hadn't written a decent sentence all day. I was working really hard on this scene between Olivia and Uncle Otto, the grizzled, wheelchair-bound brother of her mother and mentor in the art of hand-to-hand demon combat. He was a new character I'd just written into the plot. Uncle Otto was supposed to reveal a dark family secret. It was a turning point! An epiphany! It

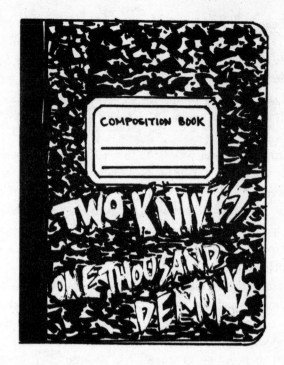

would blow the lid off the book so far. The only problem was, I had no idea what the secret was.

Looking at the pile of paper boulders at my feet, I realized I wasn't writing about demon slaying at all. Uncle Otto was a sham. I was writing about Mr. O'Shea and his secret past. What sort of person leaves all these clues for a thirteen-year-old girl to find? What sort of secrets could he be hiding?

Mr. O'Shea always seemed like an okay guy. He'd pretty much made my first couple weeks at Sticksville Central bearable. He'd even been interested in my writing, which was pretty bad, if today's output was an indication. Maybe I didn't really want to solve this mystery. Maybe I wouldn't like what I found.

I packed up my bag and headed home.

☠

"Okay," Yumi said, jabbing her grape slushie with the red spoon-straw thing. "Top five."

"Top five what?"

"Top five crushes," Yumi stated, as if this was a game we played all the time, or like this was the obvious default meaning for top five.

I nearly shot my orange slushie out of my nose. "Seriously? Are we doing this?"

"Come on, it's fun. I need to get my mind off ghosts. Would you just play along?"

"This is stupid. I don't *have* a top five. Can't we talk about *Ghostbusters* or something?" I knew I should have played along, and to at least try being a good friend to Yumi, who must have been losing her mind after maybe seeing a ghost last night. But Yumi's top five game was just embarrassing.

"Sorry. I didn't realize you'd had a stroke. I'm trying to get my mind *off* ghosts."

"But —"

"Are the Ghostbusters your five? Is that it? That's four. The Ghostbusters plus who? Rick Moranis?"

Yumi eventually revealed her top five, which I guess had been culled after many nights spent awake in bed, considering and contemplating. Below, I present Yumi's top five, comments and emphasis my own:

1. Johnny Depp (*so* obvious)
2. Morrissey (understandable, but seriously? He'd be an insufferable boyfriend)
3. Stuart Townsend (I didn't really know who this was, but I pretended I did)
4. Bruce Campbell (circa *Evil Dead 2*)
5. Stephen Colbert

"Stephen Colbert?" I was horrified. At the very least, confused.

"Whatever. You can't make fun if you're not going to play, Miss I'm-Too-Proper-To-Have-Celebrity-Crushes."

"Are you really going to call Bruce Campbell a celebrity? And why are there no Asian guys on your list? Race traitor!"

"Hey, trashface. There'd be some Asian guys on my list if there were some male Asian celebrities in North America other than Jackie Chan. Don't blame me; blame your white suprema-cist entertainment industry."

"Race traitor!" I shouted again, probably too loudly, because the male half of the Korean duo who owned the convenience store came out and began sweeping the sidewalk uncomfort-ably close to where we were standing.

"You ready to go?" said Yumi.

"Bustin' makes me feel good!" I sang, because I am, appar-ently, a total nerd.

Padding down the maroon carpet that covered the aisles of the Sticksville Mews, I spotted my five ghostly friends oc-cupying the back row on the right side of the theatre. Derek and Morna waved spastically, so I had to distract Yumi before they drew too much attention to themselves. I pointed out the fire exit at the far right ("That's where we go if the theatre's on fire!") and rushed Yumi past where the dead kids were sitting, shooting them an evil glance as I did. Did they not remember that Yumi could see them? Kirby should have remembered at the very least. I guided Yumi to two seats close to the screen (as far from the dead kids as we could sit without being conspicu-ous) and sat down.

"Wow. I don't think I've seen this movie since I was five," said Yumi.

"What? I watch it every couple of months. It's the best, Yumi. The best."

"I thought they'd be showing horror movies this close to Hallowe'en. I was hoping they'd have *Evil Dead*."

Yeah, and now I knew why that was. "It's great. You'll like it," I said. "Do you mind if I run to the washroom?"

"Yes. I expect my friends to wear adult diapers."

"BRB," I said, in case you needed a reminder I was a nerd.

I hurried to the rear of the theatre and shoved Kirby over, who was planted in the outermost seat.

"Moving pictures!" blurted Cyril.

"You guys have seen these before, right?" I asked Derek. "You're not going to flip out if a car drives toward the screen, are you?"

"Why are you whispering? The film hasn't even started yet."

"I'm excited," Cyril declared. "We almost never get to see moving pictures. Is this one good?"

"Is it scary?" chimed Morna.

Talking to five dead kids — or these five dead kids — at the movies was like talking to a classroom of hyperactive third graders who'd been on a field trip to the all-you-can-eat cupcake buffet.

"Slow down, and be quiet!" I said. "Yes, this one is good. You'll like it, Cyril. And no, it's not scary, Morna. Try to be quiet, please. It's a Hallowe'en special screening, so maybe no one will notice you, even if they can see you, but I'm here with Yumi, and she was really freaked out the first time you met. Remember, Kirby?"

"So you're not gonna sit with us?" said Tabetha.

"No. But after about a half hour, I'm going to come back here and get you, and we're going to run over to the storage area. Check out unit 305, 'kay?" I had to squint to find where I'd left Yumi, and wandered back down the aisle.

"Fine! We didn't wanna sit with you, neither!" shouted Tabetha, totally not following my instructions.

Right as Raymond Stanz and Egon Spengler were rolling up to the Ghostbusters' firehouse HQ in the beat-up ambulance that would become their vehicle, the Ecto-1, I excused myself. I'm sure Yumi must have thought my bladder was the size of a dime or I'd been mainlining Taco Bell since breakfast or something, but I couldn't worry about that now. I staggered through the dark to the last row, and dragged Kirby out of the theatre by force, trying not to arouse suspicion. I'm sure a girl exiting the theatre backward with her arms outstretched wasn't a super-common sight. The other dead kids followed where Kirby was taken against his will. We took the back exit and I began walking toward You-Store-It.

"What is your problem?" I asked under my breath. "I told you we'd have to leave."

"Ya' invite us to the movies, then ya' don't sit with us," said Tabetha.

"I told you. Yumi is scared of ghosts, so I couldn't sit with you. And you were never going to get to see it all, anyway. You need to investigate unit 305." I pointed toward the fence around You-Store-It. This was as far as I went, and I needed the kids to get me inside the unit, metaphorically speaking. Rather, I needed them to bring me the contents of that unit.

"That movie rots," added Kirby.

"We were bored!" yawned Cyril.

"Whatever. It's so good," I said, defending *Ghostbusters*.

"The depiction of ghosts is *soooo* inaccurate," said Kirby. "Green slime? Really? Are you going to go with green slime? This is ghost exploitation at its worst. It's *ghostploitation*."

"It's hilarious is what it is, you dead know-nothing. Now be quiet and find out what's in Mr. O'Shea's storage unit. Meet me back here in five minutes. If I stay out much longer, Yumi's going to wonder where I am."

"This is not as fun an excursion as I'd anticipated," muttered Derek, and he and the other dead kids sullenly walked through the concrete walls of the storage centre.

☠

I could outline how I spent the next five minutes freezing my butt off, waiting outside the locked storage centre — I really should have brought my jacket with me, but Yumi would have noticed — but those details are probably not important. The important stuff happened when the dead kids returned minus Tabetha.

"What happened in there?" I whispered. The intersection was deserted, but I didn't want to look like I was hearing voices if anyone happened to walk by. If I had a cell phone, I suppose I could have pretended I was on the phone, but Dad bought me a book for my birthday. I think a cell phone for his daughter was out of his price range. "Where's Tabetha?"

"She's coming," Cyril said. "She had to go round the other way, so she could bring the diary we found. We can't just walk it through the wall."

"You found a diary?"

"A diary, a bunch of newspapers from the 1960s, and family photos," Derek said. "There actually wasn't much in the storage unit besides those."

Why did Mr. O'Shea have a half-empty storage unit filled with newspapers and family photos? Why weren't his family photos at home? Everything about Mr. O'Shea's home life was exceedingly strange. Tabetha rounded the corner waving the diary in her hand.

"I believe y'all be wantin' this?"

I held the diary in my hands like it was a newborn kitten. I don't know what I expected, maybe a beam of light and truth to come shooting out as I opened the book, but nothing happened. And worse, the book was in French. Why was Mr. O'Shea's diary in French? I know he taught the language, but this was taking things too seriously.

"It's in French," I said.

"Yeah, and so were the newspapers," Derek said. "Mean anything to you?"

"I should remind you that I am fluent," Kirby said. "I could easily translate."

"Okay, but not now," I closed the book and made a beeline for the Mews again. "I need to get back to Yumi. We can translate this later tonight in the cemetery."

☠

Soon after everyone's eyes had adjusted to the house lights and the credits rolled into those boring categories like "drivers" and "second unit direction," I realized something totally horrible: Ashlie Salmons, she of the ultra-skeeze persuasion, she of the wide belts and perfect bangs and skinny legs, was sitting just two rows behind us, with her entourage of hateful girls. She was always horrible, but she'd become truly insufferable since she'd started dating Devin McGriff, guitarist of Phantom Moustache, the guy I'd seen her with that night at the basketball courts.

From the twinge of excitement in Ashlie's eyes — like that look a housecat gets when it sees a bird with a broken wing in the backyard — I was sure she saw us. Well, that and the fact she was looking straight at us.

"Look who they let out of their cages," said Ashlie with an arch of her finely shaped eyebrow. She must have drawn them on every morning. "You girls get day passes from the garbage dump?"

"That doesn't even make sense," murmured Yumi.

"Your face doesn't make sense," the little girl with the big laugh retorted.

"You girls win," I said, raising my palms in surrender. I was in no mood to fight with Ashlie. She'd probably just threaten to stab me again. "You're our superiors. Okay? Ashlie, can we stop fighting for a second, so I can ask you about something in private?"

Ashlie stood there with her hips thrust out to one side, and squinched her eyebrows together, but she eventually followed me out to the theatre lobby.

☠

In one corner of the minimalist theatre lobby, decorated only with posters of movies that most sane people had stopped caring about months ago, Ashlie and I had a private chat. Yumi was standing with Ashlie's cronies in the foyer, but they were just outside of earshot, while the dead kids, who were entirely bewildered by this spectacle, stayed just inside the open doorway of the theatre, shuffling their feet. I guess I should have been thankful they stayed there and out of Yumi's sight.

"What do you want, Zombie Tramp? I'd rather wash my hair with cyanide than talk to you for three seconds."

"It's about that night I saw you outside the gym. The night Mr. O'Shea died," I said. I hadn't really thought this whole conversation through. Ashlie would probably make me get on my knees and beg, or worse.

"You mean that night that you didn't see me," she reminded me, gesturing with her fist in a slow stabbing motion.

"Ashlie, I don't care what you were doing, but I think something happened to Mr. O'Shea."

"Yeah. He died."

"Okay," I said. "But I don't think it was an accident. I think someone did it to him." And with that, I fell down the rabbit hole of total insanity. No longer would I be the harmless Zombie Tramp in Ashlie's eyes, but a total psychopath.

"Listen, I know you're the child bride of Dracula or whatever and probably really into death and murder," she said. "but that's just sick. You are, in fact, sick."

"Please, Ashlie," I couldn't believe I was begging already. "Did you or Devin see anything strange that night?"

"What night?" she asked, a broad sneer cutting across her pale face. "I don't know what you're talking about."

"This is important."

"And it's important to me," she said, eyes narrowing, "and important to my Crown attorney mom that our encounter that night never happened. Nothing happened."

"You're a liar."

"Am I?" she asked, showing her sharp eyeteeth.

"You're also a potato-faced garbage bag."

That was when Ashlie's little triangular palm shot out and struck me right across the mouth. Instinctively — and I swear it was just instinct — I grabbed for her shoulders, but that's about as far as my instinct took me. I could feel the tears building under my eyes, and all the heat in the room rushing to my cheeks. Unsure of what to do next, I kind of shoved forward and pushed Ashlie to the ground, but I went down with her. At this point, Yumi and Ashlie's she-wolves were on the scene, pulling at the two of us, trying to pry us apart, but still we were thrashing at one another. Stupid scarecrow, so worried about her mom she wouldn't help me find out who killed Mr. O'Shea, you'd better believe I was going to give her a thrashing. A red-vested usher stood ten feet off and shouted impotently. "Hey, now. Stop that!"

The dead kids must have seen our scuffle and rushed over, careful not to get punched or elbowed by accident. But I guess Morna couldn't resist. She lifted a complimentary theatre magazine, rolled it into a misshapen tube, and brought it crashing down on Ashlie Salmon's nose as she was rising to her feet.

But, of course, Yumi saw it — saw Morna, an immigrant Scottish girl from 1910, roll up a magazine and smack Ashlie in the face — and Yumi completely lost it. Who knows if she saw the other dead kids, too, but what happened next suggests she saw at least a couple of them.

Everyone froze as Yumi Takeshi shrieked like a baby caught under a lawnmower.

"Ghosts! Ghosts!"

☠

16

Following the big theatre donnybrook, I had to do some emergency trauma care on poor Yumi. On the bus ride home, I assured her that she wasn't going crazy and that the ghosts probably wouldn't hurt her and stuff like that. Of course, I had to pretend I didn't see the ghosts myself, that I didn't know what she was talking about while she described Morna MacIsaac and Kirby LaFlamme almost to perfection.

After the bus deposited me a block from my house, I made sure to call Stacey first thing. I told him about the incident at the theatre and that he should probably be a good friend and give Yumi a call. Stacey was a bit offended we didn't invite him to watch *Ghostbusters*, I could tell, but it seemed he understood the situation was way beyond who invited whom to what movie. I hung the phone up and waited for Dad to fall asleep.

☠

A couple of majorly boring television shows later, Dad was sawing logs something fierce, so I collected my jacket and the diary from Mr. O'Shea's storage unit and went to the cemetery. By the time I'd arrived, it was clear the dead kids had been waiting for some time. Several board games had been discarded around the clearing.

"Sorry," Morna began. "I'm so sorry. I didnae know . . . I jes' saw tha' girl hitting ye, and I wanted ta help."

"It's okay," I said. "Yumi's going to be upset for a while, but she'll get over it. Right now, I need Kirby to help me translate this French."

Though I aced most of my French assignments, or did while Mr. O'Shea was still teaching me, I figured Kirby's French was far superior. I mean, he always bragged about it, so his French should be pretty killer. I cracked open the diary and laid it flat against the closest level tree stump I could find.

"This book says it's the property of Henri LaFleur," I said, stating the obvious. His name was all over the front of the book. "And it's from decades ago. These dates are all from 1968 and 1969. Are we sure this is Mr. O'Shea's?"

"The storage unit was listed under the name Henri LaFleur, whoever he is," Derek said. "Maybe he was a friend of your teacher? Anyways, start reading."

"Here," Kirby said, flipping ahead to the very end. "Let's spoil the ending. This was Henri LaFleur's most recent entry. What does it say?"

I steadied the diary on the stump, and luckily the moonlight was shining bright enough to read by. I squinted and tried to translate.

"After what happened at the . . . what is this, Kirby?"

"Stock exchange."

"Stock exchange, I . . . understand I must . . . leave . . . uh, something about Quebec . . . um . . . change my . . . change my . . . what's this word, Kirby?" My vocabulary was horrible. If only I needed to conjugate some verbs, my French skills would come in super-handy.

"Identity."

"Identity . . . Identity?" I repeated, coming to a very unpleasant revelation. "You think . . . you think Mr. O'Shea changed his name? From Henri LaFleur? Why would he do that?"

"Keep reading," said Kirby. His French was about as good as he boasted, and he'd already finished reading the journal entry.

"And most of all . . ." I read on, "that after what happened . . . passed? . . . I must separate and . . . distance . . . myself totally from the F-L-Q?"

I looked at Kirby in amazement, and he stared back meaningfully. It was clear; this was the clue that we had been searching for. The key to all understanding. But I had no idea what it meant.

"What's the FLQ?" I asked.

"I have no idea."

"What?" Tabetha asked. "What didja' find? What's it say?"

So I told her and all the dead kids that the diary seemed to suggest Mr. O'Shea, my French teacher, may have once been known as Henri LaFleur and may have once lived somewhere in Quebec. Furthermore, it suggested that he had changed his name and identity when he decided to leave something called the FLQ, whatever that meant. Additionally, a woman named Celeste had expressed great desire to plant kisses all over his body, and he was going to really miss that, but I edited that last part out of my description. I couldn't see how that fact would assist in our investigation. I wished I could edit it out of my mind.

"Have any of you heard of the FLQ?"

The dead kids answered me with blank stares.

"Derek," I said. "You and I are the only ones who might remember anything about it. The diary was written in the late 1960s. Does the FLQ ring any bells for you?"

"I have a vague recollection of something . . ." he mumbled. "I think they were French . . . and dangerous."

French and dangerous. *Français et dangereux*. Like the foreign legion and tongue kissing. It was not a lot of information for us to go on, and I guess everyone realized it.

"This don't help us at all," Tabetha gloomily remarked.

"In some ways it does," I said. "We know Mr. O'Shea changed his identity for some reason. Changing your name is pretty serious business, unless you're an actor or something. Maybe he made some enemies with his old name. Some enemies in the FLQ. What if some 'friend' of Henri LaFleur came calling?"

"Or maybe he changed his name to become an actor, and that's how he knows this Phoebe Cates," Cyril remarked.

"I'm pretty sure he didn't know Phoebe Cates," I said.

Nevertheless, my first suggestion was a decent "what if," but my theory didn't erase the fact that the police had determined Mr. O'Shea's death was an accident at his own hands. If someone came calling, how would they even get into the auto shop? And that someone would need to know about a lift — that you'd need to break it to cause it to drop a car on Mr. O'Shea. That was a lot of coincidences. The dead kids and I needed a plan of action and not just a vague, swirling mass of unfinished theories.

"I'm going to need to talk to Mr. Page. He's my history teacher. If something happened in Quebec in 1969, it's like his job to know what it was. I can ask him after class. I'll meet you back here tomorrow. In the meantime, Kirby, you read that diary cover to cover!"

☠

When I returned to the sliding door, my dad was waiting for me, bleary eyes, dirty bathrobe, and all. I thought I had honed my skills at sneaking out of the house to, like, ninja level. Dad must have had a particularly bad night and realized I was gone when he woke up. One of the dangers of leaving him asleep on the couch.

I pulled the door open and it sounded like the airlock of a spaceship in the movies. It's like I was about to leap into the harsh environment of outer space. Dad, in his sleeplessness, already had a lot of time to prepare a series of questions. And so, the inquisition began.

"What were you doing out there?" he demanded.

"Just . . . figuring things out," I peeped.

"Figuring things out?" Then he pretended to laugh. It was unsettling and weird. "Do you have any idea what time it is?"

"One o'clock?" I ventured.

"Try two." So close.

"Dad," I ramped up into teenage whine mode, a mode I often turned to, as it sometimes worked quite effectively. "I like it in the cemetery. I go there to think. And sometimes I like to go there at night."

"Uh-huh," Dad said, but the expression on his tired face suggested that he didn't understand as much as his "uh-huh" led me to believe. "You know who else likes the cemetery at night?" I could guess that the answer did not include earthworms and funeral directors and harmless things like that. "Criminals. *Murderers*. Child-snatchers." He nodded his head, as if agreeing with himself.

"Dad," I pleaded.

"October, I know how much you like it in the cemetery. The cemetery is an important place for you. I get that. But I don't like you going there by yourself at night."

But I'm not by myself, though I couldn't tell him that. I wondered what Dad would say if I'd told him the real reason I was out so late.

Dad stared at me for a few seconds, as if he didn't understand who I was or how I had appeared in his kitchen late at night, then softened. "I'm sorry, October. I shouldn't get so agitated. But with Mr. O'Shea dying the way he did . . . in my auto shop . . . I couldn't sleep, and when I realized you weren't here . . . I can't handle all this. . . ."

"I'm sorry," I said. I tried to think of how he must have felt, waking up and finding his only daughter missing at two in the morning. He might have had a point.

"So, I need you not to go into the cemetery at night. Not now. Can you understand that, October?"

I reluctantly nodded. Dad sullenly shuffled back to his bedroom.

"You can meet some very strange people out there in the cemetery, pumpkin."

Yeah, I thought. People like me.

☠

October was so crestfallen over her conversation with her father that she had real difficulties extracting herself from bed on Monday morning. She was envisioning a future barred from the cemetery, where she never saw any of the dead kids ever again, a future where Mr. O'Shea's enigmatic death remained half-solved. It was not a happy future. Not like the one on *The Jetsons* with robot servants and anti-gravity boots and all that stuff. She stared at the ceiling and started to feel more sympathy for her dad all the mornings he couldn't get out of bed. Luckily, that morning happened to be one of those days for her dad too, otherwise he'd be banging on her door, harassing her for still being in bed a half hour before school started. Seize the day, and all that garbage that parents say.

Eventually, October reasoned that her dad had a chemical imbalance, and she simply had a bad night . . . and sometimes spoke with dead children . . . so she had better get out of bed. She had no excuse. Off to school it was.

Things hadn't improved much for Yumi since the movies. Sitting in the cafeteria like a drenched navy officer the rescue boat didn't have room for, her usual humour and energy had been replaced with reserve and paranoia. Her eye sockets were deep purple caverns and it was clear she hadn't slept at all in two nights. October slouched into the bench across from Yumi and Stacey and opened her lunch bag.

"How are you doing?"

"Okay," Yumi said. She sounded dehydrated, her throat

175

packed with sand.

"She's been a bit squirrelly since the visit to Mr. O'Shea's," Stacey adroitly explained. "She, uh, kind of flipped her wig in the darkroom in art class."

"I thought Mr. Alito was a ghost," Yumi insisted.

"And what was splashing photo developer on the ghost of Mr. Alito supposed to accomplish, exactly?" Stacey asked.

Yumi was so embarrassed she turned red, but October was grateful for the colour. She had been so grey and lifeless, October half-expected Yumi to be a zombie herself. At least this was proof blood still pumped through her circulatory system.

"Sorry. Bad joke," Stacey said. "I know things are difficult."

"You saw it, right?" Yumi said eagerly, her eyes latching onto October's in a desperate stare. "You saw them, too, October. At the movies? And at Mr. O'Shea's house? Didn't you? You must have seen something."

October hesitated — she was just about to lie, say no, she didn't really think they had encountered anyone from the spirit world — when Ashlie Salmons jammed herself into the gap in their intense conversation.

"So," Ashlie said, "Kung Fu Zombie Tramp made it to school after seeing a ghost and going completely mental? I thought ghosts and vampires were what you Zombie Tramps were all about. Don't you want to get to second base with the undead or something?"

Ashlie had recently taken to calling Yumi "Kung Fu Zombie Tramp," so as to differentiate her from October, the non-Asian Zombie Tramp. It wasn't overly creative, but potato-faced spoiled brats so rarely are. Ashlie's friends snickered and laughed, even though they had heard the Kung Fu Zombie Tramp joke, like, a zillion times.

"I always knew you goth losers were crazy. What about you," she faced October. "You ready for round two, foxy boxer?"

There was no Mr. O'Shea around anymore to chase the bad lady away. October and Yumi had to sit there and accept the abuse until Ashlie got bored of insulting them, like a young boy tiring of pulling the legs from a spider.

"Piss off," said Stacey from out of nowhere.

Ashlie and her friends were dumbstruck, as were October and Yumi, if not more so. Goose Neck's head whipped back in amazement. Big Laugh and Novelty T-shirt (whose message of the day was "Unicorns FTW") couldn't speak, their mouths slightly parted but silent.

"What?"

"You heard me. Piss right off," he elaborated.

The statuesque and wide-belted Ashlie Salmons shifted her gaze to the fey and awkward tall boy who sat next to Kung Fu Zombie Tramp. She hadn't devised a name for this one yet; she hadn't honestly been aware of his existence until now.

"Who are you, slug? You're telling me to piss off? *You* piss off, you pansy."

The awkward, tall boy whom we all know better as Stacey got to his feet, then began shouting at the top of his lungs. "No, Ashlie! Not here! I am *not* going to make out with you in the middle of the cafeteria! Our love and our groping are special; I'm not going to share them with anyone!"

The Sticksville Central cafeteria must have been starved for some humour, because the crowd at the surrounding tables was immensely appreciative of the comic relief. The concrete walls quaked with laughter. A few joyous whoops rang out. Ashlie narrowed her beautiful green eyes into cold slits.

"You're dead."

October knew a lot of people who were dead, and Stacey Whatever-his-last-name-is was not one of them. Ashlie Salmons made a hasty retreat from the cafeteria, shouts and catcalls trailing behind her like toilet paper that had stuck to her shoe. Ashlie's gang of girls hesitated, unsure whether they should follow or run away. A few agonizing moments later, they hurried after their ringleader.

Yumi turned to Stacey and grinned for the first time all day. "Wow, Stacey," Yumi was flabbergasted. "When did you grow a spine?"

"I think," he scratched his chin as he mused, "that was just before I grew a moustache, and shortly after I had you two kids."

History class moved by in real-time for October. She felt that the Canadian troops in 1916 couldn't possibly have spent more time in the swampy, leech-filled trenches of Belgium and France than she spent sitting, waiting with anxiety in that little square room. But then, maybe she was exaggerating.

When the final school bell rang, October hurriedly jammed all her things into her backpack and rushed to Mr. Page's desk. Mr. Page was dropping things into his bag, too. The only difference being that his bag didn't have things like "NIN" and "The Cure" scrawled in whiteout all over it. He noticed October Schwartz hovering in front of his desk and looked up from his end-of-day packing.

"Oh, October," he said, surprised, as few students ever opted to linger in his class more than a few seconds beyond the final bell.

"Mr. Page, can I ask you a history question?"

"Sure," he said. "I guess that is my area of expertise. What do you want to know?"

"Do you know what the FLQ is?"

"Yes, of course," Mr. Page said. "But why are you interested in the FLQ? We're only covering World War I now. The FLQ doesn't crop up for at least forty-odd years."

"Well, I, uh . . . I saw something on the CBC news about it, but they didn't really explain it too well."

For the first and last time in her life, October Schwartz was thankful for the CBC's television programming.

"Oh. Do you have some time?"

"Does it look like I have friends?" October said with a slight smile. Readers, that is so mean to Stacey and Yumi, not to mention the dead kids. Thank goodness they weren't here to witness October's betrayal.

And so, Mr. Page dimmed the lights, lowered the screen above the chalkboard with a snap, and, by the blazing light of the overhead projector's bulb, told October everything he knew about the *Front de libération du Québec*.

"The FLQ is the acronym for the *Front de libération du Québec*," Mr. Page explained. Sorry. I just spoiled that for you, didn't I?

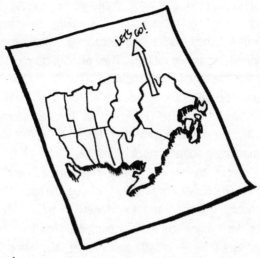

Fig. 1

"The group formed some time in the early 1960s, and their goal was to separate the province of Quebec from Canada. They felt that Quebec and French-speaking Quebecers had been wronged throughout Canada's history, and wanted to create a separate nation. They aimed to bring about this separation through violent revolution, attacking federal government and English-speaking institutions within the province.

Fig. 2

179

"The FLQ planted bombs in mailboxes in Westmount — which was a wealthy, mostly English-speaking neighbourhood in Montreal — they wrote and broadcast manifestoes, they started committing armed robbery. They planted bombs at McGill University and the stock exchange, too."

October mentally scratched McGill off her ideal list of Canadian universities. The University of Toronto seemed less explody. October remembered that Henri LaFleur's diary did mention something about a stock exchange.

"It's difficult to say how many members were in the organization. The police continually broke up the group, and the FLQ continually reformed and found new members. But there could have been anywhere from a couple dozen to a hundred members at any time — mostly political radicals, union leaders, and French-speaking students."

French-speaking students? If Mr. O'Shea really once was Henri LaFleur, he would have been a student in the 1960s.

"Some people felt the FLQ were ruthless terrorists. Many thought they were freedom fighters, defending Quebecois rights when no one else would.

Fig. 3

"Then in October 1970, the FLQ kidnapped two politicians: the British trade commissioner and the Quebec labour minister. In exchange for their release, the FLQ wanted a large ransom, safe passage from Canada, and publicity for the cause. They . . . well, they say there's no such thing as bad publicity, but that was probably the exception to the rule.

Fig. 4

"The province — the *country* — was in a panic, right? What was there to do?"

October wondered why Mr. Page directed these questions at her. What did she look like? The prime minister?

"The prime minister at the time, Pierre Trudeau — wore roses on his lapel, his wife hung out with rock stars like the Rolling Stones — instituted something called the War Measures Act, which meant that all Canadians' rights were suspended. The government could arrest whoever they felt like arresting with no evidence. Even if they just didn't like the look of you or had a bad feeling about you.

"The army was sent to Montreal to calm the chaos and arrest suspects. It's usually regarded as one of the darker moments in

Canadian history. It actually increased resentment in Quebec toward the federal government. At least, that's what a whole bunch of people much smarter than me say."

"But what happened to the politicians who were kidnapped?" asked October.

Fig. 5

"Well, the day after the army rolled into town, the body of the labour minister was found in the trunk of a car. Over a month later, a deal was made with the kidnappers for the British commissioner's release. That . . . particular chapter in Canadian history is named the October Crisis. Heh . . . it's kind of a funny coincidence."

Yeah, laugh it up, October thought.

"So," October said aloud, trying to summarize a long, overly informative lecture — even with the visual aids, "the FLQ was a terrorist separatist group in Quebec who once killed a labour minister?"

"Well, I would probably call them terrorists. But a lot of people in Quebec might take issue with that. And they killed more people than that one labour minister. The October Crisis was the most sensational of the events connected to the FLQ, but their bombs killed at least six people and injured dozens of others."

Henri LaFleur could have planted any of those bombs, October reasoned. He could have kidnapped those politicians, could have killed one to seven people. And the diary mentioned the stock exchange. That would theoretically be a very good reason to change your name and life, and a good reason for someone to murder you, too. How could the kindly old man with an Irish name who taught October French and curling and lent her musty old horror novels be mixed up in kidnappings and bombings and international intrigue? This history lesson was illuminating an entirely new realm of possibilities about Mr. O'Shea, and October didn't think she was going to like exploring them all that much.

"October, I have to leave now," Mr. Page said. "If you want to find more information about the FLQ or the October Crisis, you might want to visit the library or search on the internet. I'm not an encyclopedia." With that Mr. Page hoisted his unadorned bag over his head and shoved his head into a yellow bicycle helmet. "I'll see you in class tomorrow."

Her old teacher may have planted bombs for the FLQ, her best living friend was petrified with fright, her dad was preventing her from seeing her dead friends, and she still had no idea who really killed Mr. O'Shea. At times like these, October wished she had normal problems, like that fourteen-year-old girl in her class who got pregnant and had to drop out of school.

☠

Following her tutorial with Mr. Page, October had supplemented her FLQ knowledge (after another installment of the infinite Santuzzi detention) with a general internet search at the school library, so she was a veritable FLQ expert, by her own estimation. But — and here's the problem — her dad had expressly forbidden her from going to the cemetery at night. Yes, the very cemetery where she could share her new-found knowledge and strategize with the dead kids. If she couldn't set foot in the Sticksville Cemetery again, solving Mr. O'Shea's mysterious death would be nigh impossible, no matter how much information about the FLQ she had.

Did Nancy Drew ever have to cope with a disapproving and clinically depressed father? Maybe. October had never bothered to read any of those books, so she honestly didn't know. But whatever. Nancy Drew had her own car — a jalopy or something — so her father's potential disapproval was beside the point. October was still three years from driving lessons.

That night, full to bursting with FLQ factoids, October fidgeted in the kitchen while Mr. Schwartz marked biology tests. She was almost certain that given the right conditions — and she wasn't ruling out knocking her dad out with chloroform — she could sneak into the cemetery again, but she also knew that tonight, the risk was too great. If she was caught sneaking out the very night after she'd been reprimanded, her dad would be hurt and insulted, and October couldn't fathom the punishment that would result. She needed an alternate plan.

"Restless, pumpkin?" her dad asked, not quite peering up from the biology papers. "Why don't you make some tea?"

"Uh, that's okay," October said. "Actually, do you mind if I just grab my driver's licence? I think left it outside in the mail. I'll just be a second."

"Don't be long. You know I don't like you lingering outside at night."

If you were paying attention, you'd notice October's question was a work of total genius. It accomplished two things. One, it established that Mr. Schwartz wasn't entirely paying attention. October just turned thirteen; she doesn't have a driver's licence. And even if she could drive, why would her licence be in the mail? Two, it allowed her to go outside for a few minutes. October grabbed her trusty notebook and a marker and hopped outside.

Minutes later, a page torn from the *Two Knives, One Thousand Demons* was speared on the cemetery gates. Written on that paper, in black block letters, was a very important message: "CAN'T VISIT. COME TO BACK DOOR @ 12."

☠

The dead kids did, indeed, come to the back door just minutes after midnight. October's dad was snug in his bed, dreaming of crystalline solids or molar mass or whatever dreams biology tests inspire, by the time Cyril gently rapped at the sliding glass door. Keeping watch at the kitchen counter, October hurried to the back door and unlatched it before her dad could hear.

"Don't come in," she whispered.

The dead kids, all about to step inside, felt snubbed.

"My dad doesn't want me going into the cemetery late at night anymore, so we're going to have to work around it."

"So, what's an FLQ?" Kirby asked.

She patiently recounted everything Mr. Page had told her earlier — everything she could remember:

"The FLQ were a group of political dissidents active in the 1960s and 1970s. They kidnapped some government guys and then killed one of them, and the prime minister instituted martial law. The army was in the streets and all legal rights were suspended as they tried to find these FLQ people. So I guess they were pretty dangerous."

Cyril was already lost, being fuzzy on the concept of a prime minister, as there wasn't a prime minister in the era during which he was alive. "So the FLQ killed someone?"

"A bunch of someones, probably," October said. "They planted bombs all over Montreal."

"Scoundrels," said Cyril, slamming his fist into his open palm.

"Shhh," October insisted.

"And it looks like your French teacher was one of these . . . scoundrels . . . no?" said Kirby. "Don't worry, I'm sure he had a very good reason for planting bombs."

"I don't know," said October. "But it's our only realistic lead . . . and it would be a good reason to change your name . . . and a good reason why someone might want to kill you, if they ever found out."

"So, ye think one of yer other teachers found out yer French teacher was part o' this group once, then killed 'im?" Morna asked.

"Well, someone at the school, I guess. How else would they have been able to unlock the auto shop?" October wouldn't have put murder past some of the teachers at Sticksville Central. She was sure Mr. Santuzzi must have killed some people in his day: enemy soldiers, hoboes, nosy shoeshine boys. And he was distinctly un-saddened by Mr. O'Shea's death, spreading rumours about what happened. And what about the school janitor, who also had keys to the auto shop?

"Sounds a hair far-fetched," said Tabetha.

"Far-fetched?! Thanks for grounding me in reality, ghost girl," spat October. "What if someone at the school had a relative harmed by the FLQ?"

"So, what do we do now?" Kirby whispered. "Are you sure we can't come in?"

October's plan sprung out fully-formed, like the goddess Athena from Zeus's head. Check out your Greek myths, kids. Those stories are messed up to the extreme.

October ignored Kirby's request to enter. "The five of you meet me at the usual spot tomorrow at nine."

"What about yer father?" Morna asked.

"Don't worry about it. I'll figure something out," October answered. "We're going to break into the school. Everyone at the school is a suspect. Teachers, office staff, even the students. We need to get the teacher address book, and you need to interrogate the janitor. He has the other set of keys to the auto shop where Mr. O'Shea died. We've only got a few days left, so we're kicking into maximum overdrive. I hope you aren't above a little breaking and entering."

A few of the dead kids expressed their pleasure at the prospect.

"Ain't *breakin'* and enterin' if you just walk through the walls," corrected Tabetha.

☠

October had a plan figured out, but "panic" was the word of the day when she woke up. It ran through her mind, doing wind-sprints from one end of her skull to the other. And why?

Panic #1: It was Tuesday morning, October twenty-eighth. Friday night — Hallowe'en — was the last night she'd have the dead kids' help in uncovering the mystery of Mr. O'Shea's death until November 27 (I looked it up). No matter the progress they'd made, that didn't give them much time.

Panic #2: Mr. O'Shea's killer was most likely another teacher at Sticksville Central, which meant a full-blown murderer was in her midst every weekday. The only teachers that she knew for certain were at the high school that night were her dad (who was obviously not a murderer), the principal, and Mr. Santuzzi. She might have some idea if any other teachers were around the school that night, but stupid Ashlie Salmons couldn't be a halfway-decent person and tell the truth for once in her life.

Panic #3: As was mentioned, Hallowe'en, perhaps the best holiday ever devised — man, those pagans could party (if you doubt it, watch *The Wicker Man*) — was only four days away, and guess who hadn't made her costume yet?

The only bright spot in her panic-stricken life was that Mr. Page had provided her with much-needed historical information that could crack the Mr. O'Shea case wide open.

So that Tuesday morning, October shuffled out of her bedroom and down the hall to knock on her dad's door. It opened before she could knock and her dad popped out, already showered and dressed in a checked shirt and boldly-striped tie. She wasn't comfortable with her father's occasional refusals to leave his bed or shave or bathe, but the pre-coffee perkiness was a strange surprise. Maybe her dad was on drugs?

"Pumpkin! I'm glad you're up. Yes . . . I wanted to talk to you this morning."

"Really," she said.

"As you know, I've been concerned about you spending so much time in the cemetery. I know you like to work on your book out there — the spooky atmosphere and all that — but I think spending too much time out there might be unhealthy."

Her book? October had barely worked on her book in weeks — not since Mr. O'Shea died, save for one horrible passage about Uncle Otto, if you'll recall. One thousand demons lay un-slain, and two knives, severely underused. *That's* what her dad thought she was doing in the cemetery, she realized, although she didn't quite understand how he imagined she could write in the pitch black of night.

"I also realize that you're probably still having a hard time meeting people here in Sticksville. It can be lonely in high school. I know. I've been there. So tonight . . . we're having Father-Daughter Night!"

"Father-Daughter Night?" October said, trying not to sound utterly disappointed. This was his great solution to being new in town?

"Yes. You and I will spend tonight together. We can order a pizza. I don't know — play some Scrabble or something."

"No!" shouted October. When she saw how offended her dad looked, she quickly backpedalled. "I mean, not that it doesn't sound like a lot of fun. Everybody likes pizza, right? . . . But I can't tonight. I already made plans."

"With Yumi?"

"Yes. Yumi." She silently thanked her dad. Life was so much easier when he assisted in her lies.

"That's not a problem," he said, as chipper as before. "I'll talk to her today at school. She's invited, too!"

With everything worked out and squared away, Mr. Schwartz patted his daughter on the shoulder and strolled into the kitchen for breakfast. October, meanwhile, shuffled back to her bedroom and tried to determine why her dad, who seemed to like her, was so intent on ruining her life.

☠

Father-Daughter Night was mentioned a few more times before October left for school; it seemed there was no escaping it. Indeed, tonight promised to be the Schwartz event of the decade, but it also meant she'd be unable to meet up with the dead kids at nine, as planned. Maybe she could sneak them a message, and have them search the school on their own. Feeling guilty about her lack of work on *Two Knives, One Thousand Demons* (despite its inherent danger), she took it with her and reread what she'd already accomplished on her stroll to school. It wasn't much.

When October arrived at her locker, Stacey Whatshisname was waiting for her. Not that he had anything specific to say. He just had nothing better to do.

"Yeah, usually I wait by Yumi's locker," he explained. "But your dad wanted to talk with her."

October felt a brick in her throat. Yumi was going to be very confused by the conversation she was having with Mr. Schwartz, especially since she didn't know about the plans for tonight she had supposedly made with October.

"Is Yumi doing all right?" she asked. "With the ghosts and everything?"

"Yeah," said Stacey. "A lot better. Apparently she's sleeping with only the bedside light on now."

While they talked, October couldn't help but notice a few bristles of light hair on Stacey's upper lip. She stifled a laugh. When will high school boys ever learn that they'll never look good with a moustache? The answer: pretty soon, if they have Yumi Takeshi for a friend.

Yumi came barrelling down the hallway. Her legwarmers were patterned with pentagrams, and she nearly tripped over them on her way to October's locker.

"Stacey! Where did you go? Oh, hi, October," she said. "Your dad is acting really psycho, you should know. He invited me to something called Father-Daughter Night, then got really flustered when I told him I had to go to my grandma's birthday party tonight. He knows I'm not his daughter, right?"

October blushed, but Yumi failed to notice. The recent addition to Stacey's face was much more noticeable.

"How old is Granny Takeshi turning?" Stacey asked, unaware of Yumi's growing revulsion.

"What's on your face?"

Stacey hesitated. "I'm . . . growing a . . . moustache."

"It's supremely icky," Yumi decided. "You should shave it. Like immediately."

The class bell rang and Yumi and Stacey left for their first period class, whatever that was. October should really know her friends' schedules by now, shouldn't she? Stacey's hand obscured his mouth from fellow students as he walked away. October headed to class as well, but French was the least of her worries. October was already steeling herself for second period, when she'd force herself into a little discussion with Mr. Santuzzi, prime suspect numero uno.

☠

October decided to wait until the very end of math to test out her hunch. Given a worst-case scenario — Mr. Santuzzi realizes she's onto his crime, breaks his chalk pointer into a sharpened stake and chases her around the math room — she could flee and still know the evening's homework. Practical thinking, no doubt. That said, waiting also had the distinct disadvantage of no witnesses being left in the classroom. It may not have been the wisest idea to wait, however, as she spent the entire period not envisioning objects in three-dimensional space, as she was expected to, but envisioning Mr. Santuzzi cackling like a witch with a poor hairpiece, kicking in a switch with his patent-leather dress shoes, and dropping two tons of German-engineered steel onto poor Mr. O'Shea, then making a hasty retreat with plenty of time to devise a nefarious pop quiz on cross-multiplication.

Mercifully, the bell rang and the other math fanatics left the classroom like they were being chased by angry bees. Only October lingered and limped her way over to Santuzzi's desk. He was seated, scanning a math textbook for dirty pictures or rude messages that mischievous students may have added.

"Ms. Schwartz?" he said without moving his gaze from the page he was carefully eyeballing.

"Oh . . . uh . . . Mr. Santuzzi," she said nervously. "I just wanted to ask if I could have an extension on tonight's assignment. See, I have a big history essay due —"

"No extensions," said Santuzzi with finality. He still hadn't made eye contact with October. "What's the issue? You need more time to come up with creative insults for me?"

He still hadn't gotten over the whole dirtbag thing. *Sensitive.* She knew Santuzzi would never grant an extension, even if she'd asked while trying to prevent her own entrails from spilling out of a 10-inch gash in her stomach. The question was what professional confidence artists call a "ruse." Observe, my friends.

"Okay," said October. "It's just this paper on the FLQ — 'Terrorists or Freedom Fighters?' We have to decide —"

Mr. Santuzzi's head snapped toward October and finally made eye contact. Searing, searing eye contact.

"Freedom fighters?" said Santuzzi derisively. "Is that what that bike-riding hippie Page is teaching you kids? I can write your essay for you right now, Ms. Schwartz: Freedom fighters don't put bombs in mailboxes like snivelling little cowards. Period."

With the period, he banged his meaty fist on the table. "Brevity is the key to effective communication, Ms. Schwartz. Don't waste too many words on those degenerates."

"Well," said October, retreating from the room cautiously. "That will certainly help in my essay. Thanks, Mr. Santuzzi."

Thanks, Mr. Santuzzi? October almost puked all over herself as she exited the room. She could hear her math teacher muttering about "bleeding-heart liberals" as she continued down the hallway to her locker. Case closed, October thought. If Santuzzi had known Mr. O'Shea was once in the FLQ, she had no doubt he'd have killed him. October personally feared for her own life, and all she'd done was mention the FLQ by name. She doubted that he'd use so impersonal a method as dropping a car on Mr. O'Shea. A good, old-fashioned neck-wringing seemed more like Santuzzi's style.

Nevertheless, mere hatred alone wasn't proof enough in any legal sense. If only she could establish some kind of connection between Mr. Santuzzi and the FLQ — maybe he had lived in Montreal at the time? He did look a bit young to know about the FLQ first-hand. Furthermore, she'd jumped to conclusions about the FLQ. She had no definitive evidence that Mr. O'Shea was once a French Canadian political radical — as far as she knew, he could have stolen LaFleur's diary.

Maybe the case wasn't quite as closed as we all thought a paragraph ago. False alarm, intrepid readers. At least the dead kids' trip to the high school wouldn't be a total waste.

☠

Arriving in the cafeteria with her lunch in a little plastic shopping bag, October encountered a scene of unadulterated horror: organized fun. At the top of the room, organized fun was being overseen by the benevolent dictators of the student council. A giant wooden bucket sat at the front of the cafeteria, spangled with orange and black streamers and filled to the brim with murky water and apples.

Yumi was also frozen in horror, just a couple paces before October. October sidled up beside her. The student council president was holding a microphone and valiantly trying to attract participants. A few brain-dead student council members had already volunteered and were waiting patiently in a short line of contestants.

"Are they actually bobbing for apples?"

"I used to really like Hallowe'en," said Yumi.

One of the misguided souls in the contestant line was,

October recognized, Novelty T-shirt from Ashlie Salmons's friends. Across her chest, it read "Makeout Queen." She motioned to the mannequin with the microphone and pointed to October. Before she could move, October's name was being bellowed over the cafeteria P.A.

"October Schwartz! October Schwartz, get in line!"

Traitorous Yumi shoved her forward. Some friend.

"There's no escape, October Schwartz!" she laughed.

So there she was, standing in line, behind some student council member with an improbable name that began with "Z," while a disinterested cafeteria audience booed and jeered. October went into a slight trance, blocking out the crowd and other students, and imagined she was Olivia de Kellerman, the brassy protagonist of *Two Knives, One Thousand Demons*.

She watched the mesmerized victims of Charybdis, the water-demon, as they queued in the eerie cavern before her. In turn, they gazed into Charybdis's watery lair, and were dragged face-first into the deep. Her turn came, she dunked her head into the water, seeking Charybdis's throat with her incisors. She clamped her powerful jaws down and wrenched her head back to the surface, tearing out the demon's throat.

As October's head resurfaced, a mealy McIntosh apple clenched in her teeth, the cafeteria's sights and sounds rushed back, flooding her senses.

"Yeah, Schwartz! Wooooo!" came a piercing cry from the back of the room. Yumi at work.

October flicked at the wet black cloth of hair covering her eyes. Directly in front of her was the very dry and very fashionable Ashlie Salmons, a green apple in her hand.

"Wow. Who knew that Zombie Tramp would be so skilled at eating without her hands?"

October released her jaw's hold on the apple and it hit the water like a stone.

"Oh, wait," said Ashlie, answering her own question. "All dogs eat that way." She tossed the green apple at October's skull and hit her mark.

"Let's calm down now," advised the student council member with the microphone, as effective as an eraser on ink.

Yumi rushed to the front of the cafeteria, pulling Stacey away from his tuna sandwich. October needed moral support.

"Make up your mind, Ashlie. Am I a dog or a tramp?" said a very wet and very irritated October.

"I think in that Disney movie, they were the same thing, fatty. You must know that movie, given that you're a kid."

Yumi shook her tiny fist to salute Ashlie's cleverness. Stacey merely struggled to down the tuna and bread he'd stuffed in his mouth.

"Okay, just be calm," the council member at the mic reiterated. Two other council members had already left to find teachers.

"Do your ugly little friends know?" Ashlie pulled the microphone out of the student council guy's hand to amplify her insult. "That you only just turned thirteen? That you're a little baby?"

"You're *thirteen*?" Yumi exclaimed.

Stacey choked a bit more on his lunch.

The cat was out of the proverbial bag. Now the entire cafeteria was aware that October was only thirteen — even though probably only thirty of them knew who she was in the first place.

195

She could write off meeting any boys (except for creeps) forever, as well as making any new friends. Even the two living ones she'd made might find better things to do, probably with other similarly aged fourteen-year-olds.

"My mom thinks your dad is crazy to put a thirteen-year-old in high school," Ashlie continued, dropping the mic and kicking some errant apples on the ground. "But, of course, your dad *is* crazy. It's pretty much a fact." She slid behind October and whispered in her ear. It felt like someone had poured cold cream of wheat into her aural canal. "Everyone knows your dad should be in a rubber room. I heard all about his breakdown back in your old town."

October's old home was hours away and it was unlikely any of the students in Mr. Schwartz's fated chemistry class had transferred to Sticksville. How could Ashlie know? Casting aspersions on October's lust for the undead and revealing her age to the entire cafeteria was one thing, but making fun of her dad's illness was unforgivable in October's mind. In a snap decision, she gave Ashlie a sharp elbow to her conveniently placed belly. Stacey nearly spat his chewed-up tuna across the cafeteria.

"Ow, you *psycho*! You stupid fat lard!" shouted Ashlie. She gripped October's head and pulled at it like she was trying to twist off a bottle top. Her white press-on nails left scratches across October's face, and the pair staggered across the cafeteria like a drunken couple.

Mrs. Tischmann appeared at the cafeteria double doors with another student council member and began shouting. Stacey moved to break up the combatants but slipped on a wet apple and fell on October and Ashlie instead. All three crashed to the ground and rolled right into Mrs. Tischmann and tore her leg off, just below her knee. The leg sheared right off like it was put through an invisible buzz saw and it dropped to the ground like a ham hock. If I were there, I would have barfed — for real. Tischmann grasped at the hapless council member and both fell to the floor. Several students witnessed the legless Mrs. Tischmann and began shrieking and yelling — generally flipping out, like most people when witnessing an accidental amputation.

Principal Hamilton leapt onto the scene. He pried Ashlie's claw-like hands from October's face.

"To the office, *now*!" The way he shouted it, everyone in the cafeteria was prepared to march down to the office, although he was speaking only to Ashlie. "Ms. Takeshi, would you please take Ms. Schwartz to the nurse? And tell her to come to my office at the end of the day. And someone help Mrs. Tischmann up and return her leg!" He took hold of Ashlie Salmons's left arm and pulled her behind him like a rebellious kite on the way to the office.

By this point, everyone in the cafeteria was either looking at October or at the leg, which had rolled in front of the pop machine. Ashlie's clique of killer vixens were particularly shocked and dismayed by the recent lunchtime developments. The little girl with the big laugh was certainly not laughing. October got to her feet, wiped her runny nose with the back of her pale hand, and sat down at a table. She opened her lunch bag and began to eat her turkey sandwich.

Over by the soda machine, Stacey, a boy with a stronger stomach than I, gingerly approached Mr. Tischmann's leg. Upon closer inspection, he discovered it was wooden — thankfully — and brought it to the music teacher, who had been propped up on a cafeteria bench by some students. Leg returned, he walked over to the table where October ate. Mrs. Tischmann screwed her leg back on like she was putting in a light bulb.

"Holy cats, Schwartz! You wanna go to the nurse?" Yumi asked October, almost frightened to talk to her. "You're bleeding a little."

The cuts Ashlie's razor-sharp talons had made began to seep red.

"I'm fine," October insisted. "Let's just eat."

Music class was awkward, but strangely peaceful. Mrs. Tischmann — who knew she had a wooden leg? — was shaken by lunchtime's fracas, which led to some subdued instruction. Ashlie Salmons was absent, which made class infinitely more enjoyable. The few students who had seen the fight either glared at October or nodded and smiled. Those who didn't know were kind of afraid to ask October about the damage to her face.

The relative peace of music class betrayed the dread October felt about the end of her day. Not only did October have Father-Daughter Night to "look forward to," but she also had that meeting in the principal's office. There was no way Ashlie hadn't told Mr. Hamilton about her elbow smash attack.

Back up just a second, friends: since when does Mrs. Tischmann only have one leg? Why does nobody care about this but me? Luckily, Mr. Page informed October of the story behind the missing limb before history class:

"I heard about the fight at lunch," Mr. Page said to October as she walked in the door.

"Yeah . . . uh . . . it wasn't my fault."

"I hear you knocked off Mrs. Tischmann's wooden leg. She's pretty embarrassed about it."

"Why? And since when does she have a wooden leg?"

"I can't believe I didn't bring it up yesterday. Mrs. Tischmann was a runner at the Montreal Stock Exchange when she was just a teenager. An FLQ bomb went off and she lost her leg."

Um, and this is not vitally pertinent information how, Mr. Page? In a split second, prime suspect number one switched to the kindly, yet flaky music teacher. An eye for an eye, a life for a leg.

"Mrs. Tischmann doesn't like to talk about it, which I'm sure you understand. But it's so strange it would come up at school just after we talked about the FLQ. What are the odds?"

October wasn't a betting woman, largely because it was illegal for someone her age to gamble in her province, but if someone asked her who killed Mr. O'Shea, she'd now put all her money on Eileen Tischmann. She'd lost her leg to those French Canadians. But October remembered that Mr. O'Shea carted Mrs.

Tischmann's son around to concerts, which complicated things. Maybe she was, like, keeping her enemies closer or whatever?

At the end of the day, October put the books she needed into her backpack and closed her combination lock. Stacey and Yumi came by her locker and offered to buy her a slushie, but October declined, explaining she had to talk to Principal Hamilton. Moments later, she found Hamilton standing behind the front desk of the school office, searching through some of the grey industrial filing cabinets.

"Ms. Schwartz," he said. "Just the young woman I wanted to see. Come with me."

October nodded and followed Principal Hamilton to his private office behind the main reception. He settled himself in his black leather chair and smoothed his brown blazer. Then he motioned for October to sit in the chair across the table.

"Ms. Schwartz, I have to be honest. I'm more than a little concerned about you."

"The fight was . . . I mean, I guess I started it, technically . . ." she fiddled manically with her necklace.

"The fight is just one instance of a pattern, the way I see it," said Principal Hamilton. "Teachers have been telling me things for weeks."

"Teachers are telling you things about me? What are they saying?" October felt more violated than anything else. Who were these teachers to talk about her? They should mind their own business.

Principal Hamilton raised his hand. It was not, sadly, a request for a high five. He was trying to slow October down. "They noticed you took what happened to Mr. O'Shea very poorly."

Poorly. *Poorly.* As if she was being graded on her response to death.

"Several teachers said you were quite disturbed by Mr. O'Shea's passing . . ."

"Death."

". . . and that you demanded to know where the funeral was. Then there was today's fight with Ashlie Salmons. She told me you started the aggression by elbowing her in the stomach. Now,

199

I don't know whether to believe that or not, but the fact remains that you were fighting in the school cafeteria."

October felt like a criminal being read a list of charges — although she saw herself more as a political prisoner. She hadn't done anything wrong from where she was standing.

"Then there was the math test Mr. Santuzzi told me about. We're concerned, October."

We? Did Mr. Hamilton become royalty when she wasn't looking? October wanted to escape the office as soon as possible.

"I . . . uh . . . appreciate your concern, Mr. Hamilton, but I have to get going —"

"Slow down, Ms. Schwartz," Hamilton prevented her from rising from her chair. "I've scheduled you an appointment with our school physician, Dr. Lagostina, on Friday afternoon. Not only is he our physician, he's also a practising therapist. Death is a difficult thing."

It didn't seem too difficult for the five teenagers who loitered in the cemetery behind her backyard daily. She wanted to scream. She accepted Mr. O'Shea's death; she just didn't accept that it was an accident.

She didn't scream, and instead silently took the appointment card Principal Hamilton had filled out and actually thanked him for it. Hamilton smiled like he had just successfully programmed the clock on his microwave and helped October find her way back to the front office.

School therapist, October thought to herself. Ashlie Salmons was right — her dad was crazy, and it ran in the family. Not that October felt she had mental health issues, but then again, the people that have them never think they do. And though she knew these kinds of things were real illnesses you had little control over, she also knew what it would look like to Ashlie and the hundreds she'd probably tell if they ever found out she was leaving classes to see a therapist. Crazy like her dad, is what they'd think.

The thought made her far colder than the remorseless autumn wind that whipped at October's back as she walked home alone.

☠

Vendetta.

With double points on the "V" and a double-word score, it was thirty points. On top of that point explosion, I got a bonus fifty points for using all my letters. Eighty points! My dad was feeling that where it hurt.

Even though I was totally occupied with solving a murder mystery and all, Father-Daughter Night was not as embarrassing as I'd initially feared. It was nice being forced to relax. If it weren't for the matter of Mr. O'Shea's killer being on the prowl or my dire need to tell my dead friends about Mrs. Tischmann's amputee lifestyle, I might have even enjoyed it. Pizza is rarely an indication of a bad night, and my Scrabble matches with my dad had always been fierce battles. He didn't seem to notice that all the board games other than Scrabble had mysteriously vanished, which was a miracle.

Dad had turned up the oldies station so he could sing along with all the songs that he knew from the '60s, long before I was even born. Unfortunately, he knew most of them.

He kept singing about Carrie Anne and if he could play her game. I think it was a song about a girl who worked at a carnival or something.

Aside from that tragic musical interlude and others like it, things were okay. Like I said, Scrabble matches between Dad and me were often barnburners, and the results were usually controversial. After all, Dad may have been older and a teacher, but I was the writer in the family. At least, I *had* been the writer before I started hanging out with dead people. Not to be conceited, but I had at my command a rather impressive vocabulary, although my dad knew all the sneaky, made-up scientific terms, which all too frequently made use of high-scoring tiles like "Q" and "X." I was never really sure that he wasn't fabricating the words entirely. How far could I trust my dad? Could I *xenon* trust him?

We were both sprawled out on the living room floor with the Scrabble board in the centre of the carpet. I was lying on my stomach, aimlessly brushing designs into the carpet's grain. I sipped from my glass of Mr. Pibb and again rearranged the seven tiles on my frame. My mind wasn't quite in the game, though, to the total detriment of my score. Oh, how I missed the halcyon days of "vendetta." I mean, my mind would flit back to unusual vocabulary now and then, but I was preoccupied with other mysteries.

I now had two prime suspects: the clearly homicidal Mr. Santuzzi and the probably angry, vengeful, and legless Mrs. Tischmann. Who was the more likely culprit? Santuzzi was more likely to kill a man than he was to tip at a restaurant, and he did express great distaste for these FLQ people. But the FLQ had also cost Mrs. Tischmann her leg. You could never underestimate what the loss of a limb might do to a seemingly normal, though flighty, person like Mrs. Tischmann.

More than anything, I needed to tell Cyril, Tabetha, Derek, and Morna — even Kirby — about Mrs. Tischmann's missing leg and just how it had happened. But there was no conceivable way I could extract myself from Father-Daughter Night without arousing Dad's suspicion.

My dad was busy singing away to Tommy James and the Shondells. Could I ever tell him about my bizarre extracurricular activities? I was pretty sure he wouldn't be thrilled his daughter was conducting clandestine murder investigations. It didn't seem like the kind of thing dads like to hear.

"It's only a few days until Hallowe'en," Dad interrupted my thoughts. "Have you thought of a costume yet?"

"Mostly. I just need to make it." The lack of costume was

a sore spot. I know I've said it before, but Hallowe'en equals the best holiday of the year. Me not having a costume was like someone who likes parties sleeping through New Year's.

"It's only a few days away, you know."

"Yeah, I know, Dad. Maybe you should focus on making a word over there."

"Sorry." His eyes ran left to right across the tiles, then back. "Can I ask you a question?"

I twirled the "T" tile in between my fingers. When Dad has to ask permission to ask a question, I start to get nervous.

"I know how much time you've been spending in the cemetery, and I know that your time there is important — for writing and reading — but I'm still a little bit worried."

"There's nothing to worry about, Dad," I insisted.

"And I can't help but think you were less than honest about having plans tonight with your friend, Yumi. I never liked to spend evenings with my parents either, so I don't blame you too much for that."

I could predict where this story was going, and I really wasn't prepared to answer the question that he was bound to ask.

"When you started wearing black makeup and dyed your hair last year," Dad said, "I understood. I mean, I'm not so old that I don't remember Siouxsie and the Banshees and Robert Smith, the whole goth thing. But you're in that cemetery more of your waking hours than anywhere else, save for the school. It seems a little . . . *morbid*? I guess I'm just wondering why you spend so much time there."

"No reason, Dad," I said. "I just like it there." I couldn't tell him the truth. He had enough problems of his own without worrying that his daughter was delusional, speaking to ghost children on a nightly basis.

"It's not . . ." Dad hesitated. "You're not upset about your mom, are you? Maybe I shouldn't have said anything."

"It's not about Mom. I mean, I miss her, yeah, but I barely remember her. The cemetery is quiet and calm . . ." I explained, fully aware that after dark the cemetery was also the rec room of some late, lamented teenagers. But Dad didn't have to know that. "You don't have to worry about me, Dad. I'm okay." I gave him a sheepish smile to help him relax.

Dad returned it with a smile of his own. "I know you are. But Principal Hamilton told me you got into a fight at school."

That dastardly sneak. My dad had obviously known about the fight all night and just let me drink Mr. Pibb and eat pizza and trounce him in word-related board games, waiting for the right moment to reveal this information.

"Um . . . it wasn't really a fight," I explained. "More like a misunderstanding."

"Oh, I see," Dad said, fluffing the corduroy pillow he was resting on. "So Ashlie Salmons's stomach misunderstood your fist?"

"My elbow actually."

"Principal Hamilton tells me he recommended you see the school psychiatrist?"

"Yeah. I'm supposed to see him on Friday." I could tell how upset he was, how upsetting it was, the possibility that his daughter was as messed up as he was.

"Okay. Well, good luck. I'm sure it will be fine. I — what is that?"

I laid my final tile down on the board with extreme decisiveness — a devastating "equine" (of, or relating to horses) off of Dad's "barium." Triple-letter score on the "Q."

"We're playing best two games out of three, right?"

We needed more titles, so I fished around in that unbelievably, classy velvet bag they give you to scramble the tiles.

"No more tiles left."

"What did you do with them? There were about a dozen after I took my last batch."

As a demonstration, I turned the bag inside out.

"I swear there are more," Dad said. "Look around. Maybe they fell out onto the floor."

I lifted the pizza box and the Scrabble box off the floor, and pushed a few magazines around the coffee table in the hopes of finding some stray letter tiles. When I finally got to the end table at the far side of the couch, I discovered where the missing pieces had gone.

"Found them!"

"What are they doing way over there?"

What they were doing way over there became clear when I looked down at the end table. Someone had clearly left a message for me:

KUM UPSTAIRZ

Either one of the illiterate kids wrote that message, or they were running short on tiles. But I got the gist. "Dad, I have to run to the bathroom," I said, stuffing the tiles back into their velvet container. "Don't cheat."

"There's a bathroom downstairs, too," Dad reminded me, but I had already reached the top of the staircase.

☠

When I entered my bedroom, I locked the door so my dad wouldn't have any first-hand accounts of ghosts himself. The five dead kids sat huddled in the corner, and I was amazed by how well they fit the general atmosphere of the room, a room I hadn't cleaned in weeks. It was a bit embarrassing. Piles of clothes and Jenga-like stacks of CDs and books covered almost every inch of floor space.

"So, this is your room," said Tabetha.

"It's not very nice."

"And certainly not too clean."

"There's a lot of black in here. Have you thought about adding some colour?"

"Okay, thanks, dead interior decorating squad," I said. "Now can we get to it? I can only pretend I'm in the bathroom for so long before my dad thinks I have dysentery or something."

"Why weren't you at the cemetery at nine?" asked Derek. "We were waiting. We've only got a few days left and then we're gone."

"I know — my dad won't let me escape. There's a father-daughter thing happening. I'm going to have to be more careful about sneaking out in general."

"Then what about tonight?" Tabetha asked.

"I need you to do some mystery solving on your own. Please."

Grim faces all around. It was like I was teaching remedial English and just asked who'd like to start the oral presentations. They'd never been the most enthusiastic detectives, but I was hoping for more than this. "Come on, it'll be fun. Ghosts' night out! Leave that fleshy ball and chain at home!"

"What do you need us to do again?" Cyril was unfazed by this sales pitch.

"Go to the high school. Look at the crime scene and if the janitor's there, try to find out what he knows."

"So, we get to interrogate somebody?" asked Tabetha. Things were looking up.

"Yes," I said. Then I remembered something about Cyril that could help me. "The crime scene is in the auto shop. *Cars*, Cyril. Automobiles. Motorcars."

"All right, we'll do it," said Kirby. "Now how do we get there?"

"I can take us," said Derek excitedly. "I went to Sticksville Central."

Given how easily Derek navigated the way to the police station and the storage area, I was a little less than confident about his ability to find his old high school. But I didn't have time to draw them a map.

"Great! Thank you, thank you, thank you. Also, I need you to find Mrs. Tischmann's address. Eileen Tischmann. There should be teacher addresses in the main office."

"Eileen Tischmann?" asked Morna.

"She's my music teacher. Her leg was blown off by an FLQ bomb in the sixties. And get Mr. Santuzzi's address, too. I don't remember his first name . . . Lucifer? Damian? Something."

Dad started calling from the first floor.

"I have to go back."

An hour later, the dead kids were in the front office of Sticksville Central High School. In a lucky exception, Derek actually had a pretty good sense of direction when it came to finding it. The school office was also a disorganized shambles, which made finding an address list of the Sticksville teachers a great deal more difficult. And as only Derek and Kirby could read, Cyril, Tabetha, and Morna stood around feeling about as useful as beach umbrellas in Siberia.

After a few minutes, the beach umbrellas started to grow restless. Derek and Kirby were taking ages to dig anything up.

"Let's go," goaded Tabetha. "How hard could it be to find two addresses?"

"Sorry," Kirby said. "Tabby, why don't you help us out — oh, wait. I forgot. You're *ignorant*."

While attempting to construct a stinging rebuttal, Tabetha heard a melodic whistling, followed by the sounds of squeaky wheels rolling by. "Everyone hide! Be quiet!" she yelled.

Tabetha, Cyril, and Morna dove straight through the front desk so they could hide behind it. Kirby and Derek crouched in the shadows where they were standing. The whistling and rolling tires grew louder, and through the large bay windows of the front office, the dead kids could spy a janitor wheeling his cart of mops and yellowish cleaning supplies around a corner of the school atrium.

"The janitor," Morna whispered with a note of anxiety in her words.

Cyril Cooper was crouched beside her, behind the front desk.

"What do you say, lass? Shall we scare him away together?"

Morna blushed a light, grey pink and clasped her hands together. She liked it when Cyril called her "lass." She looked at her shoes and couldn't think of anything to say. Then Kirby's head suddenly appeared between her shoes at her feet, and she let out a small scream.

"Oh, don't get your knickers in a twist," he said as he heaved himself up through the floor. If Morna's knickers had been in a twist, Kirby would have been in prime viewing position. "It's just me. Derek has the book."

Across the room, Derek's silhouetted figure raised an arm and waggled the address book.

"Hey! I heard that!" shouted the custodian from the atrium. "Is someone in there?"

"Looks like we got a believer," said Tabetha with glee.

"Good," whispered Cyril. "We still need to check the crime scene and question that groundskeeper, so it helps that he can see us. Derek, take me and Morna to the auto repair shop. Kirby and Tabetha, you scare that man until he talks. You spill your guts until he spills his. Understood?"

"Why'm I always saddled with fat boy?" said Tabetha.

"You need a saddle, horse-face," answered Kirby.

"Be quiet," said Cyril. "Now let's go."

"Maybe they should come to the shop with us first," suggested Derek.

"Why?"

"To . . . I don't know . . . pick up some tools?"

A few words about the school custodian: The custodian was a kind man, liked by the students of the school. His chocolate brown hair was splashed with grey and his face was the texture of an oft-used baseball glove, but the kids could see a young spirit behind those superficial signs of age. Those who gave it some thought, that is. In general, most students didn't think about him at all. The administration also appreciated his presence. He worked hard, worked late, and was most often of a friendly disposition.

So neither the administration nor the students had the faintest clue why the custodian quit the following morning, why his cart was found unattended in the middle of the hallway when school resumed the following day, or why he'd provided no explanation for his departure. But you're about to find out why all that happened.

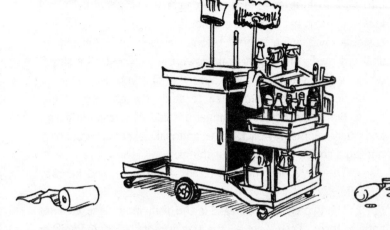

The custodian headed for his closet to put away his cart and empty his bucket of ammonia and water, before heading to his old muscle car to drive home for the evening. He absent-mindedly whistled an REO Speedwagon tune as he pushed the cart back through the school atrium. He wondered if he needed some sleep. Just minutes ago, he'd imagined a shout and movement coming from the office, but when he searched the room, it was empty. Suddenly, a strident voice soared through the atrium, interrupting his whistled power ballad.

"No! Don't do it! I'll call the police! Nooo!!!"

The screams were panicked and horrible. The custodian turned and kissed the crucifix around his neck. Agonized screams continued, and seemed to emanate from one of the hallways jutting out from the atrium: the computer hall. Cautiously, he edged his cart back the way he came, inching toward the hallway, silently praying the screams would end. Then . . . they did. Frozen at the corner, the custodian swallowed deeply and looked down the hallway. He was met with a scene of unspeakable horror.

But let's speak about it anyway.

Lying on the ground, just inches from the computer lab, was a young teenage boy in suspenders and short pants. Kneeling beside him was a young girl in pigtails and a tattered plaid dress. She was methodically taking the boy's head off with a coping saw. The boy again howled in pain as the serrated edge bit deeper and deeper into his throat, severing his flesh in a crazy quilt pattern. The girl looked up from her task and said nothing. She didn't have to. The custodian was down the hall before she could open her mouth, and was madly shoving his cart down the hallway to the closet, where he fully intended to lock himself until daybreak.

If he had taken some time to study the gruesome scene before him in an objective manner, instead of screaming curses and careening his way back to the janitorial closet, he would have noticed a couple of conspicuous things:

1. The boy's neck did not bleed as the girl sawed her way through.

2. The two children engaged in the dismemberment were not entirely there. They were a little translucent, like holograms or something.

3. The boy was remarkably vocal for someone whose neck was no longer attached to his head.

Kirby picked himself off the floor and securely screwed his head back on.

"Holy cats," he said. "Could you saw a little straighter next time, Tabby? I look like a jigsaw puzzle."

"Is there a problem?" she asked.

"It's a bit jagged, cool-hand," he said, fingering the zigzag cut across his throat. "This'll take hours to heal," he added and wobbled his head.

"Cry me a river, slave trader."

"Cyril is the slave trader — and we don't even know that for sure."

"Whatever. Come on. Our job isn't done."

Complete darkness surrounded the custodian in his closet, where he had curled himself into an impenetrable ball in the corner. Convinced, with the logic of a frightened four-year-old, that the horrible children couldn't hurt him if he was asleep, he shut his eyes and prayed for serenity.

The back of his eyelids suddenly went blood red. Someone had turned on the light. When he opened his eyes, he realized the night was just beginning to get sinister. The murderous and (apparently) murdered child loomed over him, the girl twirling the ugly coping saw, the boy cradling his severed head in his arms, the eyes staring his way.

"Oh, mother! Please leave me alone! Don't hurt me!"

Tabetha hissed and spat like oil in an overheated saucepan.

"What do you want?"

"Information," moaned the severed head.

"Yes! Yes! I'll tell you anything you want!"

Kirby's head was distracted by one of the closet's posters, a half-naked woman advocating a brand of iced tea.

"He'll tell us anything we want!" cackled Tabetha, slapping Kirby's arm with the saw.

"Ow!" Then, in his false baritone. "Who killed Terry O'Shea?"

"Terry O'Shea?"

"The French teacher," Kirby lowed.

"Him?" the janitor said. "Nobody killed him! It was an accident! The lift broke!"

"How did he access the auto repair shop?" said Kirby.

"I don't know! I don't know! Someone must have let him in!"

"Someone like you?" Tabetha brought the saw blade dangerously close to the janitor's prodigious nose.

"Oh no! No, no, no. No! I didn't even know he was there 'til I found the body!"

"Who else possesses the keys?"

Possesses the keys, he said. Was it Kirby or horror show impresario Vincent Prince leading the interrogation?

"Just me, the principal, and the new auto shop teacher — Schwartz!"

"That's it?!" shouted Tabetha.

"I think!" he hesitated. "The old auto shop teacher might still have keys — *Mr. Moustache!*"

"That sounds like a fake name," bellowed the head.

"I don't remember his name! The teacher with the moustache. That's all I know! Please let me go!"

211

The head and the deranged black girl eyed each other for a half minute, then parted, leaving an open pathway to the closet door.

Human history has not recorded a man moving as fast as the custodian, who bolted out the front door of the school and a quarter of the way across Sticksville before slowing down, leaving his car abandoned in its parking spot.

☠

Everything was still completely taped off in the auto shop — yellow police tape was strung like popcorn at Christmas. But it proved no impediment to Cyril, Morna, and Derek, who searched the room, which had now sat empty for weeks, with great verve.

In one corner rested a mangled pile of metal that must have at one time been the lift. Mr. O'Shea's car had long since been impounded. At first, the three could detect nothing of interest in the room. Only Cyril — who found all automobiles of great interest — noticed some things worthy of his attention, including a Jeep and a Volkswagen Beetle parked in the shop, also cordoned off with police tape. But it wasn't long before Derek discovered something of note about the lift itself. It had two switches, one of which had been smashed in.

"Guys, look at this."

"The police report said the switch was smashed in," Morna asked. "What are ye showing us?"

"See how there are switches on either side?"

It was true, a switch bordered both sides of the lift area.

"Whoever did this smashed in only the right switch. So?" Cyril didn't see the big deal.

"Morna," Derek said. "Did you bring the diary? Open it up, see what hand Henri LaFleur wrote with."

Morna propped the diary open. Blue ink smudged over the words on the left side of the paper. "He's left-handed!" Morna shouted. "Henri LaFleur wrote wi' his left hand! Derek, you're a genius."

"That means if Mr. O'Shea was Henri LaFleur, he didn't do this himself," Derek stood in front of the lift. "If I'm left-handed, and standing here, I'm going for this switch. And it's untouched. Let's see if we can find any other clues."

Immediately, Derek and Morna began looking for other evidence, opening closets and toolboxes. Cyril looked for a bit, too, but was soon entranced by a set of keys dangling from a rack inside a cabinet just beside the teacher's desk.

☠

The coping saw tinkled on the ground outside the front of the high school. Kirby and Tabetha waited impatiently for the other three to arrive.

"Derek has the address book," noted Kirby. "Think there's an actual Mr. Moustache?"

Tabetha just glared.

"Me neither. But at least we know someone else has a key to the auto shop, and Mr. Hamilton, the principal, too."

"A dumb waste a' time is what that was," said Tabetha. "Stupid janitor didn't know nuthin'. Only worthwhile thing I did was cut off your head."

"Maybe Derek, Cyril, and Morna found something," said Kirby, adjusting his suspenders.

"I doubt it," said Tabetha, gesturing. Kirby followed her outstretched arm to see what she was pointing at. A bubble-shaped car carrying their three friends was barrelling around the corner of the parking lot. Had he died twenty years later, Kirby would have recognized the automobile as a Volkswagen Beetle.

Kirby and Tabetha caught a glimpse of Cyril behind the wheel as the automobile veered all over the road (and lawn and sidewalk) at a frightening speed. Even at a great distance, Kirby could see the looks of horror etched on Derek and Morna's faces.

"Let's hope no one in Sticksville is out for a late-night drive," said Kirby. He and Tabetha sprinted down the sidewalk in the direction of the speeding car, which had just exited the school parking lot.

☠

Inside the Volkswagen Beetle, things were a bit out of control.

"Jumping Jehoshaphat!" shouted Cyril. "This is so much faster than any horse!"

"Yeah. Too fast," said Derek. "Slow down! Bring us back to the school!"

"I can't believe I waited this long to drive one. This is phenomenal!"

Morna, meanwhile, sat in the back with her hands in front of her eyes, murmuring prayers to herself. One shouldn't be scared of much when already dead, but if you were in a car with a teenager from the 1700s whose accelerator foot seems to be magnetized to the floor, you'd start praying, too.

Derek knew the evening was over when, scouring the crushed hydraulic lift for more clues, he heard a car's ignition and saw the headlights of a Volkswagen Beetle flare ablaze with life. He leapt through the closed door of the running car. Morna was already seated in the back, her little white hands crossed over her mouth.

"What are you doing?!" he shouted. Then he turned to Morna. "Did you allow this?"

"Nae . . . but Cyril was looking at all the motorcars and saying how great it mus' be tae drive one, and then I told him I'd been in a car an' it wasna' tha' exciting — just like a train wi' no track — and then he said he'd never been on a train and I got all sad an' . . ."

"Cyril, you don't know how to drive! And you're dead! What if someone sees us!"

"No one will see us," said Cyril, cocking his tricorn hat back. "It's three in the morning."

"No. No one will see us because we're ghosts!" shouted Derek. "And instead, they'll see a car zipping around without a driver!"

"Which one of these makes it go?" Cyril blithely ignored Derek.

After turning on the emergency flashers and changing the radio station several times, Cyril found the gas pedal with his foot and the car lurched forward, bashing through the aluminum garage door and coasting into the school's rear parking lot.

"Oh no," Derek moaned.

"Remember what you said, Cyril," said Morna, growing exponentially more terrified of the joyride. "Just a wee trip and then we bring the car right back. Okay?"

"And this must determine direction," Cyril muttered. He twisted the steering wheel and jammed on the accelerator again. The small car spun to the right and rocketed down Riverside Drive.

"You're on the wrong side of the road. You're on the wrong side of the road."

"What?" said Cyril, who was having a hard time hearing anything over the blaring radio he'd inadvertently turned on. The singer Meat Loaf was screaming about a "Bat Out of Hell."

"You're on the wrong side of the road!" shouted Derek. "Get on the other side of the yellow line."

Cyril swerved into the right lane. Morna yelped. Surprisingly, Cyril was a pretty good driver. Despite the speed at which he drove, and his reckless disregard for lanes, road signs, traffic lights, and the division between the road and the sidewalk, he managed to avoid colliding with anything that might seriously damage the car.

"Somebody's going to see us," said Derek. "Let's go back."

"C'mon, Cyril," pleaded Morna from the back. "We shoul' go back. It's been . . . fun . . . but we shoul' head back."

"No one's going to see us!" he insisted. "There are no other automobiles on the street."

"You're going to hit something!"

"I can drive," Cyril answered, with all the confidence of a first-time marathon runner who hasn't trained for the big day. "I've been on boats. I know how to steer."

"This doesn't have a rudder."

"Look out!" shouted Morna. The Volkswagen Beetle quickly reshaped two garbage cans and disassembled a real estate sign for Diamandas Realty at the speed of 80 kilometres an hour. Derek stomped on the brake from the passenger seat and the car shuddered to a halt in the middle of the lawn outside a pleasant two-storey house.

The three dead kids sat in the car in a slight daze. A massive dirt trail charted their pathway into the lawn, and deep furrows had been cut into the earth by the Beetle's tires.

"So, you can drive, eh?" said Derek, being a total smart aleck.

"What're we going ta' do?" yelped Morna. "Somebody musta' heard that. We gotta' get out o' here."

The front door of the pleasant two-storey house swung open and Alyosha Diamandas leapt onto the porch. He had been pursuing some late-night cleaning at one of his properties (said pleasant two-storey house) when he heard a crash from outside. His face turned licorice red with rage as he noticed the demolished For Sale sign and the damage an old Volkswagen Beetle had done to the pristine lawn. He was estimating the cost of emergency landscaping when he noticed three instantly recognizable figures inside the beached car. "You!" he shouted. "You kids!"

Morna was the first to notice the man with the thin moustache hopping down the front steps. "It's Mr. Diamandas. We'd better run!"

"We'll drive," asserted Cyril, and he slammed on the pedal again. Not a very gentle driver, that Cyril. The car spun its wheels in the deep dirt and remained stationary. Diamandas ran up to the struggling car and banged on the windows with his fists.

Alyosha had a flashback to that townhouse that was practically sold, until the prospective buyers saw the kitchen cabinets opening and closing of their own accord. And the three-bathroom, five-bedroom estate that was a surefire sale before messages began mysteriously appearing on the basement wall. The dead kids always appeared in October. He thought they had gone away. He had sold houses without supernatural interference for the past four years, but now the ghosts were back to pick up where they'd left off — ruining Alyosha Diamandas's life.

"You stupid ghost kids! You ruin my life!"

"He's kinda right," Morna admitted.

"Don't agree with him, Morna," Cyril said. He kicked the gas pedal again and the car lifted out of its rut and zoomed back onto the road. Cyril continued down the street, and Alyosha Diamandas was left in the car's vapour trail, cursing the day the children had died.

☠

It was now five o'clock in the morning and the sky was just beginning to brighten. Cyril, Morna, and Derek returned to the cemetery looking pretty rough, even for dead bodies. Tabetha and Kirby had been waiting in the Schwartz's backyard for the joyriders' return.

"We caught a little of your wild adventure," said Kirby, hands in pockets. "We tried to catch up to you, but you were moving too quickly. That looked . . ."

"Amazing?" suggested Cyril.

"Stupid."

"Did anyone see you?" Tabetha asked.

"There was a minor incident with Alyosha Diamandas," Cyril said. "But nothing important."

"I have the teacher address book," said Derek, who looked like he'd just run up a mountain. "I'll leave it with October before it's light. I've already taken down the address for our first teacher, Mrs. Tischmann."

"Where did you leave the car?" Tabetha asked Cyril.

"Where I found it, of course."

☠

I arrived at school on Wednesday morning to find an unimaginable mess. A badly damaged Volkswagen Beetle was parked directly across from the front doors, with police busy taping off the vicinity and pushing curious students back. Once I shoved my way through the crowd to get inside, the chaos continued. Rumours were rampant about some inexplicable and severe vandalism in the auto shop, and how the janitor had some sort of severe breakdown and left the school in a panic. Most people assumed he was the one who'd driven the Beetle on a crazy rampage through the auto shop and most of Sticksville.

Call me suspicious, but I just naturally assumed it had something to do with the dead kids. A teachers' address book was on my dresser when I woke up in the morning and I doubted its appearance and the broken-down Volkswagen at the entrance to the school were unrelated.

☠

By lunchtime, I was in such a horrible mood, I felt like smashing my face against the cafeteria's grill. I'd just finished class with one suspected killer. He hated the FLQ, was at the school during Mr. O'Shea's time of death, and all he wanted to talk about was common denominators. And after lunch, I had class with another suspected killer to look forward to. Mrs. Tischmann had serious motive, having lost her leg to the FLQ, but she said she didn't really know Mr. O'Shea. But then why was he picking up her kid from the concert at the Y?

Sometimes I wished I'd stuck with writing and curling as hobbies. But then, curling and writing could conceivably be considered the cause of all this mess. Could curling truly be the root of all evil?

I collapsed on the cafeteria table and unloaded my damp, unappetizing turkey sandwich onto the table. Yumi and a now cleanly shaven Stacey tumbled onto the bench across from me.

"Sorry about yesterday, October," Stacey said, looking down at yet another sad-looking tuna sandwich. "I'm sure you didn't want the whole school to find out how young you were."

"It's all right," Yumi decided. "Right? It's a year. No big deal."

"Yep. No big deal," Stacey added.

"Yeah," I said, a bit less convinced.

"So, you'll be, like, graduating before you can get your driver's licence?" Stacey asked.

"Shut up," Yumi hissed, elbowing him in the gut.

"Whatever. Can we just forget yesterday's lunch ever happened?"

Did they have to be so weird about it? It's not like I was secretly eight or forty or something. I was a year younger than them! Ugh.

"Well, speaking of yesterday's lunch never happening," Yumi said, producing my battered composition book from her bag. "You forgot this when you rushed out of the cafeteria at the end of lunch. Don't you need it?"

"Not exactly . . . it's just this book I was trying to write."

"Book? Cool. What's it about?" asked Stacey.

"It's a horror book."

"Nice. Can I read it?"

"Uh . . . when it's done. Sure. Thanks for finding it, Yumi."

Considering I hadn't worked on *Two Knives, One Thousand Demons* for ages, it would probably be a very long time before Stacey ever cracked its spine, which was for the best, really. He would probably turn into a werewolf or something.

"October," said Yumi, seemingly remorseful. "There's something I need to tell you."

"What?"

"Your dad has been calling my house a lot over the past couple of weeks. Always late at night. He's been looking for you, and I always tell him I don't know where you are. Is that why he invited to me to Daughter night or whatever it was called?"

"I know. It's all right. That's what Father-Daughter Night was about. I've been . . . well . . . we're friends, right?"

"Of course!" said Yumi, insulted that I'd think otherwise.

"So I can trust you when I tell you this . . ."

Yumi nodded and I knew she could be trusted. Yumi was one of those girls to whom nothing in life is more important than her friends. If a mystical being appeared before her, offering her the ability to fly and read minds and shoot beams of pure love from her chest if she'd only give up a friend's secret, Yumi would probably happily remain bound by the laws of gravity and physics. And as for Stacey, what other people did he even know?

"I like to sneak out and hang around the cemetery at night. It's right behind the house. I know it's weird. . . ."

"Weird?" Yumi said. "That's the greatest thing I've ever heard! I want to hang out in the cemetery at night!"

"Wait, aren't you afraid of ghosts?" a clearly continuity-concerned Stacey asked.

"Yes, okay," she admitted. "Maybe I don't want to do it myself, but I support this action, in theory. Is it cool in the cemetery? I can't believe you live beside a cemetery! That is so great!" Yumi was practically shouting, which was making me a little uneasy. This was supposed to be a secret, after all. The cafeteria already got their fill of October Schwartz secrets yesterday, during the lunch that I had convinced myself never happened. Stacey, meanwhile, methodically chewed his tuna sandwich and stared at something interesting on the cafeteria wall. I began to suspect Stacey was part cat.

"Yeah, my dad isn't too keen on it though. He thinks I'm

disturbed or depressed or something."

"Whatever. Listen, this totally negates whatever issues I might have had about your age."

"You had issues?" Stacey said.

"Can you take me to the cemetery sometime?" Yumi asked. "Maybe after I'm totally over this ghost thing. It's still a little fresh."

"Sure," I said. I didn't know what I was worried about at the start of lunch. I even considered that one day I'd introduce Yumi and Stacey to my dead friends. Maybe.

☠

The rest of the day was mega-uneventful. In music, the students were all treating Mrs. Tischmann with overt niceness and devotion. Ever since they had discovered her wooden leg they seemed to have a new respect for her, as if she weren't a huge flake but was actually some kind of wise oracle deserving of their respect because she had part of a tree for a shin. Not that I had anything against people with wooden legs, mind you. I just wanted people to remember that amputees can be jerks like the rest of us. Maybe even murderers. Meanwhile, Ashlie Salmons was completely absent from school.

By nightfall, it was with no small amount of anticipation that I waited for Dad to fall asleep. As soon as I could get to the cemetery I'd finally find out what had happened at the school last night. Plus, I now had virtually complete access to every teacher's house, thanks to the address book and the dead kids' "break and enter" techniques. I was confident that I'd figure out what happened to Mr. O'Shea in no time.

Sneaking out was a cinch, but all the same, I had no intention of staying out any later than I absolutely had to. I was thirteen, and I'd been repeatedly caught sneaking out and getting into fights. If Dad found me coming in late once more, he'd probably make me join a convent or go to military school or something. That's probably how Mr. Santuzzi got started. The moon cast odd shadows in the graveyard, and as I approached the usual clearing a strange clacking sound became louder and louder. The sounds became totally obvious when, one second later, I walked in on the middle of the dead kids rehearsing some play. Cyril and Derek were intensely engaged in some sort of sword fight with cut tree branches. Tabetha and Kirby were arguing, again — something about the stage direction for the scene. Morna, to all appearances, was simply scoping Cyril out. I finally figured out that Morna might have been a little bit boy-crazy; in the mood for a little United Empire love.

Despite her focus on Cyril's pantaloons, Morna was the first to see me.

"October!"

The sudden halt in the dramatic production resulted in Derek's wooden stick slicing down through Cyril's face, but it was okay. He was dead; he couldn't feel a thing.

"What's going on? A play? What about my mystery?" I was more than a little concerned that they'd moved onto rehearsals. Had they abandoned Mr. O'Shea? This wasn't some kind of part-time detective agency.

"Don't worry," Tabetha said. "We went ta' the school. Got yer address book."

"Yeah, I saw. Thanks! And the auto shop? Did you find anything?"

"We found the switch that was broken," Derek said.

"And then you trashed the auto shop?"

"Ye heard abou' tha', huh?"

"I don't want to know. The less I know, the better," October said with a wave of her hand. "I can't stay long — what did you learn?"

Derek outlined his theory about the switches. He told October that if Mr. O'Shea had smashed the operating switch himself, he would have had to be right-handed. And Henri LaFleur wasn't right-handed, according to their extremely unprofessional handwriting analysis.

"Was Mr. O'Shea left-handed?" Morna asked. "Can ye remember?"

I tried to picture him writing in class, but no images came

to mind. I was, with some effort, able to remember him curling, though. He threw the stone with his left hand. I was sure of it.

"He was left-handed. I'm almost positive."

"Well, that doesn't prove he was Henri LaFleur," Derek said. "But it's almost irrefutable proof that he didn't drop that lift on himself."

The dead kids also told me about their question period with the custodian.

"That explains how they found his cart this morning. You don't think he did it?"

"He was pretty scared," Tabetha said. "I think he'd a' told us any secrets he was hidin'."

"Does the math teacher have a moustache?" Kirby asked.

"Yeah. Mr. Santuzzi has a moustache, but so do half the male teachers at Sticksville Central. It's almost like a uniform."

"Well, what do ya' want us ta' do?" asked Tabetha.

"Search Mrs. Tischmann's tonight. My music teacher seems like the best suspect. If you find anything, leave some kind of message for me when you get back."

"What are you going to do?" Cyril asked.

"If it looks like she might have been involved? Just watch me."

☠

October was awakened the next morning by a sharp stabbing poke in her thigh. Of all the ways to be awoken, this is one of the worst ones. I speak from experience. She rubbed at her crusted-over eyes and noticed it was still very early — barely even six. Her alarm wasn't set to go off for another hour or so. Shuffling off her covers, October stood up and found a crisp envelope in her pyjama pants. "Living Girl" was scrawled across the front, and October realized, with a start, that one of the dead kids must have stuffed it into her pocket overnight. It was sort of her fault since she asked them to leave her a note, but this was getting a bit personal, she felt. Would you want Kirby LaFlamme stuffing things in your pockets as you slept? Doubtful.

She also realized the dead kids probably didn't own any stationery. They must have stolen it from Mrs. Tischmann. Normally, she was against petty larceny, but if Tischmann was involved with Mr. O'Shea's death, October hoped they took *all* her stationery. Pens, too.

October read the letter:

> *Dear October,*
>
> *We searched the music teacher's house and we think you may be on to something. On the kitchen counter we found newspaper articles of the stock exchange explosion and photographs of her and your French teacher at some party. They were obvious, laid out on the counter, like they'd just been viewed. We*

225

didn't have to search at all. Maybe you want to call the
police or something.
  Yours,
  Derek Running Water

  P.S. If we solve this mystery early, will you take us to the
movies again?

October's world crashed down around her like a poorly secured series of mobiles. Maybe it wasn't old man Santuzzi after all. Each word, each letter, each stroke of ink on the paper — "From the desk of Eileen Tischmann" — was like a chisel to October's brain. All signs rationally pointed to Mrs. Tischmann being Mr. O'Shea's killer. And though that brain chisel was difficult to ignore, October tried. Mrs. Tischmann was never going to win an award for educator of the year — not even among the dismal candidates at Sticksville Central — but could she really be a murderer? A murderess? This decision, she decided, wasn't something a bunch of old photos and a wooden leg alone could determine. October had to take the investigation into her own hands from here.

☠

October arrived at music class a bit later than planned on Thursday afternoon — the result of an involved debate with Yumi over Mr. Tim Burton's take on the Headless Horseman — so she missed the chance to talk with Mrs. Tischmann before the period began. She wasn't sure that would have been the best time to confront her, anyway — she could imagine the palpable tension: October knowing, Mrs. Tischmann knowing that she knew, her murderous intent, each downward stroke of her conductor's baton a wishful knife in October's belly.

From the instrument room, October retrieved her trombone. She assembled the slide and bell before inserting the terrifically cold mouthpiece. October blew silently into the mouthpiece to warm it on her way back to her seat. She waved to Stacey, armed with his mallets, and sat down in the back row. Ashlie Salmons, back from yesterday's absence, swung around in the front row, and glared at October. It was the first time she'd seen Ashlie since giving her a friendly elbow to the stomach. Ashlie's pointy face split into two grinning rows of near-perfect teeth, which is not the normal sort of reaction a person has to someone who recently physically assaulted her. Understandably, October was a bit apprehensive.

Mrs. Tischmann opened the class by leading the students in a few scales. Everyone was still treating her like an untalented but well-liked relative at karaoke. All polite smiles. She flapped her arms joyously to the beat Stacey provided, her wild hair bouncing in time.

"Okay, everyone!" she sang. "Now for a little fun, take out 'Dancing in the Street.'" Apparently, Mrs. Tischmann's dictionary had a different definition for fun than yours or mine. "Remember — put some *soul* into it." Mrs. Tischmann winked and made a strange grimace, and October hoped she'd never have to see that face again.

Two and a half minutes into the class's soulless version of "Dancing in the Street," their musical momentum collapsed. October saw the devastation as an opportunity, and shot her arm up in the air. Now, she thought, was the time to arrange a meeting with Mrs. Tischmann so she could ensure an intervention of sorts after class. Mrs. Tischmann, her head still reeling from the class's butchery of Martha and the Vandellas' hit single, spied a pale hand above the brass bells and horns.

"Yes, October?"

"Sorry, Mrs. Tischmann. I know this doesn't have anything to do with the song, but could I talk with you about something after class?"

"That would be fine," said Mrs. Tischmann. "I guess I'll just have to wait to discover what secret topic it concerns."

"It's probably about her appointment with the school therapist," offered Ashlie Salmons, at a decibel level the entire class could enjoy. The scamp. "Principal Hamilton's set up a bunch of therapy sessions for her."

Now, October had learned from her dad that seeking

professional help for one's problems was nothing to be ashamed of. Unfortunately, Ashlie Salmons was not so enlightened, nor were many of October's classmates who began to whisper to one another and snicker. Stacey crashed his cymbals together raucously, which seemed to be a misguided, but somewhat sweet attempt to drown out the gossip and laughter. Or he just liked making loud noises. Hard to say with him.

"That's enough! Stacey! October! Ashlie!" shouted Mrs. Tischmann, attempting to regain control of the class. "Ashlie and October — pack up your instruments. You're both going straight to the office. You can talk to Principal Hamilton about your little feud."

"But I didn't do anything!"

"October," she continued, turning her attention to the goth girl whose face had turned an unfortunate shade of bright red. "I can meet with you at the end of the school day if you still need to talk. But right now you need to go to the front office with Ashlie."

October nodded her head trying not to cry, yet again. Maybe she could make it through a full week without bawling like a thirteen-year-old who was not yet ready for high school. She followed Ashlie Salmons out the door — two prisoners unwillingly chained together on their way to execution.

They only made it about twenty locker lengths before the accusations started.

"Why can't you just leave me alone? I already have to see the school therapist because of you!"

"Think you're the only one, Zombie Tramp?!" Ashlie snarled back, her accusing finger in October's face, the nail splashed perfect Vanilla Dreams white with polish. "Did Mr. Hamilton not inform you of the good news? We're talking with Mr. Lagostina *together*."

"Oh, barf," October said. It seemed the day couldn't get any worse.

"I know, right? Zombie Tramp attacks me and I need to see the therapist? In some sort of group therapy session? Cry me a river, Schwartz."

"Why won't you leave me alone? I only wanted to know what you saw that night Mr. O'Shea died. No one cares about you smoking!" October was on the verge of the verge of tears. Not quite there yet because fury was now her dominant emotion. "I hope you *never* pass grade nine."

"You shut up about that," seethed Ashlie. "You don't know what you're talking about."

"I think Mr. O'Shea was killed, and I need your help!" October exploded.

If not for the music students who were currently destroying "Love Shack," the outburst surely would have disrupted classes along the art hall. October turned around to face some terrible grade ten art projects in the hallway's display case. No way was she going to cry in front of Ashlie Salmons. She'd love it too much. There was a very real possibility, dear readers, that Ashlie was energized by the tears of unpopular girls.

"Are you serious? Are you still on about this?" she asked.

"Yeah," October sniffed. "I know it's stupid."

"You should really tell my mom about this," she commented. October couldn't figure out why Ashlie had instantly become her closest confidante.

"You don't . . . think I'm crazy?"

"I do," Ashlie admitted. "But I can't imagine you'd keep bugging me about this crap if you didn't have good reason. You'd be a glutton for punishment," she reasoned.

"I guess."

"I'm *horrible* to you and your stupid friends."

"Yumi and Stacey."

"Those are both girl's names. Is Yumi Kung Fu Zombie Tramp?"

"Yeah," October said, calming down a bit.

"So, she's not even Chinese?"

"Who cares?" October said, exasperated.

"I mean, why even talk to me at all if you could avoid it, right?" Ashlie reasoned.

Drained of weeks and weeks of anger, October aimlessly attempted random number combinations on nearby lockers while she waited for Ashlie Salmons to respond with something, anything that could explain her actions.

"Listen," she said. "I hate my mom," she said, rifling through her little green purse for gum. "She said I can't date Devin. She's still angry with me for flunking last year. *Witch*. So I'm a little self-conscious about getting in more trouble; I don't want Crown Attorney Salmons finding out her daughter was smoking and drinking in the parking lot when she was supposed to be in volleyball practice, okay? She's already all over me about schoolwork. You wouldn't understand. You're like some ten-year-old whiz kid, right? Stupid baby."

"I'm thirteen."

"Whatever. Let's call a truce. You don't tell anyone about Devin and me at the school that night, and I can tell you everything you need to know. Full eyewitness account."

"Really?"

"Yeah. What do you want to know? Who was at the school that night? Everyone on the volleyball team, your dad, Mr. Hamilton, Mr. Santuzzi, Mr. Page, the janitor, Mrs. Tischmann . . . a lot of teachers, actually." She looked toward the sky as she counted, as if the answers were all written somewhere over the particleboard ceiling panels.

"Uh . . . thanks. I guess."

"Whatever. Listen, if I do this, you've got to repay the favour. Stop being so crazy. Elbows flying. Weird niner guys with bad moustaches shouting at me in the cafeteria. When my mom finds out about this therapy session, she's gonna have a kitten. Give birth to an actual cat, you understand? So calm down. I know I mess with you, but you're a freak. Just deal with it like a Spartan, okay? And let's try to get out of this therapy session as unscathed as possible."

"Okay . . ."

"And there's no way I'm going to Kaiser Hamilton's office. We're skipping the rest of the period and we're not saying anything to anyone. And then we're good," Ashlie concluded.

Well, I don't think any of us were expecting that about-face. Ashlie Salmons: unlikely ally to our heroine? I had just assumed she'd be unmasked as some sort of robot programmed by her math teacher to torment October until graduation. If you're writing your own book feel free to take that idea and run with it.

"So you won't make fun of me anymore?"

"I really can't promise anything, kid."

☠

History class provided October the perfect opportunity to plan her interrogation of Mrs. Tischmann. Mr. Page had a certain amount of faith in October, much like Mr. O'Shea once had. She was sometimes able to spend entire classes doodling, writing in her book, or — more commonly the case in recent days — mentally exploring the possibilities and motives involved in Mr. O'Shea's murder, without so much as a peep from Mr. Page.

Reminded of her budding authorial career by Stacey during yesterday's lunch, October had begun writing down notes for questions to ask Mrs. Tischmann in her *Two Knives, One Thousand Demons* notebook. Occasionally, she'd add a few lines about Olivia de Kellerman, demon-slayer extraordinaire, and her ongoing battle with incredible evil. So she hadn't really abandoned her novel *entirely* entirely. Her attempt to write in Thursday's history class created an unholy hybrid of horror and a game plan for questioning her music teacher:

That was intense. Never before had Olivia de Kellerman seen the Toronto Symphony's timpani player turn blood-red, grow fangs, and sprout bat wings from his back. As she wrenched her blade from his collapsed skull, she could see silhouettes of the lower brass section near the back of the auditorium. The long shadows and blood pouring down her forehead obscured much of her vision, but Olivia could almost swear she watched the baritone players shed their human skins and slither into the instrument room.

Um . . .

Something about something — then she shoved her knife deep into the conductor's cummerbund region and pulled upward until she hit bone. The demon-witch howled in pain.

"Why did you kill him?" Olivia demanded. She was up to her hilt in the rancid flesh of the demon-witch who had devoured her mentor, Uncle Otto. "Why did you do it?!"

"I don't know what you're talking about," shrieked the demon-witch, clawing at Olivia's right hand.

"You didn't kill him? The man who took your eye?" (Oh yeah. The demon-witch only had one yellow eye. And was totally unhappy about it.) *"You had the opportunity! The motive!"*

Okay, the story was getting a bit ridiculous. October realized this, too, just as she realized the shadow suddenly casting itself across the desk was that of Mr. Page.

"October, may I ask what you're doing? Because whatever it is, it certainly doesn't seem to involve the Treaty of Versailles. And instead, involves . . . *demon-witches*?"

October's best answer was a shrug of her shoulders.

"Mmm-hmm," said Mr. Page. "Well, if you could not do that in history class, I would appreciate it."

October gave a little sheepish grin of agreement, and was returned a tight smile from her history teacher. So much for a little faith.

☠

"Is it true?"

October was shoving books and binders into her narrow locker when an excitable and fast-talking Yumi Takeshi approached, demanding verification of the truth of it, whatever *it* was. The chains and bracelets Yumi wore jangled and clanged, so physical was her enthusiasm.

"Is *what* true?"

"You know," she dropped her voice to a conspiratorial level. *"That you're in therapy."*

"Yes," October looked around to see if anyone nearby was listening. "Where did you hear that? And why are you so excited about it?" She pushed Yumi, only somewhat jokingly. Stacey arrived at October's locker moments later.

"Everyone's talking about it. Stacey told me how Ashlie announced it in music class, but I just figured she was lying. Besides, it's kind of cool."

This was news to October. While her dad had always maintained therapy was perfectly normal and all that, he never tried to make the practice seem hip. Only Yumi could think it was cool. Her cousin was probably in therapy or something.

"Cool?" October said.

"Yeah. I mean, it's undeniable proof you can't be boring, right? Do boring people need therapy?"

How do you argue with that kind of perfect logic?

"People in a catatonic state need therapy and are pretty boring," said Stacey, arguing with that kind of perfect logic.

"Whatever," October said, closing and securing her locker. "The only reason I'm seeing the school therapist is because Principal Hamilton is making me. And the only reason he's making me is because I hit Ashlie Salmons. And I have to take the therapy session with her."

"What a witch," said Yumi, in awe of her total witchery.

"Seriously," said Stacey. "It's those of us who aren't injuring Ashlie Salmons on a regular basis who should see a therapist."

"Come on . . . she's not . . . that . . . bad," October said, ashamed. She felt an unjustified need to defend Ashlie since their awkward truce.

"Maybe Principal Hamilton was on to something," Yumi decided, for October had clearly lost all sense of right and wrong.

Wait a second. *Yikes!* Hearing his name aloud, October realized what I already had: that Principal Hamilton was still a major suspect. He has the keys to the auto repair shop. He was on site that night it all went down. What if the therapy sessions were Hamilton's way of keeping October off the case? What if he was trying to discredit her because he was involved in Mr. O'Shea's death? That would be pretty nefarious, wouldn't it?

"Sorry, guys. I have to run," said October. "I have a meeting with Mrs. Tischmann."

October swiftly strode down the arts hallway to Mrs. Tischmann's door. It was slightly ajar, which was a good sign she was still there, waiting for October. But waiting *how*? Might she already suspect why October wanted to speak to her? Think like Olivia de Kellerman, girl. WWOdKD? She'd interrogate the stuffing out of Mrs. Tischmann — her and her wooden leg. She'd strap her down and open a jar of termites. Mrs. Tischmann could be lying in wait behind the door, ready to bash a guitar over October's head like she was in the front row of a Sex Pistols show (circa 1977). October couldn't take a chance like that; she definitely needed to keep her head intact. The only logical course of action was to sprint into the music room and take Tischmann by surprise.

October burst through the door to find a very confused Mrs. Tischmann at the blackboard, octaves and bars marked in white. If she hadn't been convinced of October's need for psychiatric help before, this had surely changed her mind.

"October, are you all right?" Mrs. Tischmann looked concerned. "Is someone chasing you?"

"Uh . . . no. Just . . . practising for the track and field team."

"We don't have a track and field team."

So much for quick thinking. After all the excuses she'd made recently, you'd think October would get a little better at it.

Mrs. Tischmann ignored the fact that her student believed she was on the school's nonexistent relay team and apologized for the day's music class. "I'm sorry about what happened today, October. I'm sure Principal Hamilton reprimanded Ashlie and I don't think it will happen again. Now, what did you want to talk about?"

It was now or never, October reasoned.

"Your leg."

"My leg?" Mrs. Tischmann was taken aback. "What about it?

You know now that it's wooden. But I don't like to make a big deal about it." The curls of her hair bounced as she rapped her knuckles against the faux leg.

"I would," October gulped. "I would make a big deal about it . . . if I lost my leg in the bombing of the Montreal Stock Exchange."

Mrs. Tischmann stared at October as if her head had begun dispensing a strawberry milkshake. "How do you know —"

"Did you know that Mr. O'Shea was once a member of the FLQ, Mrs. Tischmann?"

Mrs. Tischmann looked like October had taken that strawberry milkshake, thrown it at her, then slapped her — Mrs. Tischmann's face was now a hundred shades of red. "I don't think we should talk about this," she said. "I think you should leave, October."

October's heart was like a hummingbird caught in a mailbox. She was now certain Mrs. Tischmann had something to do with Mr. O'Shea's death, but she didn't know what to do, what question to ask next, how to act. She needed to make her move fast, because Mrs. Tischmann was pushing her out through the door.

"No, please!" October begged. "I just want to talk to you about Mr. O'Shea!"

"I will not just sit here while you speak ill of the dead," she tried to angle October out of the doorframe without manhandling her. "Mr. O'Shea was a very kind, very special man."

"I agree," said October desperately. "And I want to know why someone killed him!"

"Killed him?" Mrs. Tischmann stopped trying to force the door closed. "Do you actually — oh my, you think I . . . ? Come in. Close the door."

October did as she was told, though she feared she might regret closing herself in a room at the far end of a hallway after school hours with a possible killer. But such are the impulsive choices one makes in life.

"Come here. Sit here," Mrs. Tischmann whispered, and sat down in one of the plastic orange chairs that normally comprised the flute section. October joined her. "What makes you think Mr. O'Shea was killed? It was a horrible way to die, but it was an accident."

Either Mrs. Tischmann didn't kill Mr. O'Shea, or she had a second calling as a drama teacher. Still, October thought it wise to limit what information she revealed; for example, explaining how she found Mr. O'Shea's storage unit or that she knew what the official police report said might be problematic.

"My dad was questioned by the police about it," she said, which wasn't a total lie. "Mr. O'Shea was crushed by his own car, when the switch for the mechanical lift was broken."

Mrs. Tischmann winced, as if the car was crushing her instead. Sorry, kids. That was a really insensitive way to describe it.

"How could someone crush himself? And the right-hand switch was the broken one, but Mr. O'Shea was left-handed, right?"

"You're right," Mrs. Tischmann gasped. "I thought that too. When he died, I said to myself, Terry wouldn't be so careless. So stupid. And he'd never take his own life. But then I thought I was being ridiculous. Who'd want to kill Terry?" Mrs. Tischmann looked wistfully into space.

October didn't know if she was going to continue speaking, so she interrupted. "Uh . . . I thought *you* might."

"Never! Oh, I would never . . ."

"But you knew he was part of the FLQ? They took your leg!"

Mrs. Tischmann then explained how she and Mr. O'Shea had been good friends, precisely because he had been part of the FLQ. This confused October at first, but made more sense as she continued her story.

When Mrs. Tischmann landed a teaching job in Sticksville, Mr. O'Shea realized within a month who she was, where she had worked, and most importantly, why her one leg was wood and screws instead of flesh and bone. A couple of months later, he asked Mrs. Tischmann out for coffee so they could speak privately. Over hot caffeinated beverages, Mr. O'Shea told Mrs. Tischmann everything — his old name, his old life as Henri LaFleur, his unwitting membership in the FLQ, how he had purchased the timer for the Montreal Stock Exchange bomb, how he'd left Quebec, and changed his identity. Most importantly, he told her that he'd spent every day of his life since the explosion trying to atone for his actions. He'd studied the newspaper clippings and magazine articles about the stock exchange bombing and he knew the names of all twenty-seven people injured that day.

Mrs. Tischmann had been shocked. She hadn't thought about the attack in years, and now this colleague was informing her that he was somehow responsible for the lack of feeling below her knee. Mr. O'Shea said he wouldn't beg for her forgiveness; he felt he didn't deserve it. But he wanted her to know what he had done. Immediately after he told her, she just stirred the cream in her coffee and could think of nothing to say. It was all too painful and strange. Mr. O'Shea simply apologized, left five dollars on their round table, and left. About a week later, she forgave him — not that she ever told him she had. Instead, she just became a close friend.

"And you kept his secret?" asked October, amazed, not only by Mrs. Tischmann's story, but by the whole world of the hidden lives of teachers. Every teacher could have a story like this — a secret life she'd never know.

"Yes. I never told anyone, not even my ex-husband. Not my parents."

"But . . . I mean . . . wasn't that dangerous for him?" October stammered. "You could have turned him in at any time."

"I could have," she said. "But the way he told me everything, without even knowing me, really, and without any regard to how it could affect his life . . . I think he was suffering his own personal punishment."

Mrs. Tischmann looked serene after confessing. October would bet her eye teeth — whichever ones those were — that her music teacher had told the truth, but some aspects of her story still made no sense.

"You never seemed too close to Mr. O'Shea. You weren't even upset when he died," October said.

"Ha. Leave it to teenagers to be blunt. Mr. O'Shea and I tried to keep our friendship something of a secret. I thought it would be the best way to keep his past hidden . . . but maybe . . . maybe it was a cold thing to do."

Mrs. Tischmann began to cry into her hands, and then October felt really horrible. She didn't know what to do. If it was her dad or Yumi or someone crying, she'd hold that person and say soothing things like, *It's all right* or *No, lots of people like you*, but this was her music teacher. She wasn't going to hug her.

"It's okay," October said, and awkwardly patted Mrs. Tischmann's head like she was a dog she'd just been introduced to. She waited for an appropriate lapse of time before asking another question. "Mrs. Tischmann, what if someone else found out Mr. O'Shea was in the FLQ and helped make that bomb? Would they maybe want to kill him?"

"October," she said, wiping her eyes and smoothing her tangled hair. "How would anyone else find out?" Uh, *hello*. October found out, music lady. "And even if they did, they'd just call the police. Why would they want to murder him? I'm sorry, dear, but I really do think this was just an accident. Accidents will happen."

She began to cry a little again, and October clumsily excused herself and left the classroom. It can be very uncomfortable to watch adults cry.

Rows of pumpkins lined the stoops of Riverside Drive as October made her way home. The good news was that she could cross one suspect off her Sticksville Central suspect list. Mrs. Tischmann was too much of a wreck to be Mr. O'Shea's murderer. She was probably still blubbering in her classroom, playing "Memories" on the piano and breaking down after a few bars. The bad news was that October had no other convincing suspects, just a laundry list of all the other teachers who were there that fateful night.

In her mind there was and had been only one real suspect: Mr. Santuzzi. Almost everything fit. October was going to enjoy nailing his butt to the wall, even though the thought terrified her. Terrifying but also enjoyable — like a roller coaster where you have to stand up during the ride. Or hot dogs you buy on the street.

☠

To top off a week of horrible things, Hallowe'en was just one night away — the signs of jack o' lanterns and cotton-ball spiderwebs were all over the lawns — and that meant the dead kids would soon be saying farewell. In just over twenty-four hours, my five dead friends would be crawling back into the soil of the cemetery, or fading from existence, or something like that. I wasn't entirely clear how it all worked. But I knew I wouldn't have five valued ghost detectives at my service for a while. I needed to find the real murderer and needed to make it snappy.

Adding insult to injury, I still didn't have a costume.

Dad walked in the front door around five, and I sprang a request on him before he'd even taken off his coat.

"Dad. I know you're probably really tired after a day of school and you probably have a lot of marking to do . . ."

"But . . ." he said.

"But do you think you could help me with a Hallowe'en costume? Maybe?"

"You don't have a costume yet? October, do you not own a calendar? Have you not seen the pumpkins? It's Hallowe'en tomorrow. But I guess I can help you out. What's the costume?"

"Cthulu," I said. It had taken me a long time to come up with the perfect costume, and I was proud of myself.

"Okay, and who or what is that?"

"It's an ancient demon featured in the stories of H.P. Lovecraft."

239

"Okay . . . and what does Cthulu look like?"

"Like the embodiment of extreme evil, pretty much."

"October," Dad sighed. "I'm going to need you to be a lot more specific."

☠

The night was colder than it had been earlier in the week, so when I left the house in jacket and gloves — after toiling for hours on a Cthulu costume with Dad, more about that later — it felt more like December than October. The only thing souring my mood was that little problem of never solving the mystery of Mr. O'Shea's death before the dead kids, well, died again.

Those very dead friends seemed surprised to see me in the Sticksville Cemetery that night.

"October?" said Derek. "I thought you couldn't leave the house anymore. We were going to come visit you."

"Good news, corpses! I wore my dad out making him build my Hallowe'en costume. He'll be unconscious until seven in the morning. But maybe we should meet inside. It's freezing out here."

They probably didn't notice how icy it was, being dead and unable to feel extremes of temperature and all, but I doubted I could last ten minutes outside in the cold wind. If we were going to discuss the case — and we had no time to dawdle; there was only one day left — we needed to find some shelter.

"Lead the way," Cyril said.

"Oh no. You're not coming to my house. My dad's already stressed that I'm going to the school therapist."

"School therapist?" said Derek.

"Yeah. I'll explain later."

"How about in here?" Kirby said, walking through the door of a tomb as if he owned the joint. He didn't; I checked.

Seconds after Kirby's ghostly form disappeared behind the stone door, we heard an incredibly loud scraping through the wind. The stone door slowly opened and Kirby's sallow face appeared from within. "Come on in," he said. "Leave the door open for some light."

The dead kids filed in pretty readily, but I wasn't super-keen to follow. There was a dead person in there; someone's grandpa or something. It felt wrong.

"I don't know about his," I said, creeping hesitantly to the door.

"What? Like this gent is going to mind?" said Kirby jokingly. "He doesn't need all this room."

"Talking to the dead is one thing, but violating tombs? I don't know . . ."

Once inside the dark stone tomb, however, I was way more thankful for the shelter from the wind than I was committed to not breaking into dead people's final homes. The tomb was a lot warmer than it was outside, but it was also very dark. Even with the tomb door wide open, I could really only see half of each of the dead kids. The other half was completely obscured by the shadows. I had the strange sense that we were like a gang of fugitives huddled together in the dark, hiding from multiple divisions of law enforcement, or sort of like the singing von Trapp family from *The Sound of Music* pressed together behind convent pillars as Nazi soldiers panned spotlights back and forth.

"Did you have any trouble getting into Mrs. Tischmann's?" I asked.

"Girl," said Tabetha. "After hiding in the trunk of a carriage for months to get to this country, breaking inta' some ol' white lady's apartment was a breeze."

"Okay," I said. I chose to ignore that Tabetha was probably the only dead kid who'd spent an extended period of time silent in a box (unless you counted their caskets). "So, no problems?"

"No problems," said Cyril.

I followed Morna's gaze, realizing something had happened. Morna had unconsciously focused her eyes on Cyril's forearm, its grey flesh gnarled and torn.

"What happened to your arm?"

"Okay. One problem."

"Turns out, your teacher's yappy little dog could see us," explained Tabetha. "Cy here offered the use of his forearm as a doggie treat ta' keep it quiet. Just snapped his own arm off like a stalk of celery and fed it ta' the mutt."

"He was very brave," said Morna.

Tabetha rolled her eyes and I stifled the strong urge to vomit after hearing about Cyril's stomach-churning bravery.

"It should be fine," Cyril said, apparently referring to his chewed arm. I was more concerned for the little dog that had been gnawing on his dead flesh.

"The bad news," I said, swallowing some upchuck, "is that Mrs. Tischmann didn't do it."

"What?!" the dead kids all said, in some form or another.

"But she knew your teacher's past," said Derek.

"Yeah, but she'd known for years. She seemed really broken up by the whole experience. Trust me."

"She did have a lot o' photographs of her and yer teacher. They looked happy," Morna said.

"And the further bad news is that we have no evidence that links our remaining suspects to Mr. O'Shea's death, and it's Hallowe'en tomorrow. We have one more day to solve this mystery, and we have no useful clues whatsoever."

"Listen, lady. We did our best," Tabetha had prepared their defence.

"Shut up, Tabetha," Derek replied.

"I know you've all done your best — I'm just so mad it's ending like this. We'd come so far . . ."

"We still have another day," suggested Morna. "An' we can come back in a month."

"Yes," Cyril said. "What about what the custodian said? An instructor with a moustache — what about that Italian fellow you suspected? Sarducci?"

"*Santuzzi*. But just having a moustache isn't enough. It's like a moustache convention at my school. Even my friend Stacey tried to grow one. We don't have any evidence on Santuzzi, aside from the moustache and his dislike of the FLQ.

Though he was there the night Mr. O'Shea died."

"Who cares 'bout evidence?" said Tabetha, rolling up her dress sleeves. "You think it's him. Let's get the bum."

"I don't think we should rule out any of your other teachers, either," said Cyril.

"Tomorrow is Hallowe'en," I said. "Let me snoop around at school a bit and I'll come to the cemetery as soon as it's dark. Mr. Santuzzi's probably our best bet, but I want to make sure before we waste too much time on him. We're going to need all the remaining hours we can get. No waiting around until midnight."

"Won't people see us if we leave too early?" Morna asked.

"Everyone will be in costume for Hallowe'en — you'll probably just look like rich kids with really elaborate and expensive costumes. We can walk around wherever we want."

Tabetha was pleased. "I always wanted ta' look like a rich kid."

"What did you say about a school therapist?" Derek hesitantly asked the question that I'd truly hoped he'd forgotten.

"Yeah . . . uh, the principal thinks I'm creepily fascinated with Mr. O'Shea's death. He wants me to see a therapist." I crumpled inward into a little black ball.

"Therapist? What does that mean?" Cyril asked, and looked to Kirby and Derek. I guess he normally looked to them whenever he encountered some strange, futuristic new term.

"Uh . . ." said Derek, probably thinking of a way to describe the concept that didn't make me seem crazy.

Kirby stepped in to assist. "They think she's crazy," he said, and twirled his index finger beside his temple, the universal symbol of insanity. "And the therapist is going to try to fix her."

Everyone understood the concept of crazy.

"They think she belongs in an asylum," said Cyril.

"Fix her?" laughed Tabetha. "Might as well teach a pig to waltz. There ain't no fixin' a crazy woman."

I noted that the 1860s view of mental illness was not exactly enlightened. Seeing my death stare, Tabetha added, "Not that I think you're crazy."

"So, what're ye going to do?" asked Morna, not the least bit fazed that she was nearly touching knees with me, a bona fide lunatic. I decided I probably liked her the best, though I liked all the dead kids for different reasons. Even Kirby. I'd miss them, come November.

"Try to convince them I'm not," I said.

☠

I spun around a bit in my bedroom mirror, checking out the tentacles and bat wings at the rear of the suit. This marked the only time I'd ever been glad about having the mirror in my bedroom. True, I had some serious misgivings about wearing such a bulky outfit on my final mystery-solving day, but come on! It was Hallowe'en. Not wearing a costume was like robbing an orphanage on Christmas Eve. Well, probably not that bad.

No matter. My dad and I had made a mega-cheap Cthulu costume in one night, using mainly pipe cleaners, spray paint, electrical tape, and green nylon stockings stuffed with newspaper. Sticksville Central, say hello to the Lovecraftian ideal of evil!

"You look like a melting dragon," Dad commented, standing out in the hallway. His costume was pretty weak: a cowboy hat and plaid western shirt. He wasn't even in cowboy boots. "What's the matter, October? You look confused. Oh . . . *fine*. You look like 'the extreme embodiment of evil.'"

It was impossible to disguise the distress distorting my face from the stupid cowpoke in the hallway. Hallowe'en, usually so fun, was a convergence of several miseries this year — a therapy session with Ashlie Salmons, the end of my working relationship with the dead kids . . . I could probably count on breaking a limb somewhere in there, too.

"I completely forgot what today was," Dad said. "It's your appointment with the therapist. It won't be so bad, pumpkin." He sat me down on my bed and rubbed the greenish sludge on my back. "Trust me. I know a thing or two about therapists. Though you may want to rethink your costume."

"It's not that, Dad, it's . . . I don't know," but I couldn't continue. I didn't even know how to begin. There was too much I couldn't tell him.

"Whatever happens, you'll be fine, October. And just remember, going to see a therapist is no big deal."

On the way to school, I kept stumbling over some of my low-lying tentacles, nearly falling face-first into the damp leaves all over the sidewalk. Going to see a therapist had been no big deal, back when I was sure I wasn't mentally ill and was also certain a teacher at Sticksville Central was responsible for Mr. O'Shea's death. Now I was at a dead end — there was no real evidence that any teacher was involved, just my hunch that Santuzzi had a part in it. No one else, save the dead kids, believed me. There was a solid possibility that I was, in fact, *super*-mentally ill. How else could you explain my delusional beliefs that my math teacher was a killer?

I stared at the pile of pumpkins decorating the front entrance of the high school. How could I have been so wrong? Was Mr. O'Shea's membership in the FLQ a complete fluke? It seemed to have no connection to his death whatsoever.

☠

The corridors of Sticksville Central were filled, half with believers and half with blasphemers. Vampires, hippies, and zombies shared locker bays with the usual popped-collar jocks and thugs in training. And of course, there were the requisite number of sexy nurses, sexy cats, and even a few sexy fry cooks. My costume received a fair number of looks and catcalls ("What are you? A garbage dump?"), so I was relieved when I saw two friendly faces at my locker — Superman and Lois Lane — usually known as Yumi Takeshi and Stacey . . . maybe Lane *was* his last name?

And yes, they had gone the extra mile for costumes. You'd imagine Stacey would be the guy with the "S" on his shirt, but the reality was the exact opposite. Yumi stood about 5 feet in a full Superman suit, cape and all. Her short black hair was gelled into an impressive spit curl in the front. Stacey wore a lavender blazer and skirt the same colour black as his bobbed wig.

"Holy cow, Stacey. You planning on getting your teeth kicked in today?" I asked. It's like the guy went out of his way to be an outcast.

"Not the plan, but I recognize it's a definite possibility."

"Yes, I'm very proud of our boy Stacey," Yumi announced. "All appearances to the contrary, he's turning into a real man."

It wasn't all that daring. I mean, he *was* wearing flats.

"So, what are you?" asked Stacey. "A garbage dump?"

"No," I huffed. "I'm Cthulu — an ancient and very evil demon."

Yumi and Stacey's blank stares were interrupted by the morning bell.

☠

Surprise, surprise. Fun-loving Mr. Santuzzi arrived in math class sans costume. Though the pink tie, light grey slacks and vest he wore were something like a costume, I guess. He had worn them the week before, and the week before that, so it was like he had dressed up as . . . himself.

The alleged murderer/math instructor was teaching a lesson on triangles — the method by which you prove that two triangles are congruent, not to sound like a textbook or anything. Mr. Santuzzi was in the mood to test if his earlier lessons on congruency had made any great impression on us.

"Somebody . . . anybody . . . *October Schwartz*," Mr. Santuzzi locked me in his crosshairs and fired. I dropped my face into my upturned fist. "Can the walking garbage dump tell me what proofs are required to demonstrate Triangle ABC and Triangle DEF are congruent?"

"Two angles and one side, or two sides and one angle, or all three sides," I recited.

Of course my answer was correct. On top of being a crack

detective and friend to all sorts of dead children, I also happened to be a pretty darn good student. So Mr. Santuzzi could chew on that.

"That's right," Santuzzi said. "Remember, everyone. In math you must find your proofs before demonstrating congruency."

Maybe I wasn't mentally ill after all. It seemed probable before, but now, sitting in class with that hulk of a strange and threatening man, Mr. Santuzzi seemed more and more like a suspect. Maybe he had hidden his proofs too well; made it impossible to find his angles and sides. Aside from a serious distaste for the FLQ and an almost comically villainous handlebar moustache, Santuzzi had left no evidence. At that moment I hated math class with more verve than any of my fellow costumed classmates slumped at their desks like so many sacks of laundry.

As I approached our cafeteria table at lunch, I was greeted by the cheers of Yumi and Stacey, already seated and halfway through some hybrid of lasagna and sloppy joes. Tomato sauce dotted Lois Lane's left cheek.

"Here she is!" shouted Yumi.

"Entertainment! Entertainment!" applauded Stacey, with mock enthusiasm, like a parody of someone who got excited about things.

I tried to suggest, as loudly as I could with my eyes alone, that the two of them should politely shut up as I sat down beside the *Daily Planet*'s best reporter. That's Lois Lane, by the way. Clark Kent is a total ambulance-chasing hack.

"What are you two applauding about?"

"Lunchtime is always so entertaining when you join us," Yumi explained. "Fake moustaches, catfights over apple bobbing . . . I have my money on a live animal attack today."

"Rejects," said a random Roman centurion as he passed by the table.

I was about to protest my new reputation, but then I accepted it might not be entirely undeserved. Ashlie Salmons and her female entourage coasted by. Her friends were all dressed as variations on the "sexy" theme, but Salmons herself was positively understated as Daphne from *Scooby-Doo*. Maybe she chose it because the costume allowed her to wear a large pink belt.

"Nice costume," I remarked as the group stalled beside our table.

"We should have come to school dressed up together," said Ashlie with a plastic smile. "Could have been a group thing. I'm sure you could fill out Velma's costume. Or you could skip a costume altogether and go as the dog."

"You look nice," I said, as Ashlie's group floated on toward the front of the cafeteria.

"Was that sarcastic?" Yumi asked.

"I don't know." I was confused myself. What was happening to me? "What are you two doing for Hallowe'en?"

"Stacey's coming over and we're watching all of the *Exorcists*. Even the crummy new one. Wanna come?"

"Maybe," I said, fully aware that my Hallowe'en pursuits would all involve last-minute searches of teachers' houses with the dead kids. "I'll have to see how the therapy session goes."

"Oh, yeah," said Yumi, flinging away her red cape to reach into her bag. "Stacey and I got you something."

She then presented me with a bright yellow card, featuring a photograph of a golden retriever puppy in sunglasses and the words "Good Luck!"

"Thanks, but it's not a test or something," I said, quickly concealing the card in my backpack. "I don't think there's any luck involved."

"Okay. We just wanted to say something," Yumi said, then pouted.

"Thanks, guys, but I'll be fine."

Maybe I shouldn't have hidden the card so quickly. After all, it was really nice of them to think about me. I'd have never thought about getting either of them a gift for their upcoming appointments, whatever they might be. I realized I didn't even know their birthdays. And, yeah, I told them I'd be fine with the therapy session, but I barely believed that myself.

☠

24

Just before music class, I made the solitary walk to the office of the school physician and therapist (same guy). I totally didn't approve of the school saving a few dollars by doubling up on two-for-one specialists, but I really doubt Dr. Lagostina cared. The corridors around me felt like they'd been dialled to slow motion. I couldn't hear the other students talking in their costumes, just a general roar of sound. Dread must have been slowing everything down, utter dread about what might happen behind the psychiatrist's door with Ashlie Salmons. Who knew what terrible secrets she'd reveal?

"October," said the doctor behind the door. "I'm Dr. Lagostina. Ashlie has already joined us. Please have a seat."

Dr. Lagostina must have really wanted to remind us he went to medical school and had an M.D., because he was dressed like a surgeon, with seafoam green scrubs and latex gloves, a parabolic mirror strapped to his forehead, and a stethoscope around his neck. And this Hallowe'en costume was to supposed to inspire confidence in his therapy skills?

Dr. Lagostina's office was unusually designed for something inside a high school. His desk faced a wall, and, aside from his chair, the only other pieces of furniture were two burgundy armchairs, one of which I assumed I was supposed to sit in. Ashlie was already seated in the far chair. She was slouched into its corner, almost camouflaged in her super-sleek Daphne costume. Her eyes shot at me like a poison dart and she fidgeted with her little lavender boot. Everything about this setup told me I was walking into a trap, but I took my seat anyway.

The doctor was suspiciously tanned, considering it was fall here in the Northern Hemisphere. He wore oversized glasses on top of his oversized nose. (It was big, okay?) His tightly curled black hair crept out from under his surgical cap and up from his surgical scrubs or whatever they're called. Dad never told me what went on during his therapy sessions, so my only impression of therapists came from the movies. I half-expected Dr. Lagostina to whip out some ink blot tests and ask Ashlie and me what we saw.

Dr. Lagostina swivelled in his chair, and I got a little jealous. Why couldn't my chair swivel? Could Ashlie's chair swivel? I tried vainly to commiserate with her — *sucks about our non-swivelling chairs, am I right?* — but she just looked back with total disdain.

"Girls," Doctor Lagostina said, again swivelling. "Do you know why you're here today?"

"I think it has a lot to do with me elbowing Ashlie in the stomach."

"I agree," Ashlie said. "I, too, think it has a lot to do with her elbowing me in the stomach."

I wasn't so glad we'd made our truce at that point.

"That's certainly true," he said. "But there's more to it than that. Teachers and students have noticed a pattern of behaviour in the both of you. One of you shows no interest in schoolwork, is frequently tardy, and more frequently reported bullying other girls, while the other one of you is fighting, arguing, making inappropriate remarks on tests, and wallowing in inordinate sadness and gloom."

"You made inappropriate remarks on a test?" Ashlie asked, slightly impressed.

"Regardless," Dr. Lagostina said, interrupting a real bonding experience. "We feel these . . . tendencies . . . only amplify when the two of you are together. And we fear both of you may be seriously troubled but you don't know how to ask for help."

"Everything's fine, really," I said, speaking for us both.

"May I ask the two of you some personal questions?" he

asked, and opened two manila file folders flat upon his desk. I wondered what it said about me in that stupid folder; I resented that I'd probably never know.

"I guess we won't get anywhere if you don't," I mumbled. Dr. Lagostina chuckled a little and his stethoscope rattled.

"Everything we say in here is secret, right?" Ashlie asked. "Otherwise, I'm *not* okay with that."

"October, your dad teaches science here at Sticksville Central. Great teacher. How about your mom?"

"My mom ran away when I was a little kid."

Dr. Lagostina nodded and began scribbling in the file folder with a fountain pen. Ashlie and I glanced at each other. That would get annoying fast. But seriously, what kind of incomplete, half-baked file did he have if he didn't even know my mom left?

"How old were you when that happened?"

"Like, three or something."

"Did it bother you, growing up without a mother?" Dr. Lagostina inquired.

"Not really. I mean, I always wondered what happened to her, but my dad told me a little while ago."

"What do you mean, *what happened to her?*" he asked.

"Where she went. She just disappeared on my birthday and my dad never heard from her again. I don't think they're even divorced."

Again, Dr. Lagostina scribbled enthusiastically in the file folder.

"Now, Ashlie," he swivelled toward her chair. "Not to embarrass you, but your grades are rather poor. You were left back last year."

"So?"

"No reason," he said. "And you live alone with your mother, who is a Crown attorney, correct?"

"Yes, *and?*"

"Well, that must be difficult," he theorized. "I'd think a mom who is one of the chief lawyers in the area could be especially strict."

"We get along fine."

"Maybe we should change the subject," he decided, faced with Ashlie's stonewalling. "October, many of the teachers have said that you've acted strangely since Mr. O'Shea's death. He was your French teacher?"

"Yes."

"And when he died, that made you sad."

"Yeah. Of course."

"Of course, of course. But some people said it was more than sadness. They said that you were 'overly depressed' or 'morbidly fascinated' by Mr. O'Shea's death."

I could feel the anger inching through my veins. What teachers were saying this? And did Dr. Lagostina have to get into this with Ashlie right beside me? I just knew she was filing this stuff away for future reference.

"Several teachers said you made a series of attempts to attend Mr. O'Shea's funeral. Your eye makeup was smudged all over your face for the majority of the day. I hear you've been hanging out at the cemetery, too. What is this all about?" he said, and, looking up from the folder, lowered his comically large spectacles.

My dad had apparently turned on me, ratted me out. That stool pigeon! If I was ever going to prove I wasn't a total basket case, I might have to tell Dr. Lagostina something about my whole murder investigation. If I sat here, as silent as Ashlie Salmons for the whole session, it would just lead to more appointments.

"Okay, I'll tell you, but I don't want you to think I'm crazy," I squirmed in the burgundy seat. Ashlie straightened her back and leaned forward for the juicy details. Given who was in the room with me, I figured it was probably a good idea to gloss over the whole super team-up with five dead kids. But it was hard to figure out what to say. It was just as important to reveal that I wasn't morbidly obsessed with Mr. O'Shea's death — only justice. That sounded pretty wicked, actually.

"Of course not," Dr. Lagostina laughed again. "Nobody's crazy here."

Ashlie arched her eyebrows. At least the monster had a sense of humour.

"I thought . . . at first . . . that Mr. O'Shea's death wasn't an accident."

"You suspected foul play?" I surprised him. "But why would anyone want to kill Mr. O'Shea?"

I tugged at a loose thread in the chair's arm, but the look on Dr. Lagostina's face showed he wasn't in love with my attempts to de-thread his nice chair. "That's what I was trying to find out. I mean, how do you drop a car on yourself when you don't even have a key to the room? And I know it probably made me look ghoulish and morbid and all that, but I don't think that Mr. O'Shea was killed anymore . . . I, uh, closed . . . my investigation."

Dr. Lagostina began writing again in the file folder. At first, I appreciated the lull; I could relax and stop spilling my guts for a second. But once it started looking like he was working on a term paper, I got concerned. He must have believed I was so completely insane, he had to take down every word for posterity. I must have been the most fascinating psychological profile since that guy whose personality changed when he got a railroad spike shot through his brain.

"What?" I asked.

"What *what?*" he said.

"What are you writing? What are you thinking? There's a lot of writing happening."

"I don't think so," he decided.

"No, she's right," Ashlie said, popping a stick of gum into her mouth. "That's a lot of writing."

"Do you want to know what I think of your 'investigation?' My quick first impression?" he asked, briefly placing his fountain pen in his mouth before realized he'd put the writing end between his lips. "I think this mystery may be a delusion, a displacement related to your mother's abandonment. And perhaps it relates to your discomfort of not fitting in, being too young to handle high school, getting teased by some of the older, more socially adept girls like Ashlie here."

She smiled.

"And since you can't possibly make sense of all that discomfort or your mother's sudden disappearance from your life, you've transformed your teacher's accidental death into a mystery so you can try to solve it. To make sense of it."

Okay, so I really resented a couple things about that:

1. That Dr. Lagostina thought I was delusional and making things up.

2. That Dr. Lagostina thought I couldn't possibly figure out why Mom had left and where she went. I mean, that was all part of my uber-secret long-term plan.

"But why would I make it a mystery if there was no possible way I could solve it? If Mr. O'Shea's death was an accident, or I was just deluding myself, wouldn't that just frustrate me more?" I asked.

"I know," he said. "I don't understand that aspect at this juncture. We'll have to revisit it in later sessions, as there are two of you here today, and I can't let you hog all the time."

"Hog," Ashlie snickered.

Our truce was not working as planned. Dr. Lagostina was already talking about future sessions, plural.

"It's fine," I said, trying to salvage things. "I'm over it. Like I said, I decided it was an accident. My delusions are gone."

Dr. Lagostina seemed completely unfazed by my miraculous mental recovery. Instead, he wrote a few more lines in my folder, then swivelled over to Ashlie again.

"Ashlie, let's talk a bit about your previous year here at Sticksville."

"No, thanks," she declared.

"Then let's talk about the two of you together," he said. "We know how your conflict exploded that time in the cafeteria, but when did this little feud between the two of you start?"

"October ran into me after volleyball practice one night," Ashlie explained, leaping over whole weeks of her calling me Zombie Tramp. But I guess we were sticking to the truce, trying to get out of this therapy session with as little fuss as possible. I held my tongue. "I *might* have been smoking out by the basketball courts with my boyfriend, but that stays in this room, Dr. Lagostina. And October *might* have seen me. So we got into a little fight."

"October is against teenage smoking?" Dr. Lagostina asked, confused.

"No," she sighed. "I figured she was going to tell her dad about it because she hates me because I'm so awesome. Her dad coaches me in volleyball. I just knew the cutting volleyball to smoke thing would pop up at some parent-teacher night with my mom, so I *maybe* threatened her a little."

Dr. Lagostina turned back to me. "October, is that how it happened?"

"Almost exactly," I said, swallowing my self-respect. "And I probably would have told my dad, too. That was smart thinking of Ashlie, threatening me like that."

"My mom is strict, like you say, Dr. Lagostina," Ashlie explained. "So I can't take any chances of her finding out about any of the . . . uh . . . liberties I take. I'd already had a close call that night when Mr. Page saw Devin and me."

"Mr. Page, the history teacher?" Dr. Lagostina asked. "He saw you smoking on school property, too?"

"Yeah. At first I thought I was busted and Mr. Page would call my mom or give me detention or something destructive, but he just asked me for a cigarette and kept walking."

Dr. Lagostina went back to the manila folders with a vengeance. He added lines and lines to Ashlie's file, but her psychiatric record was still like a haiku compared to the epic poetry of my mental problems. More distressing to me was that Mr. Page was acting like some mid-life crisis on legs, borrowing cigarettes from students. I couldn't be sure if Ashlie was telling the truth about this or not.

"So, Mr. Page borrowed a cigarette from you, while you were smoking on school property," Dr. Lagostina said, verifying the statement.

"Yeah, I *know*," Ashlie said, shrugging her shoulders.

"I'm afraid I'll have to talk to Mr. Page about this," he said.

"I thought this was confidential!"

"He'll be here soon to change his bandages," Dr. Lagostina warned. "I need to check on that electrical burn of his. He hasn't had one of those since he stopped teaching auto shop."

Whoa, Dr. Lagostina. Way to be doubly not confidential. It was like he was a doctor of gossip. But in a more important way, he was like my hero, because he, with the help of Ashlie Salmons, had just provided a pantload of clues. Mr. Page was at the school the night Mr. O'Shea died, and he has an electrical burn. And he used to teach auto shop? I could have kissed Dr. Lagostina on his elephantine nose.

☠

25

Second sessions with Dr. Lagostina were scheduled for the following week, though luckily Ashlie and October no longer had to tag-team and take therapy sessions at the same time. October shook Dr. Lagostina's latexed hand, hastily split from Ashlie Salmons, and made her way to music class, now half over, all the while fearing that her delusions, as Dr. Lagostina had so kindly put it, were returning.

She flubbed note after note and choked on her big trombone solo during rehearsal because her mind couldn't stop rapidly building a case against her history teacher, Mr. Page. She now knew that he was the former auto shop teacher, he had a moustache, and, possibly, a key to the room. He was also at the school around the time Mr. O'Shea died and was apparently sporting a wicked electrical burn, concealed under his clothing, October guessed. Was it possible, she wondered as she opened her trombone's spit valve and shook saliva onto the carpet, could Mr. Page be the murderer? He had seemed so caring after Mr. O'Shea died, and interested in preserving his memory — but that's exactly what a clever murderer might do! And if Mr. Page was any kind of murderer, he would be a *clever* murderer.

Ms. Tischmann interrupted October's train of thought, chastising her for playing when she had only asked the woodwinds to play during the coda. Come on, woman! October can't think about codas. She's trying to solve a murder!

October's stomach dropped. If Mr. Page was, in fact, a clever murderer, he would know October was onto him. She had asked *him* about the FLQ. He had told her about Mrs. Tischmann's missing leg. This could all be terrible, horrible, very bad news. That is, it would be bad news if she could actually picture the goofy, curly-haired, bike-riding Mr. Page as a murderer, which was near impossible to do. Did Darth Vader ride a bike to work? Did Jack the Ripper think history was "neat"? And there were still suspects like Mr. Santuzzi and Mr. Hamilton to consider. Still, Mr. Page had a moustache, so it wouldn't hurt to have the dead kids stalk him.

☠

During history class — the most intense and harrowing history class October could remember, the intensity of which had almost nothing to do with the discussion of the federal election at hand — Mr. Page told October he needed to see her after class about her latest assignment, "Immigration to Canada in the Early Twentieth Century." Suspicious of his motives, October said she couldn't stay because she had to volunteer with the legally blind. Oh, why did she drag the legally blind into her web of lies? But, truthfully, she couldn't take any chances. Mr. Page had a slight chance of being a sociopathic, French-teacher-killing, meddling-thirteen-year-old-skinning machine, and a private after-school visit seemed far too risky a proposition.

"Then after the weekend? Monday after class?" he smiled.

"Sure," said October.

☠

October's afternoon limped along like it had been hit by a garbage truck. Why couldn't night fall at four in the afternoon? She began to think night would never arrive, and never before had she so desperately needed to speak with the five dead kids adjacent to her backyard. *Exorcist* movies with Yumi and Stacey had been discarded in favour of investigating the Mr. Page lead, but she regretted that she could have been watching Linda Blair projectile vomit instead of working through her homework on a Friday afternoon, killing time as best she could. She should have agreed to meet Mr. Page after class, just to have something to do. Even if that something was getting stabbed.

Her homework was intermittently stalled by infrequent trick-or-treaters who had started their rounds before the sun set, many of whom wondered aloud why October was dressed as a garbage dump when she answered the door to dump candy into their waiting bags. Mr. Schwartz's car rolled into the driveway at about five o'clock. Moments after he entered the front door, October was already pestering him about dinner, claiming she was famished.

Unfortunately, her dad was immune to her nagging — at least, he was that afternoon — so they didn't eat dinner until well after six.

Conversation centred on October's appointment with Dr. Lagostina, but only in the vaguest terms. Mr. Schwartz knew not to press too hard, and October didn't volunteer that she had been diagnosed as delusional. During the chit-chat, October could observe the colour draining from the backyard, shadows falling beyond the sliding glass kitchen door. Mr. Schwartz, upon finishing his meal, remarked that he was exhausted, and asked October if she wouldn't mind cleaning up on her own. And, of course, she didn't. Things couldn't have worked out better if she'd drugged her father. Soon he'd be napping in his office or bedroom: the perfect opportunity to hold an emergency meeting with the dead kids.

Mr. Schwartz retired to his office and October collected the sullied plates and silverware for washing. Never had she washed the dishes so quickly before in her life. October rinsed plates, bowls, pots, and glasses without wasting any time with soap, then gave them a slight pat with the checkered dish towel before lobbing them into whichever cupboard was closest at the moment. She flipped the lights to make the house look unoccupied. The bane of every serious trick-or-treater is the empty house, or house that is trying very hard to look empty. October hoped the darkened rooms would keep any eager kids from ringing the bell and waking her dad. Then she donned her jacket and cracked open the sliding door to the backyard.

And that was the moment her dad walked back into the kitchen.

Frozen on the kitchen tiles, he stood in disbelief. He couldn't have looked more disappointed if October had just announced she was dropping out of school, joining a nudist cult, and selling her kidney for a really cool collection of bottle caps. A half-graded lab report rested in his left hand.

"I thought you were sleeping . . ."

"October, I thought we had discussed this."

"Dad," October moaned. "I can't explain this, but I really have to go to the cemetery right now."

"October," he said. "I don't want you in the cemetery after dark. That's the end of it. I don't care if it's Hallowe'en."

"Dad," she pleaded. "This is a life and death situation."

"I know it must seem like that now, but whatever it is, it can wait."

Oh, the irony of his remarks!

"Please trust me," she begged.

"How can I trust you, October? You told me you wouldn't do this anymore, and yet, here you are!"

October had no response to that. How *could* her dad trust her? She was probably delusional.

"You're not leaving. End of story."

"I have to. I'm sorry, Dad." With those words, October made a break for it. She left the kitchen door ajar and galloped down the wooden steps, hopping the cemetery fence, and running into the impenetrable darkness. Thankfully, she'd had the sense to remove her bulky Cthulu costume before dinner; otherwise, she'd never have cleared the fence and would have ended up face down in the dirt. Her dad's shouts followed her flight:

"October! October! Come back!"

She didn't like to disappoint her dad, but it wasn't the end of the story, as her dad believed. She still had a mystery to solve. But, man, did she hope she was right about Mr. Page. She'd hate to be grounded forever because of a red herring.

She bolted through the aisles of tombstones. Her lungs felt like they might ignite like a box of matches. She ran at full speed, right past the big willow tree and nearly into Derek, who was explaining the process of safely driving an automobile to Cyril.

"Hold up, Living Girl. Where's the fire?"

The fire, at that moment, was in October's lungs. She puffed and panted, and it was a few seconds before she had enough breath to speak in complete sentences. "I was . . . need you . . . look . . . in history teacher's . . . house." Almost complete.

"Your history teacher?" said Cyril. "He wasn't even one of your suspects."

"Please," October gulped. She was bent over, holding her sides where the pain busily burrowed its way through her muscles. "I need your help to do this as early as possible. We only have a few hours left."

"Agreed."

"And I need to go with you."

"I do not think that's the best idea you've had," said Cyril.

"If I'm right about this," she said, "then Mr. Page knows that I know, and we'll need to call the police immediately."

Derek looked sombre. "I'll get the teacher address book. Round up the gang, Cyril. We've got a date with history . . . or the history teacher."

The two dead boys ran deeper into the forest. October remained in place and tried to catch her breath as it nimbly dodged her clumsy grasp.

☠

As the teacher address book revealed, Mr. Page lived not far from October's house, in a quaint little home on Overlea Drive. Well, the address book didn't reveal the size or quaintness of the house; that had to be discovered first-hand. It made a great deal of sense: Mr. Page biked to work every day, and October would sometimes see him pass during her morning trudge to Sticksville Central.

Huddled behind a large green power transformer at the end of Overlea Drive, October and all five dead kids surveyed the street. A few trick-or-treaters snaked their way down the curved road — a pirate, a scuba diver, and even a purple plush triceratops. The porch light at Mr. Page's illuminated the entrance where the plush dinosaur and scuba diver went to retrieve candy.

"That's his house," October said. "He's home. Be careful."

"We're always careful," said Tabetha.

"You stay here, October," Cyril demanded. "We'll see what we can find inside."

October agreed and lay in wait behind the cold, metallic cube of the transformer, quietly humming away. She monitored her surroundings at all times, twice being startled by kids in costume. She had an irrational fear that Mr. Page would leap out of the nearby hedge wielding a butterfly knife or nunchucks. October reasoned that the dead kids would probably find nothing of any consequence inside Mr. Page's home, and they'd all head home. The dead kids would disappear at the stroke of twelve and the mystery would remain unsolved.

The longer she waited, the more convinced October was that she was wasting her time. Mr. Page wasn't a murderer. He was the nicest teacher at Sticksville Central, save for poor Mr. O'Shea. Why would he kill Mr. O'Shea? To ensure the "nicest teacher" title was his and his alone? Besides, he had no connection to the FLQ. He was, like, twenty years younger than Mrs. Tischmann, and as clever as he was, he wouldn't have told her that much about the October Crisis if he had something to do with Mr. O'Shea's death. That'd be insane. This whole search was probably just, as Dr. Lagostina had warned, fuelling her delusions. Dr. Lagostina did seem like a perceptive guy, aside from when he accidentally tried to eat his pen. Remember that? Classic.

It felt like three years passed before she saw the ghostly figures of five children running toward her. "What did you find?" she said in her loudest stage whisper.

Tabetha spoke first, "He had a newspaper in his office."

"It was from the sixties. About a bomb at a shoe factory in La Grenade," added Kirby. Weird, huh? That the bombing happened in a town called La Grenade. You can't make that stuff up.

"Some old woman died, and the FLQ took credit. It's from 1966," said Derek.

"I can't believe it," October said, her hand involuntarily rising to her face. "He knew Mr. O'Shea was Henri LaFleur, and he said nothing. He's got a moustache and an electrical burn! All signs point to guilty! It must have been Mr. Page."

"What must have been Mr. Page?" someone asked.

October saw Morna's big white eyes climb above her head. Cyril started to shout when October felt a sharp poke between her shoulder blades. She spun around to find the real estate agent, Alyosha Diamandas, standing there in his wrinkled grey suit, pinking shears in hand. I don't think any of us expected that. What was he doing here?

"My old friends, the little dead children," he grimaced just at their sight. "And the daughter of one of my clients."

Then, boom! The butt of a rifle slammed into the side of Alyosha's skull, and he dropped to the lawn, completely out cold. The assailant turned the gun around in his hands to showcase the bayonet. Holding the rifle was Mr. Page in full World War I Canadian military regalia, his crystallized breath pouring from his open mouth.

"Yes. What must have been Mr. Page? And what was that about dead children?"

☠

"What must have been Mr. Page?" he asked again, rather innocently, though he hadn't moved the rifle's little knife thing, which was like a centimetre from my chest. I suddenly realized that my suspicions were correct. Mr. Page had definitely murdered Mr. O'Shea.

"Uh, nothing," I said, wondering if Mr. Diamandas was still breathing. "That's a great costume, Mr. Page . . . you should have worn it to school . . . a-ha . . . is that a real gun?"

This Mr. Page who'd surprised me in the dead of night, right after cold-cocking a real estate agent, was definitely not the goofy, curly-haired, smiling Mr. Page of Sticksville Central. While his hair hadn't changed, and he certainly looked goofy with his old-timey army fatigues, helmet, and machine gun or whatever, I was nearly peeing my pants with fear. He was smiling, but he definitely wasn't happy. His grin was fish-hooked into a distorted imitation of his usual face.

"Do you like it?" he asked. "It's an antique from World War I. Ross rifle. It doesn't fire, but the pointy knife on the end still works. Who were you talking to?"

October wondered who she was talking to, too. She suspected the dead kids were still behind her, but they hadn't said a word since the slightly disturbed Mr. Page arrived.

"You were talking about an Henri LaFleur. And you're here on my street in the middle of the night, talking with a plainclothes police officer."

"I think that was a real estate agent," I said. If this was how he treated someone trying to sell a house, what was he going to do to me, accusing him of murder?

"What were the two of you doing?"

"Trick or treat?" I offered.

"In class, you asked me about the FLQ. What do you know, October?"

It would have been a good time to plead ignorance, but I had a foolproof plan. "I know that you killed Mr. O'Shea, and soon the police will know."

Mr. Page's eyes widened. "It was an accident! An accident! You can't know!" he insisted. His left hand shot out and clamped onto my arm. I recoiled, but couldn't break free from him.

"Cyril! Derek! Tabetha! Everyone! Attack!" I yelled. "Attack!"

"We can't," whispered Morna, who appeared at my right side.

"Do something!" I shouted. My foolproof plan was blowing up in my face. Derek, Morna, and Kirby held onto me, and by all pulling together, I was just barely able to break loose of Mr. Page's grasp.

"Looks like your imaginary friends have left you," Mr. Page said. He couldn't see the dead kids. "Now, please, let me explain!" His voice was strained, desperate.

"Help! Help!" I shrieked.

"Shut up! Please! You're making a scene. Please, be quiet!"

"*Help!*"

The last thing I saw was the end of that Ross rifle coming toward me much too quickly. Then everything went black.

☠

When I woke up, I was extremely distressed to discover that I was blind. I was blind? Mr. Page must have clocked me harder than I'd remembered; my chubby rat paws would have to be my eyes now. I was having a lot of trouble using my hands, though. What was I going to do? Seconds later, I realized I only had a blindfold on and that I had been bound to a chair.

"Cyril?" I whispered. "Morna? Derek? Anyone?"

"We're right here." It was Kirby's voice that answered.

"We?"

"Morna, Tabetha, and me," he said.

"What's happening?" I asked, completely frantic. The last thing I remembered was a bug-eyed Mr. Page with a bayonet, and I didn't think he'd just vanished. Somebody blindfolded and bound me, and it wasn't the dead kids.

A doorbell rang in the distance.

"You're in the history teacher's house. He has you all tied up, but he's in the other room. I think he's tryin' to figger out what to do next," Tabetha said.

"Actually, I think he's answering the door and passing out candy," Kirby said.

"He hit ye' in the head," said Morna's voice, somewhere in the darkness. It was like listening to music while asleep.

"You should be quiet," suggested Kirby. "He doesn't know you're conscious yet."

"Why don't you dead kids *do* something?" I begged. What was the point of having these dead kids as friends, anyway? "Punch him in the neck. Use your ghostly supernatural powers!"

"We canna'," Morna said.

"What are you talking about?"

"We can't consciously harm a living person," said Kirby. "Remember?"

I don't remember anything about that, and I even wrote down all their lame ghost rules.

"You think you could have reminded me of this *before* my history teacher attacked me with a bayonet?" I whispered.

"Oh, it's not like he hit you with the sharp end." Kirby: a portrait of sympathy.

"Well, you can do *something*, can't you?" I whined. "Scare him away?"

"He canna' see or hear us, but Cyril an' Derek are working on tha'," said Morna.

"Okay, good." I tried to collect my racing thoughts. It was like trying to keep three hundred rats in a shopping cart. Why was Mr. Page the one person who couldn't see the dead kids? Seemed like every other moron in town could. "Dial 911 on the telephone," I told them.

"They won't hear us," said Morna.

"Doesn't matter," I shook my head. "Just call and leave the phone off the hook. Maybe they can trace the call and find me here. Happens all the time on television." I was assuming that was really what happened, though maybe it was too much to assume that the Sticksville police had those capabilities.

I heard Kirby dash off to find a telephone and the next thing I knew, Mr. Page, looking very panicked, was tugging the blindfold from my eyes.

"Talking to yourself again?" he asked. I refused to even look at him, the monster. "I don't know why I bothered to blindfold you. You know what I look like . . . and you know where I live."

"If you're going to kill me, you should just do it," I said defiantly. Then I thought I maybe shouldn't be quite so forceful. I should probably stall for time, if either the telephone trick or Cyril and Derek's mysterious plan were going to work. Besides, I was in no rush to be dead, really. Luckily, it seemed Mr. Page wanted to stall for time himself.

"I'm not going to kill you," he said. He was sweating quite a bit. The collar and armpits of his shirt were soaked through and his hair was ruffled into an impressive bird's nest. Even his moustache looked askew. "I'm not. I'm . . . I don't know what I'm going to do . . . but you can't tell anyone what you know. Understand?"

The doorbell rang again.

"No!" He raked his fingers through the bird nest. "You stay here and be quiet."

Mr. Page swiftly made his way around the corner, leaving me alone with the dead kids in what I could now identify as the laundry room. My chair was chained to a sink. From the front door, I could hear Mr. Page appraising the trick-or-treaters' costumes, "Ooh, what a brave little fireman. And a donkey? Oh, okay. A *bunny*." Would it have made any sense to yell? I mean, if there were any, like, strapping adults with strong arms or semi-automatic weapons chaperoning the kids, that could really have helped me out. But before I could wonder much more, Mr. Page was back, rubbing his tired, red eyes.

"Maybe . . . maybe . . . if I just *explain* what happened — how it was an accident — you'll understand."

Then, it was like I was suddenly transported into one of Usher's music videos. The lights flashed on and off and the strobe effect gave Mr. Page's face and gestures a demonic appearance. Morna and Tabetha were rapidly flicking the light switch, trying to distract Mr. Page, but he barely noticed. They ran to the kitchen and I could hear them smashing the dishes, sending soda glasses and wine goblets to smash on the tile below, but my history teacher had one focus only, and unfortunately, that was me.

"Yes, I found out who Mr. O'Shea really was. Mr. Henri LaFleur. *Phoney!* . . . I've always been interested in the FLQ and the October Crisis. My grandmother was one of the first casualties of their stupid, useless war. You'd think being a receptionist for a shoe factory would be . . . would be risk-free!"

The FLQ killed his grandmother? But Mr. Page couldn't have been old enough to know her if she'd died in 1965. Maybe that's why he couldn't see the dead kids, because he had no real connection to her, so it was bizarre how enraged he was about this dead grandma he'd never met. Maybe he felt he'd missed out on years of pinched cheeks and hard candy.

The doorbell.

"Leave me alone!" he shouted at the ceiling. But with the second bell, he dutifully retrieved the bowl of fun-sized candy and answered the door. "Wow! A mummy . . . look at you! And some football players!"

I decided I should definitely scream, strapping adults or not. "Help!"

The front door crashed closed and Mr. Page blasted into the laundry room like a battering ram. He crammed my old blindfold into my mouth. The freak nearly choked me with it.

"Be quiet! Be quiet!" he panted. "You're just lucky it was only three idiot teenagers at the door. . . . So, where was I? *Yes!* Mr. O'Shea was Henri LaFleur. I even did my thesis on the FLQ at Western University," Mr. Page said, totally oblivious to the kitchenware still shattering away in the next room. "And when I discovered that Henri LaFleur — a name I'd been familiar with for years — was now Terry O'Shea, my co-worker . . . well . . . a fellow teacher! Teaching *French*! The gall of him. I . . . well, I lost control a little."

"*Hypflk ddd ufyonnnow?*" I tried to ask, the more important syllables interrupted by the gag in my mouth. Mr. Page plucked the cloth from my mouth. Thick gobs of my spit fell to the laundry room floor. I wanted to puke. "How did you find out?"

"Through the mail."

I certainly didn't think that was going to be his answer.

"In the office, each of us teachers has a mailbox. A few weeks ago, I received an envelope addressed to Henri LaFleur," Mr. Page explained. "I guess because I'm the only Henry at school, the receptionist thought it was close enough. But I read it with some interest, having seen the name before in my somewhat obsessive research on the FLQ. It was from someone named Celeste Boulanger."

Celeste. That was the burning kisses lady Henri wrote about in his journal.

"In the letter, she said she was dying. Apparently, she wanted to write her old boyfriend Henri one last note — seemed like she was writing all her old boyfriends — and had somehow figured out what school he taught at; but not, I guess, his new name. Or she didn't bother to use it, at least. Oh, if I'd never seen that letter —" Mr. Page stared at the floor a long time before continuing.

The doorbell rang again. And again, he shoved the dirty cloth back into my mouth and headed for the front door.

"Oh, Superman and Lois Lane!"

"Mr. Page? Why are you dressed like history's first G.I. Joe?"

"It's Hallowe'en! I'll see you kids Monday."

Yumi and Stacey! How could I warn them? But it was too

270

late. Slam went the door, and out came the gag again.

"Celeste — she enclosed an old photograph of herself and Henri, and I recognized Mr. O'Shea immediately. I couldn't believe — here — evading the — the — and my *grandmother*? I didn't know what to do."

Listen, I'm really sad for your grandmother, I thought, *but you killed my French teacher, you psychopath.* Tabetha and Morna rushed back into the room, looking mega-distressed. I couldn't help them out. If the man wasn't scared of poltergeists, I was out of luck, and probably about to join the ranks of the dead kids myself. How I hoped that phone call trace thing wasn't just a TV trick.

"I'm sorry!" Morna said.

"What is this guy, deaf?" said Tabetha, and kicked the wall in disgust. Mr. Page didn't hear that, either.

"I sent him a few anonymous letters, informing him that someone knew his FLQ secret, threatening him to get him to quit and turn himself in to the police. But my letters didn't seem to have any effect."

Mr. Page had threatened Mr. O'Shea. That explained how he'd had time to leave clues, like the map and the picture of Phoebe Cates. It was still weird that he left them for me, though. I'd helped him find his glasses at an ice rink; it's not like I had a degree in advanced criminology or something. Mr. O'Shea must have had a lot of misplaced faith in me. It would have been sweet if it didn't make me so sad.

"So . . . so I stayed late that night. I confronted Henri LaFleur in the auto shop. I left the door unlocked so he could get in to see his car. I didn't want to — I never meant to kill him," he pleaded and pulled at his collar, like he needed more oxygen or something. Maybe I'd be lucky and he'd pass out. "I was just going to threaten him with the lift. Maybe I'd . . . I could have called the police, locked him in the shop with my keys. I don't know!" He howled. "I shouldn't have threatened him with the lift, because once I saw his perfectly calm face, I just wanted to smash it in! I shouldn't have even been there!"

From the garage, I could hear an engine start and a car

horn honk wildly. That must have been Derek and Cyril's master plan, but Mr. Page was super-deep into his confession now. He didn't even glance behind him when the car engine started revving.

"I don't know what I was thinking," Mr. Page wailed. "I wanted to give him a scare. I wanted to destroy the youthful bomb maker, but Mr. O'Shea was just an old man. If he left that auto shop, I knew he'd leave Sticksville forever, and I couldn't let that happen. *Couldn't.* I'd changed my mind. It wasn't fair, after what he did to my family. I shoved him under the lift and kicked the switch until the car dropped!" As Mr. Page tried to continue his story there was a loud knock at the front door.

"More trick-or-treaters! Use the doorbell!" Mr. Page was exasperated.

Could it be the police already? The knock seemed insistent. Purposeful. Maybe the noise Derek and Cyril were making had attracted a few irate Sticksville homeowners, concerned about the rapidly plummeting charm of the neighbourhood. Mr. Page just ignored the door.

"It was happening too fast. My hands were on him, shoving him before I knew what I was doing — the lift dropped too fast. And I was kicking . . . It — it was an accident!" He tore the blindfold from my mouth like he was starting a lawnmower. "I never meant to — You understand, don't you?! You know about his past. He's a killer!"

The insistent knock persisted.

"There's someone at the door," I said.

"And?"

"Don't you think you should get it? You answered the door for all the other trick-or-treaters."

"How stupid do you think I am?" he laughed. "You want me to answer the door? I'm not answering it. Hallowe'en is officially over. Don't get distracted. Do you understand? It's not my fault. It's *not*."

Tabetha ran to the front hallway, doing Mr. Page's job in his absence. She must have opened it, because the knocker stepped inside the house.

"Hello? Henry?" My dad's voice was the one echoing down the hallway. "Henry, are you home? I was on your street . . . looking for October. She's kind of run away, and I'm looking for her . . . but I walked by your house and heard this racket in your garage. Came by to check on you. Are you okay?"

I started crying, and this time I didn't care that I was breaking my stupid no-tears pact. I'd never been so grateful to have a concerned and nosy parent before in my life. I mentally promised to bake Dad a pumpkin pie if the two of us ever escaped from Mr. Page's house alive. I started to scream, but Mr. Page muffled me with the balled-up, saliva-soaked cloth he'd been using.

"You stay here," Mr. Page whispered, as though there was anywhere I could go. He picked up his World War I rifle from the corner, secured his helmet, and slowly stalked down the hallway.

Morna, the only dead kid left in the laundry room, God bless her, helped me extract the gag from my mouth.

"Dad!" I screamed, but Cyril and Derek's unfortunately timed second attempt at the car horn made my screams completely inaudible. "Untie me," I choked. Now that Mr. Page was no longer within prime choking distance, this seemed the best option. "Morna, he's going to kill my dad!"

☠

Mr. Schwartz called out again, but he was mostly drowned out by a final horn blast from the garage. "You haven't seen October, have you, Henry? Your car is making some strange sounds . . . " He explored the house with an inordinate amount of caution. No idiot, he realized something weird was going on from the explosion of car sounds in the garage to the front door that magically opened by itself.

Kirby, Tabetha, Cyril, and Derek reconvened in the laundry room, running through the overturned baskets and detergent bottles to surround October, bound beside the dryer. Derek and Cyril had abandoned the garage once they recognized their "haunted car" ploy was failing miserably.

"Help Morna untie me!" she whispered to Cyril, now concerned it was too late to warn her dad. Screaming would only make Mr. Page do something horrid and irreversible. "Derek, Tabetha — take care of my dad! Don't let Mr. Page hurt him!"

Cyril and Kirby set to work with Morna, quickly loosening the ropes that bound October, and Derek and Tabetha sprinted out of the room, not bothering with the door.

Further down the hallway Mr. Page hid in the corner like it was a foxhole, readying his antique rifle. The calls from October's dad increased in volume as he neared Mr. Page's hiding spot. The dead kids could hear his light footsteps just around the corner. They scurried around the bend unnoticed by Mr. Page and saw Mr. Schwartz, only steps from the unhinged soldier and the business end of a 1914 vintage bayonet. Mr. Schwartz's sad eyes searched the dimly lit household for any sign of his colleague.

"Henry?" he shouted. He thought he could hear noises closer to the back of the house.

Henry — that's Mr. Page to you kids — leapt out from the dark corner and held his weapon in front of him like a magical wand. He was quivering with a volatile cocktail of anger, panic, and regret — and itchiness. The old uniform was made of wool or something terrible like that. The rifle's blade was old, but still looked sharp enough to classify as an instrument of death. Mr. Schwartz lifted his hands defensively, and tried to figure out what dreadful situation he'd walked into.

"Sorry to do this, Schwartz," Mr. Page said, "but I don't know what else to do." He was visibly shaking. With a deep breath, Mr. Page thrust forward with the bayonet at October's dad's very soft and vulnerable chest.

At that moment, Tabetha and Derek bent down and each took one of Mr. Schwartz's thin ankles, then pulled with all their might. With a loud thud, Mr. Schwartz rudely greeted the floor and nearly lost consciousness. The bayonet stabbed at the vacant air and missed Mr. Schwartz completely.

Mr. Schwartz groaned. Tabetha shouted, "Pull!"

In front of Mr. Page's disbelieving eyes, the prone body of October's dad was pulled backwards along the wooden floor by unseen forces at an astonishing rate. Mr. Page upturned his bayonet and stabbed at the floor, hopping like an indignant leprechaun.

"We're lucky October's dad doesn't weigh much," said Derek, yanking on Mr. Schwartz's pant leg. "Otherwise he'd be a pincushion by now."

"We're luckier he's wearin' a belt," said Tabetha, also tugging on a pant leg. "Or he'd be stabbed and pantsless."

Mr. Page took a wild stab at Mr. Schwartz's head and narrowly missed his neck, which was careening backward along with the rest of Mr. Schwartz all over the long, narrow hallway. The blade's tip lodged in the wooden floor and Mr. Page couldn't, for the life of him, free it. As he struggled with the rifle, he witnessed Mr. Schwartz's body, legs in the air behind him, slide over the threshold of his front door and into the front yard. He let out an anguished cry of desperation and left the rifle jammed into the floor as he chased his new nemesis outside.

Meanwhile, October grew impatient with the glacial slowness with which three dead bodies attempted to untie her from the chair. She had no idea how long she'd been unconscious, but apparently it was long enough for Mr. Page to unleash some of his prize-winning knots.

Cyril deftly loosened the knots that bound October's legs. Morna and Kirby were having considerably more difficulty with the ropes around her waist and arms.

"Cyril, you like to drive, right?" October asked.

"Yes, ma'am," he said, moving on to her arms.

"Is Mr. Page's car still running?"

He nodded.

"When I'm free, can you drive his car into the street and put on the emergency lights? Did Derek show you where those were? The button looks like a triangle," October said.

"I got the waist!" shouted Morna in delight as the ropes slid down October's sides.

"Not to question your authority," said Cyril, still working on the ropes binding her arms, "but why did you send a girl with Derek to help your father and leave me here fiddling with ropes?"

"Tabetha can handle things," October said, sincerely hoping that Tabetha and Derek were, indeed, handling things. "Besides, you're a shipbuilder, right? I needed your expertise with knots."

He made a facial expression that blended a grimace with a smile. "Well, you've got it."

That second the final knot came undone, and October jumped to her feet. Cyril dashed to the garage, while she sprinted down the hallway. October grabbed a broom standing in a dusty corner, sidestepped the free-standing bayonet in the corridor, and leapt out the front door. Morna and Kirby tailed close behind.

On Mr. Page's front lawn, she saw her history teacher dressed like all was quiet on the western front, swinging his fists at her dad, who was staggering to his feet like an optimistic drunk. Derek and Tabetha were at her dad's side. They'd kept him alive this far; now it was October's turn. Morna and Kirby dashed ahead of her and bowled over Mr. Schwartz, who was getting pushed around quite a lot. Mr. Page, fists clenched, stalled for a second, trying to comprehend Mr. Schwartz's sudden collapse, but his thought process was quickly interrupted by the sensation of his left knee exploding, splintering, and yowling in agony as October swung the wooden broomstick against it.

Mr. Page joined his fellow teacher down in the leaves and grass of his front lawn, deciding it was far too painful to move in any way. His heart was pounding, his authentic costume now drenched with authentic sweat, and he could really use a rest. Though his vision was a bit blurry, he could see his student, October Schwartz, standing above him, jet black hair flopped over one eye, blood running down her forehead and a push broom in her hand.

"That explains things," he gasped. "You're a witch."

Mr. Page's garage door, previously so innocuous, squealed and groaned and finally burst apart as a battered minivan tore through the aluminum and swerved out into the street. The four-way flashers blared on, and Cyril left the van running as he joined the collection of living and dead people scattered on the lawn.

October followed the dead boy's lead and hurried over to her

278

dad, whom the dead kids had dragged a safe distance from Mr. Page. When she looked down at him, she found he was muddied and bruised, but mostly okay. The dead kids exchanged inscrutable glances and quietly retreated to the darker nearby areas of Overlea Drive. In a couple hours, it would be midnight, and they had a strict curfew tonight.

"Oh, Dad. You're okay," October said, and dropped to her knees to hug her father.

"October, you're bleeding," he said, noticing the red trail along her forehead. "Wait. Did Mr. Page — you were in his house?" October's dad began to understand some things. He had an undeniable urge to get to his feet and stomp repeatedly on the history teacher's crotch.

"It's okay, Dad," she said, recognizing that urge in his facial expression. "I'm okay." Tears came to her eyes again, partly due to the overwhelming situation, but mostly because the dramatic action of dropping to her knees had caused way more pain than she'd anticipated.

"October, I'm sorry I got so —" Mr. Schwartz started, but the rest of what he had to say was swallowed by the blaring sirens of the police cruisers that rolled noisily into Overlea Drive and scattered the few rubbernecking trick-or-treaters who'd stumbled onto the bizarre late-night tableaux.

☠

28

Death Be Not Prompt

The good news — you know, aside from my dad and I not dying and Mr. Page being caught — was that the police bought my made-up story. Ghosts didn't come up at all. But the bad news was it was nearly eleven o'clock and in about an hour, the dead kids would disappear from my life . . . at least for a couple weeks. Sitting in the police station, waiting for my dad to explain his portion of the story, I couldn't help but think about Mr. Page and Mr. O'Shea.

If Mr. Page had been telling the truth, he murdered Mr. O'Shea in a moment of anger that got out of hand; he hadn't planned to kill Mr. O'Shea. If I hadn't figured things out, he would have continued to teach history competently and be a law-abiding, tax-paying citizen for the rest of his life — a citizen with one deep, dark secret. Was he really so different from Mr. O'Shea?

Mr. O'Shea had inadvertently committed a terrible crime in his youth — maybe even killed Mr. Page's grandma and blown off Mrs. Tischmann's left leg — and he hadn't turned himself over to the proper authorities. He ran, hid, changed his name and his entire life, and lived with his secret. If I'd known what Mr. O'Shea had done, would I have turned him in, too?

I guess I should have just been glad I never had to make that decision. Though, in a way unfortunate way, the arrest of Mr. Page was certainly going to bring Mr. O'Shea's dark secret to the forefront. Before, his students just thought he was bad with a mechanical lift. Soon they'd know he was a teenage mad

281

bomber. I hadn't really thought about that when I was obsessed with finding his killer. Justice can really be the worst sometimes.

☠

Only due to my dad's complete exhaustion was I able to sneak back into Sticksville Cemetery one last time before November. We got back home around 11:30 and my dad faceplanted into his pillow like he'd just come home from a fun run across the Himalayas. I waited all of two minutes (maybe not my most cautious decision) before making a break for the cemetery gates.

Everything had happened so quickly, I hadn't had the chance to say goodbye to the dead kids. The earliest I'd see them would be the next full moon and they'd just saved my dad's life . . . seemed really awful to let them vanish or get sucked back into hell or whatever happens to them without so much as a thumbs-up. But trudging through the darkness, I couldn't help but notice the reason this roller coaster of mystery had all began. So even though the clock was ticking, I took a minute to finally say goodbye to my poor, complicated French teacher: *Au revoir*.

Before, I'd avoided Mr. O'Shea's gravesite on purpose. I mean, I'd been to the cemetery nearly every evening since Mr. O'Shea died, but this was the very first time I'd stopped to visit his grave. It seemed wrong to even dare to go near it while the mystery was still unsolved. But with his killer in custody, I felt like it was maybe time to see my French teacher and curling coach again.

The headstone was rooted in a plot of mostly unoccupied land. In time, other bodies and coffins would move in, begin to crowd Mr. O'Shea, and surround his marker with newer, modern, flashier headstones. But for now, Mr. O'Shea was alone, I guess kind of like he'd been for most of his life.

I started to head toward the clearing where I expected the dead kids to be, but as soon as I turned, I found Sticksville Cemetery's five best detectives behind me, helping me keep Mr. O'Shea company in his final resting place.

"Thanks for joining me, guys," I said. "Sorry I'm so late."

"So this is him?" Derek asked.

"This is he," Kirby corrected.

"Nice to finally meet the guy we went to all that trouble fer," said Tabetha.

"You need more time?" asked Cyril as he turned to leave.

"No," I answered. "I think I'm okay."

The six of us moved slowly through the cemetery, even though only ten minutes separated us and midnight, wading through a shag carpet of dead leaves, gradually making our way back to the massive willow tree.

"You know, ya' did pretty good with that crime-solvin' stuff," Tabetha said. "For a livin' person, that is."

"Mmm," agreed Kirby. "I'm impressed with what someone like . . . you . . . was able to accomplish."

"Thanks," I nearly blushed at the idea. I felt like I had made mistakes at nearly every turn. Surely a good detective wouldn't nearly get herself and her dad killed by a century-old rifle. But maybe I did all right. "I have to thank each of you, too, for all your help. And, y'know, saving both my life and my dad's."

"Don't mention it," said Derek, though he, too, was clearly blushing.

Morna broke into a big, toothy smile. "It was fun."

"I owe you all so much," I said nervously, "and I know you don't have much time. It's almost midnight. But I'd like to repay you somehow. I want to help you solve your mysteries." I only half-believed the words pouring out of my mouth myself.

"What mysteries?" Tabetha said.

"You were all killed, but you don't know how or why. That's why you're ghosts, right? Wouldn't you like to find that out?

"Kirby," I continued, "why did you die at thirteen while all your siblings lived? Tabetha, you have your suspicions about what happened to you. Wouldn't you like proof about who cut your time in Sticksville so short?"

I was wearing the dead kids down, I could feel it.

"Cyril," I turned to the boy in the tricorn hat. "I know you're dying . . . figuratively, of course . . . to know what

283

happened that night in 1779 or whenever. And Morna, if I were you, I'd want to know the name of the monster that left my body in a cold, snowy alley. Derek, your killer might still be out there. We could find whoever it is and bring that person to justice."

I finished what I thought was a pretty rousing speech and took a deep breath.

"So you've found some way to travel through time?" asked Derek Running Water excitedly.

"Uh . . . no."

"Well," huffed Tabetha, who crossed her arms. "Then how exactly do ya' intend to find this stuff out?"

"Uh . . . well, it will be like I'm travelling through time with my . . . um, research and . . . uh . . . personal interviews . . ." I lamely offered.

The dead kids were *not* impressed. I don't wear a watch, but there must have been five minutes left to midnight. Why were they making things so hard?

"Okay," I said. "How have you been making out on your own?"

From their total silence, I could tell they hadn't made any progress solving their own murders. Most of them had probably given up on knowing decades ago, though the mysteries must have still bothered them, like pebbles in their ghostly little shoes.

"Are we not the Dead Kid Detective Agency?" I asked, officially naming our weird little club. "When I raise you next time, it's not going to be all about board games. Let's solve some mysteries! What do you say?"

"Yer going ta raise us again?" Morna asked with hope in her eyes.

"Of course. Next chance I get," I said. "I can't imagine what the next month will be like without you. I'll be here with my book at the next full moon."

"November 28th," Kirby informed the group. "Mark your calendar."

"Just one last thing," I said. "Right now, it's my one mystery to your five. Seems a little lopsided."

"Oh, what now?" blurted Tabetha.

"Was another of your teachers killed?" Kirby asked. "Do you have several suspected murder cases on the go? I just knew the girl who frequented the cemetery would be really creepy." This from a talking corpse in a boys' school uniform.

"No," I said. "Just one more case to even things out. After I help you solve your mysterious deaths . . . I want you to help me find out where my mom is . . . she ran away ten years ago. Can you help me find my mom?"

Cyril, without consulting the other ghosts, immediately agreed.

"What time is it?" Derek asked. He looked around, a bit skittish.

"Can't be too long until midnight," I answered.

There was nothing left to talk about. In moments, the dead kids would vanish and I'd be alone in the cemetery and no matter how many times I read my book, they couldn't come back until late November. And though it was only a few weeks, it seemed like it would be forever. In so many ways, Cyril, Tabetha, Morna, Derek — even Kirby — were as close to me as Yumi and Stacey. Closer, even. And soon they'd be vanishing from this mortal plane or sphere or whatever the phrase is. Who knew if reading that passage from *Two Knives, One Thousand Demons* aloud would even work on November 28? I'd added pages to the book in the interim; was that against the rules? These ghost rules were totally random.

Either way, the dead kids were disappearing soon. At least for a month. Possibly forever. Knowing myself, dealing with that absence was going to be a bad scene. Coping with loss, as I ably demonstrated with Mr. O'Shea, was not my specialty.

"I think it's happening," Cyril gulped.

Before I could say anything or do anything — what was I going to do? Grab at their hands? Fall to my knees in agony? — my five dead friends started disappearing from the feet up. Outmoded and ragged footwear vanishing, followed by knee socks and pantaloons, until only their sad, ashen faces remained floating in the dark.

"Please come back," I called. But they couldn't answer. Nothing remained. Not even Cyril's stupid hat or Tabetha's braids. I'd have even killed for an insult from Kirby.

The total lack of ceremony — no light, no music, no ominous wind — made me nearly as sad as the actual dead kids' absence. Not knowing what else to do, I walked back to the house, resolved to do the only thing I really knew how to do when I cared about someone: solve their mystery. First chance I got, I was hitting the history books at the library.

☠

Just like that, the Dead Kid Detective Agency wrapped up its very first case and set off on, let's assume, a long career of uncovering the most pernicious crimes in the town of Sticksville's history. A beautiful yet morbid friendship had been cemented.

But I suppose you'll want to know what happened immediately afterward.

Police business first. Mr. Page confessed to the murder of Terry O'Shea, but October Schwartz didn't press charges for the whole abduction thing. Currently, Mr. Page is in prison awaiting his trial, at which he intends to plead guilty. He was in a wheelchair for a month due to his injured knee. And he was fired from Sticksville Central, obviously.

Second, the father-daughter stuff. Following that terribly exciting Hallowe'en night, and after Mr. Schwartz slept for a million years, October and her dad had a very quiet weekend recuperating at home. Saturday morning, October could be found at the kitchen table with a half-eaten bowl of Quaker oatmeal, scribbling away in her *Two Knives, One Thousand Demons* notebook. She wasn't penning the adventures of Olivia de Kellerman anymore. Instead, she was recording what she could remember of Mr. O'Shea's mystery and how the dead kids helped her solve it. Maybe the adventures of the Dead Kid Detective Agency would prove to be a more inspiring topic. October had a crazy idea that once she'd typed the story up, she could use it to help Cyril, Tabetha, and Morna learn to read. A simpler book, one that didn't use big words and phrases like "liberation" and "Phoebe Cates," would have probably been more appropriate, but what did October know? She was thirteen and certifiably delusional.

Mr. Schwartz casually placed the maroon Scrabble box in the middle of the table and noticed his daughter toiling away in her book.

"Haven't you had enough knives for one weekend?"

"That was a bayonet," October replied.

"I know you're working on your book, but can I interest you in a game?"

A few words into the game, Mr. Schwartz began to ask his daughter the questions he hadn't been able to ask late last night while he lay prone on Mr. Page's neatly trimmed grass. His colleague had killed another colleague, who was once a member of the FLQ, as far as he understood it. Not the kind of Hallowe'en memories he wanted his daughter to treasure.

"October," Mr. Schwartz said, linking "V-E-I-L" to an "S." "Were you spying on Mr. Page? Is that why you were over there?"

October wondered how much she should tell her dad. If he was worried about her spending time in the cemetery, he'd probably be way less enthused with her cloak and dagger work. And any mention of dead kids was surely off-limits. Besides, she missed them too much to even think about mentioning their existence. As far as her dad was concerned, October decided, his ignorance was her bliss.

"Why would I spy on my history teacher?" October said, acting offended by the mere insinuation. "I ran away after our . . . fight . . . and when I was walking down Overlea, I ran into Mr. Page, running around in his costume."

"Really."

"He must have already gone mad from guilt or something. The unit on the October Crisis was coming up in class."

"Well, the important thing is that you're okay now," he said, rising from the table to make some tea. "That must have been very scary for you. I know I was terrified. How's the forehead?"

"Fine," she said, touching the bruised area of her hairline. "Still hurts when I touch it. Or when Voldemort is near."

"Don't say his name out loud," her dad whispered.

"I mean You-Know-Who."

Mr. Schwartz placed the full kettle onto a stovetop element. "The strangest thing about last night is that I really felt like I was moving under someone else's power. Like somebody was shoving me out of harm's way."

October watched her dad grow more and more flustered as he tried to explain the phenomenon without getting, you know, overly spiritual.

"Look at me," he said. "Your clinically depressed dad's going to need a new batch of pills. That's what you're thinking, right? I'm just telling you how it felt."

"Maybe you have mental powers," October said, fishing a bag of chocolate fudge cookies out of the kitchen cupboard.

"Like ESP?" he asked. "I thought about that. I mean, my body moved where I wanted it to move, somehow evading Henry's attacks. I suppose it's possible. But I would have thought I'd have a little more control over it. Y'know . . . like floating through the air instead of sliding backward on my face."

October nearly choked on a mouthful of cookie, she laughed so hard. "Can you pour me some tea?" she asked.

"You know, another thing I can't get my head around is how the police never suspected Henry."

"It did look like an accident, I guess."

"Yes, a case of Occam's razor, I suppose," her dad said, filling two mugs. He handed the one with a black cat on the side to his daughter.

"What? Occam's razor?" She'd never heard of Occam before, not to mention his shaving products.

"It's a science term. A principle, really," her dad, captain of the nerd team, explained. "It says that for whatever results you achieve in an experiment, the simplest explanation for those results is most likely the correct one."

October nodded as she emptied four — no, five — spoonfuls of sugar into her mug.

"So, the police saw what looked like an accident, could find no evidence to the contrary, knew of no enemies of the victim and concluded it *was* an accident. Occam's razor."

"But that wasn't what happened at all."

"Well, Occam's razor isn't a hard and fast rule," said her dad. He sighed, scratched at last night's five o'clock shadow — now much more like a solar eclipse — and drank from his "Scientists Do It Methodically" mug.

Once you befriend dead kids and discover your teachers are former Quebecois bomb makers and murderers, Occam's razor must not apply. Simple explanations jumped out the window the moment October first saw Morna MacIsaac in the Sticksville Cemetery.

"I hope you're not worried," Mr. Schwartz said to his kid. "This sort of excitement isn't typical in Sticksville, I'm sure."

A semester hadn't even passed and already October had been found out as a baby, labelled a basket case by most of her peers, and nearly been impaled by her bayonet-wielding history teacher. Things could only improve. But with five dead kids scheduled to make a return appearance outside her backyard within a month, she imagined things in Sticksville were only just beginning to get unusual.

☠

Monday, November 3rd was October Schwartz's first day back at Sticksville Central, and despite the absence of Mr. Page, things remained pretty much the same as they'd always been.

Rumours about Mr. Page started inching through the school by nine o'clock. There were rumours that he had been arrested. Rumours that he was wanted for arrest, but he'd fled to the United States and adopted a new identity and was currently working in a high-end dog grooming salon or washing dishes in a Malaysian fusion restaurant. Reports varied. But as to what he was or wasn't arrested for, there were a multitude of theories. Most assumed he was a child-snatcher. Wouldn't you?

But Mr. Page wasn't the biggest news after the weekend. Travis Belluz puked down Megan Davies's shirt while getting to second base at some costume party on Friday night, and that was way more scandalous. And revolting.

Other kids continued to talk about October behind her back, but now they talked about her rumoured involvement with Mr. Page's arrest, in addition to her suspected mental illness and her age. Ashlie Salmons was still the devil, and continued to make October's life intolerable, and Mr. Santuzzi was just as strict and unsettling a teacher as ever. October honestly had trouble not thinking of him as a murderer. It seemed so right! Occam's razor, proven wrong again. When did the stupid thing ever work?

Waking her from a daydream in Monday's math class with a shout, Santuzzi reminded October, "In Singapore, they have public canings for people who can't pay attention."

Okay. That guy was *really* not a murderer?

Yumi and Stacey were still the same people they had always been. When October met them in the cafeteria, they had countless questions about Mr. Page's arrest and the rumours that surrounded it. Yumi, in particular, was eager to glean everything she could.

October told them about how she'd been kidnapped by Mr. Page, about the bayonet and soldier's costume, and about how Mr. Page had caused Mr. O'Shea's "accident." Again, the crucial aspects of her murder investigation and the presence of a certain number of dead kids were omitted from the narrative, but the details she revealed were shocking enough for Yumi.

"What? That's for real? I thought that was just his stupid history-based Hallowe'en costume. I didn't think he'd gone insane."

"We went trick-or-treating at his house," Stacey said.

"We didn't go *trick-or-treating*," said Yumi, smiling over Stacey's memory gaps, embarrassed to be sitting with a trick-or-treating loser. "Don't listen to him. He's a drummer. He finds the board game Risk fascinating."

"We did too go trick-or-treating."

"Oh no! You were probably there! All chained to a drainpipe or locked in a cupboard or something," she said. "I'm sorry! We *were* there. I'm so sorry."

Yumi had greeted this new information with an equal measure of horror and joy — horror that her good friend had experienced such a frightening imprisonment, but sheer joy at knowing someone involved in something so cool. Yumi would definitely be one up on her cousin now, in the information department at least. Stacey, as usual, was rather blasé about it, and treated October as if her big revelation had been that she was originally from Iowa. October sometimes felt Stacey was like a taller, less dead, slightly more masculine version of Morna in that respect. She wondered if they could be related, but she couldn't remember Stacey's last name at the moment.

"So, are you free Friday night?" Stacey asked.

"Um, I think so. Why?"

"There's another concert at the Y. Yumi and I will be in attendance, and there's an extra working seatbelt in my dad's car."

"Oh, *please come*," Yumi insisted.

"Well, my dad's a little strict about me leaving the house after the kidnapping," October smiled. "But I'll see what I can do."

"Hey, Zombie Tramp," shouted Ashlie Salmons, interrupting a totally perfect Kodak moment. "I heard you and Mr. Page were going to elope when the police busted him. Honeymoon in Niagara Falls. How'd that work out for you?"

What a hosebeast. Things were definitely back to normal at Sticksville Central.

☠

That afternoon, October strode into the Sticksville Public Library, coasting across the carpet like a heat-seeking missile aimed at the history section. She found several books on the pre-war era, Canada's involvement in World War I, and the country's immigration waves. She photocopied every scrap of information she could find about Sticksville, Ontario, in the early twentieth century. She even pocketed a pamphlet offering a walking tour of the historic pubs and restaurants of Sticksville and its surroundings.

She needed everything she could find. After all, a dead Scottish lass was counting on her.

☠

October Schwartz: she's the protagonist of the book. If you're having a hard time keeping track of her, you should probably put the book down right now. Enrol in a remedial English course or something.

Mr. (Leonard) Schwartz: October's dad and a teacher at Sticksville Central High School. He teaches auto repair and biology, and probably important life lessons to October, or whatever. He's also been clinically depressed since October's mom left the both of them.

Yumi Takeshi: October's best friend at Sticksville. She shares October's interest in black clothing, eyeliner, and horror movies. She also comes as part of a two-friend package deal with Stacey.

Yumi Takeshi's cousin: Yumi's mythical older cousin and an oracle of sorts on all matters pertaining to local Sticksville teenage gossip.

Stacey [Last Name Unknown]: friend to October and constant companion to Yumi Takeshi. A lanky boy with an affinity for mismatched vintage clothing and percussion instruments.

Ashlie Salmons: terror of the unpopular ninth grade girls at Sticksville Central High School. Loves include belts, boots, bangs, and bullying. She leads a small crew of mostly unpleasant young ladies. Salmons was left back a year for reasons unknown. (She probably just didn't study enough or something totally unmysterious.)

Mr. Hamilton: new principal of Sticksville Central High School, he's a recent transfer from Central Tech High School in Toronto.

Mr. Terry O'Shea: October's French teacher, who coaches the girls' curling team and introduces October to the writing of H.P. Lovecraft.

Mr. Henry Page: history teacher at Sticksville Central High School. He's an enthusiastic bike rider and local historian. And stamp collector, let's say. I don't know for sure, but it sounds right up his alley.

Mrs. Eileen Tischmann: the well-meaning but somewhat flighty music teacher at Sticksville Central High School.

Mr. Santuzzi: stern mathematics teacher at Sticksville Central High School, noted for his tight leisure suits, alleged toupee, and military past. He says things like "roger" and "lock 'n' load" when teaching lessons on factoring.

Cyril Cooper: unofficial leader and oldest of the dead kids. He was from a Loyalist family who fled to Canada during the American Revolution, and had a possibly promising career in shipbuilding cut short by a mysterious assailant. Cyril is fascinated by automobiles.

Morna MacIsaac: youngest of the dead kids, Morna was a Scottish immigrant who came with her family to Canada in 1910 for work and affordable land. Instead of finding much of either, the MacIsaacs lived in squalid tenement housing until Morna was killed outside a local pub. She's the first dead kid October ever encounters and the one who leads her to the others.

 **Tabetha Scott:** dead kid who had to escape slavery in the American South before arriving in Sticksville. She left Virginia via the Underground Railroad and settled in town with her dad. Bickers endlessly with Kirby and never hesitates to share her opinions.

Kirby LaFlamme: dead kid and one-fifth of the not so famous LaFlamme quintuplets. During the Depression, he and his siblings were the inspiration for the LaFlammetown theme park. He was outlived by all his brothers, and is fluent in both French and English. (This becomes totally crucial.)

Derek Running Water: the most recent of deaths among the  dead kids, Derek lived with his mother in Sticksville, but became politically committed to the Mohawk Warrior cause with the 1990 standoff in Oka, Quebec, the events of which led to his death. Derek can be relied upon to provide explanations to the other dead kids for modern technology and terminology. But he's not great with directions.

Alyosha Diamandas: one of Sticksville's most persistent realtors. Alyosha feels a healthy real estate market is indicative of a healthy democracy. He thinks *Glengarry Glen Ross* is a documentary and is the sometime nemesis of our dead kids.

Olivia de Kellerman: fictional heroine of October's horror opus, *Two Knives, One Thousand Demons*. Fated to fight alone (with occasional help from her wheelchair-bound Uncle Otis) against hell's hungry hordes, Olivia likes sharp things and dislikes evil.

Dr. Lagostina: Sticksville Central High School's resident twofer: part physician, part therapist. He, unlike most normal people, likes listening to people's problems.

a-ha: only the biggest Norwegian rock band of all time! Known best outside of Norway for their mega-hit "Take On Me," which boasted one of the coolest music videos of the 1980s. (The girl falls into a comic book, and then the hot guy in the comic book escapes into the real world!)

Blaise Pascal: a seventeenth-century French mathematician best known for inventing calculators while still a teenager, and devising the Pascal Triangle. No relation to the Bermuda Triangle.

Bruce Campbell: the square-jawed and legendary B-movie actor who plays Ash in the *Evil Dead* movies (see below). He was also Brisco County in *The Adventures of Brisco County, Jr.*, but I really doubt you'll know what that is. He does make a cameo appearance in every Spider-Man movie, as a wrestling announcer, snooty usher, and waiter.

Darth Vader: one of the main villains of the *Star Wars* movies. Big guy with a deep voice and dresses in black. You probably have seen him. Carries a lightsaber and (spoiler alert) is the dad of that Luke Skywalker kid.

Encyclopedia Brown: boy detective in a series of children's mystery novels written by Donald J. Sobol.

***Evil Dead* movies:** a trilogy of horror movies directed by Sam

Raimi and starring Bruce Campbell that feature the many horrible things that can go wrong when you open the *Necronomicon*, the book of the dead. Over the course of the films, the tone grows gradually more comic, but all three should really not be viewed by anyone without a strong stomach for pencil stabbings and gushing blood.

French foreign legion: an especially elite branch of the French army known for their military skill and intense bond. Its soldiers come from many different countries.

G.I. Joe: name for a series of toys (and later, television series) developed by Hasbro, featuring figures representing the various sectors of the American armed services. More generally, "G.I. Joe" referred generically to American army servicemen during World War II.

Glengarry Glen Ross: a play (and later film) by David Mamet about the desperate lengths real estate salesmen go to in order to avoid being fired. Amazing and glorious in its use of profanity. It's like the Sistine Chapel of the F-word.

H.P. Lovecraft: early American author of particularly weird horror stories, many of which featured ancient demons, the horror of the abyss, and unholy summonings.

Jackie Chan: if you don't know who Jackie Chan is, drop this book immediately and go rent *Police Story 2* or *Project A 2* or something. Forget *The Karate Kid* and *Rush Hour*. Go for the Hong Kong stuff. You'll thank me later.

Jack the Ripper: notorious serial killer in Victorian London who terrorized the neighbourhood of Whitechapel in 1888 with a series of particularly gruesome murders.

The Jetsons: animated television series from the early 1960s about a family living and loving in the futuristic utopia of 2062.

They have a robot maid, floating cities, anti-gravity boots, and many other things we aren't anywhere close to having yet. (If you sense bitterness, you're not mistaken.)

Jefferson Airplane: psychedelic rock band that originated in 1960s San Francisco. Headed by lead singer Grace Slick, they recorded "White Rabbit" and "Don't You Want Somebody to Love?"

Johnny Depp: do you really need to be told who the sexiest man alive is?

Kodak: at one time, photographs had to be taken on film. There were no digital cameras, just film ones. Kodak was a manufacturer of film, and they had a whole advertising campaign about "Kodak moments," heartwarming memories captured on film to treasure forever.

Linda Blair: the actress who portrayed the kid who gets possessed by the Devil in *The Exorcist*. You know, the girl whose head spins around and who projectile vomits all over her mom as the priests try to save her.

Little Rascals: a group of impoverished neighbourhood children who were the subject of a series of early film comedies, and who had such colourful monikers as Spanky, Alfalfa, Buckwheat, and Stymie. Most of the child actors died under unusual circumstances before the age of forty.

Martha and the Vandellas: Successful Detroit-based R&B group who recorded in the 1960s and early 1970s with Motown Records. Best known for hits "Heat Wave," "Nowhere to Run," and "Dancing in the Street."

Meat Loaf: one of the greatest rock 'n' roll vocalists of all time, known for his hit *Bat Out of Hell* albums. Got the nickname of Meat Loaf due to his considerable girth.

Morrissey: the enigmatic lead singer of 1980s British rock group The Smiths, who is known for his melodramatic lyrics, pompadour, and controversial opinions. He sings like an angel, my friends. An angel!

Mr. Pibb: a knock-off version of the soft drink Dr. Pepper. Popularized by Chris Parnell and Andy Samberg in their song, "Lazy Sunday," with the line, "Mr. Pibb and Red Vines equal crazy delicious."

Nancy Drew: famous fictional teenage detective who appeared in a series of novels first published in the 1930s by Carolyn Keene. Here's a mystery solved: did you know Carolyn Keene wasn't a real person? Just the pseudonym for a syndicate of ghostwriters. Much like 'Evan Munday.'

Neil Diamond: legendary Jewish singer-songwriter, and the man behind such hits as "Sweet Caroline," "Solitary Man," "Girl, You'll Be a Woman Soon," "I'm a Believer," and many others. Sometimes known as "The Jewish Elvis," and no, I'm not making that up.

REO Speedwagon: have you ever said "I can't fight this feeling anymore?" Well, so did this rock band from Champaign, Illinois. And they set it to music, and turned it into one of the biggest singles of all time.

Rick Moranis: a Canadian comedic actor probably best known as the dad who shrunk his kids in *Honey, I Shrunk the Kids*. But he also played Louis Tully in *Ghostbusters*, an unlucky sap who gets possessed by a spirit and turned into a demon dog over the course of the movie.

Robert Smith: lead singer of the popular goth rock band, The Cure. Best known for his mop of black hair and penchant for hastily applied lipstick. The voice behind "Lovecats," "Friday I'm in Love," "Just Like Heaven," and all those songs.

Roy Orbison: beloved American musician with an unusually powerful voice. He looked a bit like a shop teacher from the 1950s on his way to a funeral and wore sunglasses at all times of day. He was the singer of songs like "Oh, Pretty Woman," "Only the Lonely," and "Crying."

Scooby-Doo: Long-running cartoon series from Hanna-Barbera that follows the adventures of four unlikely friends/meddling teenagers (Fred, Daphne, Velma, Shaggy) and their inexplicably talking dog, Scooby-Doo, as they solve supernatural mysteries. Haunted houses are investigated, teenagers are chased, large sandwiches are eaten, Velma's glasses are lost, and the ghost or monster is invariably revealed as a crochety old carnival owner or somebody like that.

Sex Pistols: pretty much the most important punk rock band of all time. You should learn the names Johnny Rotten, Sid Vicious, Steve Jones, and Paul Cook soon, because it will come up later, I'm sure. The band behind the songs "God Save the Queen" and "Anarchy in the U.K."

Siouxsie and the Banshees: well-known early British goth rock band active from the late 1970s to the early 1990s. Lead singer Siouxsie Sioux is, like, the template for female goths the world over.

The Sound of Music: a musical by Rodgers and Hammerstein based on the real-life experiences of Maria Von Trapp and the Von Trapp family singers. A nun named Maria leaves the convent, becomes an au pair for an Austrian military man, teaches his kids to sing, but then they must all flee due to the rise of Nazism. That old story. The movie version stars Julie Andrews (Mary Poppins) and Christopher Plummer (General Chang).

Stephen Colbert: American comedian and satirist best known for his fake news show, *The Colbert Report.* Have you noticed that weird elf ear he's got? He likes those *Lord of the Rings* books, too. Maybe he's part elf?

Stephen King: uh, just about the biggest horror writer of all time. Have you ever heard of *Carrie*? *The Shining*? *Salem's Lot*? *Pet Sematary*? Well, he wrote them all.

Stuart Townsend: that Irish actor who played Lestat in one of those vampire movies and Dorian Gray in that terrible *League of Extraordinary Gentlemen* movie. He's okay, I guess.

Thunderdome: back when Mel Gibson was cool, he was in a series of Australian post-apocalyptic movies in which he played the character Mad Max. In the third film, Mad Max encounters Thunderdome, a steel-caged gladiatorial arena. The only rule: "Two men enter, one man leaves."

Tom and Jerry: cartoon cat and mouse duo who attempted to kill or maim one another in a series of cartoons produced by Hanna-Barbera. They were the inspiration for the much more homicidal Itchy and Scratchy, who appear on *The Simpsons*. Jerry, the mouse, typically got the upper hand.

Tommy James and the Shondells: American rock 'n' roll group of the 1960s who recorded hits as often as you or I eat hot breakfasts. Their best known songs include "Hanky Panky," "Crimson and Clover," "I Think We're Alone Now," and "Mony Mony."

Usher: recording artist Usher Raymond IV, who you might remember from such jams as "U Got It Bad," "Yeah!," and "Confessions, Part II." For the sake of the book, you only need to know his videos have high production values and could induce epileptic seizures.

Vincent Price: totally creepy actor who starred in countless horror movies over his career. His money-maker was his distinctive and authoritative voice. If you've ever heard Michael Jackson's "Thriller," Price provided the spooky voice during the bridge.

The Wicker Man: cult classic British horror movie about a devout Christian policeman who is sent to an island of Celtic pagans to find a missing girl.

Acknowledgements

Thanks to forever-friends Callie and Molly for reading and enthusing about way-early drafts of this book, which were probably not even that good. Thanks, too, to Stacey May Fowles, for being incredibly supportive of this book before even reading a word of it. Many thanks to Elise Cole and the Oakville Public Library's teen advisory group for acting as an early focus group for *The Dead Kid Detective Agency*, and to the Toronto Reference Library for giving me an ideal spot to write the first draft.

I also want to thank the whole amazing ECW crew, especially editors Erin Creasey and Michael Holmes, for believing in this book and making it all it could be (kind of like my own personal U.S. Army), Jenna Illies for publicizing and promoting the snot out of it, Jennifer McClorey for doing a bang-up copyedit, and Jen Hale for correcting all my errors, making invaluable suggestions, and giving me a reason to make videos of myself watching *Buffy the Vampire Slayer*. Thanks to David Gee and Rachel Ironstone for making the novel look three million times more dazzling than I could have imagined, and to reader Hadley Dyer, who helped give the book its shape and structure.

Finally, thanks to all my friends and family for being supportive about all my inane, ridiculous ideas (book-related and otherwise). Superhuman thanks go out to my parents and my brother Andrew (who is looking more and more like Crispin Glover), to the gang at Coach House Books – especially Alana, Leigh, and Christina – for teaching me almost everything I know about book publishing, to my fellow illustrators in SketchKrieg! for making sure I'm always drawing, and to my number one lady, Grace, for everything else.

Here's a sneak peek at Book Two of

The Dead Kid Detective Agency

1

Nobody could replace Mr. O'Shea. Until someone did.

That part shouldn't be overly surprising. With a French teacher dead and a history teacher imprisoned, Sticksville was the place to be for the ambitious yet unemployed teacher on the go that November. What *was* surprising was that October Schwartz encountered said French replacement in the town's public library that Sunday. October couldn't fathom why the new instructor — Ms. Fenstermacher — was spending her Sunday with all these books and severely outdated computer terminals. Wasn't that like a police officer spending his vacation reading courtroom transcripts?

"October!" Ms. Fenstermacher called as loudly as the regulations of the library would allow and waved both hands, like she was treading water.

October had really wanted to hate Ms. Fenstermacher: it would have been so much easier for her cognitive processes if Mr. O'Shea's replacement had been someone despicable or even someone forgettable and bland. The trouble was, October couldn't help but find her anything but . . . well . . . kind of awesome. Suspiciously so.

Okay, so I recognize that teachers, as a species, are never awesome. But check this evidence: Ms. Fenstermacher's hair was nearly as black as October's and defied all gravity and logic, she wore thick framed glasses, and referenced *Battlestar Galactica* in front of October's class three times in her first week of teaching. She certainly wasn't going to be mistaken for Mr. Santuzzi. October looked up from the historical atlas of Sticksville spread across the study group table and returned the wave as noncommittally as possible. It was encouragement enough: in moments, Ms. Fenstermacher was standing over her shoulder.

"What brings you to Sticksville Public Library this dazzling Sunday afternoon?"

Let's assume that was an ironic usage of the world "dazzling." Though the weather forecasts called for overcast skies, chilly temperatures, and light rain on November 27th, Mother Nature had exceeded all expectations, pulling out a truly miserable day in the clutch. Outside the floor-to-ceiling length library windows, it looked like sewer water was being hosed down from the rooftops.

"Oh, stuff," October answered. And by "stuff," she meant, "some last-minute research on Sticksville in the early twentieth century and the MacIsaac family in particular because I've slacked off all month and I'm raising a few friends from the dead tomorrow night so we can figure out who killed one of them." "Stuff" was more concise.

"I won't keep you from your stuff," Fenstermacher said — finally, a teacher in Sticksville with a sense of personal space. "Besides, I've got movies to borrow. I just wanted to say hello."

With that, Ms. Fenstermacher — clearly vying for "cool grownup" status, and in a much more hamfisted way than Mr. O'Shea ever had — departed for the DVD section, leaving October to her historical cartography. And not a moment too soon: the instant her new French teacher had caught her eye with that awkward hand greeting, October Schwartz uncovered what she'd been searching for over the past hour: the address of the boarding house where a living Morna MacIsaac had done that living about a hundred years earlier.

As insinuated earlier, October hadn't dedicated as much of her free time that November to historical research as she'd originally planned, and the calendar indicated that the full moon was only one night away. She was glad to have at least one shred of evidence she could present to Morna when she resurrected her, alongside Cyril Cooper, Tabetha Scott, Kirby LaFlamme, and Derek Running Water. She didn't want to look like a *total* deadbeat.

October eyed the plain wall clock above the library's checkout desk. She still had a couple hours until her dad expected her back at home and the address she'd found in the atlas for The Crooked Arms boarding house wasn't but a fifteen-minute walk from the library. Granted, that fifteen minutes would be spent in the frigid, filthy acid rain being vomited from the grey clouds above, but it was an easy walk otherwise. (And yes, The Crooked Arms was the name of the boarding house. It's totally conceivable as a boarding house name.)

She clapped the dusty atlas closed, wiped her likewise dusty hands on her black jeans and pulled her black umbrella (dust-free at the moment) from her backpack. She hoped the current owners of whatever The Crooked Arms was now were friendly. Or not murderous, at the bare minimum.

☠

Where are my manners? I apologize — we just leapt into the fray (if a public library can ever be described as a "fray" of any sort) without so much as a welcome. So, welcome, dear readers, to the second adventure of the Dead Kid Detective Agency. Ta-da! You can expect much of the same — our plucky heroine with a penchant for black clothing and her five most deadest BFFs uncovering dark secrets that rock the quiet town of Sticksville to its secretly rotten core and doing so in the zaniest possible ways. But one thing you can't expect is yours truly.

Tragically, I won't be around to comment on what's happening with October and her dead friends in the here and now. Instead, I'll be magically transported back in time, like some modern-day Marty McFly or Scott Bakula, to 1914, the year when our favourite ghostly Scottish lass Morna MacIsaac met her untimely end. I'll be relegated to describing horse-drawn coaches and coal chambers and other such terrible things, but it's not all bad. There's a mystery, after all, and a mystery that involves (spoiler alert) illegal immigrants, suffragettes, saboteurs, and famous inventors, just to namedrop a few highlights. But I still have the opportunity to set the scene in contemporary Sticksville, so let us continue.

✄

The Crooked Arms was at the end of a sad street named Turnbull Lane. The surrounding neighbourhood wasn't one October frequently visited, and given that she was a thirteen-year-old without a crippling gambling addiction to off-track betting and no need for a condemned pawn shop, one can understand why she wasn't familiar with the area. She was, however, determined to become familiar with it, if this was Morna's old stompin' (and dyin') grounds. She trudged through the rising mud puddles, passing deserted storefront after deserted storefront, her umbrella just barely maintaining its integrity in the wind and driving rain. Given the dismal conditions, it was impossible to tell if the weather or downtrodden state of the street accounted for the complete lack of people.

At Turnbull Lane's end, facing an empty, garbage-strewn lot that rose to a hill, stood The Crooked Arms. Three storeys tall, it had seemingly been built by carpenters with crooked arms themselves (hence the name?), or perhaps a crooked construction company. The winds appeared to be the only force keeping the clapboard walls from toppling over. October scanned every single one of the old boarding house's shuttered windows and determined it had long ago been abandoned. The home where Morna had grown up now looked so eerie, it could have been the inspiration for the Bates Motel. October wondered if it had been as dilapidated when Morna had slept inside its walls.

October also noticed one other crucial feature of the lot during her quick visual inspection of The Crooked Arms: a large sign planted in the brown grass and weeds that informed residents that the house was scheduled for demolition early the following year.

✄

The next afternoon, Sticksville Central High School's favourite dictatorial math teacher, Mr. Santuzzi, dismissed his second-period class with an ominous warning: "This Thursday is our unit test on the Pythagorean theorem. Don't let it be your last."

Their last test on the Pythagorean theorem? Their last test ever? Was capital punishment on the table for math class? Had it ever really *not* been on the table with Mr. Santuzzi as teacher? The questions were endless, so the cryptic threat stuck with October all the way to the cafeteria, where she met with Yumi Takeshi and Stacey Whatshisface. The month that had intervened between that fateful Halloween night when Mr. Page was arrested and now had certainly not witnessed any spike in the trio's popularity. They remained about as desirable to most classmates as back acne. They stood as the final bastion of the outcast table, like astronauts in a capsule from which mission control had cut off all communications.

Yumi and Stacey were attempting to rein in massive smiles when October sat down across from them. They weren't a humourless bunch, but grins of that magnitude were cause for some alarm.

"What?" October demanded, picking a label off her apple with her ragged black fingernail. "What did I do? Did I get eyeliner all over my mouth again?"

Yes. That had happened. Two weeks earlier, "Zombie Tramp" was briefly replaced by "The Bearded Tramp" for a short spell.

"No. Nothing like that," Stacey insisted. "It's good news. I swear."

"Who's got two thumbs and a radio timeslot?" Yumi asked. Then, jamming her thumbs toward her face: "This guy!"

Yumi and Stacey folded into the cafeteria table with laughter.

"I don't get it," October said.

"You're sitting across the table from the new Thursday lunch-hour DJ of Radio Sticksville High. I'll be playing all your favourite hits — or, more accurately, all *my* favourite hits — for my adoring cafeteria audience every Thursday afternoon."

"Since when does this high school have a radio station?" October asked. A fair question, since they were currently seated in a completely music-free cafeteria environment.

"We're starting up Radio Sticksville in December. The radio station equipment was always there," Yumi explained. "There just weren't any teachers willing to supervise."

"And who's supervising it now?" October asked, chomping into her Red Delicious. "Not that really old guy who took over for Mr. Page?"

"No," Stacey said. "It's your hot new French teacher."

Ms. Fenstermacher was trying way too hard; she really needed to tone down the whole 'hip teacher' act: develop a weird facial tick or wear sweaters from Northern Reflections or something.

"She's not that hot," Yumi argued.

"She is — and I don't make this designation lightly — a stone cold fox," Stacey rebutted.

"That's great, Yumi. How did you get the DJ job?" October asked, ignoring the total grossness Stacey was currently demonstrating.

"They wanted a grade nine to DJ one timeslot, and I guess I had the best music selection."

"You were the loudest," Stacey corrected.

"Yeah, yeah. Listen to your Walkman while I perfect my DJ name," Yumi said.

As instructed, Stacey returned to his Walkman while October and Yumi brainstormed the ideal DJ moniker. By the end of lunch hour, they'd narrowed it to two choices: DJ Yu-sless and DJ CD-Ramen, though they agreed the latter might be kind of racist. Who should interrupt this pivotal decision-making process but Mr. Schwartz, arriving without warning or apology in the cafeteria doorway. He had callously abandoned one of his science classes to make the trip downstairs.

"Heads up," Stacey warned, pulling out his earbuds. "Dad alert, October."

The warning came too late. Mr. Schwartz had already beelined to the outcast table, and pretty much every other table with any level of social standing degenerated into giggling, finger-pointing, and general derision for October and her whole "rogue dad" situation.

"October!" Mr. Schwartz exclaimed, brushing his chalky hands on his brown slacks. Do people still say slacks? That's what they were. "I'm so glad I found you."

"Dad," she stage-whispered through clenched teeth. "Could

this not wait until after school?"

"Sorry, pumpkin," he said, almost as if he was taking some perverse pleasure in his daughter's suffering. "But that's what I need to talk about. I have to stay extra-late today for volleyball. Our girls are on a roll. We could make it to the championships!"

"That's great, Dad. Really," she wanted to be proud for him, but more importantly, she wanted him to be gone. She directed her dad to the door with a dramatic roll of her harshly outlined eyes. "I'll see you later tonight?"

"Your friend Ashlie Salmons is really a phenomenal player," he continued, an unstoppable embarrassment machine. "Behaviour issues aside, she's going to take us to the regionals, I'm sure."

October no longer wanted to be proud for her dad. Her friend, Ashlie Salmons? October nearly blew apple chunks all over her dad's chalk-streaked shirt. Instead, she merely frowned and arched her brow.

"Okay. I get it," Mr. Schwartz relented, finally getting it. "Dad. School setting. Bad idea. I understand. See you at home."

He tried to exit as speedily as possible, but the damage had been done. It makes no difference how fast or slow you drive away from a car accident once you've committed vehicular manslaughter.

"That was embarrassing," October said.

Yumi and Stacey presented expressions that were all like, *tell me about it*.

"Tell me about it," echoed Ashlie Salmons, sidling up to October's table. "Doesn't your dad care about your social status? Oh wait, does Zombie Tramp really count as a status?"

Ashlie brought a manicured finger to her lip, as if she were actually considering this philosophical quandary. Standing beside the dishevelled trio clad in unwashed black rags and whatever mismatched thrift-shop mess Stacey was wearing, Ashlie looked like another species in her perfect jumper and gray leggings.

"Uh —" Yumi started, either to answer or to deliver a stinging comeback.

"Don't even start with me, Kung Fu Zombie Tramp," Ashlie barked. "You're already on my list for stealing that radio timeslot. It should have been Devin's."

"You're still seeing that guy from Phantom Moustache?" October asked.

"Like he'd ever leave me," Ashlie answered. "And now, with DJ Kung Fu Zombie Tramp at the mic, we'll have to listen to funeral marches every Thursday."

Tired of playing with her food, Ashlie Salmons drifted back toward her usual table. Ashlie's appearance was traumatic and on another day, her dad's visit might have crushed her spirit completely, but October was unflappable this Monday. This Monday was November 28th, the first day — according to the dead kids' own extremely unscientific reckoning — when she could summon the dead kids back to this mortal plane or wherever it was where she and Ashlie and her dad and the members of S Club 7 lived. After tonight in the cemetery, good times were going to roll.

Ignoring the destructive interruptions, Yumi returned to where her and October's conversation had dropped off.

"What are you up to tonight, Schwartz?" she asked. "Want to come over my place and listen to some funeral marches?"

"You know me," October said. "I love me some funeral marches. But I've got to get some work done on this thing." With that, October lifted the battered composition book she kept with her at all times, the one labelled *Two Knives, One Thousand Demons*. "These demons aren't going to stab themselves to death. Someone's got to write it," said October, succinctly explaining the writing process. "I'll be in the Sticksville Cemetery until it gets too dark to see."

The bell rang, and October packed up her things for music class.

"If you get bored," Yumi said, "just give me a call."

"On what phone?" The three friends passed the soda machine where just a month earlier, Mrs. Tischmann had misplaced her leg.

"Yeah, I need a phone, too," Yumi added. "Life would be so much easier with a cell."

"Don't look at me," Stacey said, feeling the keen weight of the conversation upon his shoulders. "I'm still working with a Walkman."

☠

Half a day later, Mr. Schwartz was sound asleep, unable to inflict much in the way of embarrassment in his near-catatonic state, and his daughter October, now quite adept at sneaking out, was standing in the middle of a clearing in the Sticksville Cemetery, that same *Two Knives, One Thousand Demons* notebook in her outstretched arms. Overhead, the trees, shorn of all their leaves by this point in the year, looked like skeletons reaching up to the heavens, grabbing at the full moon like it was a frisbee and all the dying trees were part of some ultimate tournament.

The entire cemetery — from the majestic, show-off tombstones that measured far above October's height to the lowly paupers' graves marked only with a roughly cut stone — took on a bluish, deathly sheen. But it's not unusual for a graveyard to look a little deathly.

October was lucky she'd brought her black peacoat, because it was positively freezing in the graveyard. She hadn't anticipated the cold. October was bad enough; could she really visit the dead kids night after night in the middle of December? Maybe she could sneak a space heater onto the cemetery grounds somewhere, hide it behind a rarely visited tomb.

The cold was little deterrent, though. October was warmed from top to tail by confidence. (Fun fact: confidence produces no heat energy whatsoever.) Once she read the mystical phrase she had somehow written into her still-unfinished demon-slaying epic, her five dead friends would be with her. She'd tell them about The Crooked Arms, investigative hijinks would ensue: clues would be discovered, suspects would be interrogated, property (let's face it) would be damaged, and in no time at all, they'd solve the mystery of who killed Morna MacIsaac. A few degrees below zero on the thermometer wasn't going to slow her down.

October thumbed the lined pages of the composition book until she reached the fatal verses. Watching the vapour escape from her own mouth in the frozen air, she drew in a deep breath and recited the words:

As Nature turns twisted and dark,
To this dread graveyard I donate my spark.
As tears begin to blind mine eyes,
The innocent young and the dead shall rise.

Then nothing — absolutely nothing — happened.

☠

Evan Munday is an illustrator and the cartoonist behind the self-published comic book *Quarter-Life Crisis*, set in a post-apocalyptic Toronto. He works as a book publicist for Coach House Books. *The Dead Kid Detective Agency* is his first novel. He lives in Toronto, ON.